CHALLENGE THE IMPOSSIBLE

Books by Edward D. Hoch
Published by Crippen & Landru

The Ripper of Storyville and Other Ben Snow Tales. Available as a Kindle e-book

The Velvet Touch. Available as a Kindle e-book

The Old Spies Club and Other Intrigues of Rand. Available as a Kindle e-book

The Iron Angel and Other Tales of the Gypsy Sleuth. Available as a Kindle e-book

Diagnosis Impossible: The Problems of Dr. Sam Hawthorne. Available as a print book and as Kindle e-book

More Things Impossible, The Second Casebook of Dr. Sam Hawthorne. Available as a print book and as a Kindle e-book

Nothing Is Impossible, Further Problems of Dr. Sam Hawthorne. Available as a print book and as a Kindle e-book

All But Impossible, The Impossible Files of Dr. Sam Hawthorne. Available as a print book and as a Kindle e-book

Challenge the Impossible: The Final Problems of Dr. Sam Hawthorne. Available as a print book and (forthcoming) as a Kindle e-book

CHALLENGE THE IMPOSSIBLE

The Final Problems of Dr. Sam Hawthorne

BY

EDWARD D. HOCH

INTRODUCTION BY

JOSH PACHTER

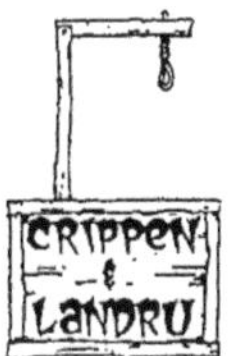

CRIPPEN & LANDRU PUBLISHERS
Cincinnati, Ohio
2018

Cover Design by Joshua Luboski

ISBN (limited clothbound edition): 978-1-936363-30-8
ISBN (trade softcover edition): 978-1-936363-31-5

FIRST EDITION

Printed in the United States of America
on recycled acid-free paper

Jeffrey A. Marks, Publisher
Douglas G. Greene, Senior editor

Crippen & Landru Publishers
PO Box 532057
Cincinnati, OH 45253
USA

Email: crippenlandru@earthlink.net
Web: www.crippenlandru.com

CONTENTS

INTRODUCTION

Edward Dentinger Hoch was – and remains today – a legendary figure in the history of contemporary crime fiction. He published almost a thousand short stories, appeared in every issue of *Ellery Queen's Mystery Magazine* from May of 1973 until after his death in 2008, created a village of unforgettable series characters (including Nick Velvet, Captain Jules Leopold, Jeffrey Rand of the Department of Concealed Communications, Michael Vlado, Simon Ark, Ben Snow, Alexander Swift, Stanton & Ives, and of course Dr. Sam Hawthorne), won an Edgar for his 1967 story "The Oblong Room," was the Mystery Writers of America's Grand Master in 2001 ... the list of his accomplishments goes on and on.

Yes, Ed Hoch was a legend. But he and his wife Patricia were also my friends.

In 1955, when Ed made his first professional sale to *Famous Detective Stories*, I was a toddler. Thirteen years later, when I was sixteen, I made my own debut, in EQMM's "Department of First Stories." I immediately joined the MWA and – when I came home to Long Island from the University of Michigan for Christmas breaks and summer vacations and other holidays – I trained into New York City for its monthly cocktail parties. I was too young to drink the cocktails legally, but regular bartender Chris Steinbrenner slipped them to me anyway, and I got to meet and talk with many of my idols, such as Stan Cohen, Lawrence Treat, Bill Brittain, Dorothy Salisbury Davis, Donald Westlake, John Lutz ... and Ed and Pat.

Ed in particular took me under his wing, and, when I signed up to attend the MWA's annual Edgar Allan Poe Awards Banquet in 1970, he arranged for me to sit with him and Pat right up at the front of the ballroom instead of tucked away beside a kitchen door at the back, and afterwards he and Pat brought me along to an after party at Mary Higgins Clark's penthouse apartment overlooking Central Park and made sure to introduce me to Mary and the many luminaries in attendance.

My first three contributions to EQMM were tales of the Griffen family, whose eleven children were all named after famous fictional detectives: two about E.Q. Griffen and one about his younger brother Nero. For my fourth story, I left the world of imitation and created characters of my own – but for number five I turned to parody. Ed Hoch's Nick Velvet stories were always titled "The Theft of the ________," and his Rand stories were almost always titled "The Spy Who ________," so I wrote a spoof about master thief Vic Nelvet and codebreaker Bland of the Department of Congealed Communications (and threw in homicide cop Leo Pold for good measure) and called the result "The Theft of the Spy Who." It appeared in the September 1972 issue, and Fred Dannay introduced it by saying that "one indication that an author and his characters have 'come of age,' have 'arrived,' is when another author writes the first parody or pastiche," and sandwiching it – inevitably – between a new Nick Velvet story and a new Rand story.

In 1973, I attended my first Bouchercon. I wasn't originally planning to go, but I changed my mind at the last minute and showed up unexpected. At the conference hotel's front desk, I left a coded message for Ed, announcing my arrival:

> Jim,
>
> Once she heard, Patricia asked Charles. He told everything.
>
> Richard.

I thought I was being clever, with the first letter of each word of my message spelling out my name – but what I forgot was that Ed was a guy who crafted short stories about Rand the codebreaker, not a codebreaker himself, and my message – especially because I included Pat's name – made the two of them uneasy rather than amusing them. I spent the rest of the weekend apologizing for my dopey practical joke.

From time to time, my travels brought me through Rochester in upstate New York, and I would always stop to visit Ed and Pat. More than anything else, I remember their finished basement, its walls lined floor to ceiling with long rows of white bookshelves that held ten copies of each publication in which Ed's work appeared – so that, in that pre-computer age, he would have plenty of tear sheets available for the marketing of reprint and foreign rights. I can't recall any of the various street addresses at which I lived during the 1970s, but the Hoch's Rochester address remains etched in my memory. (Since Pat still lives there, I won't mention it here – but I remember it, right down to the ZIP code.)

Around the middle of the '70s, I was in NYC for another Edgars, and Ed invited me to join him and a group of fellow crime writers for a drink at the Algonquin Hotel. There were about eight of us in all – and, yes, we were seated at a round table – and I nonchalantly whipped out the first fan letter I'd ever received and proudly displayed it to the gang. And, one by one, each of the other writers sheepishly reached into his jacket pocket and drew out an almost-identical letter from the same sender. I may be inventing this next bit, but in my memory the others were all disappointed to discover that their "fan" was in fact nothing more than an autograph hound who it ultimately turned out had sent the same basic letter to dozens of writers, while only Ed and I saw the humor in the situation.

In 1979, I moved overseas to Amsterdam, and for the next dozen years my interactions with Ed and Pat were restricted to snail mail. By 1984, I'd relocated to what was then West Germany and came up with the idea for a short-story collection to be titled *Partners in Crime*, for which each story would be written by two people working together ... and one half of each pair would be me.

The first person I invited to participate was Ed, and he wrote me back to say that he never wrote collaboratively ... but (and this will tell you more than anything else I've said thus far what a wonderful and generous soul – and what a wonderful and generous friend – he was) that he'd make an exception in my case.

He was interested in reviving Robert Louis Stevenson's idea of a suicide club, he said, and if I could come up with a satisfactory plot for a story that would feature his Jeffrey Rand character and could be titled "The Spy and the Suicide Club," he'd do the actual writing himself. So I plotted, and Ed wrote, and the story that resulted appeared in the September 1985 EQMM.

I moved back to the United States in 1991, having missed the entire Reagan presidency, and I saw Ed and Pat various times over the years that followed. Those visits still hold a very special place in my heart, and I only wish there'd been more of them.

On January 18, 2008, I woke up and logged into Facebook ... to learn that Ed had passed on the previous day, a month short of what would have been his seventy-eighth birthday.

That's now ten years ago, but I still think of Ed and Pat often – and soon after this volume is published, I plan to drive up to Rochester to hand-deliver some copies to Pat, whom I haven't seen in far too long.

Speaking of this volume — the fifth and last of Crippen & Landru's collections of the Dr. Sam Hawthorne stories — I was honored and delighted when Doug Greene and Jeff Marks asked me to share some reminiscences about my friendship with the Hochs, although I have to admit that Dr. Sam is not my favorite of Ed's characters. For reasons I'm not sure I can put into words, I like Nick Velvet the best of the village of familiars Ed populated over the half-century of his writing career.

But Dr. Sam runs Nick a close second, and the stories you're about to read aren't tales that weren't good enough to make it into the first four volumes of this series. Since C&L has been releasing the stories in the order of their original publication — and since they were written beginning with Dr. Sam's arrival in Northmont in the early 1920s — what you're about to read are the last of the Hawthorne stories, set during the WWII era, and it is in fact in this final grouping that you'll find the good doctor at what is — at least in my opinion — his best, as he solves his last fifteen cases, including the death of a visiting movie star, the bizarre appearance of a walking snowman in the middle of the summer, a locked-room murder whose only suspect seems to be Dr. Sam's old friend Sheriff Lens, and a dozen more equally baffling "problems."

So settle back and prepare to be entertained and astounded once again as the impossible is made not only possible but inevitable by the astoundingly inventive mind of my dear friend, Edward D. Hoch.

Josh Pachter
May 2018

THE PROBLEM OF ANNABEL'S ARK

I haven't really told you much about the other doctors in Northmont (Dr. Sam Hawthorne said as he took down the wine bottle and poured the traditional small libation for himself and his visitor), because when I arrived in 1922 I was the only one in town. The situation greatly improved in '29 with the opening of Pilgrim Memorial Hospital and the arrival of some good new residents, among them my friend Lincoln Jones, the town's first black doctor. By September of 1940, Linc had married and was raising two children in Northmont, and his son Nat was at an age where he wanted a pet dog for the sort of companionship his kid sister couldn't provide.

It was the Saturday after Labor Day, and between patients my nurse Mary Best and I were discussing the week's big news. President Roosevelt had traded fifty overage destroyers to Britain in exchange for 99-year leases on eight strategic sea and air bases in the Western Hemisphere. "We're moving closer to war all the time," Mary decided. "I'm just afraid we'll be in it a year from now."

"That all depends on Hitler," I responded. "I can't believe he's foolish enough to try invading England."

Linc Jones poked his head in the door at that moment. "What's this? Are you two talking about the war? Business must be slow."

"Well, what are you doing strolling around the doctors' annex?" Mary challenged with her usual grin. She liked Linc. "Don't you have any patients to see?"

"All cured and on their way home. My biggest concern right now is Turner, Nat's pooch. He's got a bad case of diarrhea, and I can't convince the boy that I only treat two-legged patients."

"Sam will help you."

"Thanks, Mary," I grumbled. Then, turning serious for a moment, I asked, "Didn't I hear of a veterinarian opening a place on the way to Shinn Corners?"

Linc nodded. "I'm on my way there now, soon as I pick up Turner. Want to come along?"

"It's a woman, isn't it?"

"So I hear. Annabel something. Calls her place Annabel's Ark."

"Cute," was all Mary could say. "You two run along and have your fun."

"Am I clear till two o'clock?" I asked her, making a pretense of being businesslike.

"All clear. If the lady vet delays you two, let me know."

Linc Jones was a tall, handsome man in his mid forties, maybe a year or two older than I was. We took his car ("You don't want Turner messing up your Buick, Sam.") and drove out to Town Line Road where he and Charlene had purchased a house a few years back. His wife was a dark-skinned beauty, and they made a handsome couple at social events around town. It was Charlene, now, who came out of the house carrying Turner, the sick mongrel pup, wrapped in a towel. I wondered for the first time if Linc had invited me along to ease the tension of a black man calling on a white woman veterinarian.

"How are you, Sam?" Charlene called out as Linc hurried to take the dog from her.

"Can't complain on a day like this." I replied. "I guess poor Turner could be better, though."

"Maybe the new lady vet can fix him up," she said, "if she's not too busy with cows and horses."

I got the job of holding Turner in his blanket while we drove the rest of the way out to Annabel's Ark. It was about halfway to Shinn Corners, a perfect location for drawing customers from both towns. The white cinder-block building was one story high, about the size of a small house, and a milk box near the door contributed to the homey feeling. A small sign with tasteful gold letters identified it as *Annabel's Ark—A Shelter For All Creatures.* There were only two cars in the parking lot when we arrived, a sleek little Lincoln-Zephyr coupe and a black Plymouth sedan. I figured anyone who'd name her place Annabel's Ark had to be driving the Lincoln-Zephyr.

We rang the bell and walked in to be greeted by a variety of woofs and snarls.

There were half a dozen dogs and cats in separate cages and they didn't seem happy to be there. A young woman wearing a white coat came out to greet us. "You must be Dr. Jones," she said to Linc. "Your wife called in about Turner. I'm Annabel Christie. Don't mind my patients. They'll calm down in a moment."

Close up she looked more like a movie star than a veterinarian. It wasn't that she was beautiful, exactly, but her blond hair, hazel eyes, bright smile, and sharp features all contributed to an almost magnetic attraction. I was embarrassed that I couldn't keep my eyes off her. "You can call me Linc," he was telling her. "This is my friend Dr. Sam Hawthorne."

She turned her smile on me, full force. "I've heard about you, Dr. Hawthorne. You're the local Sherlock Holmes."

"I like to think of myself more as Dr. Watson, though he didn't have much of a practice."

"Same initials as Holmes, though," she persisted.

"That's been pointed out to me before. And you're A. Christie, like that British mystery writer."

"Annabel Lee Christie, not Agatha." She turned her attention to Turner, examining the mongrel pooch with a tender hand. "What's the matter, boy? Not feeling good?" The dog whimpered in response.

"He's had this diarrhea the last few days," Linc told her. "He was running around the fields Monday when we had a few people in for a Labor Day barbecue. I suppose he ate something that was bad for him."

She nodded. "A thoughtless guest or just some bad weeds out in the field. I've seen worse cases." She finished her examination. "I'll give him an injection. Then mix this powder with his food for forty-eight hours. He should be back to normal by then."

"Thank you, Dr. Christie. How much do I owe you?"

She shrugged. "Let's call it ten dollars. Professional discount."

"I'll have to remember that," I told her. "I'll come see you the next time I have a case of distemper."

She eyed me with a smile. "You do that, Dr. Hawthorne."

A young man came out of the back room carrying a slim Siamese cat. "She's a bit perkier now," he announced. "I think we can move her to a cage out here."

"That's good. Ray Perkins, my assistant, this is Dr. Jones with his dog Turner, and Dr. Hawthorne."

"Pleased to meet you," he said, placing the cat in one of the empty cages. The nearest dog immediately started growling, and Perkins moved the Siamese to a different cage facing the front door. The young man was tall and slender, moving with the awkwardness of youth. I guessed him to be in his early twenties, probably ten years younger than Annabel Christie.

"This Siamese has a blockage of some sort," she explained. "Just the opposite of Turner's trouble. We may have to operate if she's not better by Monday."

Linc paid her the ten dollars, and I scooped up Turner in his blanket. "Nice meeting you, Dr. Christie," I said. "That's a neat-looking Lincoln-Zephyr you've got outside."

Annabel Christie laughed as we departed. "Things aren't always what they seem. My car's the Plymouth."

* * *

My meeting with Northmont's first veterinarian might have amounted to no more than that, except for what happened the following Monday. I'd risen early on Sunday, brought in the milk and paper, and read the latest news about a huge daylight air raid in London. After weeks of bombing by the Luftwaffe, the British government had issued an invasion warning, convinced the Germany was about to strike across the English Channel. The September seventh raid only heightened that fear. Some 300 German bombers and 600 fighter planes hit London's dock area with deadly accuracy. Guided by the still-blazing fires, the planes returned that night for another attack.

"If they do invade England, we're in it," Mary Best said somberly as we discussed it at the office the following morning. "I feel I should be doing something."

"You are doing something, right here," I reminded her.

"I mean something more, for the war effort." She turned away for a moment. "I was reading that the army needs nurses."

"Mary—"

She waved me off. "I'm just thinking about it. I haven't made any decision yet."

In the five years that Mary had been my nurse, our relationship had developed into far more than that. I sometimes escorted her to dances and parties, and we'd even taken a vacation with another couple. I felt closer to her than to any other woman I knew. But before we could discuss the matter further the telephone rang and she reached across the desk to answer it. "Dr. Hawthorne's office." She listened and said, "Just a moment, please."

"Who is it?" I asked.

"Dr. Christie," she replied, passing the phone to me without changing her expression.

Annabel Christie's familiar voice came on the line. "I'm sorry to bother you like this, Dr. Hawthorne, but I wonder if you might be out my way today or tomorrow. I have a little problem here that may call for your detective skills."

"If you've had a break-in, Sheriff Lens should be notified."

"There are no signs of a break-in, but that Siamese cat you saw the other day seems to have been strangled in its cage."

I hesitated a moment and then said, "I'm making a house call on Mrs. Rawlings this afternoon. It won't be any problem to swing by the Ark."

"I'd appreciate it."

When I told Mary about it she scowled. "A dead cat? She called you about a dead cat?"

"There seem to be some mysterious circumstances. I think she wants my opinion."

Mary started working on the bookkeeping and said no more about it.

* * *

Mrs. Rawlings was a farm widow like so many of Northmont's older residents. Her husband had died in his sixties, and she'd been left with farmland rapidly going to seed. Her only son, Gordon, a milkman who lived in town, came out when he could to help her with the place, but his heart wasn't in farming. Though I treated Rose Rawlings for a variety of minor complaints, she mostly summoned me as an audience of one for a litany of her woes.

"Why don't you sell the place and move into town, Rose?" I asked her on that day's visit. "You'd be closer to your sister." It was not the first time I'd made the suggestion. Dr. Flagel, a widow herself, was Rose's only sibling. Dora's late husband had left no relatives, and she lived by herself in town.

But Rose only shook her head. "Randy put his life into it, and I know someday Gordon will want to farm it too. He spent his boyhood back in those woods, catching grass snakes with a snare at the end of a long pole."

"Catching snakes as a child is different from growing a hundred acres of corn as an adult, Rose."

"He'll come back someday," she said with a sad smile. "I want it to be here."

It was not my job to deflate an old woman's dream. I gave her some pills and went on my way.

Annabel's Ark wasn't really close to the Rawlings farm at all, but I figured Dr. Christie wouldn't know that I'd gone out of my way to visit her the same afternoon. The sun was pushing up the late summer temperature as I pulled into her small parking area. This time there were four cars there. Inside I had to wait while Ray Perkins delivered a happy puppy to one man and a fat tabby cat to a woman I knew slightly from town.

"Is Dr. Christie around?" I asked the young man when we were finally alone.

"She's with the monkey," he replied.

"Oh. Do you think she'll be long?"

"I'll see." He went into the treatment room, closing the door behind him.

After a moment Dr. Christie appeared, wiping her hands. "Sorry if you had to wait, Doctor. I was treating someone's pet for wasp stings. It wasn't easy."

"I'll bet it wasn't." I smiled at her. "You know, this 'Doctor' business isn't necessary among colleagues. Let's just be Annabel and Sam."

"Fine by me, Sam."

"Now what happened here?"

She indicated the empty cage opposite the door, where I'd seen Perkins place the cat on my visit two days earlier. "This is where I found her dead, as soon as I walked in this morning," she told me in a flat voice. "The Siamese named Sabbath. She belonged to Mrs. Flagel."

"Flagel? Not Dora Flagel?"

Annabel nodded. "Do you know her well?"

"She lives a block away from me in town, but we're just casual acquaintances. Her sister is a patient of mine. In fact, I just came from a house call there."

"I phoned Dora as soon as we found Sabbath's body this morning. She's very upset."

"I'm sure she is. Judging by the size of her house and yard, she's a woman who values her possessions. But what made you think I could help?"

"The place was locked up tight and there was no sign of a break-in. The cage was also shut." She pulled the knob of the spring latch to open it, then swung the door shut until the latch snapped into place.

I went over to examine the front door. It was a solid piece of wood without any window, and the lock was the latest type of Yale. I asked for her key and she produced a ring of them from her purse, indicating a shiny new one. It slid into the lock with ease, and the door's bolt worked smoothly. "Does anyone have a key besides you and Ray?"

She shook her head. "I have the only key. Ray's just worked here three weeks. I haven't had a duplicate made for him yet."

"The animals are left alone at night?" I asked.

"Usually, unless there's a special problem with one of our patients." She motioned toward the closed door to the back room.

"Ray said you were with a monkey."

"I wish it were that simple. Come back with me. I want you to see Sabbath's body anyway."

"Dora Flagel hasn't picked her up yet?"

"She doesn't want to. Says she wants to remember Sabbath as she was. I'm to dispose of the body. I told her I'd bury it out in back."

She led the way into the rear room, where Ray Perkins had his hands full. This was no monkey but a large long-armed ape some five feet tall, thrashing about violently as Annabel's assistant attempted to lock him in his cage. "What is it?" I asked in alarm.

She shook her head sadly, but more over Ray's shortcomings as a handler than the great ape's antics. "I'll do it," she told him, moving in quickly with a broomstick to prod the creature back into its cage far enough so she could slam the door and slip the hasp over its metal staple. Then she put a padlock through the staple without locking it. Belatedly, she answered my question. "It's an orangutan named Pedro."

"Who'd have that as a pet?"

"A retired seaman named Vespa over in Shinn Corners. He brought it back from Sumatra, but now the poor creature's been stung by wasps. I'm treating him the best I can."

"Don't you lock him in?"

"He won't get out of there. If I locked it and there was a fire, how could they rescue him? At least the front door and windows could be smashed in. Actually, I'm pleased to be treating something larger than dogs and cats. The folks around here haven't quite trusted me with their bulls and cows and horses yet."

I turned away from the great ape and went over to the examining table. The dead cat lay covered by a white cloth that I carefully lifted off. Annabel came to my side and pushed away the fur at its neck to show me the thin red line around the throat. "She was strangled by a cord or wire."

I picked up one of the dead cat's paws. "There's dried blood here too. One of her claws was partly torn out. The killer may have a scratch on him."

"Why would anyone do something like this to a helpless cat?' she wanted to know.

"The question that puzzles me is how they did it. The front door shows no sign of tampering." My eyes roamed the examining room, taking in a refrigerator and a narrow cot beneath a single small window with a view of the backyard. I walked to a rear door covered by an inner door of heavy mesh screening. "Is this the only other entrance?"

"Yes, it's for supplies. You can see the door itself is padlocked on the inside, and I had this mesh screen door installed so we could circulate the air in summer without the danger of any animals escaping. It's also padlocked, though I may open it if this heat keeps up."

"The windows?"

"There are only two, one in each room, and both were firmly latched on the inside.

We went back out front, leaving the orangutan beating at the bars of its cage and looking quite healthy to me. Ray Perkins was tidying up and preparing to feed the patients. He took a quart bottle of milk from the refrigerator and filled four small dishes for the remaining cats, then produced a bag of cat food. I smiled at Annabel. "Is there any chance you walk in your sleep?"

"None. And the key never left my ring. It's a tricky think to get off." She showed me.

"No one could have stolen it long enough to make a copy?"

She shook her head. Ray finished his job and joined us. "Still trying to figure out how the cat was killed?"

"Any ideas?" I asked him.

"Beats me. No one got in here during the night, that's for sure."

"Did you two leave together?"

"We always do," Annabel answered for him, "unless I have to stay late with the animals."

"Does that happen often?"

"Only once in the six weeks I've been open. That's what the cot in the examining room is for, in case I have to sleep over."

"But you weren't here yesterday?"

"I stopped by to feed the animals and administer some medication. Sabbath was fine then. I think she must have been killed early this morning. When I arrived at eight and found her, the body was still warm."

I turned to the assistant. "What about you, Ray? Were you here too?"

He nodded. "I drove in a minute or two before her. I was waiting in my car, like always."

"But you didn't see anything unusual?"

"Nothing." There was only a little milk left in the quart bottle. He drank it himself, washed out the bottle in the sink along one wall, and pulled open the milk box to add it to the other empties. Then he asked Annabel, "Do you want me to bury the cat?"

I could see it was a distasteful decision for her to make. "Oh, I suppose so." She turned her eyes to me. "This is the first death I've had. It wasn't my fault, but I suppose I'm responsible."

"Let me look into it," I told her. "Strangled cats are a bit out of my line, but this does seem to be a locked-room mystery of sorts."

I wanted to call on Dora Flagel, but first I decided to stop by the sheriff's office and inquire about any other mysterious break-ins around the area. Sheriff Lens gave me a warm welcome, as always. He was my oldest friend in Northmont, but he couldn't help me with break-ins. "Other than a couple of missing chickens it's been a quiet time, Doc. You got something I haven't heard about?"

I outlined the cat killing at Annabel's Ark and Sheriff Lens gave a little snicker. "I never knew you to be so interested in the death of a cat. But there's no doubt our new vet's a handsome young lady."

"She asked me to look into it and I am, Sheriff. Someone strangled that cat and I'm wondering why. And how."

"From what you tell me, I'd question her assistant some more. Seems like he's the most likely suspect."

"How'd he get in to do it?"

"Maybe the cat wasn't dead when they came in, only sleeping. While Doc Christie was checking on her other patients he quietly opened the cage and strangled the cat."

"The cage is facing the door, not six feet away. It was the first thing she saw when she walked in."

"Well, Doc, one thing I've learned from you in eighteen years is that things aren't always what they seem."

"Annabel Christie told me the same thing when I met her Saturday."

* * *

I drove over to Dora Flagel's place after that. It was a handsome Victorian house, one of the oldest in Northmont, with a large rock garden in the side yard that produced a variety of small blossoms almost all summer long. Both garden and grass were well tended. Mrs. Flagel, a widow like her sister, was a stout woman in her early sixties with graying hair and a pleasant manner. She wore thick eyeglasses, and it took her a moment to recognize me. She was surprised when I indicated I was looking into the death of her cat Sabbath, and she led me inside to the living room.

"I know you have a reputation for solving unusual murder cases, Dr. Hawthorne, but my poor cat hardly qualifies."

"She certainly died under unusual circumstances, Mrs. Flagel. Do you know of any reason why someone might want to kill her?"

"Certainly not! She never bothered another living creature." She amended that to add, "Except for an occasional bird, of course."

"Do you know a young man named Ray Perkins?"

She frowned in thought. "I don't believe so."

"He's Dr. Christie's assistant at the Ark."

"Oh! I met him when I brought Sabbath in, but I didn't remember his name. He seemed like a nice chap."

"You've received no threats of any kind? Nothing unusual?"

"Of course not." She seemed about to add something, but hesitated. When I prodded her a bit she told me, "Last week I lost a valuable diamond from my best dinner ring. It looked as if two of the prongs holding it in place got bent somehow. I've been searching the house, but I still haven't found it."

"Could you have had a burglar?"

She snorted at the idea. "A burglar would have stolen the entire ring, wouldn't he?"

I glanced around at the spotless living room. "Do you have a cleaning woman to help you here, Mrs. Flagel? Or a gardener for outside?"

"My nephew takes care of the lawn and garden. A cleaning woman comes by every fortnight, but she wasn't here last week. There was no robbery, but I just wish the diamond would turn up. It was an anniversary gift from my late husband."

"Is it insured?"

"Of course. If I can't find it I'll have to notify the company."

"When was Sabbath taken ill?"

"On Friday, the day before I took her to the Ark."

"Had Dr. Christie treated her before?"

"I believe Sabbath was the Ark's first patient. My Siamese had a bit of distemper right after it opened."

"You've been very helpful, Mrs. Flagel," I told her. "I'll do everything I can to locate the person who caused Sabbath's death."

"That would be a great consolation to me. Doctor."

* * *

I took the back road over to Shinn Corners next, traveling some fifteen miles before I topped Holy Hill and saw the village nestled in the wrinkled valley a mile below. Finding a retired seaman named Vespa in a place this size shouldn't be too difficult, I reasoned, and it wasn't. A gas station attendant directed me to a small house a few blocks down the street, cautioning me to watch out for the ape.

There was a man in his sixties in the yard, wearing the peaked cap of a naval officer. His weathered face left little doubt that he was the one I sought. "Mr. Vespa?" I asked, unlatching the gate to join him in the yard.

"Do I know you?"

"I'm a doctor, I've come about your orangutan."

"Is he dead? Is Pedro dead?" He seemed on the verge of tears.

"No, nothing like that. I happened to visit Annabel's Ark today and saw him. She's still treating him but he seems in good shape to me."

The old seaman's relief was immediately obvious. "Thank God! He has been my companion for two decades, on land and sea. I would not want to live without him."

I detected the trace of an accent, perhaps Italian. I knew his name was the Italian word for wasp. "Why would a former sailor settle so far inland?" I wondered.

"Because of Pedro! I wanted a little place on the coast, maybe Cape Cod, but people wouldn't allow me to keep Pedro as a pet. They said he belonged in a zoo! I had to come here to find a village where it was all right."

"Do you keep him in a cage?"

"At night? Of course, yes. Otherwise he would be swinging from tree limbs."

"Could I see where he's kept?"

Vespa was growing suspicious. "Why do you ask all this? Will you make me move again?"

"No. I can assure you of that. I'm looking into an accident at the veterinarian's place."

"Pedro?"

"Not Pedro. It was a cat."

He led me into the little cottage. It was sparsely furnished, but a large fishing net was draped over one wall and a ship's sextant rested on one table. The only picture on the wall was a print of a Winslow Homer painting showing a sailing ship against a sunset. "I keep Pedro in here at night," he said, leading the way into a back bedroom.

The cage was smaller and less sturdy than the one at Annabel's Ark, but apparently it did the job. Out the back window I could see a fenced yard and some trees for climbing. Perhaps Pedro had found a suitable retirement home here. "Has he ever had any trouble with neighbors' pets?"

"No, never! He is a gentle giant." Vespa smiled when he said it, and I hoped Annabel Christie would soon be able to reunite him with the orangutan.

But there was something I had to do first.

* * *

It was almost six by the time I got back to the office, and Mary was just closing up. "I thought you'd gone on home," she said.

"I took a ride over to Shinn Corners. Any calls?"

"Dr. Christie again. She said it wasn't important."

"I'll check with her, and I want to call Sheriff Lens, too. You can go on home."

When I reached the sheriff he was baffled by my request. "You're doing what, Doc? Spending the night with an ape?"

"I think it's the only way I can crack this case, Sheriff."

"What case? You've got a dead cat, nothing else. That's not even a felony. You want me to arrest someone for cruelty to animals? Hell, the judge would probably let him off with a hundred-dollar fine."

"Just do it as a favor. I need you out there tonight."

He gave a long sigh. "Doc, I think you've gone batty. But if you want me, I'll be there."

Next I called Annabel Christie and told her, "I want to spend the night in your back room, watching the orangutan."

"He won't be here, Sam. That's what I called to tell you earlier. I cured his wasp stings. I'm about to phone Vespa to pick him up."

"Can't you keep him one more night?"

"Is it important?"

"I think so, yes. I'll be out there shortly. Maybe we can get something to eat and then you can lock me in with Pedro for the night."

"Not alone," she told me. "If you stay, I stay."

"That's hardly necessary."

"Look, Sam, it's my place. I'm just getting started here in Northmont, and I have an investment to protect. I can't afford to lose another animal."

"You won't. I'll be out there in a half-hour."

It was dark when I reached the pet hospital, and she was waiting for me out front. We drove to a nearby roadhouse that served good food at a reasonable price. Over dinner she remarked that she'd never been there before. "You'll have to show me more of Northmont's sights."

"I'd be happy to. Any new patients today?"

She shrugged. "Just a dog with ticks, I'm still waiting to make a house call on a cow."

I couldn't help laughing. "You will, sooner or later."

"At least I haven't killed anyone yet." Then the smile vanished as she remembered Sabbath. "I'm sorry. I spoke without thinking."

"You weren't responsible for her death, and I intend to prove it. Did Ray bury her out back?"

She nodded. "But I can't turn the place into a pet cemetery. In the future I'll make arrangements with a crematorium in the city if the owner doesn't want the body."

The food was good, and we even had room for some chocolate cake for dessert. Then it was back to the Ark. "I'll park my car down the road," I suggested. "Maybe you can move yours too."

She looked at me quizzically. "What do you think is going to happen?"

"Nothing, I hope."

I was pleased to see that the cages out front were all but empty. Most of Annabel's cats and dogs had been sent back to their owners. In the back room she joined me on the cot facing Pedro's cage. The great ape sprang up and clung to the bars but soon tired of showing off for us.

"Is this proper?" she asked. "We're spending the night together seated on a cot."

"All in the interest of research," I assured her. "Is that padlock the way it was Sunday night?"

"That's right. Through the staple but unlocked. Are we waiting to see if he can get out of that cage?"

I didn't answer directly but took a flashlight from my jacket pocket. "Could you turn out the lights? And unlock the back door? But don't let me doze off."

She did as I asked and returned to the cot. Outside, the moon cast its glow across the backyard. "Haven't I read this story before?" she asked after a few moments' silence. "A killer orangutan?"

I nodded in the darkness. "Poe. And you're Annabel Lee. Don't think I didn't make the connection."

"My mother was a romantic."

"Annabel Lee died in the poem."

"That's why I don't use my middle name."

Across the room from us Pedro rattled his bars.

We were both silent for a time. "Are you awake, Sam?" she asked finally.

"Just barely."

"What are we waiting for? Pedro didn't kill that cat."

"Of course not. He might have gotten out of his cage, he might even have opened Sabbath's cage, but he wouldn't have used a cord or wire to strangle her."

"Then who–?"

That was when my eye caught the movement of a flashlight in the Ark's backyard. "There he is!" I whispered urgently. "Come on!"

We were out the back door in an instant, targeting him with my flashlight. "Stop right there!" I shouted.

The man was tall and dressed in black. He dropped his shovel and stood where he was, perhaps fearful that we were armed. A car's headlights swept in from the road as Sheriff Lens appeared from his hiding place.

"But who is he?" Annabel asked. "I've never seen him before."

"You've probably seen him several times since you opened your Ark. You just never noticed him."

Sheriff Lens came running up, puffing a bit. "Is this is the fellow I'm supposed to arrest, Doc?"

The tall man turned to me with a slight smile. "Arrest me for what? Trespassing? Cruelty to animals?"

"The theft of your aunt's diamond," I said simply. "Annabel, let me introduce you to Gordon Rawlings. He's your milkman."

* * *

An hour later, back at the sheriff's office, I explained it all to Annabel and Sheriff Lens. "It seemed obvious from the beginning that the motive behind the crime had to be something more than the killing of Dora Flagel's cat. If someone wanted to strangle a cat, there are enough stray ones around. Whoever went to the trouble of killing Sabbath in that locked animal hospital had to be after something else."

"But what?" Annabel asked. "And what was this mention of a stolen diamond?"

"Sabbath belonged to Dora Flagel, and when I spoke to her I learned that she'd lost a valuable diamond from her dinner ring. It seemed to have happened just before her cat took ill. I remembered your telling me, Annabel, that Sabbath was suffering from some sort of blockage. That seemed more than a coincidence. I began to consider the possibility that the Siamese cat had swallowed the diamond, causing the blockage."

Annabel Christie shook her head. "Cats don't swallow diamonds."

"They might if it was inside a bit of cat food." I leaned forward on the sheriff's desk. "Even though two of the prongs holding the diamond on the ring seemed to have been bent open, Mrs. Flagel refused to accept the possibility of robbery. What burglar, she asked, would take the time to remove the diamond from its setting rather than steal the whole ring?"

"She's right there," Sheriff Lens agreed.

"Not entirely. Suppose the thief was a member of her family, someone who frequented the house and had a perfect opportunity to steal the diamond. If the ring itself was left behind, Mrs. Flagel might not notice the missing gem for weeks or months. Remember the thick glasses she wears for her poor eyesight. She told me her nephew cuts the grass and tends to her yard. Certainly he would have been inside the house on these occasions, if only to use the bathroom. I'm speculating, but I think that's what happened last Friday. She must have walked in on him just after he removed the diamond from the ring. He feared she might accuse him and even ask him to empty his pockets. So he fed the diamond to Sabbath with a bit of cat food.

"Before he could return later to retrieve the stone, Sabbath was shipped off to Annabel's Ark with intestinal problems."

"You still haven't told us how you knew who he was," Annabel said. "Or how he killed the cat inside my locked building."

"Knowing family relationships made the first part easy. Dora Flagel has one sibling, her sister Rose Rawlings. And Rose has only one child, her son Gordon, a milkman. I remembered that Dora's late husband left no relatives. So the nephew who tended to Dora's yard had to be Gordon. I remembered that the Ark fed the cats milk, and it was left in the milk box by the front door. Could that milkman have been Gordon Rawlings? I remembered that Sabbath's cage was opposite the front door, only a few feet away, and the milk box was next to the door. Rose Rawlings told me just the other day that when Gordon was young he used to catch grass snakes using a long pole with a snare at the end. Could such a pole have been used to kill Sabbath? Indeed it could. I noticed your assistant, Ray, pull open the milk-box door yesterday to place an empty bottle there. There was no snap or lock on the inside. Gordon simply opened the outer door, pushing open the inner door and saw Sabbath in her cage. He must have brought the snare or noose with him for just such an eventuality. The snare on the end of the pole could easily be used to pull open the knob on the cage door. Then he looped it around the cat's neck, not to kill her but only to steal her. Sabbath clawed at the cage for a foothold—remember the torn claw?—and hung on. Gordon kept pulling and the cat strangled. He still couldn't get her out, even in death, so he freed the snare, pushed the cage door closed with his pole until the lock clicked, and got out of there."

"How'd he close the inside milk-box door?" the sheriff asked.

"Usually you can grip the edge and swing them shut. It didn't have to be a right fit."

"And tonight?"

"I knew he'd come back for Sabbath's body. His aunt must have told him it was being buried behind the Ark. I suppose Annabel thought I wanted to watch the orangutan's cage, but I was really watching out the back window for our cat killer to return."

"It still didn't have to be the milkman," Annabel argued. "Anyone could have stuck that pole through the milk box."

"Not during the night when it was dark inside the Ark. It had to have been done shortly after daylight. Remember Sabbath's body was still warm when you found it. Who else could safely tamper with a milk box along that road in the early morning without fear of being noticed? Only a milkman."

* * *

After that I went home for a few hours of sleep. When I arrived at the office in early afternoon, Lincoln Jones was chatting with Mary. "How's the pooch?" I asked.

"Fine. Good as new. But you look tired. Have a hard night?"

"I was sitting up with a patient."

"Anyone I know?"

"A fellow named Pedro. He's going home today."

THE PROBLEM OF THE POTTING SHED

It was the second Saturday of October, in 1940, that my nurse Mary Best gave me the news I'd been dreading. She waited until midafternoon, when our shortened office hours were ending, to tell me she'd decided to join the navy as a nurse. Only a few days earlier, Secretary Knox had announced a limited call-up of the naval reserve, and nurses were in short supply. (Even now, all these years later, Dr. Sam Hawthorne seemed to remember the pain of that moment. He poured his guest another small libation and continued.) I can't say it was a complete surprise, because she'd been talking about it for a month, trying to decide between the army and navy. But it was a blow, nevertheless. Mary had been more than a nurse to me. She was a close friend and companion, a friend to my friends. She'd even kept up an occasional correspondence with my former nurse April, after April married an innkeeper in Maine.

"You've been with me more than five years," I told her. "They've been happy years for me."

"And for me too, Sam. But I was just passing through Northmont, remember? I was always on my way to somewhere else."

"I thought we might—"

She hushed my lips with her fingers. "The war won't last forever. Maybe I'll be back."

But I already knew that Mary Best was the sort who always moved forward, never back. "When are you leaving?"

"Will November first give you time enough to find someone?"

"I don't know," I answered honestly. "That's just three weeks."

Our conversation was interrupted by the telephone, and since I was closest, I answered it. I recognized the raspy voice of Sheriff Lens at once. "Doc, are you free right now?"

"I just finished with a patient, Sheriff. What is it?"

"Can you get out to the Oberman place on Old Farm Road? We've got something here that's right up your alley."

"What is it?"

"Douglas Oberman is dead inside a locked potting shed. If you can get here right away we won't break in till you arrive."

"My God, Sheriff. The man might be still alive!"

"No chance, Doc. We can see through the window that he's been shot in the right temple. There's lots of blood."

"All right. I'll come right out."

I hung up and told Mary about it. "I'd better get out there and see what's happened. We can talk later."

* * *

The Oberman place had still been a working farm when I came to Northmont with my medical degree in 1922. After the parents died around 1930, their only son Douglas sold off all of the fields and barns until only the homestead and a fairly extensive garden remained. He was an automobile mechanic by trade, and he'd used the money from the land sale to erect the largest gasoline station in Northmont. Douglas and his wife Angie were well off by local standards and now, after eight years of marriage, they were expecting their first child. Angie was a petite, friendly woman whose tomboyish youth had hardly prepared us for the take-charge woman she'd become. I'd watched her grow larger and happier through the summer, and I was pleased for her, even though she'd chosen a doctor over in Shinn Corners as her physician. Now I only hoped she'd be able to withstand the shock of whatever had happened to her husband.

It was after four when I reached the house, and I recognized the sheriff's car parked in front, along with one of his deputies' vehicles. There were two other cars in the driveway, one of them belonging to Oberman. As I hurried up to the front porch, Sheriff Lens himself opened the door. "Glad you could come, Doc. We've got ourselves a bad situation here."

"How's Angie Oberman?"

"We put her to bed. Maybe you can give her a sedative."

"I'd better check on her husband first." Despite the sheriff's assurance that he was dead, I had to see for myself. I nodded to Felix Quinn, Lens's deputy, and followed them out the back door. The potting shed was a small green structure at the end of the garden, set against a low hedge that effectively marked the boundary of the property. Perhaps Oberman wanted no visible reminder of the family of farm he'd sold off a decade earlier.

Another deputy was standing outside potting shed with a stocky man I recognized at once as Howard Oberman, Douglas's brother. "What happened, Howard?" I asked.

"I don't know. My wife and I stopped by for a visit, and their neighbor came over too. The five of us were sitting around having a drink when Douglas said he had a pot of mums for us in the potting shed. He was gone a few minutes when Tomley–"

"Tomley?"

"Their neighbor from across the road. He went home, but I thought he was coming back. Just after that I hear a shot from outside and I went out to the potting shed to see if everything was all right. It was locked from the inside and Douglas didn't answer my knocking. Sandra came out of the kitchen to join me."

I tried the door but it held firm. There was no padlock in the hasp. "Is there a window?"

"Around here."

He showed me a tiny window, little more than a rectangular slit less than a foot wide and nine inches high, nearly six feet up in the shed's wall. I had to stand on my toes to peer through it. Douglas Oberman was lying on his back on the stone floor, staring at the roof with blue eyes open but unseeing. From the bloody wound with powder burns around it, there could be little doubt that he'd been shot in the right temple with a gun held very close to him.

"When I phoned Sheriff Lens I said it looked like suicide," the dead man's brother said.

The sheriff grunted. "If he shot himself, where's the gun?"

"We can only see a small portion of the floor from here. It might be under him, or under the window."

"Can you see what's holding the door closed?"

"It looks as if the padlock from the outside's been attached to something. We'll have to break in the door. Unless we can smash this window."

"No one here could fit through that space," Sheriff Lens said, and I had to agree with him. A child maybe, or a small adult. "Let's break it in."

The two deputies hit the door together with their shoulders and the wood splintered. Once inside, I knelt by the body and established for certain that Douglas Oberman was dead. Almost at once I spotted the revolver, just inches from his outstretched right hand.

"Don't touch it!" Lens cautioned. "Fingerprints." He took out a handkerchief and lifted the weapon carefully by its barrel. "A revolver with one shot fired, Doc. I guess maybe I got you out here to investigate a suicide after all."

I went over to study the splintered door. A hasp had been screwed into the wood on the inside, and the padlock secured it to a metal staple in the doorframe. It was identical to the hardware on the outside of the door. "He unlocked the padlock, brought it inside, and locked himself in."

"Why would he do that?" the sheriff wondered.

"The most likely explanation is his pregnant wife," I suggested. "He locked the door from the inside because he didn't want Angie to suffer the shock of finding his body." But I could see that the finish on both hasps had dulled with time. There may have been some other reason for locking the potting shed while he was inside.

"Where you goin' now?" Sheriff Lens asked.

"I should look in on Angie." I left him there with his deputies and returned to the house.

Howard Oberman's wife Sandra was upstairs with her pregnant sister-in-law. She was a tall woman in her forties, beginning to develop a middle-aged spread. "It's a terrible shock," she told me softly. "She won't let me touch her."

Angie's body was almost buried beneath the covers of her bed, though I could see she was still partly dressed. "It's Dr. Hawthorne, Angie," I told her in case she didn't remember me.

"Where's Douglas?" she managed to ask, turning her tear-streaked blue eyes toward me.

"There's been an accident. I have a sedative for you, but I'd like to examine you first, to be certain the baby is all right."

"No. I have my own doctor in Shinn Corners. I'm all right." Then, "He's dead, isn't he? Douglas?"

"I'm afraid so."

A shudder seemed to run through her body. "That shot I heard. Did somebody shoot him?"

"We don't know. The sheriff thinks the wound may have been self-inflicted."

"*No.*" It was almost a scream. "No no, no, no! He would never have done that. He had the baby coming. We'd waited for so long and now—"

I opened my bag and took out a powdered sedative. Sandra brought me a glass of water and I poured it in, stirring it well. "Drink this, Angie. It'll help you sleep."

"I don't want—" she began, but I put it to her lips and she drank. She was asleep within minutes, as much from her exhaustion and fear as from my powder.

"How far along is she?" I asked Sandra.

"About eight and a half months. It could come any time now."

"Who's her doctor?"

"Boynton, in Shinn Corners. He's very concerned about her. He phoned this morning to see how she was doing. She talked to him briefly."

"If she doesn't trust anyone else, you'd better get her over to him tomorrow. This shock might induce premature labor."

"I'll drive her there myself."

"We'll try to sort this thing out and determine what happened."

"Do you really think he killed himself?"

"It looks like it," I told her. "Were the rest of you all together when you heard the shot?"

She thought about that. "Not really. Angie and I were in the kitchen preparing a little snack. The men were in the living room. Pretty soon Douglas came out and took the shed key off its hook in the kitchen. He said he wanted to get something. Angie had been uncomfortable all afternoon, with the baby getting so big, and she went up the back stairs to the bathroom. I was fixing little sandwiches and a pot of tea when I heard the shot. I knew right away it came from the potting shed."

"Was the door to the shed open or closed?"

"It was closed then. I was busy with the sandwiches and didn't see him go in. Right after I heard the shot I saw my husband walk over to the shed to see what had happened. He tried the door but it wouldn't open."

I nodded. "Douglas took the padlock and locked the door from the inside. Had he ever done that before?"

"I have no idea. Perhaps Angie would know."

"She's not in any shape for questioning right now. Where is this neighbor, Mr. Tomley?"

"I don't know."

I left her with Angie Oberman and walked across the road to the Tomley place. I knew Herb Tomley vaguely by name, but we'd never really met. He raised chickens and did some harness racing at county fairs around the state. I suppose he was something of a gentleman farmer, and he looked every bit of it when he came to the door. A muscular, middle-aged man with graying hair, he wore jodhpurs and riding boots with a fancy shirt open to the waist. "What's up?" he asked.

"Mr. Tomley? I'm Dr. Sam Hawthorne. There's been a tragic accident at the Oberman's house."

He squinted into the afternoon sun. "I saw the sheriff's car. What happened?"

"Douglas Oberman's been shot. He's dead."

"I was just over there having a drink with them less than an hour ago."

"Howard Oberman thought you were coming back."

"No, I'm not much for drinking in the afternoon. One's my limit."

"Did you hear a gunshot shortly after you left?"

"I might have. I wouldn't have paid much attention. Folks around here are always shootin' at those damned chicken hawks circling around. I do it myself."

"Did Douglas act strange or depressed while you were there?"

"Not so's you'd notice. We were just chatting."

"All right," I said. "Sheriff Lens will probably talk to you later."

"I'll be here." He'd made no effort to invite me in, so I retreated hastily. The news of his neighbor's violent death certainly hadn't upset him noticeably.

Sheriff Lens met me as I crossed the road. "Did you give Angie a sedative?"

I nodded. "You can question her later. What does it look like?"

"Everything points to suicide, Doc. It couldn't be anything else."

Still–

"Would your deputies do an inventory of everything in that potted shed?"

"Sure, I guess so. But if it's suicide, what's the point?"

"I just want to cover all the angles."

* * *

The sheriff came by my place on Sunday morning as I was fixing breakfast. "How about some bacon and eggs?" I asked.

"Already ate at home. I just came to drop off this inventory you wanted."

Before I looked at it I told him about Mary Best's plan to enlist as a navy nurse. "I hate to see her go, but her mind is made up."

Sheriff Lens shook his head sadly. "This war is changing everyone's lives. If we really get into it, they might even want you, Doc."

"I doubt it they're looking for too many forty-four-year-old men," I said with a laugh. But we both knew that draft registration was starting that very week, with the first young men to be chosen by month's end.

The sheriff passed me a single sheet of paper. "Oberman had nothing but a handkerchief in his pockets. Here's the inventory of the potting shed. One of the flowerpots had mums in it. I guess that was what he was going to give his brother and sister-in-law."

I ran quickly down the list, then studied it more carefully. There were the expected garden supplies, flowerpots in various sizes, bags of soil, fertilizer and peat moss, two shovels, a rake and a hoe, a lawn mower, a trowel, a rolled-up sleeping bag, some loose tulip bulbs, a box of grass seed, worn canvas gloves, and a dog-earned gardening book. "That's everything?" I asked.

"That's the lot. Except for the revolver and the padlock, of course. What did you expect to find, Doc?"

"It's just my locked-room instincts again. I wanted to be sure there was no evidence of a firecracker or something that might have been mistaken for a gunshot."

"Nothing like that. It had to be suicide. The revolver was his. Angie said he kept it to kill varmints."

But something was bothering me, something I couldn't quite put my finger on. "Why would he do it? He had everything to live for. Their first child was about to be born."

"Who knows why people suddenly turn crazy, Doc. It's something we just have to accept."

After the sheriff left I tried to put Oberman's death out of my mind, but it kept gnawing at me that afternoon while I was out raking leaves in my yard.

Finally I took a break and went in to phone his widow. There was no answer at the Oberman home, which wasn't surprising in view of the tragic event. I phoned Douglas's brother and had better luck.

"Angie's really in a bad way." Howard told me. "Sandra phoned Dr. Boynton in Shinn Corners and he said to bring her right in. He has an extra room at his house where she can stay until the baby arrives. Sandra and I will handle the funeral arrangements and take that off her mind, at least."

"You didn't remove anything from the shed after we broke in, did you, Howard?"

"Remove anything? Of course not. What would I remove?"

"I'm just thinking out loud. Call me if you hear anything about the baby."

"Of course."

I hung up and went back to my yard work. Fifteen minutes later I was phoning Sheriff Lens at home. "Sheriff, Douglas Oberman was murdered."

"How do you figure that?"

"There was no key on your inventory list."

"Key? What key?"

"He always kept the potting shed padlocked, and Sandra told me he took the key off a hook in the kitchen when he went out there yesterday. He undid the padlock and shifted it to the inside hasp. He locked it. But where's the key?"

"You don't need a key to lock a padlock. You just snap it shut."

"But he needed the key to unlock it. Where did it go? Not into his pocket, nor anywhere in the potting shed."

"Maybe he handed it back to Sandra and she forgot to mention it. We'll probably find it on the kitchen hook."

"Do you have the key to the house?"

"No reason to, Doc. It's suicide, remember? I suppose his brother has a key."

"Can you get it and meet me out there?"

"Now? It'll be dark in an hour."

"I'll be there in thirty minutes."

* * *

Sheriff Lens was there ahead of me, grumbling about the waste of his time. He unlocked the front door and I followed him in. The house had only been closed up since morning but already I could sense the musty odor of death. I walked first into the kitchen and snapped on the light. There were four hooks by the door for keys and one of them was empty. It was obvious that none of the remaining keys was for a padlock.

"So where is it?" the sheriff asked.

"I think Douglas took it off the hook and unlocked the shed's padlock. He may have left it hanging from the outside staple as people sometimes do. The killer arrived a moment later, took the padlock inside, and locked the inner hasp with it, probably removing the key from force of habit. Then he shot Douglas Oberman, left the gun by his right hand, and escaped."

"Escaped how?"

"Well, the floor is stone and the roof is solid. That only leaves the door or the window. Let's go look at them again."

It was almost sundown, but there was still enough light for us to examine the hasp and padlock on the inside of the splintered door. "These screws haven't been tampered with in years," Sheriff Lens observed, "and the padlock is still firmly in place. We didn't unlock it."

I smiled. "Because you had no key. Let's look at the window." I struck it with the heel of my hand and it moved a bit. With a little more effort I had it open.

"It would take a child to fit through there, and how would a child even reach it? You've got to face the fact that it was suicide, Doc."

"Then where's the key to the padlock?"

"These flowerpots are full of dirt. He could have stuck it into any one of them."

"Good luck," I said, and he started poking the trowel into the pots. I went outside to examine the ground. The earth beneath the small window was firm, showing no evidence of footprints. From there I could see the upstairs bathroom window where Angie Oberman had been when the shot was fired, but not the kitchen or living room where Howard and Sandra would have been. Herb Tomley had departed by this time, walking across the road.

I kept going in ever-widening circles, searching for what? The key Douglas might have hurled from the window before shooting himself? There was nothing. The killer might have pushed open the window and inserted the gun tied to a pole, pressed it against the victim's head, pulled the trigger with a piece of string, removed the pole, untied the pistol, and dropped it back through the window. Except what would Douglas have been doing all this time? And what had happened to the key? And why wouldn't Angie or Sandra, or the victim's brother, have seen the killer escaping after the fatal shot that they all heard?

I saw something lying in a small hollow of bare ground about thirty feet from the potting shed. At first I took it for the remains of a bird's nest, but then I realized that something had been burned there. I could identify some feathers, and I thought of the circling chicken hawks Herb Tomley had mentioned.

Sheriff Lens came out to join me. "Find anything, Doc?"

"Something was burned here, perhaps a bird of some sort. Do you have a bag I could put these feathers in?"

"I've probably got one in the car." He returned after a moment with a small brown bag and I placed the charred remains inside.

"Any luck finding the key?" I asked.

He shook his head. "It's not in any of the flowerpots, and I even checked that rolled-up sleeping bag. No luck."

'Sleeping bag?"

"Sure, Doc. It was on the inventory sheet."

"Why would anyone keep a sleeping bag in a potting shed?"

"Maybe he liked to sleep out under the stars occasionally."

I walked over and examined the splintered door again. "I still think it was murder. Someone padlocked the door from the inside and took the key out of force of habit. When you snap a padlock shut you always take the key."

"You're wrong this time, Doc. It's suicide."

"Then what happened to the key?"

"Hell, maybe he swallowed it." The remark was a kidding one, but as soon as it was out of his mouth I could see the sheriff's expression change. "That's it! He swallowed it!"

"Sheriff—"

"I'll have the coroner X-ray the body in the morning!"

* * *

On Monday morning I didn't wait for the sheriff's call. Instead I drove out to Annabel's Ark, where a woman veterinarian had recently opened a small animal hospital. Annabel Christie was attractive and affable, and I'd taken a good deal kidding about her from my nurse Mary since she opened her office a couple of months earlier.

"Sam, how are you?" Annabel greeted me, returning a fat gray tabby to its cave.

"Can't complain. Are you keeping the patients healthy these days?"

"A lot healthier than yours are. I hear Douglas Oberman shot himself on Saturday."

I smiled a bit. "He wasn't my patient. Did you know him?"

"Slightly. I buy gas at his station."

"Actually, his death is what I came about."

"And not to see me?"

"Well, that too." I opened the paper bag. "I'm not as convinced as Sheriff Lens that this is a suicide. I found these charred remains in the Oberman yard and I'm wondering if you can identify them."

She picked up a spatula and separated the larger bits. "Feathers."

"That's why I thought of you. Their neighbor says folks around there shoot at hawks."

She shook her head. "They're too small for hawk feathers, and the marking aren't right. They look like plain old chicken feathers to me."

"Why would anyone burn them?"

"Simple. They plucked a chicken and ate it, putting the feathers in the trash which they later burned."

"Chickens." My face must have shown my disappointment.

Annabel laughed. "It's not so bad as all that. Maybe the sheriff is right about its being a suicide."

I drove back to my office thinking I'd spent enough time on a case that was going nowhere. When Sheriff Lens did call, I fully expected to hear his voice gloating in triumph at the X-ray results. He surprised me with his first words. "There's no key, Doc. He didn't swallow it."

"Oh?"

"I'm beginning to think you're right about murder."

"Let me follow up another angle," I said. I was still thinking about that unexplained sleeping bag. "I'll get back to you."

My afternoon appointments were light and I phoned Oberman's neighbor, Herb Tomley, to ask if I could stop for another talk. "If I'm not at the house I'll be out in back shootin' woodchucks," he told me.

But before I went I put in a call to Dr. Boynton over in Shinn Corners. I'd met the man once during a regional conference at Pilgrim Memorial Hospital, but I knew little about him. He came on the phone sounding gruff and harried, but after I identified myself his tone became friendlier.

"Are you calling about Mrs. Oberman?" he asked.

"Exactly. Her husband's death was a great shock, in her condition."

"Well, I'm happy to report that Angie delivered a healthy baby boy at 3:15 this morning. He weighs eight pounds, one ounce, and she's named him Douglas after her late husband."

"She came through it all right?"

"Fine. The baby was nearly two weeks premature, but mother and son are both doing well. I'm going to keep her in our guest room for the rest of the week until she's able to return to Northmont with the baby."

"It might be best," I agreed. "By that time the funeral will be over. Is she able to receive visitors?"

"Not today, but I believe her brother-in-law and his wife are driving over tomorrow afternoon."

"I'd like to see her too, if I could."

He hesitated. "A brief visit only. I don't want to tire her out."

"I'll try to get there around noon."

* * *

When I drove out to Herb Tomley's place no one answered my knock. I went around back and gazed out at the empty field, hearing in the distance the sharp crack of a hunting rifle. Then I saw him, a tiny spot of red far out in the field. As I trudged toward him he lowered the weapon and came to meet me. "Damned woodchucks! I think I hit one of them."

"Do you ever have trouble with people stealing your chickens, neighbors perhaps?"

"Nothing like that. Once, a couple of years ago, a hobo off the train stole a couple of chickens out of the henhouse. I had him in my shotgun sights but I figured he probably needed 'em worse than I did."

"I wanted to ask you a bit more about the Obermans."

"I hear she's having her baby."

"Had it this morning," I informed him. "A boy."

"That's good."

"You live right across from them. Ever notice anything unusual at night?"

"Like what?"

"Did Douglas ever sleep outdoors in the summer?"

"Why would he do that?"

"Perhaps after an argument with his wife?" I suggested.

"Hell, they got three unused bedrooms in the place. He wouldn't need to go outside."

"The potting shed door could be padlocked from either side."

"Yeah," Tomley answered with a smirk. "When he was doin' his potting he didn't like to be disturbed."

"What went on there?"

"Couldn't tell you."

I took a deep breath. "You could be in big trouble unless you do. What was her name?"

He stared up at the autumn sky for a moment before answering, scanning the treetop for chicken hawks. "Risa Quinn," he answered softly. "The deputy's daughter."

* * *

Felix Quinn's daughter had been the subject of whispers more than a year earlier, in the summer of '39. Just nineteen years old and working at the soda fountain next to Northmont's only movie theater, she'd suddenly left town amidst rumors that she was pregnant. Some even said she'd been having an affair with an older married man, though no name was ever mentioned. We learned later that she indeed had a baby and was living with an aunt in Boston. I thought about all that as I drove over to Shinn Corners to visit Angie Oberman and her new baby. Was it possible that Douglas had fathered two children by two different women? Of course it was possible. It happened all the time. But I had to admit that illicit lovemaking in a locked potting shed was a new one on me.

I tried to remember what Risa Quinn looked like. Could she possibly have fit through that small window in the shed? Had she come back to avenge herself on the man who did her wrong? Or was Herb Tomley merely repeating an unfounded rumor?

Shinn Corners was smaller than Northmont, across the line in the next county. It was an area of flat tobacco farmland, of scrubby countryside leading into low hills. There was no hospital to compare with ours, which was why I'd been surprised that Angie chose to have her baby there. But when I pulled up to Dr. Boynton's place I saw a large home with a well-tended garden and stately shade trees. It reminded me of Angie Oberman's house in Northmont, and perhaps that was reason enough for her to choose it.

Dr. Boynton was a robust, red-faced man with a mole on his left cheek. He greeted me warmly and introduced me at once to his wife Elizabeth. "She assisted at the delivery," he explained. "She's a registered midwife."

"That's certainly keeping it in the family," I said.

Elizabeth Boynton smiled. "We like it that way. The Shinn Corners hospital leaves something to be desired. We hope someday soon to build a new one. Would you like to see Mrs. Oberman now?"

"If I may."

"Come this way."

I followed her up the stairs to the second floor, where I could already hear the gurgling sounds of a baby. Angie Oberman was sitting up in bed, looking small but happy, with the newborn cradled in her arms. "So good of you to come see me, Dr. Hawthorne."

"You're looking well, Angie. And Douglas is a beautiful baby." He had a tiny thumb in his mouth, with a tuft of silken hair over one of his deep brown eyes.

"Thank you. I believe he looks a bit like his father, around the mouth." The mention of her husband brought a sudden sadness to her face, as if she had just remembered. "When is the funeral?" she asked.

"On Wednesday, I think. Howard and Sandra will be here soon. They can tell you for certain."

"It'll be good to see them."

After we'd talked about the baby for a few minutes, Dr. Boynton came in to join us. "We mustn't tire her too much. She has more visitors on the way."

Angie had one more question for me. "Is it true that my husband shot himself?"

"The sheriff is certain of it."

"And you?'

"Just one thing bothers me. Why would your husband want to lock the potting shed door from the inside?"

"I don't know. I never went out there. The garden was his hobby. Perhaps when he was working there he didn't want to be bothered by Herb Tomley or our other neighbors."

"Did you actually see Tomley go back home?"

"No. I was in the kitchen with Sandra and then I went up to the bathroom." She patted her now flattened belly. "I was very uncomfortable."

"But when you heard the shot you looked out the bathroom window."

"Yes."

"Did you see anyone at all near the shed's door or window?"

"No. There was no one."

Dr. Boynton cleared his throat. "Please, Doctor—"

"All right." I took her hand. "I'll see you back in Northmont."

Elizabeth Boynton was waiting downstairs. I realized now that she had the large body and strong hands of a midwife. They were like earth mothers, guiding us across an uncharted sea.

* * *

On my way back to Northmont I recognized Howard Oberman's car and honked my horn. He pulled off the road opposite me and I crossed over to say a few words. Sandra was in the passenger seat by his side. "I've just seen Angie and the baby," I said. "They're both doing fine."

"I'm anxious to see her," Sandra said.

"What's Boynton like?" her husband asked.

"He seems very caring, a good doctor from all I could tell. His wife assisted at the delivery, which was in their home."

"How long will she be there?"

"The rest of the week, at least. It's just as well she doesn't return until after the funeral."

"Is the investigation concluded?" Sandra asked.

"I have one more person to speak to, one of Sheriff Lens's deputies. Then I think we'll wrap it up."

They went on their way and I returned to my car. Once back in Northmont I drove to the sheriff's office and found Felix Quinn seated at one of the desks. "How are you, Felix?" I greeted him.

"Can't complain. Not much doing today."

I pulled a chair up to his desk. "I need to ask you something about your daughter."

"Risa? She lives in Boston with my sister. Haven't seen her since she went away."

"I heard she had a child."

He avoided my gaze. "I guess so. My wife and I don't talk about it much."

"Do you know who the father is?"

"I got my ideas."

"Did you ever think it might be Douglas Oberman?"

His eyes shot up and locked with mine. "What do you know?"

"I've heard rumors."

"Are you trying to pin his death on me?"

"You were one of the deputies who smashed in the door of his shed. Perhaps that padlock was open and you snapped it shut."

"You know that's not so. We could see through the window that it was locked."

"But that's where he took your daughter, wasn't it?"

"If I knew that for a fact, I'd have killed him long ago."

Sheriff Lens came in then, a bit surprised to see us with our heads together in serious conversation. "What's going on?"

"We're just reviewing the evidence," I said. "Do you remember when we noticed the shed was locked from the inside?"

"Sure, we saw it through the window."

"That's how I remember too," the deputy confirmed.

I knew they were right. Quinn might have had a perfect motive, but he couldn't have done it. For one thing, he'd have had to lose about forty pounds to fit through that window. I stared hard at him, and in that instant I knew the *how* and the *who* and the *why*.

"Sheriff, you have to come with me, right away."

"Where are we going?"

"I'll tell you on the way."

* * *

As we traveled over the country roads I kept the sheriff in suspense. There was still so much to work out in my own mind. I would only say, somewhat enigmatically, "I could tell you the whole thing in three words. They explain how Douglas could have been killed in that locked shed, who pulled the trigger, and even a possible motive for the crime."

"Three words?"

"Three words."

"Will you tell me this much, Doc? Was the killer actually inside the shed with him?"

"Yes."

"And was the door really locked from the inside?"

"Certainly."

"Then Douglas must have lived long enough to snap the padlock shut after his killer left."

"Not with that head wound. It would have killed him instantly."

Sheriff Lens puzzled over it while I drove. Presently he said, "Hey, we're on the road to Shinn Corners."

"That's right. We're going to Dr. Boynton's house. I hope Howard and Sandra are still there."

"What does Boynton know about this?"

"Almost everything."

We pulled up in front of his house and I was pleased that Howard's car was still there. When Elizabeth met us at the door I could see the sudden fear in her eyes. "What do you want?"

"The truth," I answered.

Her husband was right behind her. "You've had your visit for the day. Angie has to rest now."

"I think not, Doctor."

Hearing our voices, Howard Oberman came to the head of the stairs. "What's going on here?"

"I must see Angie right away."

We went up the stairs, the sheriff trailing behind. Sandra was there with the new mother, carefully cradling the baby. She stared at us, startled. "What's going on?"

"We're here to wrap this up," I said. "I can tell you who killed Douglas, and how it was done, in just three words."

"And what are those words?" Dr. Boynton asked.

I looked for the first time at the small, slender woman in the bed and said simply, "Angie wasn't pregnant."

* * *

I hurried on before anyone could speak. "A little while ago, back in Northmont, I was questioning your deputy, Sheriff. I believed Felix Quinn might have had a motive and I was trying to figure out how he might have lost enough weight to squirm through that slit window in the potting shed. You see, that was our problem. The shed wasn't a classic hermetically sealed room. It had an unlocked window that could be pushed open with a little difficulty. But none of the people involved could fit through it."

"What are you trying to say?" Dr. Boynton demanded.

"Angie is the only one who could possibly be described as small, and she was almost nine months pregnant. Certainly in her condition she could never have squeezed through that window. But then I thought of something else. It's virtually impossible for two blue-eyed parents like Douglas and Angie to have a brown-eyed child like Doug here. You must know, Dr. Boynton, that it was not uncommon practice some years back for women to fake a pregnancy by wearing padding and then adopt an unwanted child as their own."

"Padding?" Sheriff Lens asked.

"A small pillow at first, which increased in size as the months passed. The woman wore them strapped around her middle. That's what you wore, wasn't it, Angie? And before you came here Sunday morning you burned the small one so it wouldn't be found. I identified some charred chicken feathers, a common stuffing for pillows."

"Are you saying Angie killed my brother?" Howard asked.

"I am. She must have known about his dalliance with other women in the locked shed. Perhaps she'd even heard rumors that he fathered a child by Quinn's teenage daughter. Yet she was made to imitate a pregnancy and take an unknown child into her home. It was probably Douglas's idea, and she resented it. Perhaps she even feared it was from another of his adulterous affairs."

"It wasn't," Boynton assured us. "I know the parents. They have a large family here."

"I should have been suspicious from the beginning, when you wouldn't let me examine you and wouldn't let your sister-in-law even touch you. You couldn't have us finding the padding, especially after you'd killed Douglas."

"But nobody saw her leave the shed after they heard the shot," the sheriff argued.

"I established that the shed window could only be seen from the upstairs bathroom, where Angie claimed to be. The others could only see the front door. Angie slipped down the back stairs, or perhaps never went up in the first place. She'd no doubt suggested that her husband gave Sandra the mums, and she ran down to meet him at the shed. She took the padlock inside, locked the door, and shot him at close range. Dropping the key in her pocket was force of habit, I suppose. She wasn't wearing her padding, so it was no trouble pushing open the slit window and boosting herself up and out. You'd been something of a tomboy in your younger days, Angie. You pushed the window closed and returned to the house behind that row of bushes, just as you'd no doubt practiced it earlier."

"The Boyntons knew nothing about it," Angie said, speaking for the first time. "They're good people who try to place unwanted babies with childless couples."

"And they phoned you Saturday morning to tell you the time had come."

"Yes. I had the gun ready. It was a good time to do it."

Sheriff Lens shook his head. "It's never a good time for murder, Mrs. Oberman."

* * *

All the while I was telling Mary Best about it the following morning, I could see she was brimming over with news. "I have to tell you, Sam, I think I have a new nurse for you."

"Oh?"

"You know I correspond with April. I told her I was leaving and she phoned last night from Maine. Her husband André is in the naval reserve and he's been called up for eighteen months' active duty. Someone's going to manage the inn for them and she's moving back to Northmont until he returns."

"April? Do you think she'd want to come back to work?"

"She'd love it," Mary told me.

THE PROBLEM OF THE YELLOW WALLPAPER

Much as I hated to see Mary Best depart from my office to become a Navy nurse in that glowering November of 1940, I was delighted when my former nurse April moved back to Northmont. Her husband had been called up for eighteen months of reserve duty, and she arrived on the train from Maine with her four-year-old son Sam in tow, looking not a day older than I remembered her. It would be the beginning of two of the most eventful years of my life. (Old Dr. Sam Hawthorne paused to wipe something from his eye before continuing his narrative, and his guest might not have been mistaken if he thought it was a tear.)

April had been a plump, jolly woman of thirty when I hired her shortly after my arrival in Northmont. Now, in her late forties, she was a happily married woman and the mother of a wonderful little boy. Perhaps I was predisposed to like him, since Sam Mulhone had been named after me, but a few minutes of playing with the boy at the station had made us fast friends.

"It's good to have you back, April," I told her, and meant it.

"You're sure I'm not putting someone else out of a job?"

"Far from it!" I assured her. "With Mary gone off to the Navy, I really needed somebody in the office. It was good of her to make the arrangements with you."

April nodded. "The Navy took Mary and my André at virtually the same time." She hung on to young Sam's hand as I guided them to the parking lot where my Buick waited. She smiled when she saw it. "A nice car, Sam, but I can remember your Pierce-Arrow Runabout."

"I was younger then." I opened the trunk and hoisted her bags inside.

"Weren't we all!" She helped Sam into the front seat and then slid in herself while I got behind the wheel. She'd rented a nice apartment only a few blocks from my office at the hospital, and I drove her there from the station.

I'd made arrangements for a dependable neighborhood woman to look after Sam while April worked, with the understanding that she could bring him to the office any day the woman wasn't available. April hadn't wanted to make the long drive from Maine with her son, so a friend was bringing her car down the following week, with more of her clothing and possessions.

I helped her get settled and then invited her to my house for Thanksgiving dinner the following day. "You and your son can't be alone on the holiday," I reasoned.

"Oh, Sam, we had our Thanksgiving last week!" We'd had two years of confusion and anger over the holiday, ever since President Roosevelt changed the date to the third Thursday in November instead of the fourth.

I merely smiled. "Well, I guess you could celebrate both days. A lot of people in Northmont do."

So April and young Sam had a second Thanksgiving dinner before she plunged into the daily chores of the office. After dinner that night, while her son slept on the sofa in my living room, she said, "Fill me in on what's been going on. I know you and Mary were quite close for a time."

"We were," I answered with a sigh. "It was one of those things that reached a point where neither of us wanted to take the next step. I hope that's not why she joined the Navy, but it might have been a factor."

"Is there anyone else now?"

I smiled at the question. "We have a woman veterinarian with a new place outside of town, over toward Shinn Corners. Her name is Annabel Christie and she calls the clinic Annabel's Ark. We've become friendly, that's all.

"And how's the crime rate? Are you still saving Sheriff Lens's hide on a regular basis?"

"Oh, the sheriff is a good man. He'll be happy to see you back. I still help him a little when I can."

"You are much too modest, Sam. You always have been. How about our patients? Anything unusual?"

"A Dutchman named Peter Haas claims he has a crazy wife. There's no one in town who can treat her but he won't send her away. I'm going over there tomorrow morning. You may want to ride along."

"How crazy? Does he keep her locked in the attic?"

"As a matter of fact, he does."

* * *

Peter Haas and his wife had come to America from Paris in search of a better life. They'd been fearful of Hitler's rise and what it might portend for the future of Europe. Haas had been in the diamond business, and I assumed it was the profits from those past dealings that enabled him to live with his wife in one of our town's largest homes, a lavish three-story Victorian house dating from the turn of the century, complete with kitchen and servants' quarters in the basement and a small carriage house out back. They lived there alone, though a maid came in to clean and cook for them.

Haas himself met us at the door that Friday morning, the day following our traditional Thanksgiving. He was a tall, slender man with thinning hair who wore metal-rimmed eyeglasses that he often removed as he spoke. I knew from his medical record that he was forty-four years old. His wife Katherine was twenty-nine but appeared older. I'd started treating her for nervous depression about a year earlier and her condition had grown steadily worse with time. I detected a slight hysterical tendency and urged him to seek help in Boston, where practicing psychiatrists were readily available.

Today, as I introduced him to April, he seemed especially distraught. "She's been peeling off the wallpaper in her room. I don't know what I'm going to do, Dr. Hawthorne."

"Let's go take a look."

He led us up two flights of stairs to the third-floor room that had been her bedchamber since early October when he had twice found her running nude through the garden at night. "Katherine," he called out as he unlocked the door, "Dr. Hawthorne's here to see you."

"Come in!" she sang out, almost too cheerfully.

We entered the bedroom and I felt that I was seeing it, for the first time, through April's eyes. The big double bed sat with its head against the far wall, between two barred windows that looked out on the rear garden and the carriage house. To our right were two more windows facing toward the center of town. These also were barred. One window was open a bit for fresh air, and all were covered by window screens to keep out summer insects. The wall to our left was blank, covered, as were the other walls, with faded yellow wallpaper of an unattractive flowery design. It had been ripped away in places and left dangling from the wall, exposing the bare plaster. The only other pieces of furniture in the room were a nightstand, a straight-backed chair, and a wardrobe.

Katherine Haas sat upright in the center of her bed, wearing a pink negligee tied in a bow at her throat. It was the sort of garment young woman might wear, and it contrasted sharply with the lined and haggard face above it. There was little doubt that she was ill. "I've been waiting for you, Doctor," she told me at once. "I have a whole new set of symptoms to tell you about."

"Let me give you an examination first." I took out my stethoscope and listened to her heart and lungs. They seemed fine, and her temperature was normal. We talked for a few minutes while I introduced April, then I said, "Suppose you tell me what the trouble is."

"Mainly it's the dreams, Doctor. They come on me every night, closer to nightmares than anything else. I dream there's a prisoner in these walls, inside the wallpaper, trying to claw her way out."

"Is that how it got torn?" I asked.

"I suppose so. I can't remember clearly."

We chatted a while longer and I wrote out a new prescription, more to comfort her than to do any real good. Once outside, I watched Peter Haas locking the door and asked, "Is that really necessary? Keeping her locked up only makes matters worse."

"You didn't have to chase her through the garden in the middle of the night," he replied bluntly. "I did."

"Then take her to Boston, for God's sake!" I urged. "I can give you the name of a fine man there."

"I believe she can recover better here," Haas said, running a nervous hand through his thinning hair.

"How? Locked in an attic room?"

April spoke up for the first time. "Mr. Haas, why are there bars on her windows?"

He sighed, seeming thankful for a question he could answer. "I understand the room was once a nursery, and later a playroom for small children. The owner had the latest safety devices for summoning servants in case of an emergency, and the bars were to keep the children from climbing onto the roof."

"I see."

The full import of her question suddenly became clear to him. "Did you think I had the bars installed?"

"I just wondered about it," April said. "The room seems like a jail cell."

The Dutchman turned to me with anger in his eyes. "Does this woman mean to insult me?"

I tried to soothe him. "Of course not. We're both concerned about your wife, that's all. She needs the sort of treatment I can't give her."

By the time we'd reached the door he'd calmed down a bit. "When will you be back, Doctor?"

"Tuesday morning, to see if that new prescription is doing any good."

Back in the car, I had to listen to April's views on the subject. "Sam, you can't allow that poor woman to suffer another day like that. It's like—it's like a story I read once. I might have it in one of the books I brought along."

I shook my head as I drove back to the office. "I'm at my wits' end." I admitted.

"Is there anyone in Boston who'd be willing to come here to examine her?"

Suddenly I remembered an old classmate of mine who'd become a psychiatrist. Doug Foley. I'd visited him a few years back on one of my infrequent holidays. "There is somebody, but he's in New York."

"Could he come up on a weekend?"

I thought about it. Like me, Doug Foley thrived on a challenge. He just might be willing to make the trip. "I can ask him," I decided.

I reached Doug in New York later that afternoon and he agreed to take the train up to Stamford the following Saturday morning, assuming there wasn't an early-December snowstorm. I would meet him at the station for the two-hour drive to Northmont. He'd stay overnight with me and return to New York on Sunday afternoon. Meanwhile, April had a suggestion.

"She's alone too much in that room. No wonder she's starting to imagine things about the wallpaper. Do you think we could get her a pet, perhaps a cat? They're soothing for people."

"It's an idea," I agreed.

I had invited Annabel Christie to dine with me that evening at the Northmont Inn. The old Ferry House was long gone, and this was now our only claim to a real country inn. As with most people, our conversation turned first to the war news. It had been a bad month for England, with the city of Coventry all but wiped out by German bombers. A naval battle between British and Italian warships was raging off Sardinia in the Mediterranean, but it was too soon to know the outcome.

Annabel looked especially fetching that evening, wearing a light brown dress that went well with her blond hair and hazel eyes. It was hard to believe I'd known her only about ten weeks, having met her when unusual circumstances arose at her veterinary hospital, Annabel's Ark. Over dinner I told her about Katherine Haas and her problems. "My nurse April wonders if having a pet cat might help her. Do you have any strays at the Ark right now?"

"I have a perfect little kitten, only a few weeks old. She was born at the Ark and the owners gave her to me as partial payment on their bill. I call her Furball, but that can be changed. She's mostly black with white paws."

"Do you think it would help?"

She shrugged. "It might."

"I feel sorry for her husband."

Annabel scoffed. "Any man who would keep his wife locked up like that deserves a horsewhipping, not sympathy."

"My friend Doug will be here next weekend. I'm hoping he'll have some suggestions."

I picked up the kitten on Monday morning and drove over to the Haas's house alone while April settled in at my office. Katherine was in her locked third-floor bedroom and seemed little different from the previous week. When I presented her with the black and white kitten she seemed genuinely pleased. "It's yours," I told her. "You can name it whatever you want."

"How can I thank you, Dr. Hawthorne? This is one of the nicest things anyone has ever done for me."

"You can thank me getting better. Have you been taking your medicine?" She glanced over at her husband, who stood near the door. "I have. I think it's helping me."

"How about the dreams?"

"N-No, I haven't been having them the last few nights."

It seemed to me that more of the yellow wallpaper had been torn and scratched away since my Friday visit. We left Katherine playing with her kitten on the bed and went back downstairs. "She's been at the wallpaper again," I observed.

He nodded with a sigh. "She denies it. She insists there's a woman behind the wallpaper, trying to get free. She must be having the same dream, even though she won't admit it."

I rested a comforting hand on his shoulder. "I have a friend, a classmate from medical school, who has a psychiatric practice in New York City. He's visiting me next weekend and I'd like him to see Katherine. He might be able to help her."

He hesitated a moment before agreeing. "Very well, if you really believe it might help."

"I'll telephone you on Saturday after my friend arrives. His name is Dr. Doug Foley."

* * *

The first week in December was a busy one for Northmont's hospital and medical staff. The beginning of the month, often accompanied by plunging temperatures and snow, seemed to signal the onslaught of all manner of colds and flu each year. Though the polio season was pretty much past, there were plenty of other worries for nervous parents. In a week as busy as that,

April and I gave little thought to Peter Haas and his wife.

It wasn't until Friday, the afternoon before Doug Foley's arrival, that April remembered the story she'd been going to show me, in a twenty-year-old anthology entitled *Great Modern American Stories*, edited by the author William Dean Howells. It was a horror story, "The Yellow Wallpaper," by Charlotte Perkins Gilman, about a situation very similar to that of Katherine Haas.

"What a ghastly tale," I said when I'd finished reading it. "I only hope we can save Mrs. Haas from a fate like that."

"The part about the barred windows and the wallpaper is what reminded me of it. I feel as if the story has come to life right here in Northmont."

"It is an odd coincidence," I admitted. "Can I borrow this book until tomorrow? I'd like Annabel to read it."

I let Annabel read it after dinner that evening, but her reaction was quite different from April's and mine. She closed the book and set it down. "You read this as a pure horror story?"

"Isn't it?"

"Sam, it's a story about feminine consciousness, about a woman imprisoned by male authority. The woman she imagines trapped in the wallpaper design is the nameless narrator herself. Her husband treats her like a child and is unresponsive to her needs. She suffers some natural depression following the birth of their baby, and he treats her in the worst possible manner."

I could see what she meant, and perhaps she was right. "You shouldn't be wasting your time on animals," I told her, only half in jest.

Saturday morning was cold and sunny as I drove to Stamford to meet Doug Foley's train. We were both still in our early forties, though I could detect a slight graying of his hair since the last time we'd gotten together. When I mentioned it, he laughed and said, "It's good for business. People don't like to reveal their innermost secrets to a callow youth. Every time I notice a few more grey hairs I increase my hourly rate."

"What do you think about the war?" I asked as we drove. "My office nurse just joined the Navy."

"We'll be in it," he predicted. "Maybe within a year. But you and I are both over forty. The draft doesn't want us. Now tell me about this patient of yours."

"I'll show my file on her at the office. Katherine Haas, age twenty-nine, although she looks older. She and her husband moved to Northmont from Paris a few years ago when Hitler first started threatening the rest of Europe.

They bought the largest Victorian mansion in town, but appeared very little in public. I started treating her for mild depression about a year ago, but her condition was worsened. After a couple of episodes of her running naked through the garden at night, her husband confined her to a third-floor room with barred windows. Almost from the beginning, I recommended he seek psychiatric help for her in Boston, but he wouldn't hear of it. I don't know how he'll react to your visit, but at least he's agreed to let you see her."

Doug shifted uncomfortably in his seat. It was a long ride after an hour already spent on the train from Grand Central. "Unfortunately, we're still viewed by many people as something akin to witch doctors. Freud and Jung aren't exactly the Mayo brothers."

"I do appreciate your coming all this distance, Doug. Naturally I'll compensate you for your time."

Foley waved away the offer. "It's good to get out in the country sometimes. In Manhattan, we get too many patients unhinged by a sheer pace of things. They simply can't cope with life in a metropolis." He glanced out the car window at the barren fields spotted here and there with a trace of snow. "I don't expect that's a problem up here."

Although my office was only open half-days on Saturday and April could have gone home at noon, she was still rearranging files when we arrived. "I'm waiting for my friend Ellen to arrive with my car and more of my things," she explained. "I'll be going shortly."

"I thought Mary's filing system was pretty good," I said, observing the stack of folders on her desk.

"It was, Sam, but everyone does things differently. I learned a lot managing our hotel with André."

I explained to Doug that April's husband had been called to active duty with the naval reserve and he three of us fell into conversation until her friend pulled into the parking lot with her car. After they went off, I located Katherine Haas's folder in the stack and showed it to Doug. He read it over twice with a grim, intense expression on his face. "I think we'd better go over there now," he decided.

"Don't you want lunch first?"

"It can wait."

On the way over he asked me about April. "She was a great help when I first came here to set up a practice," I told him. "She's different now, with her own way of doing things, but that's probably good. I'm lucky to have her back, even if it's only for eighteen months."

"The way the war in Europe is developing, her husband might be away a lot longer than that."

I hoped for April's sake he was wrong about that.

* * *

Peter Haas met us at the front door of his house and ushered us inside. "Pleased to meet you, Dr. Foley," he said after I'd made the introductions. "I'm afraid my wife is having a bad day."

"What's the trouble?" I asked.

He led us through the hall to the stairs, and I caught a glimpse of their maid dusting the parlor. "She won't let me come in, claims she'll hide in the wallpaper if I open the door."

At the third-floor room I knocked softly. "Katherine, are you in there?"

"Go away!" she said from the other side of the locked door. "Don't come in here."

"This is Dr. Hawthorne, Katherine."

"I know who it is. Go away." Her voice was low, but close by.

"A friend of mine is here from New York. I think he can be a big help to you."

"No!" she almost screamed it. "He'll lock me away!"

"Aren't you locked away now?" I tried to reason with her through the door. "Dr. Foley can help you."

"The wallpaper—" Her sentence was cut short by a sort of gasp.

I turned to her husband. "There's no reasoning with her. You'll have to unlock the door."

Haas took a deep breath and fitted the key into the lock. As soon as I heard the bolt slide free, I turned the knob and opened the door. I saw at once that even more of the yellow wallpaper had been peeled away. It hung in great hunks from the plaster walls.

The room appeared to be empty and I quickly looked behind the door as Haas and Doug Foley entered. "She must be under the bed," Haas said.

But she wasn't. She wasn't anywhere. The black and white kitten sat on the center of the quilt, the only living thing in the room.

I opened the wardrobe, which contained only one dress and a nightgown. I walked around the room, tapping the solid plaster walls. I tried the windows, but the bars and screen held firm.

Then, looking back at the wall opposite the windows, I noticed something that sent a chill down my spine. It was the blurred face of Katherine Haas, staring out at me from her wallpaper prison.

* * *

"Looks to me like it was painted with some sort of watercolors," Sheriff Lens said as he examined the face on the wallpaper an hour later. I'd summoned him at once, after determining that Katherine Haas had indeed vanished from that locked and barred room. "Was your wife a painter, Mr. Haas?"

"Not in a good many years. When we first met, back in Paris, she used to do watercolors along the Seine."

While we'd waited for the sheriff's arrival, Doug and I had been over every possibility. We'd searched the house from top to bottom, paying special attention to the third-floor storage rooms, but we'd found nothing. Katherine Haas had faded away as if she'd never existed.

Going over her room with me, Doug could only shake his head in frustration. "She had nothing here! No personal possessions, no books, no cosmetics, not even a mirror!" He turned angrily on the woman's husband, who stood watching us from the doorway. "Did you even allow her to go to the toilet?"

"Of course. I took her downstairs several times a day. She ate her meals with me. I just could not trust her out of my sight unless she was locked in here."

"And now where is she?"

"I don't know," he admitted. "In another world, perhaps. I hope it's a better world for her."

He gave the same answer to Sheriff Lens, and the sheriff wasn't any more satisfied than Doug Foley had been. "Did you kill you wife, Mr. Haas?"

"What? Of course not! How could I? These two gentlemen have been with me every minute."

"I mean before," the sheriff said, glancing over at me. "That voice Doc heard could have been a recording or something."

But I objected to that possibility. "She spoke directly to me through the door," I pointed out. "She answered what I said. We carried on a brief conversation."

We went back to searching the room. We poked and prodded the bed, pulling it away from the wall. We searched the wardrobe for a hidden compartment and pulled that out from the wall, too, but there was nothing.

Sheriff Lens had a new suggestion. After establishing just where we were standing in the hall while I conversed with Katherine through the door, he asked, "Mr. Haas, is there any chance you're a ventriloquist?"

"Of course not!"

I had to agree. "It was his wife's voice. I'd stake my life on it. She was in this room and now she's gone."

We went downstairs to the parlor, where Sheriff Lens was clearly uncomfortable with the Victorian bric-a-brac. After running his finger over a silver tea service, I saw him wipe away the dust with a sour expression. "What about the maid?" he asked. "I caught a glimpse of her arriving."

"She must be down in the servants' quarters," Haas replied. He walked over to the wall and called out, "Rose, can you come up here for a minute?"

I couldn't catch her reply, but when the young maid presented herself I realized it was Rose West, daughter of a local hardware dealer, who'd graduated from high school the previous June. "How are you, Rose?" I greeted her. "I didn't know you worked here."

"Hello, Dr. Hawthorne. I'm trying to earn money toward college. I'm at my dad's store mornings and I come here from two to six to clean and help prepare dinner." She glanced from me to Sheriff Lens and finally to Peter Haas. "What is it? Has something happened to Mrs. Haas?"

"She's disappeared," her employer told her. "Katherine is gone and we can't find any trace of her."

Rose's mouth dropped open. "I hope she hasn't hurt herself."

"We don't know," Sheriff Lens said. "Did you see anything when you arrived, anything unusual?"

She shook her head. "Everything was the same. I saw nothing of Mrs. Haas."

"Did you ever visit her in her third-floor room?"

"Sometimes when she wouldn't come down for dinner. I'd take it up to her. Mr. Haas came along to unlock the door."

"What can you do, Sheriff?" I asked him. "This whole situation is beyond belief."

He could only shrug. "Nothing, Doc. I can't see that any crime has been committed."

"The woman is gone!"

"A missing person. She probably squeezed between those bars on the windows."

"They're only five inches apart, Sheriff," I pointed out. "And they're covered with window screens."

"Let's wait a day. My guess is she'll turn up, none the worse for wear."

As we were leaving. Haas said, "You'd better take the kitten. There's no one to care for it now."

Driving back to my house, I could only apologize to Doug. "Looks like I got you all the way up here for nothing."

"Don't worry. It was a good excuse to get away from the city."

Annabel Christie insisted on preparing dinner for us both, and we spent a pleasant evening at her apartment. I tried to return the kitten, but she thought I should keep it. "You can call him Watson," she suggested. Later, when she mentioned the story about the yellow wallpaper, Doug insisted on reading it.

"Well?" she asked when he'd finished. "Is it a story about insanity or the subjugation of women?"

He could sense there'd been some disagreement about it. Wisely, he answered, "Both, I think."

The following day at the railroad station we shook hands. "Keep me informed of developments," he said. "I can make another trip up here if necessary."

"Thanks, Doug."

"And Sam—"

"Yes?"

"Annabel Christie is a fine young woman."

* * *

Monday passed, and then Tuesday, without any sign of the vanished Katherine Haas. When I phoned Rose West she told me that Peter Haas seemed remote and preoccupied on her daily visits. He ate very little, and even suggested he might be leaving town in the near future.

The news from Sheriff Lens was a bit more interesting, even if it seemed to contribute nothing toward solving the mystery. He'd been looking into Katherine Haas's background before she and her husband arrived in Northmont and had discovered some interesting facts. "It was her father, not her husband, who'd been the diamond merchant in Europe," he told me on the phone. "When he died, fourteen years ago, the family money was left in trust for her until she turned thirty. Checks from a Swiss bank are deposited to her account on the first of each month."

"So her money has been supporting them both," I said, thinking out loud. "That's interesting. What happens to the trust fund if she dies before turning thirty?"

"The whole thing goes to a convent of nuns in Spain. No wonder he kept her a virtual prisoner. He was afraid she'd run off."

"Perhaps." But suddenly I was thinking of another possibility. "How much will she receive on her thirtieth birthday?"

"Those Swiss banks won't release information like that, but you can be sure they wouldn't handle it unless it was a sizable sum."

"Thanks for the information, Sheriff. Any word on her yet?"

"Not a thing. I've sent a missing persons report out to police departments and sheriff's offices throughout New England and New York."

"I doubt if that'll do any good. I don't think she ever left that house."

"Then where is she, Doc?"

"I wish I knew."

April had finally gotten the files arranged to her liking, and when I hung up she had a raft of questions to ask me. One was about Katherine Haas. "What are these papers in French that were in her folder?"

"Her medical records. She brought them with her when they moved here from Paris. My French isn't very good, but it didn't really matter. She was in good health at the time."

She studied the top sheet. "André taught me French when we were first married. I can read most of this." Then, "Didn't you tell me she painted a picture of herself on the wall of that room?"

"Apparently. Haas said she used to do watercolors along the Seine when they lived in Paris."

"That's odd. Look at this." She was pointing to a French word in the second paragraph: *daltonien.*

I shook my head. "What does it mean?"

"Color-blind."

"Oh?"

"Certainly it's not impossible for a color-blind person to be a painter, but you don't find too many of them. Did she ever mention it to you?"

"No. And until recently she seemed in perfect health."

But I thought about it the rest of the afternoon. I thought about how Katherine Haas could have gotten out of that room, and where she might be. Finally, that evening, I phoned Sheriff Lens.

"I'm going to see Haas. Do you want to come along and make an arrest?" I asked.

"Yes."

"I knew it! I'll pick you up."

I didn't tell him anything else on the short ride back to the Victorian house. We parked a few houses down the street and went the rest of the way on foot, not up to the big house but around back toward the carriage house. I was guessing now, but I could think of no other possibility. The door was unlocked and we entered quietly. I could hear voices from the second floor. As we started up the steps a squeaky tread signaled our arrival.

In an instant Peter Haas appeared at the top of the stairs, holding a revolver. "Who's there?" he asked.

"Sam Hawthorne and Sheriff Lens, Peter. You'd better put down the gun."

Someone else had appeared behind him in the doorway and I saw that it was the missing woman. Her hand was to her mouth in alarm.

Sheriff Lens turned to me. "I thought you said he killed his wife, Doc."

"I believe he did. This woman is not Katherine Haas."

* * *

Perhaps my words were a charm of some sort, or perhaps Haas simply realized that it was all over. He lowered the revolver and turned back into the room as we followed. It was the woman we'd known as Katherine Haas who asked the question. "How did you know?"

We followed them into the little upstairs room and Sheriff Lens took the gun from Haas's hand. "I didn't at first," I admitted. "I went about it the wrong way, concentrating on how you got out of that room instead of the real question, which was *why*. The sheriff and my nurse April supplied me with some key facts about that. The sheriff told me that Katherine Haas had a trust fund until she reached the age of thirty. You'd both been living off that fund for years. Then April was filing some old medical records and found one from France that said Katherine Haas was color-blind. It's unusual but not impossible for a color-blind person to be a painter. That got me thinking about the self-portrait she'd painted on the wallpaper. What did she paint it with? There were no paints or brushes found in that room, no cosmetics, not even a mirror. It would be quite a trick for a color-blind artist without paints or a mirror to create a self-portrait of her face. And there were other things, too. This woman seemed older than Katherine's stated twenty-nine years. And the whole business of that locked and barred room with the torn wallpaper seemed inspired by a fifty-year-old short story."

Sheriff Lens was growing impatient. "Whatever her real identity, Doc, how could she have gotten out of that room? And why would they bother with such trickery?"

"I'll answer your second question first, because the *why* is the key to the whole thing. If we assume Haas killed the real Katherine become coming to America, it clarifies what followed. She was receiving a large monthly check from a trust fund, so it was important to him that the checks continue to arrive. It had to appear that she was still alive. It wasn't too difficult to forge her endorsement on the checks. He must have had plenty of samples of her signature. And by moving to America he avoided contact with family and friends who know the real Katherine. But there was a problem on the horizon—the real Katherine's thirtieth birthday was approaching. The Swiss bank would require proof positive of her identity, possibly fingerprints, before surrendering the trust fund's principal to her. Haas hoped the supposed mental problem would be a way to delay her appearance, but then I insisted on bringing Dr. Foley up to examine her and they knew that wouldn't work. Katherine had to disappear until they had time to work out their next move. Nothing else would do. If they faked her death the trust fund would automatically go to those Spanish nuns."

"Why couldn't he just have her run away?" the sheriff wanted to know.

I glanced in Haas's direction. He was standing in his eyes tightly shut, as if refusing to grasp the reality of the moment. "She couldn't remain missing forever or he'd be suspected of killing her. It would be a repeat of Paris, where he had to leave the country and come here with a new Katherine Haas. This way they concocted a mystery, possibly even a supernatural event, to give themselves time."

"How?" Sheriff Lens asked again.

"When Doug and I arrived at that third-floor door, she was already gone from the room."

"But you talked to her through the door!"

"Big old houses with servants' quarters had to have a way of summoning the servants when needed. Most used a bellpull, but some had a system of speaking tubes like you see on ships. You told us the family had safety devices to summon servants if there was an emergency with the children, and

I imagine this was one of them. The speaking tube was right inside the door, and by speaking loudly into it our Katherine's voice sounded as if it was on the other side of the door. We should have known the house had such a system because we saw Haas use it to summon his maid Saturday. We just didn't realize what he was doing when he walked over to the wall and called her."

"But why didn't we see this speaking tube when we searched that room?"

"That was the real reason why more wallpaper had been peeled off and hung in strips. One of those strips was hiding the speaking tube and we never noticed it."

The false Katherine spoke again. "How did you know all this? What did we do wrong?"

"Besides that suspicious painting on the wall, only one thing. When I arrived on Saturday with Doug Foley I glimpsed a maid dusting the parlor. But it wasn't Rose West, whom I recognized later, because the sheriff saw her arrive about two, her usual time. And I noticed the parlor was still quite dusty. You were lurking downstairs, dressed as a maid, until we were in position for you to use the speaking tube. Then you hurried off to hide in this carriage house, which is why Doug and I found no one when we searched the house before the sheriff and the real maid arrived."

The authorities held Peter Haas and the false Katherine while the Swiss bank and the Paris police were notified. But Paris had fallen to the Germans six months earlier and no one there showed any interest in the case. Haas insisted the real Katherine had died accidentally and there was no way to prove otherwise. They were released and quickly left town, though we heard later that the Swiss bank had hired detectives to track them down and recover the payments from the trust fund.

I kept the kitten, Watson, because it reminded me of Annabel.

THE PROBLEM OF THE HAUNTED HOSPITAL

By March of 1941 the European war had become a serious threat to shipping in the Atlantic, and the U.S. Navy formed a support force for the Atlantic convoy. My nurse April, back in Northmont while her husband was on active duty with the Naval Reserve, was beginning to doubt that he'd be home in eighteen months as promised. We were discussing it in my office on the chilly Monday when we first learned of the haunting. (Dr. Sam Hawthorne paused to fill their glasses before continuing with his story.)

"Some folks say we'll be at war by the end of the year," she was saying, and I couldn't disagree with her.

"Is André stationed aboard a ship?" I asked. Until he was called to active duty they'd managed an inn in Maine. Now April and her son Sam were back here for the duration.

"I think so, but everything is very secretive."

My former nurse, Mary Best, had enlisted in the Navy and arranged for April's return to the job. We'd speculated about her being assigned to the same ship as André, but such coincidences only happened in the movies. She was stationed at a naval base in San Diego.

My office was in a wing attached to Pilgrim Memorial Hospital, and it was not unusual for the resident doctors to drop in for a chat from time to time. On this March afternoon, our conversation was interrupted by Linc Jones, who'd caused a stir some years back as Northmont's first black physician. Linc and his wife Charlene had entertained Annabel Christie and me at dinner over the weekend and I was starting to thank him when I saw from his expression that it was not a social call.

"Sam, do you have a few minutes? There's something I'd like your advice about."

I turned to April. "When's my next appointment?"

"You promised Mrs. Dodger you'd make a house call this afternoon, but any time is all right. She's not going anywhere with that fever."

"More flu?" Linc asked as I followed him down the corridor.

I nodded. "It's the same every winter. How many cases do you have in Pilgrim?"

"More than a dozen bad ones. Mostly elderly. Every room is occupied. This is something else, though. A patient named Sandra Bright claims her hospital room is haunted."

I couldn't resist a chuckle. "That's a new one!"

Following his lead past the nurse's station, I entered Room Seventy-six. That number seemed to stir a memory, but at the moment I couldn't quite grasp it. If I'd expected to find a frail old lady propped up with pillows, I couldn't have been more mistaken. Sandra Bright was an attractive woman in her thirties, seated in a chair by the window. "Hello," I greeted her. "I'm Dr. Hawthorne."

She dazzled me with her smile. "Pardon me for not getting up. Dr. Jones says I have to take it easy for another day or two."

"Appendix," Linc explained. "Dr. Truman performed the surgery Saturday afternoon. She's coming along just fine."

"Just fine except for the ghost," she said, and I couldn't quite tell if she was serious. I pulled up a chair and sat down opposite her while Linc perched on the edge of the bed. It was only rarely that I sat in hospital rooms. Usually I was calling on my patients before office hours, standing at the foot of the bed and asking if they'd had a good night. Now, from this lower viewpoint, I became aware of the room's drabness. It was a private room with one bed. There were no pictures on the walls, and of course in those days there was no television set mounted near the ceiling. The bed, two chairs, and a little bedside table made up the only furnishings.

"Suppose you tell me about that," I urged.

She smiled at me. "Are you the resident psychiatrist, come to decide if I'm crazy?"

I chuckled at the thought. "We don't have one of those at Pilgrim Memorial. Dr. Jones just thought I might be able to help. Did you really see a ghost?"

She nodded. "Two nights in a row. Saturday they had me doped up after the surgery. But in the middle of the night something awakened me. I thought the bed was moving, and I could see a person, a hooded figure, outlined against the moonlit window. I started to say something, but then the figure vanished, replaced by the nurse asking me if I was all right. I went back to sleep, thinking it was just a nightmare induced by the drugs they'd given me."

"More than likely," I agreed.

"But then last night the same thing occurred! That same hooded figure was there again, this time crouching down by the side of my bed. I think I must have screamed. When I opened my eyes the figure was gone and the nurse was trying to comfort me."

"Could you have been dreaming?"

"No, I was wide awake. I had a pain medication but no sleeping pill. I closed my eyes when I screamed, but only for an instant. Then the nurse was there and the moonlight was coming through the window, just like the night before."

"Which nurse was it?" I asked.

"Betty Random. She and Jane Templeton are the night nurses."

I knew them both, from mornings when I made my early rounds before they went off duty at seven. Betty had been at Pilgrim Memorial about a year, Jane just a few months. "I'll have a talk with them," I promised.

"Won't do much good. They both think I was dreaming. I even made Betty look under the bed but there was no one there."

"Just rest and try not to think about it," Linc advised her. "If you want, I can prescribe a sedative for tonight."

"I just want to get out of here and go home."

"Well, there were no complications from your surgery. Usually appendicitis patients are hospitalized for a week or more, but I'll speak with Dr. Truman and see if we can get you out by Friday."

"But this is only Monday!" She seemed aghast at the idea of spending another night there. "Can you at least move me to a different room?"

"We're pretty crowded with flu cases. I'll see what I can do."

I followed him out to the desk and we quickly learned that every room in that area was occupied. Obstetrics had a couple of free beds but she couldn't be moved there. "Perhaps someone in a double room might be willing to switch with her," I suggested.

"I'll check on it," Linc promised.

* * *

I drove out through some late-winter snow flurries to make my house call on Mrs. Dodger and then went home to change clothes. Annabel and I were having dinner at Max's Steakhouse, a new restaurant in the center of town that had opened the previous fall. I picked her up promptly at seven, using my standard line. "How are all the dogs and cats today?"

"Fine," she said as I held the door for her. "But we had a sick snake that had to be put to sleep. I have trouble communicating with snakes."

"Don't we all!"

Her animal hospital, Annabel's Ark, was halfway between Northmont and Shinn Corners. Though it had been open less than a year, Annabel Lee Christie, with her blond hair and hazel eyes, was already a popular figure around both towns. We'd started going out together in the fall and by now I'd grown quite fond of her. "How was your day?" she asked when we'd arrived at Max's and been seated at what was becoming our favorite table.

I told her about the hospital haunting, which she wisely dismissed as merely an unusual reaction to the anesthetic administered during surgery. "I suppose you're right," I agreed. "But I remembered something tonight about that Room Seventy-six. Just over a year ago a man was killed there. He'd been arrested and wounded by a deputy after robbing the jewelry store. He tried to overpower the guard at his door and was shot dead."

"My! I never realized I was moving to such a lawless place!"

"Remind me one day to tell you about some of the bizarre murders we've had around here."

"I've seen a couple since I've been here," she reminded me. "Even though one of them was just a cat."

Max Fortesque came over to greet us. "How are my favorite doctors night?" He was a tall slender man with slick hair and a thin moustache. He'd owned a successful restaurant in Boston and I couldn't imagine what had made him sell it and move to Northmont, though once he'd mentioned something about an unpleasant divorce. Whatever the reason, he'd brought a touch of class and fine food to the town.

"I had to kill a snake today," Annabel told him contritely.

"You should have brought it in. I could have created a tantalizing dish from it."

"No thanks! Your beef dishes are fine for us."

He motioned toward the rear. "As soon as the weather warms up I'm going to add a party room onto the back. We'll enlarge the kitchen a bit and I think we'll be able to handle Christmas parties and small wedding receptions." He gave us his best toothy grin. "You two can be my first customers."

We laughed with mock indignation, as if this was sheer fantasy on his part. He joked with us awhile longer and then went off to greet some new arrivals. "He's getting a pretty good crowd for a Monday night," I observed.

"Don't you know why? It's St. Patrick's Day! Why do you think I'm wearing my green dress?"

"I guess I didn't think of it," I admitted. "In the hospital everyone wears white." Back in those days the nurses' uniforms consisted of white shoes and stockings, a starched white dress, and a white cap that was never removed while on duty.

"You're impossible, Sam! You need someone to tell you every morning what day it is."

I didn't pursue that opening, just said, "Anyway, I like your dress. But you're not Irish."

"My mother was. But it doesn't matter on St. Patrick's Day."

"I should have taken you out someplace for corned beef and cabbage."

"Max has it on the menu as today's special, but I think I'll pass. I'm not that Irish."

The dinner was enjoyable and we both were stuffed by the time dessert arrived. A glass of brandy topped off the evening, and it was after ten-thirty by the time we left Max's and returned to the car. "Where to now?" Annabel asked.

"You know, this is going to sound strange but I'd like to stop at the hospital and look in on Sandra Bright."

"The lady in the haunted room?"

"Just to see that she's all right tonight."

"Sure. I'll come along. On our next date I'll take you out to see my dogs and cats."

"Annabel–"

She tugged at my arm playfully. "Come on!"

We reached the hospital just at eleven o'clock, when the nurses' shifts were changing. "How's Sandra Bright tonight?" I asked Betty. I could see the other nurse, Jane Templeton, heading for one of the rooms with a bedpan.

"I don't know, Doctor. I just came on duty. But she seems to be sleeping."

I opened the door to Room Seventy-six softly so as not to disturb her. Annabel remained at the nurses' station chatting with Betty. Inside the room, the moonlight was coming through the window, falling across her bed. She seemed to be resting peacefully and I was about to retreat when something made me pause. I stepped closer for a better look.

The woman in bed was not Sandra Bright. And she was dead.

* * *

Betty and Jane quickly checked the board and discovered that Sandra Bright had been changed to Room Sixty-five during the day shift. "No one told us," Betty Random complained. "They moved Ruth Haefner in there."

"After the last two nights, Miss Bright was convinced the room was haunted. She asked to be moved."

The other night nurse, Jane Templeton, shook her head sadly. "Maybe somebody should have told Mrs. Haefner that and she wouldn't have agreed to the change."

"Who's her doctor?"

"Lincoln Jones, same as Miss Bright. I guess he's the one who arranged the move."

"You'd better call him, get him up here."

Linc was there within twenty minutes, looking as if we'd gotten him out of bed. "What happened, Sam?"

"You'd better come look. Sheriff Lens is on his way, too."

"The sheriff? What for?"

I led the way into Room Seventy-six without responding, simply lifting the sheet from the woman's body so he could judge for himself. He raised his eyes to mine, puzzled. "Are you implying she was frightened to death by the ghost?"

I shook my head, pointing to an extra pillow next to her head. "She was a vain woman, using lipstick even in the hospital."

"Many women do, to boost their spirits. What–?" Then he saw the imprint of her lips on the pillow. "Are you telling me she was suffocated, Sam? With that pillow?"

"We'll need an autopsy to be sure, but I'd say it's a strong possibility. The chart says she was in for kidney stones."

"That's correct. If she didn't improve by tomorrow Dr. Truman was going to operate."

Annabel stuck her head in the door. "Sheriff Lens is here, Sam."

"Send him in."

The sheriff was my oldest friend in Northmont, and now that the town was growing I knew that his days in office were numbered. I'd come to this town in 1922, straight out of medical school, long before the fancy steakhouses and jewelry stores. Law enforcement was a much simpler business then. Already there was talk of a candidate running against him in the November election, and I hated to see it happen. "What've you got here, Doc?" He asked as he entered. "Another one of your impossible crimes?"

"I don't know, Sheriff. A patient who spent the last two nights in this room claimed it was haunted, and now this woman died in it."

He stared down at the body. "What killed her?"

"See the lipstick smear on this pillow? She might have been suffocated."

"By a ghost?"

I had no answer for that. I got down on my knees and searched around the floor but found nothing. Under the bed, there was nothing but the heat return for the furnace. "I'm going to speak with Sandra Bright, if she's still awake."

Down the hall at Room Sixty-five I found her sitting up in bed. "I heard voices, Dr. Hawthorne. What's going on?"

There was no point in keeping it from her. "The woman who was moved into your room died."

"Died! What happened? Did she have a heart attack?"

"We don't know yet. It may have been natural causes."

But she was convinced. "She saw the ghost, same as I did."

I sat down at her bedside. "Sandra, so long as you're awake anyway I'd like you to tell me everything that happened with that apparition, both times you saw it." I had a prescription pad in my pocket and I took it out to make notes. "First tell me a little about yourself."

She sighed. "There's not much to tell. I moved here from Albany a few months back to take a job as a pastry chef."

"In Northmont? Where?"

"At Max's Steakhouse."

"We were just there for dinner tonight! Max didn't tell us his pastry chef was in the hospital."

"He probably didn't want the customers to know he had to buy desserts from the bakery while I was gone. He's a good boss. He's been to see me every day. It made me feel a little less alone. My folks live in Florida now and I haven't had a chance to make many friends."

"What about Saturday night?"

"Well, it was like I said. I was pretty much doped up after the surgery, but I came awake because I thought I felt the bed move. And there was that hooded figure in my room."

"Was the door closed?"

"Yes, but there was moonlight through the window."

"Could you tell if the figure was a man or a woman?"

She shook her head. "There was only this dark hooded shape. It was like a nightmare."

"Perhaps it was a nightmare," I suggested quietly.

But she shook her head. "I squeezed my eyes shut for a split second to make sure I wasn't imagining it. But then the nurse, Betty was there feeling my pulse. She said I'd made a noise and she looked in on me."

"Maybe it was she you saw against the window."

"No. I half believed it was a dream the first night but last night the figure was back, crouched on the floor by the side of my bed. That time I really did scream, and reported it all to Dr. Jones this morning."

It was basically the same story she'd told earlier, and I wanted to believe her. "I'll have to talk to the nurses again," I decided. "Tell me one other thing. Have you made any enemies since you came to Northmont? Anyone who might want to harm you?"

"No, of course not. I don't even have a boyfriend. Other than Max and the people I work with, I don't know many people. Working nights at the restaurant cuts down on one's social life."

Jane Templeton was at the nurses' station and I decided to speak with her first. She was a thin, self-possessed young woman, hardly attractive but with a good bedside manner. While we were speaking, Annabel came over to join me. I'd almost forgotten about her. "Sam, let me get a taxi home. I have to be at the Ark early tomorrow morning."

"Nonsense. I'll take you." I turned back to Jane. "I'll stop back later."

In the car, Annabel was apologetic. "I know that's important to you, Sam. You shouldn't leave because of me."

"What sort of a date would it be if I let you take a cab home?"

I left her at the door and hurried back to Pilgrim Memorial. By this time the body had been removed and Sheriff Lens had completed his questioning of the nurses. "It looks like another one of your impossible jobs, Doc, unless you're willing to admit that the ghost killed her."

"What ghost would that be?" I asked innocently.

"Frank Nomard, that jewelry-store bandit. Remember him? One of my deputies wounded him at the scene of the crime and when he tried to escape from this same hospital room he was killed. I remember him sprawled out dying on the floor. He looked up at me and said my deputy shouldn't have shot him, that he wasn't trying to escape. Then he just died."

"Who was the deputy?" I remembered the incident but not the specifics.

"Ray Brower. You know Ray, don't you? Good man. I investigated the circumstances at the time, but Ray was justified in shooting him."

"What about Mrs. Haefner, the woman who was killed tonight?"

"We're trying to reach her family in New York. She was driving home from Boston when this attack of kidney stones hit her quite suddenly."

"No one in Northmont knew her?"

"Not that we know of. Let's face it, Doc. She was killed because she got moved to that room."

"I suppose in the dark the killer might have made a mistake."

"Or else the room is really haunted. If we can believe the nurses' testimony, no one went near Room Seventy-six after they came on duty."

I talked to both of the nurses in turn, but their stories were the same. They'd relieved the evening shift just before eleven and started making their individual rounds. Nothing had been said about Mrs. Haefner and Sandra Bright exchanging rooms, and they hadn't yet discovered the switch when I arrived. "We handle rooms Sixty-one to Eighty," Betty explained, "and we usually start at opposite ends just to make sure everyone is all right. I hadn't gotten to Seventy-six before you arrived."

"Are you telling me that she was killed before eleven o'clock?"

"Well, no, because Maggie—the evening nurse—checked on the sheet that Seventy-six had no problem when she signed off. And we would have noticed anyone else entering that room. This whole thing is impossible!"

"I'll need to talk with Maggie," I decided.

"Maggie Wheeler." She glanced at the clock. "Probably sleeping now."

"Which is where I'm going to be," I said. "I'll catch her tomorrow."

On the way out, the other nurse, Jane, caught up with me. "One thing I forgot to tell you," she said. "There was a late visitor just leaving the floor as I got off the elevator tonight."

"Oh? Who was that?"

"Max Fortesque from the Steak House. I eat there sometimes."

* * *

In the morning I sought out Ray Brower, the sheriff's deputy who'd killed the prisoner in Room Seventy-six the previous year. He was an overweight dark-haired man whose stomach waged a constant war with the buttons on his uniform shirt. "I remember the hospital shooting, of course," I told him, "but I was over in Shinn Corners the day it happened and never heard all the details."

He shifted his belt to a more comfortable position. We were at the sheriff's office and he'd be going out on road patrol when we finished talking. "Well, you know the Northmont Jewelers," he began, launching into a story he'd probably told a hundred times. "They hadn't been open long at that time but it's a classy place for our growing town and they carry some valuable things. This bird Frank Nomard was driving through and decided to rob it. He walked in, showed them a gun, and started scooping jewelry into a cloth bag. Guess he didn't know they'd installed a silent alarm system like the banks have. The other deputies caught him in the parking lot and shot him in the left thigh. They recovered the gun, the bag of jewelry, and some burglar tools. It wasn't a serious wound, but they took him to Pilgrim Memorial to have the bullet removed and patch him up. I was assigned to guard him that night until he could be moved to the jail the next day."

"This was a year ago, right?"

"Sure. It was March third. I'm not likely to forget the date I killed a man."

"Tell me about that."

"Well, it was after midnight and I figured he was asleep. I was sitting on a chair outside the door when I heard some sort of noise from inside."

"What kind of noise, Ray?"

He screwed up his face as if trying to remember. "I don't know. Sort of metallic, not too loud. I decided I should investigate and I opened the door. The room was dark, but there was enough moonlight from the window that I could see he was out of bed and coming at me with a knife in his hand. I didn't think twice. I pulled my revolver and shot him in the chest."

Sheriff Lens says Nomard told him just before he died that he wasn't trying to escape."

"What'd you expect him to say? The knife turned out to be a screwdriver, but it could have been just as deadly if he jabbed me with it. We figure it was one of his burglar tools that we missed finding on him. He was in a hospital gown, but his clothes were in the room with him."

"Thanks, Ray. You've been a big help." I got to my feet and shook hands with him.

"Sheriff Lens said something about a ghost. You don't think–?"

"That he'll come after you? No, Ray, I don't think you have anything to worry about."

I went into the sheriff's office and found him on the phone with his wife Vera, talking about the killing. When he hung up he said apologetically, "She volunteers at the hospital and wanted to know if there's anything new."

"Is there?"

"Just the autopsy report. You were right. Mrs. Haefner was smothered, either by a ghost or a human."

"I'd bet on the latter."

"Then how did the killer get in and out of the room without being seen, three nights in a row?"

"I'm working on that," I told him, "Are you satisfied Ray Brower was justified in killing that prisoner last year?"

"Sure. He was a bit quick on the trigger, but he thought his life was in danger. I probably would have done the same thing, Doc."

"He said the stolen jewelry was recovered."

"Yeah, just about all of it."

"Just about?"

"Well, the store manager claimed there was a valuable diamond necklace missing, too, but it wasn't in the bag. He was hinting one of my deputies might have pocketed it, and I was hinting he might be padding his insurance claim."

"How valuable?"

"Fifty thousand. Don't know how he expected to sell it in Northmont. Anyway, the insurance company finally paid up and that was the end of it."

"Maybe Nomard hid it in the hospital room and his ghost has come back to find it."

The sheriff shook his head. "You know those rooms, Doc. They're so bare you couldn't hide a toothpick in them. We gave the bed and toilet a good search, just to be sure, but there was no hidden necklace."

"Toilet tank?'

"First place we looked."

"Okay, I'll see you later."

"Any idea, Doc?"

"Lots of them."

* * *

I had lots of ideas, all right, but there was still a piece missing. When I stopped at the Steak House for a quick lunch, I was hoping Max Fortesque could fill it in. "I didn't know your pastry chef was in the hospital," I told him as he led me to the table.

"Sandra? She had an emergency appendectomy, but she's coming along fine now."

"I hear you visited her last night."

He nodded. "It was after visiting hours. I had to wait till the crowd thinned here before I could get away. It was St. Patrick's Day, you know."

"I know. A patient was killed in the room Sandra Bright had occupied earlier."

"I heard about someone dying, but I didn't know it was that room. I was up there every day to see her and she told me she'd had a wild dream about a ghost in the room. The doctor moved her last evening before I arrived."

"But the nurses knew where she was?"

"Sure. That cute one, Maggie, told me she'd been moved."

Maggie Wheeler. I phoned Linc Jones after lunch and found out she came back on duty at three o'clock. I was waiting when she walked down the hall to the nurses' station, securing the white cap to her hair with a bobby pin. She was young and cute, as Max had said. "Hello, Dr. Hawthorne," she greeted me.

"I've been waiting for you, Maggie."

"Is it about last night? Betty phoned me about poor Mrs. Haefner. It's awful, and she was only in for kidney stones."

"When did you last see her alive, Maggie?"

"I like to check them all before I go off duty. It must have been shortly before eleven."

"Were there any strangers on the floor? Anyone who shouldn't have been there?"

"It was after visiting hours. Sandra Bright's boss came over from the restaurant to see her around ten-thirty and I told him it would be all right. He even took her for a little walk in the hall, though he wasn't supposed to. I shooed them back into the room as soon as I saw that."

"Was this before or after you checked on Mrs. Haefner?

"Oh, before! No one went in her room after I checked on her."

"And she was awake, talking?"

"She said a few words."

"There was no one hiding in her room?"

"Of course not! I always check the toilets, too, before I go off duty."

"Thanks, Maggie," I said, allowing her to go on her way.

I stood by the nurses' station, surveying the corridor that led in both directions. One of the day nurses came out of a room clutching an armload of dirty sheets and opened the door to the laundry chute. I watched the sheets disappear into it, bound for the basement laundry room, and decided it was worth a look. The elevator took me down two levels and I confronted a mountain of the day's sheets and towels ready for washing.

White, white, everything was white. It took me only an instant to spot the dark blue terrycloth robe near the bottom of the pile. I yanked it free and verified that it had an attached hood. There was a clatter as something fell from a pocket and hit the floor. I looked down and saw that it was a screwdriver.

* * *

"Here's your ghost," I said fifteen minutes later, laying the folded terrycloth robe on Sheriff Lens desk. I placed the screwdriver next to it.

"Where'd you get these, Doc?"

"Hospital laundry room. The killer bundled it up and dropped it down the chute. Is that the screwdriver Frank Nomard was carrying when Deputy Brower killed him last year?"

"Damned if it doesn't look like it!" He walked to a filing cabinet and took out a folder. "Since the case was closed, the dead man's possessions were returned to his family. But I kept pictures of them." He flipped through a file. "Here's the screwdriver." He laid a picture on the desk next to the tool I'd found.

"They're the same," I concluded. "See this dab of paint on the wooden handle?"

"I guess you're right," he admitted. "Maybe we've got a damned ghost after all."

"Hardly! You said these things were returned to his family. Who would that be?"

"A daughter out west someplace. I've got the address in here somewhere. Glenda Nomard, a post-office box in Omaha."

"When did you return them?"

"Just a couple of weeks ago."

"A couple of weeks ago," I repeated. The final piece of puzzle had just fallen into place.

"I like to wait a year on things like this, in case the family files a wrongful-death lawsuit or something. But they didn't, so I just put his clothes and things in a box and sent them to the daughter. You think we should contact her in Omaha?"

"That won't be necessary. She's right here in Northmont."

* * *

It was an odd group when we assembled that evening in Sandra Bright's hospital room. She was there, of course, and Max had dropped by for his nightly visit. In addition, I'd arranged with Linc to have all three of the nurses present. Maggie Wheeler was on duty, of course, and both Betty and Jane had come in early. With the sheriff and me, that made seven people crowded into the private room.

"It was obvious to me from the start," I began, feeling a bit like a movie sleuth with the suspects gathered together for the final scene, "that the intruder in Room Seventy-six, ghost or human, was searching for something. When I remembered the jewelry-store bandit shot dead in that room, and learned there'd been a missing necklace, it seemed likely that was the object of the search. But the timing bothered me. Why wasn't the necklace found by Sheriff Lens and his men, and why was someone suddenly for it now, a full year later?"

I paused, glancing around at their faces. When no one spoke, I continued. "Deputy Brower mentioned that the thief's weapon had been a screwdriver, not a knife, as he first thought. But the significance of that fact didn't really dawn on me until I found the screwdriver itself in the pocket of the blue robe the killer must have worn. Frank Nomard, the dying robber, told the sheriff he wasn't trying to escape when he was shot. He had no reason to lie at that point, so suppose we believe him. If he wasn't trying to escape, what was he doing with the screwdriver? The deputy entered the room because he'd heard a metallic sound. Suppose Nomard was merely using the screwdriver *as a screwdriver*."

"But we searched every inch of that room, Doc," Sheriff Lens protested.

"Every inch of the room, but not beneath its floor, not in the cold-air vent under the bed, where the screwdriver was used to remove the metal grille so the necklace could be hidden there."

"I never thought of that," the sheriff admitted.

"Neither did Nomard's daughter when she came to Northmont to search for the necklace herself. She knew enough about her father to realize he might have hidden it somewhere, but she didn't know where. Not until a year passed and the sheriff sent her a box of her father's belongings. It was forwarded here from Omaha, and when she saw the screwdriver she realized there was one place she hadn't looked. But now the hospital was filled with flu patients and others, with Room Seventy-six constantly occupied. She took a chance Saturday night because Sandra here was heavily sedated following surgery. But something went wrong. Sandra came awake and saw a ghostly figure wearing a hooded garment."

"Why a hooded garment?" Max Fortesque wondered. "From what you've told us already it's obvious one of these nurses is guilty. Why not enter in her nurse's uniform?"

"Because a white uniform would show up, even in a darkened room, if there was moonlight coming through the window. She couldn't be seen crawling around under the bed. You're correct about it being a nurse, though. The use of the hood confirmed that. Not only the uniform but the white cap had to be covered."

"She could have removed her cap," Sheriff Lens argued.

"No, because they have to be worn on duty. She was ready, if the patient woke up, to do exactly what she did—let the robe slip off her shoulders and fall to the floor, leaving her at the bedside in her full nurse's uniform."

Every eye in the room was on Betty Random.

* * *

She was pale and trembling, licking her lips nervously as she backed against the wall. "I came in when I heard her call out."

"No," I said, "you were there already. On the second night, Sandra asked you to look under the bed. The robe should have been there if another nurse dropped it, but you didn't report seeing it. You came back last night and smothered the patient before she could scream again, not even realizing in the dark that it was a different patient. Then you had time to locate the necklace in the cold-air return and screw the grille back down. You did it just before eleven, when you were on the floor but not yet on duty. Maggie had just checked the room and you knew she wouldn't check it again. That's why you didn't realize the patients had been changed, because when you should have been looking over the afternoon report you were busy in Room Seventy-six. You told me, at first, that the patient was sleeping, but then you said you hadn't yet checked the room when I arrived."

"Jane," she managed to say. "Jane did it. I've been here almost a year."

I nodded. "Since right after your father was killed. Sure, it might have been Jane, except that you did a foolish thing. When you needed a fake name for your nurse's license, you simply rearranged the six letters of your family name. Glenda Nomard became Betty Random."

* * *

The necklace was recovered and the woman we'd known as Betty Random made a full confession. The case was finished, and for a time the only problem confronting me as Annabel Christie. I solved that one, too. On Easter Sunday I asked her to marry me.

"Sure!" she responded with unabashed enthusiasm. "When'll we do it?"

"I'm forty-four years old, Annie. I can't wait too long."

"This year, then. Before Christmas. We can have the reception at Max's and Sandra can make the wedding cake."

We got out a calendar and turned to December. "How about the first Saturday, December sixth?" I suggested.

She grinned and kissed me. "December sixth, nineteen forty-one. It has a nice ring to it."

THE PROBLEM OF THE TRAVELER'S TALE

This was in the late summer of '41 (Dr. Sam began when their glasses were full), and Annabel and I had been engaged since Easter with our wedding date set for December sixth. It had been a warm and pleasant summer in New England, with news of the widening war still far away. Even when Roosevelt and Churchill met in Newfoundland during the second week in August, most of us viewed the American position as one of support and supply to the Allies rather than actual combat.

"We should get away on vacation," Annabel suggested on Friday evening as we were finishing dinner at Max's Steakhouse, our favorite local restaurant. "Who knows what next year will bring?"

"You think we'll be in the war?"

She shrugged. "Let's do it now while we can, Sam. Do you ever go canoeing?"

I had to laugh at that. "I've never been much of an outdoorsman, and I haven't been in a canoe since my college days."

"Then it'll be an adventure. If we get dunked, I can blame it on your inexperience."

"I've got a week free, but what about the Ark?" Her veterinary hospital, Annabel's Ark, now attracted critters and their owners from all over the county.

"Kelly can handle it while I'm gone. She's working out very well."

"All right," I agreed somewhat reluctantly. "Where are we going to do this canoeing?"

"I was thinking of the Connecticut River. There are some nice parks along the way where we could camp and—"

Before she could continue, Sheriff Lens appeared at our table. Under most circumstances I would have been pleased to see him, but just then it seemed more like a needless interruption. "I thought you two might be here for your Friday night dinner," he said, sliding into the booth next to me before I could object. He'd been putting on weight again of late, and I was aware that the edge of the table pressed against his stomach.

"Join us for dessert?" I suggested, mustering up more sincerity than I felt.

"Maybe just some ice cream. Got myself a problem over at the jail."

"What's that, Sheriff?" Annabel asked, and I nudged her foot under the table.

"Fellow stumbled in a few hours ago with the damnedest story you ever heard. Said he'd been hiking in the woods over near Shinn Corners on a route he takes every summer and he came upon an old house that he remembered being empty and deserted. Now it's fixed up nice, newly painted, with flowers in the yard and someone obviously living there. A man and woman were working around back and he decided to stop and chat with them. The woman was friendly enough, but the man went inside after a brief hello and didn't reappear. He had a beard, but there was something about his face that seemed familiar. After the hiker went on his way he kept thinking about it, and by the time he reached here he decided to report it. He thinks the man in the old house is Clifford Fascox."

I recognized the name at once. Fascox was a Chicago swindler who'd worked a Ponzi scheme on thousands of small investors, using money from new investors to pay high interest to the earlier ones, all the while promising huge profits from a mining company in Chile that didn't exist. He sued the first newspaper that tried to expose him for a million dollars, dampening the investigative efforts of others for several months. Finally arrested, he posted bail and promptly disappeared with some five million dollars of his investors' money. He hadn't been seen in two years, and it was assumed he'd fled the country.

"Have you reported this to the state police?" I asked.

"Not yet," the sheriff replied, obviously uneasy. "This hiker's story sounds sort of screwy and I'd like you to hear it before I do anything. He could be a crackpot, or just mistaken."

"So you thought of me."

"If you've got a few minutes I'd like you to see him, tell me if he seems all right to you."

I sighed and looked at Annabel. "Want to come along?"

"No, thanks! The screwy ones are all yours, unless they have four feet."

I paid the check and told her to take my car home, promising to phone her later. Then I followed Sheriff Lens out to his vehicle and crowded into the passenger seat alongside the shotgun he kept there like an extra gearshift. "Looks like you're prepared for a crime wave, Sheriff," I kidded him.

"It's no joke, Doc. Some folks think the Germans might try to land spies from submarines."

"That's pretty far-fetched," I told him, and it seemed so at the time.

* * *

The man who waited at the sheriff's office was tall and lanky, towering over me by some inches. His name was Graham Partridge and his long nervous fingers tapped constantly on the sheriff's desk as he talked. A bulging knapsack rested on the floor by his feet.

"As I told the sheriff, I live in Boston. Every August I go hiking through New England for a week, like an Australian walkabout. My route varies, but I usually try to pass through this area."

"Are you married, Mr. Partridge?" I asked.

"No, I'm a bachelor. Probably couldn't do this if I had a wife." He gave an odd, jerky laugh, and I could see why sheriff was a bit hesitant about him.

"Tell me what happened."

"I first saw the house just last year, and it was deserted then. Two stories, with boarded-up French windows. It needed work, especially painting. There was a garage in the back and a big willow tree out in front. But this year the house looked lived-in. I could even see a little piano through the French windows."

He kept fidgeting with his fingers as he spoke, and a thought suddenly struck me, "Mr. Partridge, do you play piano?"

"Why, yes. I'm with the Boston Philharmonic."

I gave him a smile. "Couldn't help noticing your finger action."

"I'm always practicing, keeping my fingers nimble."

"Go on with your story."

He described his pleasant surprise at seeing the old house repainted and rejuvenated. When he noticed a middle-aged couple in the back clearing brush, he decided to speak to them. "The woman was younger than the man, maybe in her early forties, and quite attractive. The man was older, with a graying beard and fierce-looking eyes. I told them I was admiring the job they'd done fixing up the old house. The woman was willing to talk, but after a brief hello the man retreated into the house. It was as if he didn't want to be seen. I chatted with her for a few minutes and then went on my way, but I was certain I'd seen him somewhere before. As I was approaching Northmont it came to me. Without the beard he could have been Clifford Fascox, the missing swindler."

"How sure are you?"

"Pretty sure. I saw his picture in the papers and on the newsreel."

"But that was two years ago."

Graham Partridge's face screwed up in thought. "I've got a good memory for things like that. I just know it was him."

"What do you think, Doc?" Sheriff Lens asked.

"It's not my decision, Sheriff. But I have a suggestion for a little test. You must have a Wanted poster for Fascox somewhere around the office. Can we lay out five posters with the names covered and see if Mr. Partridge can pick the correct one?"

"It's an idea, Doc. I never thought of that."

Sheriff Lens found the Wanted poster quickly enough. It showed a clean-shaven middle-aged man wanted on federal charges of fraud, using the mails to defraud, and unlawful flight to avoid prosecution. We set up the test, choosing men of about the same age. All were clean-shaven like Fascox. We covered everything but the faces and let him choose. "Number four," he said without hesitation.

"That's him, all right," the sheriff agreed, uncovering the names. "What do you think, Doc?"

"I don't know."

I could see he was reluctant to contact higher authorities until he'd checked it out himself. He scratched his chin and said, "I suppose I could take a run out there in the morning."

"I'll go with you," I suggested. I was sure that was why he'd gotten me over there in the first place.

"That would be fine, Doc. We could make it look like some sort of health inspection. I don't want to do anything until we're sure. You going to be around tomorrow, Mr. Partridge?"

The slender man nodded. "I was planning to stop at a bed-and-breakfast here overnight and then continue my walk in the morning. But I'd be happy to accompany you."

"I don't think that'll be necessary. Try Sleepy Hollow, down the street. Mrs. Maxwell has a nice place there. I'd like you to remain in town at least until noon. If you can draw us a little map of where this house is, Doc and I will drive out in the morning. If there's a problem I might want to talk to you again when we get back."

* * *

It was the first time since my engagement to Annabel that Sheriff Lens and I had been alone together, and it was natural that our conversation in his car the next morning would turn to the impending wedding. "I was your best man," I reminded him, "and I'd like you to be mine. I should have asked you sooner, but we went into this without any real plans."

"I'd be happy to," he told me. "Make you as miserable as the rest of us married fellas."

I knew he was kidding. His own twelve-year marriage had been a near-perfect one, even without the blessing of children. "I only pray I'm as happy as you and Vera."

"Annabel's a great gal, Doc. I knew it the minute she opened the Ark. Who'd ever have thought that the animal hospital would make it in Northmont? Remember that Kasper's Kennel back in 'thirty-five? Lasted less than a year."

"It was only a kennel, though. Folks around here needed a real vet for their pets and livestock. They needed Annabel."

"How's April doing, back working for you again? Does she hear much from her husband?"

"He writes her every few days, but it's not an easy life. He's somewhere at sea but he can't say where. Sometimes she hears nothing for weeks and then a bunch of letters arrive."

"I saw her in church with the boy. He's getting big."

"Sam," I said with a trace of pride. "She named him after me. Almost five now."

"You got that map, Doc? Is this where we turn?"

The map Partridge had drawn was a poor one. In an area without street signs it was next to useless. "I'm not sure. Try the next left."

But the road petered out and we ended at a cow path without encountering any houses. We retraced our route back to the main road and tried the next left, closer to Shinn Corners. After about a half-mile we came upon a house that vaguely fit Partridge's description. It seemed freshly painted and a young woman was mowing the grass.

"Hello, there," Sheriff Lens greeted her as I got out of the car and following along.

She held up her hand to shield her eyes from the sun. "Howdy."

"I'm Sheriff Lens and this here's Dr. Hawthorne. We're doing a health survey. You lived here long?"

"Since April."

"And your name is–?"

"Jennifer Logan." She turned away from the sun and dropped her hand, revealing the pleasant face of a dark-haired woman in her late twenties.

"Anyone else live here with you?"

"Only my companion, Jackie."

"Is Jackie home now?"

"Sure. We're always together."

"Could we speak with him?"

A slow smile played about her lips as she turned and called into the house. "Jackie, could you come out here for a minute?"

A tall, slender woman appeared in the doorway. "What is it, Toots?"

"They're doing a health survey."

She took the porch steps two at a time and stuck out her hand to me. "I'm Jackie O'Neill. Do we look healthy enough to pass?"

Sheriff Lens seemed confused. "We understood there was a gentleman living in the house."

"Nobody here but us chickens, eh, Toots?"

"That's right," Jennifer Logan agreed.

"This would be a bearded man, somewhat older than you." He produced the mug shot of Fascox and showed it to them with the name folded back out of view.

"Never saw him before," Jackie announced, "with or without the beard."

"Are there any other renovated houses around?" I asked.

"We keep pretty much to ourselves," Jennifer answered.

"Well, thanks for your help," the sheriff said. "Come on, Doc." Back in the car, he asked, "What do you make of those two?"

I shrugged. "I guess they're just what they seem. Wanted criminals aren't the only ones who might prefer to live by themselves."

We tried two more roads but by that time we were into Shinn Corners. "We'd best turn back and get Partridge to come out here with us," he decided.

* * *

The Boston traveler was just donning his backpack at Mrs. Maxwell's bed-and-breakfast when we drove up. "Find the house?" he asked when he saw us.

"Not a chance with your map," the sheriff informed him. "You'd better come with us, show us the way."

"If you need me," he readily agreed.

We retraced the same route, guided by Partridge's map, but he quickly agreed it was in error. "I missed this road to the right," he admitted.

"You said it was to the left."

"I got turned around. I've never been good at directions. Try this one."

We came upon a man I recognized, a patient of mine named Peter Harrison, spreading crushed stones on his driveway. How's it going, Peter?" I called out to him.

"Fine, Doc. Aren't you a little bit out of your neighborhood?"

"We're looking for a house, two-story, recently remodeled and repainted, with a big willow tree in the front yard. Sound familiar?"

Peter took off his cap and wiped some sweat from his brow. He'd never been a fast mover. "You probably want the old Stover place. Fellow from the city bought it about a year ago."

"Do you know his name?"

"Common name. Collins, I think. A woman named Mavis lives there, too. I suppose it's his wife. We don't see much of them. Stay right on this road and you'll come to the house."

It seemed like a solid lead at last, and soon Partridge pointed out the hiking trail he'd taken. Around the next curve we came upon the house as he'd described it, half hidden by the giant weeping willow. "This must be the place," Sheriff Lens said.

"Yes," our backseat passenger agreed. "I recognize it now."

The place seemed closed and deserted as we left the car and walked toward it. Sheriff Lens went up on the porch and peered through the curtained French doors that opened into the living room. "Pretty fancy place for Shinn Corners," he remarked. "Somebody put a peck of money into this."

"See anything?" I asked.

"Looks like nobody's—" He stopped in mid sentence. "Doc, come look in here!"

I peered through the lace curtains on the other side of the glass. It was difficult to make out anything clearly, but I saw what looked like a body stretched out on the carpet, its head and shoulders hidden from view around a corner. Quickly I tried the doors but they were all locked. "Let's see if we can find an open one," I told the sheriff.

In addition to the French doors, there were the front and back doors, both firmly locked, and eleven windows, likewise locked. After we'd circled the house, Sheriff Lens decided to break one of the panes of glass in the French doors. "We've got to get in there, Doc."

"Of course we do! He might still be alive."

The sheriff tapped the pane with the butt of his revolver and the glass shattered. He reached in to pull the bolt. "This guy was taking no chances," he observed. "Extra bolts on these French doors." He turned to Partridge. "You stay out here."

"Bolts on the other doors too, I'll wager." By then I knew it was going to be a locked-house killing. I'd been through these things too many times before.

The bearded man was dead when I reached him, and he would have been just as dead if we'd found him five minutes earlier. His head was almost touching an upright piano and bench that stood in an alcove. The fatal bullet had entered through the right temple, leaving a clean, clear hole that had bled just a little. A small automatic pistol, .32 caliber, was clutched in his right hand.

"Suicide, huh, Doc?"

I merely grunted as he continued to search the ground floor. He was in the kitchen when he suddenly called to me. "Come quick, we got another one!"

It was a woman this time, sprawled on the kitchen floor. She'd been shot at least twice, apparently with the same weapon, and like the bearded man she'd probably died instantly. "We'd better get Partridge in here to identify them," I suggested.

The sheriff went to the door and called him in. "Are these the people you saw yesterday?"

The slender man was repelled by the sight of the bodies. "My God, what happened?"

"Looks like murder and suicide. Are these the people?"

"Yes," he said quietly.

"You're sure?"

"It's them."

"And you think the bearded man is Clifford Fascox?"

"I'm sure of it."

"The woman is the one you talked with in the yard yesterday?"

"Yes, it's her."

Sheriff Lens nodded. "All right. Just stay in here for a moment."

Partridge wandered into the alcove and stared at the piano. He tapped his fingers over the keys as he had on the edge of the sheriff's desk, frowning when he hit one out of tune. "This is a crime scene," Lens reminded him sharply. "Don't touch anything." Then, "What do you think, Doc?"

"You'd better phone and get some men out here. I'm going to check the windows on the second floor."

"You think one of them might be open?"

"I'm sure they're all locked. He wanted us to be certain it was a murder-suicide."

"Fascox?"

"Yes. Or whoever killed them."

* * *

While the sheriff phoned his office and the state police, I made a tour of the second floor. The windows were all firmly locked, and the door to an upstairs porch was both locked and bolted, like the downstairs doors. The double bed in the main sleeping room was unmade. When I went back downstairs the sheriff was on the phone to the state police while Clifford Partridge stood nervously in the center of the room, afraid to touch anything.

I knelt to examine the bolts on the French doors, well aware that these could be sprung open if one of the doors was not secured at its base and top. The top bolt into the door frame was open, but the bottom bolt into the floor was firmly in place. Despite my pushing on it, the door did not move. Next I moved to the fireplace chimney, but I saw at once that it was too narrow for even an elfish Santa Claus to have used. And holding a match to the soot-lined walls, I could see it was undisturbed.

"Do I have to stay in here with these bodies?" Partridge asked.

"Go outside," Sheriff Lens told him. "The state police will want to question you."

There was a bill from the electric company on a desk, addressed to a Mavis Collins, but I saw nothing visible with the bearded man's name on it. Within fifteen minutes the first car arrived with Corporal Williams of the Criminal Investigation Division. We told him what had happened and he assigned someone to take the dead man's fingerprints. "We'll find out soon enough if it's Fascox."

Sheriff Lens explained about Clifford Partridge and how he'd recognized the man during his walkabout. "I suppose if Fascox thought he'd been discovered he might have decided to kill himself and take his wife with him, if it was his wife."

Corporal Williams nodded. "I'd better get a statement from this Partridge fellow."

"That's him outside by the willow."

When we were alone, I spoke quietly to the sheriff. "I don't think he killed himself."

"Why not?"

"Look at his wound again. Clean, no powder burns."

"Damn! I shoulda noticed that!"

"The woman couldn't have killed him, shot herself twice, and then walked into the kitchen to die. For one thing, there'd have been a trail of blood. And for another, that second bullet would have finished her off."

"But you told me the place was locked up tight, from the inside. Is this another one of your impossible crimes, Doc?"

"I'm afraid so, Sheriff."

Corporal Williams came back inside with Partridge. "Have you checked that garage out back?" he asked.

"Just going to do it now," Sheriff Lens told him. I followed along.

The garage had been painted along with the house, but unlike the house the door was unlocked and actually ajar. Inside we found barrels of junk, broken glass and empty paint cans, along with a hammer and other tools. A late-model Cadillac sat side by side with an old turn-of-the-century surrey. The cloth top of the carriage had been badly damaged, its clear isinglass sides cut apart as if by vandals. I wondered how many decades ago the damage had been done. "The old and the new," Sheriff Lens muttered. "This carriage must have been here when they bought the place."

I searched around a bit, looking for something that might help. There was a ladder capable of reaching the second-story windows, but I'd already established that they were all locked and bolted from the inside. "There's nothing to show the killer was ever in here," I decided. "If it was a vagrant, he probably would have stolen the car."

"We'd better wait for that fingerprint check," the sheriff said.

* * *

I phoned April in the morning and told her I'd be over with Sheriff Lens. Annabel listened to my call from the kitchen and said simply, "Sam."

"I know, we're going canoeing next week."

"I certainly hope so."

"I just want to be there when the state police phone in with the fingerprint report."

"Where's this fellow Partridge who started it all?"

"Still at Mrs. Maxwell's place. The sheriff wants him here until we get the report."

"If the dead man is Clifford Fascox it's going to be big news all over the country. He swindled a lot of people."

"His murder's going to be big news, too."

She sighed and looked at me. "You're never going to stop, are you?"

"I have a knack for it, Annabel. It's what I do."

When I walked into the sheriff's office later that morning I had a surprise. Jackie O'Neill, the lanky young woman we'd met the previous day, was standing just inside the door. "You're Dr. Hawthorne," she said, making it sound like an accusation.

"That's right."

"Jennifer and I heard about the killings at the old Stover place. I want to know if there's some sort of homicidal maniac on the prowl up there."

Sheriff Lens was exasperated. "I tried to tell her we're not even sure it was a double murder, Doc. It might have been a murder-suicide."

"That's not what I hear," the woman told us. "We came to Shinn Corners to get away from crime in the city. We had a couple of bad experiences in Boston and we don't want them repeated here."

"I assure you this was no maniac," I said. "The killer went about it in a most deliberate manner."

The sheriff joined in. "And I can tell you, Miss O'Neill, that I've assigned an extra deputy to patrol the roads in your area. You and your friend are perfectly safe."

"We'd better be." She turned and slammed out the door, still angry, just as Corporal Williams of the state police was coming in.

"What's her problem?" he asked.

Sheriff Lens shook his head. "She and her girlfriend feel the law isn't protecting them enough. What about the fingerprints?"

"It's Clifford Fascox, all right. He was a federal fugitive, so the FBI is in on it now. They have two agents driving down from Boston this afternoon."

I could see the sheriff wasn't too pleased to hear that. "Got any more good news for me?"

"The doorknobs, bolts, and window latches had all been wiped clean of fingerprints."

"Not the sort of thing a would-be suicide would bother doing," I observed.

"While we were checking, we contacted the Boston police about your traveler, Mr. Partridge."

"Oh?"

"Arrested back in 'thirty-nine for drunken driving when he hit a parked car. He plays with the Philharmonic and since there were no injuries he got off with six months' probation. He claimed he got drunk after a financial setback and swore he'd never drink again. His record's been clean since then."

Sheriff Lens looked at me. "What do you think, Doc?"

"About Partridge? If he killed them and was clever enough to get out of that locked house, he certainly wouldn't come running to you to report on Fascox's whereabouts."

"I suppose not."

"Still—"

"What?"

"I'm thinking."

"You fellows do all the thinking you want," the trooper said. "The FBI will be here around two."

* * *

They were right on time. Special Agent Frank Dunsmore was sandy-haired and clean-cut, with a neat blue suit and tie. He did all the talking, with just a hint of a Boston accent. "Gentlemen, the fingerprints confirm that the dead man is Clifford Fascox, a federal fugitive under indictment on several counts of fraud and using the mails to defraud. The woman who died with him is believed to be Rose Secondo, who was living with him when he jumped bail in Chicago and disappeared two years ago. If I understand correctly, there were no powder burns on either of their wounds, even though all the doors and windows were locked and bolted from the inside."

"That's correct," the sheriff told him.

"If they were murdered by a third person, can you explain how he or she exited the house? The chimney—"

"We examined it," I told him. "Not possible."

"The basement?"

"No way out."

He sighed, "Then maybe it was suicide."

"No powder burns," I reminded him.

He frowned at me. "Just who are you, anyway?"

Sheriff Lens answered for me. "Dr. Hawthorne has given me invaluable aid in cases of this sort. I don't know where I'd be without him."

"All right, Dr. Hawthorne, do you have any idea about this one?"

"Part of an idea," I admitted. "I have a problem with our traveler's tale."

"You mean Graham Partridge?"

"Yes. He lied in his original story. He said he could see a piano through the French windows, but the piano stands around a corner in an alcove. It's not visible through the windows."

"Does that make him a double murderer?" the FBI man asked. "It could, if we figured out how he did it."

"And why," the sheriff added. "What would his motive have been?"

"I have an idea about that, too. You told me earlier that he was arrested in 'thirty-nine for drunken driving. He'd had a financial setback that drove him to drink. Two years ago was when the Fascox swindle came to light."

"Let's get him in here again."

"If he hasn't left town already," I said.

As it turned out, Graham Partridge had left town. One of the sheriff's deputies picked him up on the highway, striding along with his knapsack. When we saw him an hour later at the county lockup, he was highly indignant. "I'm a respected citizen back in Boston. You're treating me like a common criminal!"

"I asked you to remain at Mrs. Maxwell's bed-and-breakfast," Sheriff Lens reminded him.

He glowered at us. "Only until you had confirmation that it was Fascox's body. I phoned your deputy this morning and he said the identification had been made. I assumed I was free to go."

"You weren't free to go until I said so."

"Sorry."

Special Agent Dunsmore and his assistant had gone out to visit the crime scene, so the sheriff and I were alone with Partridge. "You may be a respected citizen in Boston," I told him, "but you have an arrest record there for drunken driving."

"I received probation for that. It was a bad period of my life, but it's over now."

"You told police that financial setbacks drove you to drink. You were one of Fascox's victims, weren't you? That was how you were able to recognize him so quickly, even with the beard."

"I won't lie about it. He stole my life's savings. I would have known that face anywhere."

"How did you know he was hiding out here?"

"I didn't! I swear to you! I walked into that yard and there he was staring at me. Of course, my face meant nothing to him. I was simply one out of thousands that he'd swindled. But I knew him right away."

"And you killed him," I said. "You probably carried that little pistol in your knapsack for protection during your hiking. You followed him into the house and—"

"I was never in the house."

"You said you saw the piano. You had to be inside to see it."

"If I killed them, why would I come in here to report it? Why wouldn't I just keep on going? No one else saw me there."

It was a good question. And at the moment I didn't have an answer for it, any more than I had an answer for how he got out of the house after he killed them. But in his eyes I saw something, perhaps a glimmer of triumph, that told me I was looking into the eyes of a murderer.

* * *

"We're going out there again," I told the sheriff after he agreed to hold Partridge in a cell overnight as a material witness. "If we don't find anything this time, you'll have to let him go."

"Damn right I will! He's already threatening to sue for false arrest. The judge will turn him loose in the morning if I don't."

"He did it!" I insisted. "I could see it in his eyes."

"We need more than that."

"I know we do."

When we pulled up at the house where Clifford Fascox and Rose Secondo had died, I was dismayed to see that the FBI agents were still on the premises. As soon as Dunsmore saw us he walked over to the car. "Back again?"

"I'm holding Partridge overnight as a material witness," the sheriff told him. "Find anything?"

"Nothing."

As we stood there I noticed how the late afternoon sun was hitting the panes of glass in the French doors. "Sheriff, look at that."

"What are you seein', Doc?"

"The sun's reflection is just a bit different in that bottom pane. Come on!"

They followed along behind me as I hurried up to the doors. My fingers reached out and touched the pane. "What is it?"

"Not glass," I assured them. "Remember that broken glass we saw in the rubbish barrel in the garage, Sheriff? That was from this window. The killer broke it so he could reach through and close the floor bolt on this door, after he pulled the doors closed. He replaced the glass with a piece of clear isinglass that he cut from that old carriage in the garage. It wouldn't stand up to close inspection, and he had to nail the corners to hold it taut in the frame, but with those lace curtains covering it on the inside the almost got away with it."

"Sure," Sheriff Lens agreed. "Two bodies in that locked house, the murder weapon left in Fascox's hand. If only Partridge had remembered about the powder burns we might have taken it for a murder-suicide."

"It was a spur-of-the-moment killing," I surmised. "He came upon the house just as he said, and immediately recognized Fascox as the man who had swindled him and thousands of others. They must have shown him the garage and then the inside where he saw the piano. He took out the pistol he carried in his knapsack and shot them both. He remembered the isinglass windows on the carriage and cut out a piece the right size to fit the window frame. Then he locked and bolted everything from inside and left the gun in Fascox's hand. He carefully broke the bottom pane of the French doors, picked up the pieces, and disposed of them in the trash barrel. He closed the French doors and then reached through the opening to push that final bolt into its floor hole. The isinglass pane went into the door, not a perfect fit but good enough. He used the hammer from the garage and a few nails to hold it in place."

"But why did he report Fascox's sighting to me?" Sheriff Lens wondered.

"He probably never thought about the missing powder burns, but about the time he reached Northmont he remembered something else. It was a fatal error that would have convicted him in a minute. He couldn't chance going all the way back to correct it, so he came to you with his tale. He purposely drew us a misleading map after you said we didn't need him to accompany us. His whole purpose in telling that tale was to get back into this house with you, to cover up that fatal piece of evidence."

"What evidence are you talking about?" Dunsmore wanted to know. "Stop playing games with us."

"You saw how his fingers were in your office, Sheriff. He was constantly tapping them on your desk and I guessed correctly that he was a piano player. When he entered Fascox's house and saw that piano, he wouldn't have been able to resist playing a few notes."

"He did that yesterday with us!" Sheriff Lens remembered. "I had to warn him not to touch anything."

"Exactly! He played those few notes yesterday so there'd be a reason for his fingerprints on the piano keys. You see, he forgot to wipe them off when he was there the first time. With his prints on file from that driving arrest, he knew there was no way out."

"Let's go get a confession, Doc."

"That shouldn't be difficult," I said. "He's no hardened criminal. He killed two people simply because chance brought them together."

I was right. Graham Partridge made a full confession as soon as I mentioned the fingerprints on the piano keys and the isinglass in the window. "You people are pretty good for a small town like this," he remarked ruefully as he signed the confession. "But I'm still not sorry about what happened. It's just that I'll miss my piano."

THE PROBLEM OF BAILEY'S BUZZARD

Annabel and I were married on December sixth as planned (Dr. Sam Hawthorne informed his guest as he refilled their glasses from the decanter), and the church wedding was followed by a long and lively reception at Max's Steakhouse. There was much kidding about our wedding day being interrupted by a locked-room murder, as had happened the day that Sheriff Lens and Vera were married, but happily there was no repetition of that day's events. The sheriff was my best man and Bernice Rosen, Annabel's good friend and client, was the maid of honor.

We stayed overnight at my place, planning to catch Sunday afternoon train to Washington for our honeymoon. The war news that morning came mostly from the Russian front, where the Soviets had begun a major counter-offensive in the Moscow sector. I'd left the radio on while we packed, and so it was sometime after one o'clock when we heard the news that would change everyone's life. Japanese planes were attacking Pearl Harbor, in Hawaii. The nation was at war.

Annabel and I sat listening to the radio for the next half-hour, when we were interrupted by the ringing telephone.

It was Sheriff Lens. "Have you heard the news, Doc?"

"About Pearl Harbor? Yes, we have the radio on."

"Hell of a thing to happen when you're trying to get off on your honey-moon. Washington will probably be a madhouse. Are you still going?"

"I don't know," I told him, suddenly realizing that Annabel and I had each stopped packing when we heard the news. "I'll call you back."

We spent another half-hour talking it over, listening to the radio reports that kept sounding worse. The Japanese were landing troops in Malaya as well. This was no mistake on the part of some overeager admiral. It was a well-planned attack that had somehow caught us unprepared.

"We'd better postpone the Washington trip," Annabel said at last, voicing the words I'd been reluctant to speak.

"It's our honeymoon."

'There'll be other times, Sam. Our honeymoon is us, together it doesn't matter where we are."

She was right, of course. I phoned the hotel in Washington to cancel our reservations, then called Sheriff Lens and my nurse April. "Take the week off," she urged, "even if you don't go anywhere."

"We'll see. I may come in later in the week. I just wanted you to know I'm available if there's an emergency."

After that, Annabel phoned her friend and maid of honor, Bernice Rosen. The two chatted for a time about what was happening about the war that had suddenly been thrust upon us. When she hung, Annabel told me, "Bernice feels really bad about our delayed honeymoon. She suggests we come out on Tuesday for lunch and then go riding."

Bernice and her brother had a highly profitable horse farm just beyond Spring Glen Cemetery, and as the county's only veterinarian Annabel had been out there many times. She and Bernice were now close friends and Annabel had gone riding with her a few times. I'd been invited along but begged off. I'd never been much of a horseman. At an age when most young men of my era were imagining themselves as cowboys, I was more interested in the yellow Pierce-Arrow Runabout my folks had given me when I graduated from medical school.

But I could hardly turn down an invitation meant as a consolation for our postponed honeymoon. "Sure," I told my wife. "It sounds fine to me."

* * *

Bernice Rosen's horse farm covered some two hundred acres backing up to Cobble Mountain and the cemetery. I'd been on Spring Glen's board of trustees for the past few years and I knew that Bernice and others sometimes rode their horses up the mountain trails and into the fringes of the cemetery itself. I could hardly object to it, since I'd once picnicked there in my younger days. On Tuesday, following a delightful lunch with Bernice and her older brother Jack, she suggested we ride up that way. "You're a cemetery trustee, Sam. You should inspect the place from all angles."

"I have enough trouble staying on a horse on level ground."

"Come on, Sam," my wife urged. "I'll see that you don't fall."

I turned to Jack Rosen for support. "Are you coming along, too?"

Jack, a dapper horseman with combed-back blond hair and a slight moustache, smiled and begged off. "Not today, thanks. I want to catch the war news on the radio. My number is coming up soon in the draft lottery. I want to know where I'll be fighting."

President Roosevelt had given a stirring speech to Congress the previous day, following a Japanese attack on Hong Kong and an air raid on Luzon in the Philippines. The United States and Britain had both declared war on Japan, and by Tuesday there were reports that the enemy had captured a small island north of Luzon and an invasion seemed imminent. Wake Island and Shanghai were also under attack. I would have remained with Jack by the radio, but I could see that the women wanted to get away, if only for an hour or two.

Bernice was a small woman, and even with the heels she'd worn at the wedding she only came up to Annabel's chin. Still, in jodhpurs and riding boots, with the usual sporty scarf knotted around her neck she presented an attractive figure. Once in the saddle she handled her horse Jasper like a rodeo queen. "The war news is terrible," she said as we rode. "Jack's had that radio on for the past two days and I just can't stand listening to it anymore. What's to become of us, Annabel?"

"I don't know," my wife admitted. "So far, at least, we're not at war with Germany and Italy."

"That's only a matter of time," I predicted.

The day was chilly but clear, with some snow predicted overnight. The women headed up the trail toward Cobble Mountain, little more than a large hill, with me bringing up the rear. Geologists had said Cobble Mountain was a large outcropping of granite, not enough for us to challenge New Hampshire's claim as the Granite State, but still impressive. Riding up the trail, I was pleased that Bernice had supplied me with a gentle mare. I was still a bit nervous but trying not to show it in front of Annabel. "Do you ride this way often?" I asked, pulling abreast of them as the trail widened.

"Almost every day when I have time," Bernice answered. Her breath was visible in the cold air, and the horses likewise snorted fumes of condensation. "Sometimes I take the cemetery trail but usually I come this way."

A sudden shadow fell across our path and I glanced skyward to see a large bird dipping its wings to us. "What's that?" I asked, startled by its size. "A buzzard? It must have a six-foot wingspan."

"Looks like a turkey vulture," Annabel said, shading her eyes against the sun to study its flight path. "But they're more a southern bird."

"We see them around here occasionally," Bernice told us. "Not usually that large, though. That could almost be Bailey's buzzard."

"What's Bailey's buzzard, and who is Bailey?"

Bernice laughed. "Large birds like turkey vultures have been known to grab up living prey if it's small enough and they're hungry enough. Our foreman, Matt Greentree, says he used to see it occasionally when he worked on a ranch out West. One day a really huge buzzard swooped down and grabbed a small dog named Bailey. A cowhand shot at the bird and it dropped its prey. Bailey was all right, but it used to howl every time a big buzzard came circling overhead. They started calling the big ones Bailey's buzzard."

"Are vultures really that aggressive?" I asked.

It was Annabel who answered, as they paused their horses at the top of a rise where the trail split off into two branches. "They say during the Crimean War, after the ill-fated Charge of the Light Brigade, the vultures were so thick over the battlefield that squads of riflemen had to be posted to protect the wounded."

Rather than take the trail into the cemetery, Bernice led them up a bit further, along a sheer wall of stone, to a place where she could look down on the whole of her horse farm. "It's lovely up here," I admitted. "Thank you for showing us."

"I hope you'll come again soon," Bernice told us as we rode down the hill.

Back at the farm she introduced us to her foreman, Matt Greentree. He shook hands and asked, "Did you see that big bird circling around?"

"I know," Bernice said. "Bailey's buzzard."

"Big enough to carry off a chicken or a small child," he told them with a grin. He was about my age but thinner, with a leathery face that reflected a life lived mainly out of doors.

"Don't be ridiculous, Matt! Here, take our horses."

Back inside, we found Bernice's brother Jack still listening to the radio while he pondered a map of the South Pacific. "The Japanese have occupied Bangkok. They're sweeping across the whole western Pacific."

"Are you going to be drafted?" his sister asked.

"Looks like it."

I could sympathize with him. At forty-five I was beyond the limits for being drafted, and many doctors were getting exemptions anyway. But Jack Rosen was still in his early thirties. "If that happens, Matt and I will have to run the place," Bernice decided. "They wouldn't draft you, would they, Matt?"

Greentree smiled. "Not unless things get a lot worse. I'm forty-three."

Jack turned off the radio. "After a while I just can't take any more of it. They're worried now about the Japanese attacking our west coast!" He suddenly remembered something. "Oh, the Reverend Dulcimer phoned while you were out, Bern. He's coming by soon to talk to us about some cemetery thing."

Dulcimer, a local minister who was a cemetery trustee along with me, was a student of Spring Glen's history. I well remembered the board meeting when he'd entranced and/or bored us by reading a newspaper description of that summer's day in 1876 when the cemetery had opened to the public for the first time. Umbrellas were raised to protect the town's mayor from a sudden downpour while he read the official proclamation.

I couldn't imagine the purpose of Dulcimer's visit to the Rosens, but we were to find out quite soon. He arrived about twenty minutes later, driving his startling red Studebaker, just as Annabel and I were thinking about departing. Henry Dulcimer was a tall, sturdy man with a booming voice who presented an imposing figure in a church pulpit. Up close, his hair was graying and the lenses of his glasses were growing thicker, but he still moved with the agility of a much younger man.

"Sam," he said, greeting me with a handshake. "Didn't expect to see you here. Thought you'd be on your honeymoon." He gave a nod to Annabel.

"We postponed it because of the war. We might get away briefly over the holidays. What's going on with the cemetery?"

Bernice offered him a chair and he settled into it, fitting easily into our circle of conversation in front of the fireplace. "If I'd have known you were in town, I'd have called you about this, Sam. It's about General Moore's grave. They're talking again about moving his remains to the state capital for a more permanent memorial."

"We approved that a year ago, didn't we?" Moore, a Union general who'd died at Gettysburg, had been buried in a Northmont graveyard long ago, his remains moved to Spring Glen when the present cemetery opened in 1876. He was something of a state hero, though, and no one was really surprised when the governor got around to requesting that the remains be moved. The trustees had approved it and then, in typical fashion, heard nothing further for nearly a year.

"That's right, Sam," Reverend Dulcimer agreed. "But we suddenly got a call yesterday. They want to disinter the body tomorrow morning, and we'd like to take it out by the back entrance, through your property, Bernice and Jack, if you have no objection."

"Why is that necessary?" she wanted to know.

"With all the war news, we hardly need the local press making a spectacle of this. It was reported a year ago and no one objected except that troublemaker Frank Costain. I think we should just move him and be done with it."

"Do you expect trouble from Costain?"

"Who knows what he might do?"

I had to agree with that. Costain was a young hothead who'd become the bane of every elected official in Northmont. Bernice hesitated only a moment before she turned to her brother and said, "It's all right with us, isn't it?"

"Sure," Jack said with a smile. "So long as they don't do anything to frighten the horses."

It seemed like such simple thing, I automatically said, "I'll come out with you in the morning, Reverend, to make sure all goes well."

* * *

Annabel decided she'd be more useful tending to her sick animals at the Ark than taking another day off to watch a body being moved. I met Reverend Dulcimer at the Rosen farm at nine the following morning and the hearse sent from the state capital arrived a short time afterward. I could see Bernice out by the barn with her horses and I waved to her. We led the way up the back road into the cemetery. Happily, Frank Costain was nowhere in sight.

The state had sent a pair of morticians for the general's body and at first I didn't understand why they were needed. When we pulled up to the general's grave site the cemetery crew was already there, having uncovered the old coffin and raised it to the surface. That was when Dulcimer spotted the gleaming mahogany casket in the back of the hearse. "What's that for?" he asked them.

The head one, Wadsworth, explained that money had been appropriated for a new casket, since the original one from the Civil War days would not be appropriate. The morticians were there to transfer the general's remains to the new casket. Dulcimer and I exchanged glances. "What do you think, Sam?"

"I think they should have told us about this earlier. I suppose there's not much we can do about it now, except to ensure that it be accomplished in a dignified manner."

"You see what I mean about the casket," Wadsworth said. "If this is the original one it's almost eighty years old."

I had to agree that it was little more than a pine box, hardly suited to a war hero. We watched while the lid was unscrewed and gently lifted off. I think the sight that greeted our eyes brought a gasp from everyone present.

What we saw before us in the casket's padded interior was not the skeleton of a human being. It appeared instead to be the remains of a very large bird.

* * *

When we told them the news back at the Rosen farm, Matt Greentree's first reaction was, "Bailey's buzzard!"

"It certainly looked large enough to have carried off a small dog," I agreed. "But what was it doing in General Moore's coffin?"

That was the mystery, and it seemed beyond solution. There was no university or zoo near Northmont, yet I needed someone with a knowledge of animal anatomy to view the remains. Annabel seemed the likely one for the task, and I telephoned the Ark from the farm. She arrived within a half-hour and accompanied Reverend Dulcimer and me back to the cemetery.

After viewing the bones, she gave her opinion. "It's certainly a large bird of prey. You can tell that by its claws. The remains are in poor condition after all this time, but I would guess it was a vulture or possibly an eagle."

"I don't care about that," the mortician named Wadsworth said. "We need General Moore's remains. Where are they?"

"We'll have to research the cemetery records," I told him. "It may take a few days."

"We can't wait around here. You'll have to call us if you find the correct casket." He started for the hearse, then added with some disdain, "You can keep the bird's bones."

After the hearse pulled away Annabel asked what I was going to do. I shrugged. "The answer may lie in the old cemetery records, but going back to eighteen seventy-six isn't an easy job."

"Why would anyone bury a bird in a coffin? And how did it get to be in General Moore's coffin?"

"We have more questions than answers. Let's see what I turn up in the records."

Annabel headed back to the Ark while Reverend Dulcimer and I instructed the gravediggers to store the casket and bones in the toolshed for now. Then we drove over to the Spring Glen office. On the way he pointed toward the sky. "Look at the size of that one!"

I watched the circling bird, which must have had a wingspan of at least six feet. "Bailey's buzzard," I told him. "Maybe it's not a myth after all."

* * *

The two of us spent the rest of the day with the cemetery staff, trying to make something out of the old records, many of them handwritten in a spidery scrawl. "Here's something about the undertaker," Dulcimer said somewhere into the third hour. "He was a very patriotic citizen, used to lead the Fourth of July parades. Name was Frederick Furst. He passed away just a few months before they moved the caskets from the old cemetery to Spring Glen. The procedure is described in some detail. The deceased person's name was chalked on the lid of each casket as it was removed from the grave so there could be no mistake."

"But there was," I pointed out, "unless that bird was placed in the casket at Gettysburg."

"Doubtful. Wouldn't the lightness of it have been noticed at once, in contrast to the heavier coffins?"

We got nowhere, and by the end of the afternoon there was no clue as to what had become of the general's remains.

That night the war news was not good. The Japanese had captured the islands of Guam and landed in Luzon. Annabel told me that Bernice had invited her to go riding again on Thursday. She decided her assistant could handle things at the Ark. I was invited, too, but I wasn't prepared for my second encounter with a horse in three days.

We awoke Thursday to find about an inch of snow on the ground. It certainly wasn't surprising for December eleventh in New England, but Annabel phoned Bernice to verify that the horseback ride was still on. I went to my office and April told me Reverend Dulcimer had called. He was still looking through the old cemetery files but had found nothing helpful. Neither of us could believe that a man as patriotic as Frederick Furst would have stolen General Moore's remains and substituted a dead bird, yet no other explanation seemed likely. I wasn't about to entertain the notion that the general had somehow turned into a bird after death.

I stopped in to see a couple of my hospital patients, both of whom expressed regret that the start of the war had postponed our honeymoon plans. But many patients still thought I was away, and by noon April told me, "The afternoon is free. Why don't you and Annabel go off somewhere?"

"She's out riding with Bernice. I might take a ride out to the farm and meet them."

The temperature was hovering around thirty and none of the morning's snow had melted. I drove out to the Rosen horse farm and found Bernice's brother Jack cleaning out the stable. "They're still out riding," he told me. "I expected them back before this."

Matt Greentree came out of the house to join us. "Just listening to the war news," he said. "Nothing new."

"Give me a hand with this muck, Matt," Jack said. "We have to get the place cleaned out or my sister will have a fit."

I turned to look up toward Cobble Mountain, searching for riders, and saw a small car coming our way down the road. It wasn't Annabel or Bernice, but Frank Costain. I didn't like the idea of him snooping around the cemetery, and he certainly didn't belong on the Rosen private road. Costain was younger than me by about ten years, but he seemed to feel he was better qualified than people like Reverend Dulcimer and me to be a cemetery trustee.

"I don't want trouble, Frank," I began, but he interrupted before I could finish.

"Get in the car, Doc. Your wife needs you."

I felt a sudden jolt of panic, "What happened?"

"Annabel's all right. It's Bernice. She's disappeared."

Greentree had followed me over to the car, leaving Jack in the stable. "Bernice may be in some trouble," I told him. "This is Frank Costain, Matt Greentree."

The foreman pulled off his work glove and offered a red, chafed hand to Costain. "Pleased to meet you."

"Maybe you'd both better come along," he suggested. "We'll need people to search."

We decided not to alarm Bernice's brother by telling him what had happened. When we'd both slid into the car, I asked. "What happened?"

"I don't exactly know. I heard a rumor that you'd removed General Moore's body yesterday and I was driving through to see if his grave had been disturbed. Up this end on the back road I encountered your wife on horseback. There was a riderless horse trailing behind. She told me Bernice Rosen had disappeared. I suppose she must have fallen off her horse but there was no sign of her. That's when she suggested I drive down here for help."

Despite my dislike for the fellow, he seemed to be telling a straight story. By the time we'd reached the spot where the trail branched off from the back road, Annabel had ridden down to meet us. I hurried from the car and ran to meet her. "What happened to Bernice?"

Her face was drained of blood. I'd never seen her look so terrible. "Sam, she's gone! I can't—"

I took her in my arms. "Tell me everything that happened."

"That's just it! Nothing happened. We were riding up the path on Cobble Mountain. I was in the lead and she was about two or three lengths behind. Those big buzzards were flying around."

"Near you?"

"Well, they weren't close enough to frighten us. I heard a noise, a sort of gasp, from behind me, but I didn't look around right away. After maybe thirty seconds, when she was silent, I called her name. She didn't answer and I—I looked back. Jasper's saddle was empty. She just wasn't there!"

"She'd fallen off."

"That was my first thought, of course, but the coating of snow was unmarked except for our hoof prints. I could see down the trail about a hundred feet or more." She gave a terrible sob. "She was nowhere, Sam! It was as if one of those giant buzzards swooped down and lifted her from the saddle."

"I'm sure that didn't happen." I turned to Greentree and Costain. "I'll go with Annabel. You two start searching the other trails."

We led the two horses back up the trail, examining the hoof marks as we went. Annabel had steered the horses to the outer edge of the path on their return, so the line of tracks going up was undisturbed. My wife's horse had a gouge in one shoe so it was easy to tell the tracks apart. On one side of the trail was the sheer granite wall stretching up more than twenty feet, without handholds or vegetation. On the other side, the hill sloped down through bushes and underbrush. There was no sign that Bernice had dismounted in the snow, and she could not have leaped from her horse onto the granite wall. The wet snow had clung to the bushes on the other side, and these, too, were undisturbed.

"Sam, what happened to her?" Annabel asked plaintively.

"I don't know. Look, you'd better ride back to the farm and tell her brother what's happened. Then phone Sheriff Lens and tell him to get up here."

"You think it's something bad."

"No, I just want him here." Mainly, I didn't want Annabel there if we did find something bad.

I watched her ride back down the trail and then followed Costain's and Greentree's footprints up the other trail. They'd headed for the top of the granite wall, which seemed logical enough, but when I reached the top there was nothing to see. The light breeze had kept the snow from collecting there, and most of it was bare. I walked to the edge and peered down at the trail below. It was a bird's-eye view, and perhaps for a moment I imagined myself as that giant buzzard circling overhead, locking my eyes on the two women.

I considered the possibility but immediately rejected it. Bernice Rosen was a small woman, but she had to weigh a hundred pounds or more. No bird I knew could lift that much weight and fly away with it, not even Bailey's buzzard. And even if something like that had happened, wouldn't she have yelled to Annabel for help?

These thoughts were interrupted by some shouts from the other side of the granite ledge. I walked over, finally seeing their footprints, and started down through a tangle of underbrush. Below me I could make out Frank Costain's red jacket as he stood beside Greentree. "Down here, Doc," he called when he saw me starting my descent. "Be careful!"

Here and there were patches of snow that seemed disturbed by someone falling or sliding down the incline. I started to slip myself but they caught me at the bottom. "What did you find?" I asked, not really wanting to know.

"She's here," Greentree said quietly, pointing a bit farther down the bill. Then I saw her. It appeared that her body had rolled or fallen down, finally coming to a stop against a bush. I knelt in the snow and felt for a pulse but there was none. Her face and arms were covered with scratch marks, some of them deep, but there was very little blood. I undid the kerchief from around her throat.

"Is she dead?" Costain asked.

"I'm afraid so. It looks like a broken neck but I can't be sure."

* * *

I was reluctant to move Bernice's body until Sheriff Lens had seen it. By the time we walked back to the car and drove down to the farm, he'd arrived. "What is it, Doc?" he asked immediately, seeing my grim expression.

"Bernice Rosen has been killed. We don't know how. I can take you up to the body. First I'd better see Annabel."

She knew it, of course, as soon as she saw my face. "My God, Sam, she was my maid of honor just five days ago!"

"I know. I feel terrible." I told her how they'd found the body in the underbrush on the other side of the hill.

"There were no foot prints, nothing!" She just kept shaking her head.

"I'm going back up there with Sheriff Lens."

"I want to go too!"

"No." I said firmly. "Stay here with Jack. He'll need comforting."

The sheriff and I took my car and retraced the route up the hill. "What a day it's been, Doc, between this and the war."

"What happened? I haven't been listening."

"Germany and Italy declared war on us this morning, and at twelve-thirty Roosevelt asked Congress for an immediate declaration of war against them."

I took a deep breath. "It's another world war, if it wasn't already."

"It'll be a long one, Doc, with two fronts for us to fight on."

"A lot of young men will be going. A lot of them won't be coming back."

I drove as close as I could to the body's location, and the sheriff and I walked from there. I told him Annabel's story, and what little we'd found. He studied the body from several angles. "You think it was an accident, Doc?"

"It might have been."

"But how could it have happened?"

"Something must have lifted her from the saddle and dropped her here. I read a story once as a boy, I think in *The Strand Magazine*, about a man who was snatched up while riding a horse along a snowy path. In the story the man had been accidentally snagged by the grappling hook of a passing hot-air balloon and lifted into the sky. When his coat tore and released him he fell to earth and was killed."

"I think a hot-air balloon would have been at least as noticeable as a giant bird, Doc."

"I know. This wasn't a balloon."

"Could there have been some sort of booby trap or snare on the trail, put there by hunters?"

"You're forgetting Annabel was on the lead horse. If it was anything like that, it would have gotten her first. The scratches on Bernice's face and clothing certainly suggest a bird or some other creature, but I can't bring myself to believe it."

We returned to the farm and the sheriff made arrangements for the body to be removed. "I've instructed my deputies to take some pictures first, as possible evidence. Now I'd better get a statement from Annabel."

* * *

By the time we returned home late that afternoon, my wife and I both felt emotionally drained. The death of Bernice Rosen, however it occurred, had been a terrible event for Annabel. But I was totally unprepared for the effect it had.

She poured herself a drink and turned to me. "Sam, do you think you might have been responsible in any way for Bernice's death?"

"What? What are you talking about?"

"Don't you see? It's one of your impossible crimes, isn't it? Did someone kill her simply to challenge you? Was her life sacrificed to prove that you're not so smart as you think you are?"

"There's madness in an idea like that. Believe me, if she was murdered it was by a person with a logical motive."

"But she had no enemies! There was no ex-husband or even a boyfriend lurking around, so far as we know."

"It's what people don't know that often leads to murder. Whatever it was, it had nothing to do with me."

She shook her head, close to tears. "If I thought our whole life together was going to be like this—"

"It won't be! If I discovered that my crime-solving had anything to do with Bernice's death, I'd give it up. I'd close my practice and we could move to Boston."

She brushed the tears from her eyes and tried to smile. "What about the Ark? I couldn't give that up."

I took her in my arms. "Annabel, this isn't like you."

"I never had a close friend murdered before, almost before my eyes."

"I promise I'll find the killer, if there is one. And I'll find the motive, too."

The war news grew more serious by the day. The Japanese had attempted a landing on Wake Island and been beaten off, but the American force there was small and couldn't hold out for long. In Washington, the draft was picking up steam and the terms of all draftees had been extended to six months after the end of the war. I realized that Northmont could soon be a town without young men. A few exceptions were being granted for farmers growing essential crops, but many who hadn't been drafted in the selective-service lottery were hurrying off to enlist.

On Friday morning I met with Sheriff Lens at his office. "Is there anything new on Bernice's death?"

"Autopsy report. Her neck was broken and there was also evidence of strangulation."

"Strangulation? I saw no marks on her throat."

"You told me you'd removed a kerchief she was wearing around her neck. That might have protected the skin from abrasions."

I puzzled over it. "Buzzards don't strangle people, no matter how big they are."

"You never really thought it was a bird, did you, Doc?"

"No. It's just that there have been so many bird images involved in this—the story of Bailey's buzzard, the skeleton in General Moore's casket, the big turkey vultures we've seen overheard."

"Maybe if we knew what happened to the general's body we'd know what happened to Bernice Rosen."

"No," I said slowly, "the two things were never really related." I stood up and put on my coat. Outside the snow flurries had started again. "I guess I'll go back to the cemetery."

* * *

Reverend Dulcimer was at the cemetery office, still pondering the old handwritten records. "They called from the state capital this morning, Sam. They want to know what we're doing to locate General Moore's remains."

"I've got an idea about that," I told him. "Do you have that list of the bodies moved from the old cemetery?"

"Right here. You're better at reading the handwriting than I am."

There was one entry I remembered seeing, a young nephew of the undertaker Frederick Furst. No description was given of the individual caskets, but I was willing to bet this one was a twin of General Moore's. "He's in here," I said with conviction, pointing to the grave number. "Let's open it up."

We got a pair of gravediggers and set to work. More than an hour later the coffin in question was raised to the surface. As soon as they unscrewed the lid I know I'd been right. The remains inside were clad in the tattered remnants of a Union officer's uniform.

"How did you know?" Dulcimer asked me.

"It all had to be connected somehow with Furst himself. The large bird wasn't a vulture. I believe it was a bald eagle, the symbol of our country. Though I don't think it was illegal to kill them way back then, a man as patriotic as Frederick Furst would have been horrified if he accidentally shot one. So horrified, in fact, that he might have buried it in a casket and listed a fictitious child's name on the grave."

"But how could the caskets have been confused?"

"Furst himself was already dead by that time, remember. The name of the deceased was chalked onto the top of each casket as it was removed from the ground, but what happened then?"

"They were loaded on wagons and taken here, to Spring Glen."

"Correct! And we know from contemporary accounts that the town's mayor had to dedicate the new cemetery with umbrellas held overhead to shelter him from the rain. Don't you see it? The rain washed away the chalk marks on the coffin lids! Furst's dead eagle became a Civil War general because somebody guessed wrong. After fifteen years, no one would have thought twice about the general's coffin being lighter than expected."

"Then it had nothing to do with what happened to Bernice?"

"Not a thing. But I think I know who killed her and how and why."

"Did the weather report tell you that, too?"

"No," I replied, "but the war news did."

* * *

Reverend Dulcimer decided to come with me to the Rosen farm. I was glad to have him along. Despite a certain sense of triumph, this was the part I really hated. Any of us could have been a killer, given a different life, different circumstances. In this case, the sheer brutality of Bernice's killing could not be allowed to go unpunished.

Jack Rosen was at the kitchen table when we arrived. He looked up and gave me a sad smile. "I'm just completing the arrangements for Bernice's funeral. She'll be laid out tomorrow and Sunday, with the service on Monday. I'm burying her at Spring Glen, of course. It was such a part of her life, riding those trails."

"Is Matt around?"

"He's in the stable."

I found Greentree out with the horses, using a pitchfork to deliver fresh hay to the stalls. "How are you, Matt?"

"Okay, Doc," he said, continuing with his work.

"I wanted to ask you something."

"What's that?

"Why'd you kill Bernice? Was it just to get control of the farm?"

He turned and smiled, and without a word plunged his pitchfork into my chest.

* * *

Later that day, I was a patient at Pilgrim Memorial Hospital myself, something I'd never imagined happening. Annabel and my nurse April were at my bedside, tending to me like a pair of ministering angels. "You've got nice row of four punctures right across your chest," April informed me. "Luckily they're only a couple of inches deep."

"This is a great way to be spending my honeymoon!" I groaned.

"You'll live," Annabel said with a smile, trying to make light of it.

Sheriff Lens came in then. "What in hell did you say to that guy, Doc, to set him off like that?"

"Just that I knew he'd killed Bernice. Did you get him?"

He nodded. "He grabbed a horse after he forked you. He was halfway to Shinn Corners before my deputies caught up with him. He took a shot in the leg before he surrendered. You'd better tell me all about it, Doc. I'm still in the dark."

"It was the war news. When I drove up to the farm yesterday he came out of the house and said he'd been listening to the war news, that there was nothing new. But there was something new yesterday morning, the biggest news since Sunday's Pearl Harbor attack. Germany and Italy had declared war on us, and the President asked for a declaration of war at twelve-thirty. I didn't leave my office for the farm until noon. If Greentree really had been listening to the radio he'd have known about this before I arrived. When I remembered this, I asked myself where he'd been just before I got there, and why he'd lied about it. There was only one likely explanation. He'd been up on the mountain killing Bernice."

"How'd he do that?"

"He knew what route Bernice preferred, and he headed them off, going to the top of that granite slab where the breeze had mostly blown the snow away. Bernice was riding behind you, Annabel, as he'd guessed she would be. As she passed beneath him, he lassoed her around the neck and dragged her up out of the saddle. She was helpless to even scream. The force of it broke her neck and choked her to death, but that kerchief around her neck kept the rope marks from showing."

"We need some evidence of that, Doc."

"I can give you a couple of things. Greentree had worked on a ranch out West, where he no doubt became proficient with a lariat. And when Frank Costain rode down to tell us of Bernice's disappearance, I introduced them. Greentree took off his work glove to shake hands and I couldn't help noticing how red and chafed his hand was, no doubt from yanking a rope with a hundred-pound body on the end."

"Once she was dead, he scratched up her face and clothes to further the buzzard legend and rolled her body into the underbrush. He rode back to the farm by a different trail, avoiding the spot where Annabel was searching in vain for Bernice. When we came back later to search, he made sure to take Costain up to the granite top, trampling any hoof or footprints he might have missed earlier. Of course, Greentree was the one with the buzzard stories. Even if we didn't believe them he wanted to plant the possibility in our minds to keep us away from the truth."

"How could he have done such a terrible thing?" my wife asked.

"I think he wanted the horse farm. He knew Jack had a low selective-service number and would be drafted very soon. With Bernice dead he'd be running things, even if he didn't own the place. Jack might even be killed in the war and never come home. He could do what he wanted with the horses and make himself a tidy profit."

Later, when Annabel and I were alone in the hospital room, she asked, "Are you still going to be a detective, Sam? Didn't you learn anything today?"

"Two things. Don't believe in giant buzzards, and never accuse a man of murder when he's holding a pitchfork."

THE PROBLEM OF THE INTERRUPTED SÉANCE

Despite a few morale-boosting events like Doolittle's April bombing of Tokyo and the RAF's bombing of German cities, during those early months of 1942 the war was going badly (Dr. Sam Hawthorne told his companion when they had settled down with their usual small libations). The Japanese had taken all the Philippines, Hong Kong, and most of the East Indies. In North Africa, Rommel's tanks seemed unstoppable.

In Northmont, in the first six months of my marriage to Annabel, the war and everything else seemed far away. Gasoline rationing had begun in seventeen states in mid May, and was sure to spread soon. But the crime rate in Northmont had actually seemed to fall since December tragedy that had claimed the life of our maid of honor. Sheriff Lens had his own theory about the improved social climate, attributing it to the fact that many of the town's young punks had enlisted or been drafted. Some of the enlistments had come following the news that one of Northmont's own was missing in the attack on Pearl Harbor.

His name was Ronald Hale and he'd been a seaman aboard the ill-fated battleship *Arizona*. Though the attack angered the entire country, the blow was felt hardest in hometowns such as Northmont, and in families such as Ron Hale's. His mother Kate, a patient of mine, was devastated by the news. It was early June when she came to me for a checkup, the first since her son had been confirmed dead.

"You've had a bad time, Kate," I told her. "How are you sleeping?"

"Not well, Dr. Sam. I think about him all the time, going down with his ship in what he thought was a safe harbor."

"I can give you something to help you sleep, but the rest is up to you. How is Art taking it?" Art Hale wasn't a patient of mine but I knew him from the town council, on which he'd served for several years.

"Better than me, now, but he had a terrible time at first. Back in January and February he just went away for days at a time. Our son's death was confirmed to us in mid April, before the official casualty list was announced on May first. When Art got the news, he went through it all again. I think he was drinking heavily while he was gone, but he never admitted it." I took her blood pressure, which was higher than normal, and gave my usual words of caution. But I could see her mind was elsewhere. "Can I talk to you about something, Dr. Sam?"

"Anything at all. That's what I'm here for!" I expected some sort of sexual secret, which wasn't too unusual in my experience.

Instead she told me, "I've been to Boston to see a psychic."

"What?" My face must have reflected my surprise.

"A woman there contacted me several weeks ago and claimed she could communicate with the dead. I—I really think she might be able to reach Ron."

"Kate," I said, not unkindly, "you can't believe in such things. People like that are just out to get your money."

"I know. That's what Art told me when I suggested the possibility. I didn't dare tell him I'd already been there for two sessions with this woman."

"Who is she?" I asked.

"Her name is Sandra Gleam, or at least that's what she calls herself. 'Sandra Gleam—Lifting the Veil of the Afterlife,' She's a woman in her late forties, about my age, and she does seem to get results."

"What sort of results?" I asked with more than a little scepticism.

"She's contacted an Indian guide on the other side who says he can bring Ron to talk to me."

"And of course you paid her for this?"

"Certainly. I'd give a great deal to actually speak with my son again."

"And your husband knows nothing of this?"

She took a deep breath. "I haven't told him, and that's my problem. Sandra Gleam feels she needs to conduct a small séance at our home, with just my husband and me taking part. She says that would be the most comfortable setting for Ron."

I shook my head, more in sorrow than in reprimand. "Kate, you don't know what you're getting into here. The woman is a charlatan. She's using all sorts of trickery."

"How do you know that? You've never even met her."

"I know the way psychics operate."

"When she was in her trance I could see ectoplasm above her head."

"Gauze coated with phosphorescent paint."

"A small seashell appeared on the table as a sign from my son, even though I was holding both her hands."

"But the room was dark?"

"Mostly," she admitted. "There was a dim light so I could see there was no one else in the room."

"She had the shell hidden in her mouth, or perhaps even regurgitated it from her stomach. It's a trick some mediums are quite skilled at."

Kate Hale pondered this for a moment. "I have to do it. I have to take the chance that she's on the level." An idea seemed to light up her face. "Look here, Dr. Sam, since you know so much about this, could you attend the séance, too? If you're there to prove she's not a fake, my husband might go along with the idea."

I shook my head. "I think I'd have to say no to that, Kate. It falls far outside my duties as a physician."

She gave a reluctant sigh. "All right. Thank you for listening to me, at least."

* * *

My wife Annabel was Northmont's only veterinarian, and Annabel's Ark had become a haven for creatures of all shapes and sizes. That afternoon, following a house call at a farm near there, I stopped by the Ark on my way home and found her removing a painful thorn from a cat's paw. "Much the way Androcles would have done it," I suggested.

"I'm far gentler than Androcles, or hadn't you noticed?"

"I'm on my way home. You coming soon?"

She sighed and glanced over at the row of cages where her assistant was treating a large German shepherd. "I've got at least another hour here. Then I'll be along."

"I've got an idea. Let's meet at Max's for dinner. Say, seven o'clock?"

"Sounds perfect!" she readily agreed. Max's Steakhouse was our favorite restaurant in Northmont, the scene of our December wedding reception.

I changed my clothes and arrived at Max's about fifteen minutes early. Annabel hadn't yet come in and I was surprised to see Kate Hale and her husband seated in one of the booths. It seemed foolish to ignore them, so I said hello as I passed. Arthur Hale immediately stood up to greet me. "Hello, Doctor. Could you join us for a drink?"

"I'm meeting my wife. She should be here momentarily."

"Sit down anyway, until she comes."

I signaled Max so he'd know where I was and then joined them in the booth. "Nothing to drink for me," I told them. "I'll wait for Annabel."

Art Hale was a scholarly type who wore gold-rimmed glasses and smoked a pipe. He was around fifty, maybe a few years older than his wife, and when he wasn't busy on the town council he worked at a small printing business he owned that employed about a dozen people. "Kate has been telling me about her visits to this woman in Boston. She said she discussed it with you today. What's your opinion of it?"

I was reluctant to be dragged into a family dispute, but I felt I should repeat what I'd already told Kate. When I'd finished, she joined in. "Art feels the same way you do, Dr. Sam, and I'll admit you may be right. But what harm is there in finding out? All she's asking to come out here and hold a séance at our house is three hundred dollars, plus her travel expenses."

"Three hundred dollars is a lot of money," Hale murmured.

"To talk to our son? To hear his voice one more time?"

"Kate–" His voice was pleading now. "Be reasonable."

"If you're so afraid the woman is a fraud we can ask Dr. Sam to be present."

"I don't–"

But I'd barely started my objection when her husband's face brightened. "Would you, Doctor?"

"This is a bit out of my line," I protested.

"Nonsense! You have quite a reputation as a solver of mysteries. Isn't this is the same thing, in a way?"

"If you suspect some sort of fraud is being perpetrated you need to call on Sheriff Lens, not me."

"Maybe both of you could be there," Kate suggested.

I saw a way out of this entanglement. "If you can convince Sheriff Lens, I'll go along with it, too." It seemed a sure bet that the sheriff would have nothing to do with such a thing.

That's where I was wrong.

* * *

Sheriff Lens phoned me the following afternoon. "Hello, Doc. Still surviving married life?"

"There's nothing like it," I assured him. "Have you decided to run for another term?" It was a question I asked every four years and the answer had always been yes. He'd been elected sheriff for the first time in 1918, almost four years before I came to Northmont, and was completing his sixth term.

"In a weak moment I promised Vera I wouldn't run again this time. She says twenty-four years is enough for anyone, but hell, Doc–what would I do? Retire to a farm and raise chickens? I told her with the war on and all I had to serve one more term and she agreed."

I had to chuckle silently at that. I couldn't imagine Northmont with someone else as sheriff. "Anyway," he went on, "what I called about is this séance business with Art Hale and his wife."

"Forget about it, Sheriff. I told them I'd come if you did, but it was just a way of getting out of the whole thing. I'm sorry they lost a son, but I can't encourage them. It's obvious this Sandra Gleam is just out for their money. She wants to do the séance here so she can get a look at their home and decide how much she can get out of them."

"Isn't that all the more reason we should be there to protect them and expose her?" the sheriff argued.

"Do you really want to do this?" I asked.

"I think we should, Doc."

I sighed in surrender and asked, "When is she coming?"

"Saturday. She'll stay with them overnight and return to Boston on Sunday."

"Is she driving down?"

"Taking the train. Gasoline is scarce with the rationing and all."

As a physician, I was allowed a bit more gasoline than the average person, but I had to display the colored sticker I was issued for it on my front windshield. Train travel was becoming more popular, especially for our town, far removed from any commercial airport. "All right Sheriff. If you're game, so am I."

* * *

Art and Kate Hale met the train with Sandra Gleam on board late Saturday afternoon. As it turned out, that was June sixth, exactly six months since our wedding day, and Annabel had expected us to celebrate with dinner out or at least a private evening at home. All I could promise her was that I'd return as early as possible, and that didn't go over well.

I picked up Sheriff Lens in my Buick and we set off for our destination. "Been listening to the news, Doc? There are rumors of a big sea battle out around the Midway Islands in the Pacific."

"I hope we're winning."

I'd been to the Hale home a few times on house calls, and I was familiar with the impressive brick façade. It had once been a church perched on a hilltop at the end of Meadow Lane. No one seemed to remember what had happened to the congregation, but it had been remodeled into a private home in the 1920s. The layout was a bit awkward and they'd ended up with a windowless storage room across from the kitchen. Some thought the house had been partitioned that way to provide a so-called "thunder room" for those afraid of violent storms, but others offered a more prosaic explanation. The house had been remodeled during prohibition and a garage had been turned into the windowless room to serve as a storage area for cases of illegal scotch smuggled into the country.

In any event, it was empty to the bare walls and concrete floor now, except for a single card table and three folding chairs. An open bottle of white wine and three glasses stood on the table. A ceiling light provided the only illumination. Art and Kate Hale had been awaiting our arrival, and quickly introduced us to Sandra Gleam. As Kate had said, she was a woman in her late forties, with jet-black hair worn to shoulder length. Her figure was surprisingly trim and her dark eyes seemed to study each of us intently. She wore a long black dress with a pink scarf at her neck. It was her only touch of color. She was not the sort of woman I would have wanted for an enemy, yet she had a certain animal attraction. The three chairs around the card table told me that she had already excluded the sheriff and me from the séance.

"Dr. Hawthorne," she said when we were introduced. "Kate has told me much about you. I have looked forward to this meeting." I tried to read her eyes, but it was impossible. She might have been flirting with me, for all I knew.

"And I look forward to sitting in on your séance," I informed her.

"Alas, that will not be possible tonight. If I am to have any success in reaching the spirit of Ron Hale, only his closest flesh-and-blood relatives can be present."

Sheriff Lens didn't like the sound of that. "Look here, I have to be certain that no crime is being committed."

Sandra Gleam turned her eyes to him for the first time. "Does the town of Northmont have an ordinance against communicating with the dead?"

"Well, no," he admitted.

"Or trying to help people through their bereavement?"

"No. But we do have laws against swindling and confidence games."

The dark-haired woman turned toward Mrs. Hale and her husband. "Have I asked for any money other than my rather modest fee?"

"Certainly not!" Kate was quick to insist. Art Hale remained silent.

I had to come up with something to justify our presence. "If we can't be part of the séance, you must allow us to search this room, to make certain no sort of trickery is concerned here."

The woman shrugged. "It's their room, not mine. I am entering it for the first time."

The windowsless room was about the right size for a car, though if there had been a garage entrance it was gone now. The walls were all solid and the overhead light was too high to reach without a ladder. The card table and chairs were closely examined by the sheriff and me, but there was nothing hidden in or under them.

"Are you satisfied?" Sandra Gleam asked.

I looked at her long black dress, well aware that it could conceal all the tricks of a medium's trade. "Would you be willing to allow Mrs. Hale to frisk you?" I asked.

The woman smiled slightly at my suggestion. "Only if I could do the same to her."

"Look here—" Art Hale started to protest, but his wife stopped him.

"That's fine with me," she agreed. "Let's get to it."

While the medium stood still and raised her hands above her head, Kate Hale ran her own hands down the slender body, taking special care to feel around the legs. At one point Sandra Gleam slipped her feet out of her shoes so they could be searched as well. When Mrs. Hale lifted one of her feet she laughed. "I'm a bit ticklish there."

Then Sandra repeated the procedure with Kate Hale, who seemed a bit embarrassed by the groping hands but did not complain. "All right," her husband said, turning to Sheriff Lens. "You might as well search me as well."

When all the searching was finished, nothing unusual had been found. Sandra's purse remained on the kitchen counter and Hale had left his wallet and keys there, too. The women had no pockets in their dresses, and Hale's pockets held only a handkerchief and his leather eyeglass case.

I asked about the wine and was told that Sandra had brought it. "Some cooks drink a bit of white wine while they prepare a meal." she told. "My bottle serves the same purpose."

I held it to the light but there was nothing else in the bottle. I took a sip and agreed it was wine and nothing else. "A very good wine," I complimented her.

"Then we are ready," Sandra Gleam announced, filling the three glasses. Turning to the sheriff and me she said, "The Hales and I will now adjourn here for the séance. You may stand guard at the door if you wish."

But before they could begin, an odd thing happened. It was still daylight on this June evening, and the sound of a bell reached our ears. It was not the doorbell, but an irregular ringing that seemed to come from the street. Kate

Hale knew at once what it was. "That's the knife grinder. Sheriff, could you get those two paring knives I left on the kitchen counter and take them out to him? I left some money there, too."

Sheriff Lens seemed to hesitate at performing this household chore and I immediately said, "You stay here, Sheriff, I'll do it."

I found the knives and hurried out to the curb. Pete Petrov, the knife grinder, stopped his wagon when he saw me. "What're you doing out this way, Dr. Sam?"

"Visiting a patient," I told him. "Sharpen these two for her, will you?"

"Sure thing! He took the knives and operated the foot pedal on his grinder, holding the blade close enough to send sparks flying. After a moment he repeated the process with the second blade. "There you are! Good as new." I took the paring knives and paid him. "Say hello to Mrs. Hale for me." he called as he moved on with his wagon, pulling the bell cord to announce his passing.

"Thanks. I'll do that."

I went back inside and returned the paring knives to the kitchen counter by the stove. Sheriff Lens was standing by the closed door of the storeroom. "I heard some mumbling but now it's silent," he reported.

"Did they lock the door?"

"No, but no spirits from the beyond are getting by me, Doc."

I smiled. "You're not supposed to keep them out. Sandra Gleam wants them let in."

We waited for several minutes, listening for a sound, but all seemed quiet behind the door.

Finally the sheriff asked, "Think we should take a look, Doc?"

"It's only been about fifteen minutes so far. Séances can go on longer than that."

I paced around a bit longer, and then sat down to glance through the Hales' magazines. They had the latest issues of *Life* and *National Geographic*, along with an issue of *Ellery Queen's Mystery Magazine*, which had begun publication the previous fall. I skimmed through it and was settling down to read a story by Stuart Palmer when there was a thump from the closed room.

"Are you all right in there?" Sheriff Lens called out, but there was no answer. He turned the knob and slowly pushed the door open.

I could see that the overhead light was still on. Art Hale was slumped over, his head on the table. Kate had topped off her chair and was lying unconscious on the floor. Sandra Gleam was upright in her chair, her head back and the pink scarf a mass of blood. Her throat had been cut.

* * *

It took us a few moments to revive Kate and Art Hale. Both seemed drowsy and possibly drugged. Neither could remember anything after drinking the wine and joining hands with Sandra for the beginning of the séance.

"One of you better remember something," Sheriff Lens told them. "You two were alone with her in this room and I was guarding the only door. No one else could have killed her. And she sure didn't kill herself. There's no knife."

* * *

I'd examined Sandra Gleam and confirmed that she was dead. Now I searched carefully around the body, the chairs, and the table. There was no knife. "I'm afraid we'll have to search you both again," I told them.

Careful not to be too invasive, I went over Kate's clothing and felt along her body. She was my patient, after all, and I'd examined her body many times. There was no weapon of any sort. I watched while Sheriff Lens did the same with her husband. He removed the handkerchief and eyeglass case from Hale's pocket, sliding the glasses partway out, then going over his body with nimble fingers. There was no doubt in my mind that neither of them could have concealed a knife or even a razor blade. And why would they? What motive could they have had for killing this woman?

Still, I had to consider every possibility. I took a couple of tongue depressors from the bag I always carried and checked Art's and Kate's throats with a small flashlight. "What's the purpose of this?" Hale demanded.

"Say *ah*, please."

He did as he was told and his wife followed along, too. "I had to be sure neither of you slid a knife down your throat." I explained.

"You think I'm a sword-swallower or something?" he asked.

"I had to rule out the possibility."

"And Kate? Did you ever hear of a female sword-swallower?"

"As a matter of fact, yes," I told him. "There was a woman named Edith Clifford, around the turn of the century, who was said to have swallowed up to sixteen short swords at one time. She was with the circus. Both of you seem in the clear, though. Let's move out of here and let the sheriff call in his people."

While Sheriff Lens was on the phone, Art Hale headed for the kitchen to retrieve his wallet, with Kate close behind. "I know I didn't kill that woman and there were only two of us in the room with her. Art, did you—?"

He returned on her then. "No, I didn't, Kate. If anyone killed her, it was you."

I quickly intervened. "This will get us nowhere. We have to think this out."

Kate moved to the kitchen counter and picked up a sharpened paring knife. "Where's the other knife?" she asked.

"It's right there someplace. The grinder man sharpened both of them and I left them for you."

But there was only one knife now. The second knife had vanished. Though the sheriff and I searched the kitchen, there was no sign of it, not even in the drawer with the other cutlery. "We'd better check these two again," he said.

I agreed, and we went over Hale and his wife even more carefully the second time. But the missing knife did not reappear. "My God!" Kate Hale suddenly gasped, as if she'd just realized the full import of what had happened. "Could one of the spirit guides have taken it and killed her with it?"

Sheriff Lens scoffed. "I'd believe in an invisible man before I'd believe in spirits."

"But even an invisible man couldn't have picked up the knife and carried it into that room," I said. "You were already guarding the closed door when I returned with the sharpened knives."

"Forget the knife, then, Doc. One of these two had to have killed her."

"With what? You can't cut a throat like that with a fingernail."

"What about those wineglasses?"

We all reentered the room and examined the glasses and bottle, but there were no sharp edges, no cracks. All three glasses were nearly empty, and I sniffed them. Then I put a drop from the bottle on my finger and touched it to my tongue. "I can't be certain, but it seems likely there was something in the wine that put you both to sleep."

"Sandra poured it herself." Kate Hale told us. "Why would he want to knock us out?"

"Perhaps so she could rig up some spiritualist trickery," I suggested. "She may have planned to awaken you when she was ready."

"Come on, Doc," Sheriff Lens objected. "If you think she let another person into the room, it just couldn't be!"

"Maybe not a flesh-and-blood person," Kate said, "but she was dealing with spirits."

"Kate—" her husband began.

"I know you don't believe me, but what other explanation is there? She summoned a spirit who took my sharpened paring knife from the kitchen counter, came in here, and killed her with it."

"Why would the spirit do that?" I asked, trying to reason with her. "She was their friend."

Her husband was exasperated by the whole business. "Let's stop imagining spirits. There are none. The woman obviously cut her own throat. There's no other explanation."

"Then what happened to the knife?" Sheriff Lens asked.

"Perhaps it was made of ice that melted and mingled with the blood from her throat."

I shook my head. "Ice wouldn't have been sharp enough for that wound, and everyone was searched, remember? No one could have been hiding an ice dagger."

"She might have used a razor blade and swallowed it as she lay dying."

"After cutting her throat? Hardly, Mr. Hale." But his bizarre suggestion had triggered something in my mind. In addition to sword-swallowers, there were people who could swallow things like razor blades. Either of the Hales might have taped a razor blade to their leg that might have escaped our search. They might have used it to cut Sandra Gleam's throat and then swallowed it.

"What are you thinking, Doc?" the sheriff asked.

"If it's all right with you, I'd like to take Mr. and Mrs. Hale down to the hospital for a fluoroscope examination."

"An X-ray?"

I nodded. "Just to make certain there are no sharp objects in them."

* * *

Art Hale grumbled a bit, but I drove them to the hospital after the sheriff's deputies and the coroner arrived. I was careful not to let them out of my sight, not even for a restroom visit, until after I'd given each of them a full-body X-ray scan. There were no razor blades or any other weapons hidden either inside or outside their bodies. Whatever had killed Sandra Gleam was still in that room, or had been removed by some method I couldn't imagine. I thought about a case I'd investigated during my early days in Northmont, involving a man's throat cut by a slender fishing line. But there was nothing of the sort here, nothing that could be found in two body searches and a fluoroscope examination.

I wanted to go back and examine that windowless room again, before the Hales returned to the house. The sheriff solved the problem for me when he requested that the couple accompany him to his office to make a full statement. I asked Hale for the key to his house in case the deputies were gone from there. He took the ring of keys from his pocket and puzzled over them. "I can't see close up without my glasses. It's a Yale lock."

"This one," I said, detaching it from the ring. "I'll get it back to you." I left them with the sheriff, checking first with my nurse April to make sure there were no emergencies.

* * *

The coroner and the deputies were still at the Hale house. Watching them work, I realized how much Sheriff Lens had improved on his investigative techniques during my twenty years in Northmont. One of the deputies even took a small sample of grit he'd noticed on the concrete floor. "If it was a spook, he may have brought something over from the other side," he said. I couldn't argue with that.

"How about your measurements?" I asked. "Any chance there could be a secret panel or hidden closet here?"

"Nothing like that, Doc. These walls are solid, the floor's concrete, and the ceiling has only the single light fixture."

I carried a stool from the kitchen and climbed up to take a look at that fixture. The frosted glass globe screwed on over two light bulbs. Nothing had been disturbed. Next I went to the light switch by the door and unscrewed the switch plate. There was space enough for a small knife or razor blade behind it, though I saw nothing but a spider hurrying to escape into the woodwork.

Nothing.

The more I thought about it, the more I wondered if the answer might lie not in Northmont but in Boston.

* * *

Annabel was not happy when I told her I was driving two hours to Boston the following morning and might have to remain there overnight. I knew she couldn't accompany me. There was too much work to be done at the Ark. "Why was this woman killed?" I asked. "That's what I need to know. If Kate

Hale realized she was a fraud, why would she go to the trouble of luring her to Northmont to kill her in this manner? And why would her husband kill her without at least seeing what her game was?"

"But who can you talk to in Boston?" Annabel wondered.

"Mrs. Hale says there was a sister. Maybe I can learn something from her."

The news from Midway was encouraging the following morning, and our naval victory overshadowed a report that the Japanese had landed a small force on two of Alaska's Aleutian Islands. The weather was good for my drive into Boston, and the Sunday traffic was at a minimum. I located Sandra Gleam's address without difficulty, an apartment she'd shared with her sister in one of the big old buildings overlooking Boston Common.

Josephine Gleam answered the door. "Are you from the police?" she immediately asked. "They've already been here once."

I introduced myself and explained that I was helping the Northmont sheriff investigate her sister's murder. Josephine was attractive and probably younger than Sandra, a tall, slim woman with long brown hair and bangs.

"This has been a terrible shock to me," she said in a familiar Boston accent, "but I must tell you right off that we weren't really sisters. Sandra and I were very close, but the Gleam Sisters only existed on stage."

"Stage?"

"Vaudeville. Do you have any idea who killed her?"

"Not yet," I admitted. "We're working on it." She invited me in and I took a seat facing her. "Do you perform séances, too?"

"That whole business was a—" She caught herself, perhaps not wanting to speak ill of her friend. Then, after an awkward moment of silence, she began again. "Sandra and I had a vaudeville act together about ten years ago. That's when we became the Gleam Sisters. It was a mind-reading thing. I would wander through the audience in my spangled tights, holding up items like a pocket watch or a necklace, and Sandra would try to identify the objects while blindfolded. Of course, my patter always contained a key-word clue that we'd worked out in advance."

"You're telling me the act was a fraud?"

She grew restless, fidgeting in her chair. "It was vaudeville. We were there to entertain, just like the magicians. Everyone knew it was an act."

"All this was Sandra's idea?"

"Well, yes, I guess it was. We were both younger then. She thought having a vaudeville act was a great way to attract guys."

"You weren't married?"

"Not then, but Sandra always had guys around."

"When did she start this spiritualism business with the séances?"

Josephine shrugged. "Vaudeville died and she just drifted into, went from reading minds to speaking with the dead. I guess she viewed it as a natural progression."

"Did you help her with this?" I asked.

"No, no. I'm a secretary at the state capitol. We shared this apartment, but then we went our separate ways. I was married for a few years and when that went bad she took me in."

I consulted some notes that I'd made. "Kate Hale, the woman who lost her son at Pearl Harbor, said that Sandra contacted her about a séance. Do you know just when that was?"

She thought about it. "I could find out. She kept a record of all her contacts. Not men friends, just her spiritualist business. She watched the newspapers all over southern New England, checking the casualty lists from the war. When someone was confirmed dead, she telephoned the next of kin and offered her services."

"It was a cruel sort of confidence game."

"Sometimes I think she really helped those people." Josephine had gone to a desk in one corner of the room and while she spoke she glanced through Sandra's appointment book. "Here it is! She telephoned Kate Hale in Northmont on April twenty-fifth and invited her to attend a séance here. Mrs. Hale came to Boston two weeks later, on May eighth, and returned a week after that for a second séance."

"Did you know that Sandra was planning a séance at the Hale home in Northmont?"

"No. I was quite surprised when the police told me that. She rarely conducted her sessions anywhere but here. I know, because I usually had to stay out of the way when she scheduled one."

"Was there anyone who disliked Sandra, who might have had a motive for killing her?"

"Not that I know of."

I asked her a few more questions but learned nothing of interest. Sandra Gleam's life seemed as much as riddle as her death. I drove back to Northmont later that afternoon.

* * *

"We're up against a stone wall, Doc," Sheriff Lens told me the following morning. "Either Hale or his wife must have killed her, but what happened to the weapon? Is it possible they acted together? And what was their motive?"

"If they wanted to kill her, they would hardly have done it in their own home under these impossible circumstances. There's something we're not seeing here."

"What about that knife grinder, Pete Petrov? Might he have sneaked into the room somehow after he sharpened those knives for you?"

"Only if he could walk through walls. What about that bottle of wine? Did you have it analyzed?"

He nodded. "It contained a mild but fast-acting sleeping powder, likely put there by one of those three."

"I tasted just a drop before the séance and it seemed all right to me, but the sleeping powder might have been added later, by either Hale or his wife. Surely Sandra Gleam didn't do it."

"Only two real suspects and we can't solve this thing! Any suggestions, Doc?"

"Just that we go back to the Hale house and keep looking. Maybe something will jump out at us."

The June weather had turned unusually warm, and Kate Hale already had roses in her garden when we pulled up in the sheriff's car. "Aren't they beauties?" she asked. "This is a new bush I planted in Ron's honor. I think he would have liked that."

"We're sorry to bother you again," the sheriff told her, "but there are still a great many questions to be answered."

Her husband had noticed our arrival and joined us at the rose garden. "Any leads yet?" he asked. The bright sun reflected off the silver frames of his glasses and he put up a hand to shield his eyes. "Nothing. I'm sure it's not news that the two of you are the prime suspects. Nobody else got in or out of the room."

"We were both unconscious," Art Hale pointed out.

I shook my head. "One of you didn't drink your glass of wine until after you'd cut Sandra Gleam's throat. Let's go in the house."

They both seemed reluctant to face more questioning. "I didn't kill her," Kate Hale said. "So it had to have been Art."

He glared at her. "Kate . . ."

"Inside," Sheriff Lens ordered, herding them both toward the door.

I took the opportunity to have another look at their kitchen, where that sharpened paring knife had vanished so mysteriously. For some reason, it didn't seem mysterious at all anymore. I'd wakened that morning remembering that I'd placed the knives on the kitchen counter near the stove. Sure enough, there was a narrow space, little more than a quarter of an inch, between counter and stove. "Do you have a flashlight?" I asked Hale.

He produced one and I pointed it between the cupboard and the stove. At the bottom, resting on the floor, was the missing paring knife. "That's a mystery solved," I told them.

"It must have fallen there," Hale decided.

"Or been put there by the killer. One of you came into the kitchen after we found Sandra's body, saw the knives, and pushed one of them through the crack between the counter and stove. It could only have been the killer who did it, to strengthen the illusion of a spirit taking the knife to cut Sandra's throat."

"Which one of them, Doc?" the sheriff asked. "You know, don't you?"

"Yes, I know."

* * *

We'd settled down around the kitchen table, like old friends, and Kate was even brewing a pot of coffee for us. "You see," I began, "the motive was the key to it all. Even though Sandra Gleam might have been trying to swindle you both out of some money, that hardly made a motive for murder. You could merely have walked away, told her you were through with séances. No, it had to be something else. When I thought about my conversation yesterday with Sandra's roommate and old vaudeville partner, I knew what it was."

"How could you?" Kate Hale asked.

"The dates weren't right. According to Sandra's appointment book, she first called you about your dead son on April twenty-fifth and you attended your first séance in Boston on May eighth, returning a week later. The two of you were notified of Ron's death in mid April, but the announcement to the press didn't come until May first. Sandra watched the papers for the lists of casualties, but she couldn't have learned of your son's confirmed death as early as April twenty-fifth—not from the papers, at least. In fact, since we live in a small town two hours from Boston, it's safe to say that the only way Sandra Gleam could have learned the confirmation of your son's death at that early date was if one of you two told her."

"Wait a minute!" Art protested. "She might have found his name on an earlier list of the missing."

I shook my head. "Séances are only for communicating with the dead. One of you had to have told Sandra your son was confirmed dead. It could hardly have been Kate, or there'd have been no reason for her to carefully record calling you on April twenty-fifth. But you told me Art was badly affected by the report that Ron was missing in action at Pearl Harbor. He went off for several days in January and February and then again in April, when the tragic news was confirmed. You thought he was drinking, and perhaps he was. But I believe he drove to Boston for his drinking, and there he met Sandra Gleam, a woman always on the lookout for men."

The blood had drained from Kate's face as I spoke. I knew I was putting her through hell, but there was no other way. "He told Sandra, and she contacted you for a séance, Kate. When you finally told him about it, he must have been furious, though he may not have shown the full extent of his anger. Perhaps he got on the phone to Sandra and told her to stay away from his wife and not even think about journeying to Northmont. He knew she was after money, and what better way to procure it? I imagine she had a whole series of expensive séances in mind, and if you tried to stop her she'd have gone right to Kate and revealed you as an adulterer."

"That's a great deal of speculation," Art Hale told me. "Can you prove any of it?"

"You were the first to return to the kitchen counter for your wallet and keys, when that paring knife was made to disappear. But I can do better than that. I can show that you and only you could have murdered Sandra Gleam."

He smiled slightly, "Without a weapon? With Sheriff Lens guarding the door?"

"You had a weapon, and Sheriff Lens of all people should have guessed what it was."

The sheriff seemed baffled by my words. "I should have guessed? Why me?"

"Because Art cut the blackmailing Sandra Gleam's throat with a broken lens from his eyeglasses."

* * *

Hale's face turned ashen as I ticked off the points on my fingers. "As I noticed the other night at Max's Steakhouse, your regular eyeglasses have gold frames. The ones you're wearing now—an extra pair, no doubt—have silver frames. And in the hours after the murder you wore no glasses at all. You even commented to me that you were unable to choose the correct key up close without your glasses. The sheriff found them in your leather case, in your pocket, after the killing, but as I remember, he only pulled them partway out of the case."

"How could he have done it, Sam?" Sheriff Lens wanted to know.

"By drugging the wine after I'd taken a sip, while we were distracted by the knife grinder's arrival. He then pretended to drink while Kate and Sandra really did. When they'd dozed off, after several minutes he took Sandra's scarf, which he would have known she'd be wearing, covered his fingers while he broke a lens of his glasses, and then held the largest piece with the scarf while he cut her throat with it. The scarf protected his fingers against getting cut, as well as helping shield him from the blood. Then he drank the wine and collapsed along with his wife. Even if we'd taken the glasses from their case we might not have noticed immediately that there was a lens missing."

"What happened to the broken glass?" the sheriff wanted to know. "Are you telling me he swallowed it?"

"No, I'm telling you he ground it to dust underfoot, against the concrete floor. Ask your deputy about that sample of grit he gathered from the floor."

That was when Kate turned to him. "Art, is this true?"

"She was blackmailing me, Kate, and using our heartbreak over Ron's death to bleed us for money. After the pain of his death, I couldn't stand to have you learn I'd found comfort with another woman. If I hadn't killed her, it would have gone on and on."

It was a sad case with sad ending. Sheriff Lens and I barely spoke at first, after Art had been taken away. Finally the sheriff said, "There were only the two of them with Sandra, Doc. He must have known Kate would be certain of his guilt."

"Not necessarily, Sheriff. It was a chance he had to take. If he could make the crime seem impossible, perhaps she'd believe someone from the spirit world really had killed Sandra. That was why he hid the paring knife when he had a chance, to strengthen the impossibility of it."

When I saw Annabel that evening she told me a cat had died at the Ark that day. "I actually cried a bit, Sam. She was such a pretty thing. Do you ever shed any tears about murder victims?"

"I had no tears for Sandra Gleam," I said, and then sat down to tell her about it.

THE PROBLEM OF THE CANDIDATE'S CABIN

Sheriff Lens had decided to run for his seventh and final term of office in November of 1942, with the nation in the midst of its greatest war. He'd first been elected in 1918, nearly four years before I set up practice in Northmont (Dr. Sam was explaining to his frequent visitor and drinking companion), and I'd supported him every time since. This would be his first race since my marriage to Annabel almost a year earlier, on December 6, 1941, and she was at my side as much as possible in campaigning for him.

Her veterinary business, Annabel's Ark, the most complete in our part of the state, now boasted two assistants to help with the work load. That meant she could spend more evenings at home, and during the month of October it allowed her to join me at local rallies for Sheriff Lens. His opponent that year as a young man named Ray Anders, a pleasant enough fellow whose sole experience had been two years as a deputy sheriff.

We'd attended one of Ander's rallies to see what we were up against. It was held in the Grange Hall on a Sunday afternoon and we stood near the back of the crowded room so as not to attract attention. Anders, a dark-haired fellow in his late twenties, had a certain charm about him. Sometimes he joked about owning a log cabin at the edge of town, but he was no Abe Lincoln. Everyone knew he and his wife also had a nice home near the town square. He started out by commending our brave Marines who were still locked in the fierce battle for the island of Guadalcanal, then explained that a rheumatic heart condition kept him out of the service. Somehow this led into a call for younger men, new blood in the county sheriff's department.

"My opponent is an able, honest man," he announced, "but he has been our sheriff for twenty-four years! He is fifty-six years old!"

That was true enough. Sheriff Lens was ten years older than me. But I could feel him bristle at my side when his age was mentioned. I laid a restraining hand on his arm lest he shut out some comment. In the seats ahead of us some of Anders's followers took up the chant, "New blood! New blood!"

I steered Sheriff Lens toward the door before his rage boiled over. "Can you imagine?" he sputtered once we were outside. "I gave him his job! Two years he worked for me, and never made an arrest that I can remember.

Maybe he issued a speeding ticket or two. Now he thinks he'd make a better sheriff than me!"

"Calm down!" I pleaded. "Do you want to have a heart attack?"

"Why? Because of my age? Because I'm fifty-six?"

I sighed and pushed him along out the door. Sheriff Lens had never been my patient for the simple reason that he was remarkably healthy for his age. His wife Vera helped see to that. His health would not be an issue in the campaign, but his age was obviously becoming one.

* * *

The campaign manager for Ray Anders was a man named Cassell. His first name was Jonathan, but he liked to be known as Major Cassell, claiming he'd earned the rank in the Great War, as he still called it. A man in his early fifties, he'd been on the fringes of state politics for years. Managing a campaign for sheriff of a town like Northmont was quite a comedown for him, and I wondered what had brought him to us. Maybe it was money. Ray Anders was married to Jane Brophy, whose family had a profitable tobacco farm outside of town. Rumor had it her money was financing her husband's campaign, and that might have included Major Cassell. Certainly he was staying at their log cabin, which in a sense had been part of Jane Anders's dowry.

We talked about it that night over dinner at the sheriff's house, with Vera serving her favorite lamb chops. Annabel was convinced it was Major Cassell's strategy to focus on the sheriff's age. "It really upsets me that he'd stoop to such tactics," she fumed.

"Do you know Ray Anders?" I asked.

"No. I treated his wife's pet monkey once. She seemed nice enough."

"Jane Anders or the monkey?" Vera Lens asked, passing a plate around the table.

We all laughed and Annabel answered, "Both of them, actually."

But Sheriff Lens quickly turned serious. "How are we gonna tackle this age issue, Doc? No one's ever raised it against me before."

"That's because you weren't fifty-six before," I told him. "It's certainly not old by today's standards, but when you were born the life expectancy at birth was only around forty-six. Even today it's only sixty-two for white males. We can't make you younger. The only thing to do is to keep plugging away at your experience on the job. Give the voters statistics on the number of murder cases you've solved."

"Mostly with your help," the sheriff observed. "He'll probably point that out."

We finished dinner and smoked our cigars while the women did the dishes. At home I helped Annabel with the dishes, but I knew that Sheriff Lens was of a different generation, even if he was only ten years older than me. "You're going to win," I told him, trying to boost his spirits. "There's no way that Ray Anders is going to be elected sheriff of this county."

* * *

But as October dragged on, with a New England autumn so lovely we almost forgot about the war, Anders seemed to be picking up support. A few of the deputies who'd worked with Anders appeared at his rallies, and I could see Sheriff Lens was hurt by their defection. Vera even took a highly unscientific poll of voters by calling one hundred residents listed in the phone book. Forty were of Sheriff Lens, thirty-seven for Ray Anders, and the rest undecided. Of course some folks still didn't have phones and there was no telling how they would vote.

On October twenty-sixth, eight days before the election, there was a bad scene outside the sheriff's office. Rob Gallagher, one of the deputies supporting Anders, was handing out fliers for him in the parking lot. I happened to be driving by just in time to see the sheriff come storming out to confront him. Fearing the worst, I skidded to a quick halt across the street and ran over to join them.

"I'm off duty!" Gallagher was insisting. "And I'm out of the office. What I'm doing here is known as free speech, Sheriff. Do you want to fire me for it?"

Gallagher was a slender but muscular fellow, a bit over six feet tall and a quarter-century younger than Sheriff Lens. If they came to blows I knew who would be on the losing end. "Okay, you two," I yelled, pulling them apart. "Go back inside, Sheriff."

He started to say something but then thought better of it. He turned on his heel and retreated to the office.

"Are you going to tell me to stop, too, Doc?" Gallagher asked.

"Just move away, Rob. Exercise your free speech out of the sheriff's sight."

"I cleared this with Major Cassell. He said I was within my rights."

"I'm sure he did. But let's try to keep this election civil."

I followed Sheriff Lens into his office and closed the door. "What was that all about?" I asked.

"I don't know, Doc. I've never faced a campaign like this. Hell, half the time I've run unopposed! I even had the Democrats' endorsement a couple of times."

"It's clear that Rob Gallagher is supporting Anders. What about the other deputies?"

"A few of them are leaning toward Anders, but Gallagher's the only real problem. He's a registered Republican, but he's a good friend of Anders. He'd like to have his buddy behind this desk instead of me."

"You're still ahead in Vera's telephone poll."

"That could change overnight." I knew he was right. These last eight days could make or break him.

* * *

The following morning, Tuesday, I was awakened early by the ringing of the phone. Annabel answered and passed the receiver to me. "It's Sheriff Lens."

I groaned, still half asleep. "What time is it?"

"Almost six."

"Hello, Sheriff. What is it?"

"I just had a call from Major Cassell. He reports there's a prowler trying to break into his cabin. I have to go out there."

"Are you on night duty?"

"I'm home in bed, like you. But he phoned here, not the sheriff's office. Something's funny, Doc."

"I'll meet you there as soon as I can," I promised. Annabel buried her face in the pillow.

The Anderses' log cabin at the edge of town, where Major Cassell had been staying during the election campaign, was a sturdy, professionally built place that looked more like a vacation home than something carved out of the forest by pioneers. The eastern sky was beginning to glow with daylight as I drove up, parking behind the sheriff's car, a deputy's vehicle, and a shiny Buick that I knew to be Cassell's. The first thing I saw was Rob Gallagher on the cabin's porch with his revolver drawn. He was pointing it through the open front window.

"Gallagher!" I called out. "What's happened?"

"I'm not sure," he replied without turning toward me. "It looks like Sheriff Lens killed Major Cassell."

* * *

The sheriff was certainly ready to kill somebody by the time we returned to his office later that morning. He had not yet been formally charged, but Deputy Gallagher made it clear that he would file a full report with the district attorney. "It's an election frame-up!" he bellowed at me in his office. "Anders will do anything to defeat me!"

I tried to calm him down. "I doubt if that would extend to murdering his campaign manager. Tell me again exactly what happened out there."

He took a deep breath, attempting to settle down. "I told you he called me about a prowler. That in itself seemed odd, but I didn't want to turn the call over to Gallagher so I dressed quickly and drove out there. Cassell's car was the only one at the cabin when I reached it. He didn't answer my knock and the door was locked. I could see a light burning through the living-room window, so I went over and looked in. Major Cassell was stretched out on the floor, exactly as you saw him. I could see blood and what looked like a bullet wound to his head. I checked all the windows, looking for an open one, but they were all locked. The cabin has only the one door, and that was locked, too. Finally, I smashed the living room window, unlatched it and climbed through. He was dead, of course, and I saw a revolver on the floor across the room. I also saw that the cabin door was locked and bolted. That was when Rob Gallagher appeared at the window with his gun drawn."

"No one else was hiding in the cabin?"

The sheriff shook his head. "You were there when we searched the place. It's just a living room with a small kitchen at one end, a bedroom, and bathroom. There's no basement or attic. The only other living creature was that monkey locked in its cage."

The monkey was a chimpanzee, Jane Anders's pet that Annabel had treated at the Ark. It was big, weighing around fifty pounds. I didn't know what it was doing in the cabin with Major Cassell, but we could hardly consider it a suspect. "Gallagher's report is going to say he found you alone in that locked cabin with Cassell's body. No one else could have entered unless Cassell let them in, and in that case, how did they get out while leaving the place locked from the inside? That door was both locked and bolted, as you said."

"You know there are lots of tricks with door bolts, Doc."

I agreed, but not in this case. "That was the first thing I examined. The bolt is built into the door and locked by turning a knob. It's not the sort you can pull shut with a string or drop into place with a melting ice cube. The door had also been locked with a key, but I assume both Anders and Cassell had keys."

"The windows, then. One of the panes could have been removed and put back."

Again I shook my head. "I checked every one. They're all firmly in place, except for the one you broke to gain entrance. And the fireplace chimney's too narrow for even a midget Santa Claus."

"Could it have been suicide, Doc?" Sheriff Lens asked, the lines of his face deepening with concern.

"I don't see how. There were no powder burns and the revolver was on the floor across the room. There was one shot fired. I'd be surprised if it's not the murder weapon."

"It's not my gun! Mine was in my holster until Gallagher confiscated it. You don't think he'll switch them, do you?"

"No chance of that. I wrote down the serial numbers of both weapons." However, it bothered me that both revolvers were Smith & Wesson .38 caliber, the standard weapon for the sheriff and his deputies. The serial numbers were identical except for the last two digits, implying that they were acquired at the same time.

"They'll say I had a motive because Cassell was managing the Anders campaign and attacking me for being too old."

"Candidates don't shoot rivals for things that are said in the heat of a campaign, Sheriff."

"All they have to do is keep the doubt in voters' minds for one week, Doc. The election is a week from today."

* * *

By Wednesday morning all of Northmont was talking about it. The mayor had placed Sheriff Lens on paid leave of absence pending the outcome of the investigation. His service revolver had not fired the fatal shot, but the murder weapon was indeed one of a dozen purchased by the sheriff's office some years back. It had been kept in reserve, never assigned to a specific deputy.

"I haven't checked on those weapons in years," the sheriff admitted to me.

"Who had access to them?"

"Any one of my deputies. And maybe a couple of other people—my secretary Gretchen, for one."

It was only a few years back that Sheriff Lens had determined he needed someone to handle the paperwork. With nine deputies and increased criminal activity, he'd obtained funds from the town council to hire Gretchen Wild, an attractive middle-aged woman who'd moved here from Providence during the Depression. She was divorced, but I knew little else about her, and had chatted with her only a few times at the sheriff's office. Now, with Sheriff Lens sidelined at home, I decided to pay her a call.

She looked up from her typewriter, brushing her brown hair back from her forehead. "Dr. Hawthorne!" she greeted me with some surprise. "Sheriff Lens is—"

"I know. I wanted to speak with you."

"Deputy Gallagher is acting sheriff. Should I call him for you?"

"No, this is just a friendly chat."

"I want you to know right off that I can't believe Sheriff Lens had anything to do with what happened to Major Cassell."

"He'll appreciate knowing that. The sheriff has a good many friends in town and we're all standing behind him. What I want to ask you about is the storage of handguns here at the office."

She'd swiveled her chair around to face me, resting her hands on its arms. "The sheriff and his deputies each have their own weapons. They take them home when off duty, in case they're needed in an emergency."

"Counting the sheriff, there are ten men in the department. Some years back he purchased a dozen Smith & Wesson .38-caliber revolvers. The remaining two should be in this office."

"I don't think I've ever seen them," she admitted. "But they should be in the safe."

The old iron monster against the wall opposite the sheriff's desk had been there for as long as I could remember, and I'd rarely seen it open. Now Gretchen Wild shuffled around in her desk and came up with a combination, handwritten on a slip of paper. "Here it is," she said, and went over to twirl the dials. The old safe opened with a loud clunk as the bolts were pulled back. She opened an unlocked drawer and took out a revolver wrapped in an oily cloth. "This is one of the guns. The other doesn't seem to be here."

"Apparently it was used to kill Major Cassell," I told her.

"Oh."

"It looks like almost anyone might have had access to this safe," I observed, "if they knew the combination was right there in your desk."

"Nobody knew that except Sheriff Lens."

"But any of the deputies might have come across it accidentally. Or someone might have been here when you opened the safe."

"I'm very careful about that," she insisted.

"Did you know Major Cassell?"

"I'd seen him around town with Ray Anders. I didn't really know him."

Her telephone rang and I decided there was nothing more to be learned from her. I waved and left the office.

* * *

By Wednesday afternoon I'd tracked down Ray Anders at an election rally in the parking lot at Berman's Feed Store. His wife Jane was with him, passing out the same fliers Gallagher had been distributing. "I'm cutting this rally short," the candidate was saying, "out of respect for my manager and good friend, Major Jonathan Cassell, who was brutally murdered yesterday morning. The remainder of this campaign will be dedicated to his memory, and if I am elected sheriff next Tuesday I promise that his killer will be brought to justice."

A cheer went up as the crowd began to scatter, heading for their trucks and wagons. I caught up with Anders and asked if we could talk for a few minutes. "You're trying to get Sheriff Lens off the hook, aren't you?" he asked with a grim expression. "This is one time you're going to fail, Sam. No one else could have killed Major Cassell. No one else had a motive to kill him."

"Rob Gallagher was conveniently at the scene, wasn't he? It's as if the whole thing was set up in advance."

"Gallagher was on road patrol Monday night. The telephone operator reported a muffled call for help from the cabin. When he arrived, the sheriff's car was already there and that window was broken."

"How long have you known Major Cassell? What brought him to a place like Northmont?"

"I met him at a party fund-raiser in Hartford. We got to talking and I mentioned I'd like to run for sheriff if I had someone to manage the campaign. That was last year. When I decided to give it a try, Jane suggested I contact him. He'd done some business with her father and had a lot of party connections."

Jane Anders worked her way through a few well-wishers to join us. "I hope you're not trying to get the sheriff off," she said. "What he did was a terrible thing!"

"That remains to be proven, Jane."

"Don't try to say it was self-defense. There were no signs of a struggle in the cabin."

"You were there?" I asked.

"I had to retrieve Max, my chimp. He was locked in his cage. The body and the weapon had already been removed, but everything seemed normal except for the broken window."

"How did it happen the chimp was out there in the first place?"

"I'd been working at the cabin during the summer, getting it painted and in shape for Major Cassell's arrival. Max was along to keep me company, and the major took an immediate liking to him. He asked that I leave him there. I was glad to do it. With all our campaigning, it was one less thing for me to attend to."

"Did either of you lend the major a pistol for protection? That cabin is a bit isolated."

"Of course not," Anders replied. "The murder weapon wasn't mine, if that's what you're thinking. I turned in my service revolver when I left the force last year. I'm sure there's a record of it."

"I'd like to learn more about Major Cassell if I could. I understand he did some work for your father, Jane. Would you have any objection to my speaking with him?"

My request took her by surprise, but she readily agreed. "My father is a wonderful man, but I doubt if he'll be able to help you much."

"I suppose no one could except Max," I told her. "Your chimp must have seen the whole thing."

* * *

On Thursday morning, while they were still deciding whether to charge Sheriff Lens with the killing, I drove out to Finian Brophy's tobacco farm. For as long as I'd lived in Northmont, they'd grown tobacco nearby, covering the fields with protective sheets when the sun grew too hot. Most of it went for cigars, and it had made the Brophy family rich. Now, in late October, the crop had been harvested, dried, and sold. Except for a few livestock, the farm would have little activity until spring. I'd telephoned in advance, and Brophy himself came out to meet me shortly after one o'clock.

He was a tall, slender man who looked more like a country squire than a tobacco farmer. His daughter Jane had his greenish eyes and manner of taking charge. "I don't believe we've really met before. Dr. Hawthorne, I'm Finian Brophy. Come into the house. My wife is in town today."

We sat opposite each other in a large den decorated with deer heads and a few stuffed pheasants. I didn't need to ask if he'd shot them himself. "I don't want to take up too much of your time," I told him. "It's about the killing of Major Cassell."

"Of course. Everyone knows the sheriff is a personal friend of yours." He reached over for a cut-glass decanter half-filled with amber liquid. "Too early in the day for a little wine, Doctor?"

"Not at all. It's good for your health." I accepted the glass and said, "Sheriff Lens never killed Cassell. I'm trying to find out who did, and why. You had business dealings with the man, didn't you?"

"He did some work for me."

"What sort of work?"

"Lobbying the legislature on behalf of the state's tobacco interests."

I frowned at that news. "Cassell was a lobbyist?"

"One of the best in the state. Then last year he got into some trouble and decided he needed a lower profile for a while."

"What sort of trouble?"

Finian Brophy shrugged. "Someone accused him of bribery, passing money to one of the state assemblymen to insure passage of a bill. They're still investigating the charges."

"Not much point in it now that he's dead."

"No," Brophy agreed.

"Was your daughter satisfied with his work on the Anders campaign?"

"She certainly should have been. It was Cassell's idea to stress the age factor and call for new blood."

"Sheriff Lens says Cassell phoned him at home early Tuesday morning to report a prowler. Doesn't that seem odd to you?"

"If there was really a prowler it would be the natural thing to do."

"Rather than phone the sheriff's office?"

He waved a hand, dismissing it. "Perhaps the sheriff's home phone number was handier. How would I know?"

I glanced out the window at the distant fields. "Did you have a good crop this year?"

"Could have been better, but I've no complaints."

I left him, wondering if I'd really learned anything at all.

* * *

Ray Anders was not happy to see me when I stopped by his house later that afternoon. "I can tell you frankly, Sam, that nothing you says is going to change things. I honestly believe that Sheriff Lens shot him and I'd feel the same way even if I wasn't running against him."

There was a chattering sound from the next room and I saw the cage that was at Max's home. The chimpanzee jumped up and down when he saw me, no doubt welcoming a new playmate. "If only he could talk," I said.

"It wouldn't be good for the sheriff if he could."

"What about you? Were you at home all night Monday?"

"Matter of fact, I spent the night in Shinn Corners. I had a breakfast rally there Tuesday morning."

Jane Anders came downstairs wearing a fancy cocktail dress of a sort rarely seen around Northmont. "We're on our way to dinner and another rally," she explained. "Sorry to cut your visit short."

"I spoke with your father earlier today," I said.

"He phoned to tell me."

"I was just visiting with Max here. Does he ever get out of his cage?"

"He used to, all the time, until I put a spring lock on the cage door. Now he can get back inside by himself but he can't reach through the bars to turn the outside knob. Once he's in there we have to open it for him."

"Do you know if Major Cassell would take him out of the cage and play with him?"

"I think he did, a few times."

Max hopped up and down some more, demanding our attention.

"We really have to be going," Anders said. "We'll be late."

"Just one more question. The gun that fired the fatal shot—is there any possibility you might have acquired it while you were a deputy, kept it out at the cabin, and forgot to turn it in when you quit?"

He shook his head. "No, I told you I turned in the only weapon I had."

I walked out of the house ahead of them, wondering where to turn next.

* * *

Annabel had invited the sheriff and Vera over for dinner at our house, trying somehow to lift their spirits, but it was a dour evening. "I can't even campaign!" Sheriff Lens grumbled. "I start to speak and some heckler in the audience yells out, asking me why I killed Major Cassell."

"We can't go on like this," Vera said. "I want him to resign and let Anders be the sheriff if he's that eager."

"Resigning would just make him seem more guilty," I pointed out. "He has to fight this thing, Vera."

"It's Wednesday night, Doc," the sheriff said, in case I'd forgotten. "Six days till election."

"And three days until Halloween. We're going to win this for you, but we have to do it before the weekend so there's time for everyone to know you're innocent."

"Innocent!" he snorted. "I'd be in a jail cell already except the D.A. is on my side. He knows if I'm jailed or indicted before Tuesday Anders wins."

"Don't you have any ideas, Sam?" Annabel asked.

"Just one. Is it possible for a chimpanzee to fire a revolver?"

She sighed. "I doubt it, but I can't say for sure. Don't go wasting your time on it. Remember that orangutan in the potting-shed case? I think you suspected him for a while, too, but this isn't a story by Poe. Unless you can prove differently I'd favor a human killer."

"Perhaps I can prove differently," I said. "Maybe we can set up a reenactment at the cabin and see just what Max did Monday night."

* * *

It was a crazy idea, but I had to do something, if only to hold out a slender hope for Sheriff Lens and Vera. Pressure was mounting to arrest him before Tuesday's voting, and we all knew that would be the end of him. I started out with Rob Gallagher, since he was the acting sheriff. On Thursday morning I showed up at his office and came right to the point.

"Rob, I want to reconstruct the crime scene as it was on Monday night."

"What's the point of that?"

"There's a chance, just an outside chance, that the chimp might have killed Major Cassell."

"Oh, come on, Sam! That's crazy! Monkeys don't fire guns."

"Max is a smart chimp. Jane Anders told me he could get out of the cage by himself until she changed the latch."

"Max was locked in his cage when I arrived," Gallagher reminded me. "He was nowhere near the murder weapon."

"But Jane says he could get back in the cage by himself and it had a snap lock. Suppose Major Cassell was playing with him—"

"At six in the morning?"

"—and the chimp found that revolver. He pulled the trigger and the bullet hit Cassell. Max was so frightened he ran back to his cage and pulled the door shut, locking it."

All right," Gallagher said, "I'll tell you what's wrong with that. First, Cassell was fully dressed when he was killed. Second, he phoned Sheriff Lens about something. Does that sound like a man killing time by playing with a pet chimp? He was expecting someone, probably the sheriff."

"What about the prowler?"

"Sheriff Lens made that up."

"Why would he smash in the window and leave the door locked and bolted, making himself the only possible suspect?

But the deputy had an answer for that, too. "Because I arrived on the scene while he was in the middle of setting it up to look like there'd been a prowler. He didn't have time to unlock the door Cassell bolted after letting him in. Five more minutes and he might have gotten away with it. Remember too that there were no fingerprints or even paw prints on that revolver. It had been wiped clean. Does that sound like monkey business to you?"

"Will you at least give him a chance and allow us to reenact the crime? The answers to some of your questions might become obvious in a reenactment. Anders will have to go along with it if you say so."

Rob Gallagher thought about it. Finally he nodded. "Sure, let's give it a try. If that chimp can really fire a revolver, it might cast doubt on the sheriff's guilt. I'll call Ray now and make the arrangements."

"Everything should be as it was Tuesday morning when we arrived."

The sheriff's secretary, Gretchen Wild, had been typing at her desk while we talked. Now she turned and asked, "Will you be wanting those things we removed from the crime scene for fingerprinting?"

"What would those be?" I asked.

She brought out a labeled manilla envelope and opened it. "An ashtray with a cigar butt in it, a stopwatch, and an empty glass. All had the major's fingerprints on them. The stopwatch was still running."

"Running?" I frowned at the news. "I wonder why. How long had it been running?"

"I didn't pay attention," Gallagher admitted. "I stopped it and labeled it for prints. We found a couple."

"Just the major's prints? No other?"

"No other," Gretchen confirmed.

"Call Ray Anders," I said. "Ask him if we can use his cabin later today to reenact the crime."

* * *

It wasn't a simple thing, especially when we told him we wanted Max there in his cage. That meant Jane had to come, because she was the only one whose commands he obeyed. I wanted Annabel present, too, for her animal expertise, and of course Sheriff Lens was included.

We gathered around five o'clock: Anders and Jane, Sheriff Lens, Rob Gallagher, Annabel, and me. The cabin was as it had been Tuesday morning, except that the broken window was still covered by a sheet of plywood. Anders had carried in Max's cage with some difficulty, and placed it in the alcove off the living room. "How much does Max weigh now?" Annabel asked.

Anders sighed from the obvious effort. "Over fifty pounds. We only hope he's stopped growing. Sometimes they go up to a hundred pounds."

"If Max gets that big, it's off to a zoo with him," Jane promised.

We stood like spectators at the end of the room and Gallagher produced the revolver that had fired the fatal shot. "That better not be loaded," Sheriff Lens observed.

"It's not." Gallagher broke it open and spun the empty cylinder, then handed it to Jane. "Place it on the floor where we found it." She took it to the far end of the room and positioned it about where I'd seen it Tuesday morning. Then she went over to Max's cage and opened the snap lock. I observed that a metal plate around the door prevented Max from reaching through the bars and freeing himself.

Once freed, he hopped to the carpeted floor and left the alcove, entering the living room proper. "I'll fill in for Major Cassell," Anders said. He coaxed Max forward with animal sounds and the promise of a banana. The chimp ignored the revolver and came forward.

"You'd better help him out, Jane," I suggested.

She bent down and retrieved the pistol, holding the handle end out to the chimp. He touched it a bit uncertainly and moved away. She placed it on the carpet by his feet and retreated to the far end of the room by Gallagher and her husband. Max stared down at the weapon and finally picked it up by the barrel, peering at it. This went on for some minutes while we stood there, frozen in fascination. Finally Max dropped the weapon to the floor without ever fingering the trigger.

"What will he do now?" Gallagher asked.

"Probably go back to his cage." She raised her voice a bit. "Cage, Max!

He looked at her, took his banana, and retreated to the cage, pulling the door shut and engaging the snap lock. The performance was over.

"The chimp didn't do it," Gallagher decided.

"Probably not," I agreed. No one spoke the thought that was in all our minds. If Max hadn't done it, that only left Sheriff Lens.

Annabel and I went home after that. I couldn't face another evening with the Sheriff and Vera without any hope to offer them. In bed that night my wife asked, "Can't you do anything to save him, Sam?"

"I don't know. I've been over the case dozens of times in my mind and it was always comes out the same way. The killer had to have access to the murder weapon, a motive for killing Cassell, and a method of entering that locked cabin. Or if Cassell let the killer in, a method of leaving the cabin while locking and bolting the door from the inside."

"It was no accident the sheriff turned up there," Annabel said, voice partly muffled by her pillow. "Cassell phoned him about the prowler."

"That's something I don't understand. Did the killer force him to make the call just to lure Sheriff Lens out there?"

Both of us fell asleep before I could answer the question. When I awakened toward dawn I remembered portions of a dream in which a chimpanzee was chasing me with a stopwatch.

* * *

I'd neglected my practice far too much that week, and I'd planned to spend all of Friday in the office, but I'd barely arrived when my nurse April informed me that Vera Lens had just called on an urgent matter. I phoned her back at once. "Yes, Vera, what is it?"

"The county committee has asked my husband to withdraw from the race. They're coming out here with the mayor. They believe they can name a replacement in time for Tuesday's election."

"That's foolish, Vera. The ballots are all printed."

"I know, but try telling that to the committee. They think if the sheriff went on the radio tonight and threw his support to a new candidate there'd be a chance."

"Who's the candidate?"

"Rob Gallagher. He's the acting sheriff and he's a Republican."

"I thought Rob was supporting Ray Anders."

"Things change," she said with a sigh.

"As soon as I finish with the next patient I'll come out," I promised. "We have to do something."

All was confusion at the Lens home when I reached it an hour later. I recognized some of the Republican committee people on the front porch with the sheriff, who didn't look happy. "They want me to drop out, Doc," he said mournfully as I came up the steps.

"I know." I spotted Gallagher out in the yard by himself, staying clear of the sheriff until a decision was made. Leaving the sheriff and the others, I went out to confront him.

"Is this what you had planned all the time, Rob?"

He looked uncomfortable. "I didn't have anything planned. The committee came to me last night, after the word got around that your reenactment at the cabin was a bust."

"It wasn't a bust," I told him, with a bit more confidence than I felt. "I know who killed Major Cassell, and it wasn't the sheriff. I want you to repeat the reenactment."

"I can't do that, Sam. It wouldn't be any different the second time."

"I think it would be. I'll play the murderer myself."

He hesitated, uncertain of what course to follow. "The committee wouldn't go for it."

"Is the mayor here?"

"He's inside."

I found Mayor Tate in the kitchen, cornered by Vera Lens, trying to be firm without offending her. "It's all decided, Sam," he told me. "The party can't go into Tuesday's election with this murder hanging over the sheriff's head."

"We did a reenactment last night–"

"So I heard."

"I want to try it again today and get it right."

"What's the use? Sheriff Lens is dead politically. No one else could have killed Cassell."

"What if it was suicide?"

"The gun was too far away from the body for that."

"But it might have been moved, by Jane Anders's pet chimp."

There was a flicker of doubt on the mayor's face. "You think you can prove that?"

"Give us a chance. After twenty-four years Sheriff Lens deserves that much."

"Can you do it this afternoon? We have to wind it up today. If we announce a new candidate tomorrow, the Democrats will say it's a Halloween prank."

* * *

So we returned to the Anders cabin at three that afternoon. On the way out I tried to explain the situation to Sheriff Lens, but he wanted to no part of it. "Doc, it doesn't matter where the gun was on the floor, or if that chimp happened to move it a few feet away. There were no powder burns on the wound and the gun had been wiped clean. Whatever else happened, it wasn't a suicide."

"You know it and I know it, but I had to plant some sort of doubt in the mayor's mind to give us another chance."

"Just answer me one thing. Do you know how Major Cassell could have been killed in that locked cabin?"

"I think so," I answered, none too sure of it. "But I have to prove it to myself as well as the rest of them."

As promised, I took the part of the killer while Anders once more became Major Cassell. Jane Anders stood by Max's cage, with Sheriff Lens and Vera among the spectators. Rob Gallagher was there, of course, joined now by Mayor Tate. Gallagher had phoned his office to have Gretchen bring out the ashtray and stopwatch.

With everything in position, I began to speak. "I believe the killer phoned Major Cassell on Monday night or the early hours of Tuesday morning with a suggestion for the campaign. Cassell was expecting the killer and that's why he was fully dressed at that early hour. The plan was that he'd call Sheriff Lens at home before daybreak to report a prowler, requesting the sheriff himself respond. Then they would time his response with this stopwatch. If he didn't come personally, or if he took some time to reach the scene, it could be used as evidence that his age was slowing him down."

"I'd never use something like that," Ray Anders insisted. "It's such a low tactic it would probably lose me as many votes as it gained."

"I agree, but the killer didn't intend ever to use it. The purpose was to lure the sheriff out here where he could be framed for Cassell's murder."

"All right," Anders said, going to the phone. "Assume that I've made the call."

I pressed the stem of the stopwatch and set it on the table. "While they waited the killer walked over to the cage and let Max out. There was no time to lose because the sheriff could drive out here in twenty minutes or less. The killer produced the revolver and fired one shot into Major Cassell's head. The gun was wiped clean and dropped on the carpet and the windows were checked to make sure all were latched from the inside. Then killer made that muffled call to the operator, also reporting a prowler, so a deputy would be sent to the scene shortly after the sheriff arrived. The killer left by the only door, locking it with a key."

I did exactly that, having borrowed Anders's key to the cabin. I stood outside the door and called out in a loud voice, "Knob, Max!"

Nothing happened.

I called again and still nothing. I unlocked the door and went back inside. "I thought you'd established that Max didn't fire that gun," Jane Anders said.

I swung the door closed. "Tell him, Jane."

"This is foolish."

"Tell him. He only responds to your voice."

She looked to her husband for support, but he was only staring at her, wide-eyed. "You have to say it, Jane," he told her finally "Just to prove he's wrong."

She took a deep breath and said it. "Knob, Max."

The chimpanzee bounded across the cabin to the door, reached up, and turned the knob of the bolt. Then he retreated to his cage and closed the door.

Jane Anders collapsed crying into her husband's arms.

* * *

I explained it all later, as much as anyone can ever explain the pressures that drive a person to murder. "We know Major Cassell worked as a lobbyist for Jane's father, Finian Brophy. And Brophy told me he'd been accused of bribery in connection with his work for the state's tobacco industry. The investigation was ongoing, and I suspect Cassell was about to implicate Brophy to save his own skin. Brophy arranged for him to work on the campaign here, but that wasn't enough. I think Jane wanted to protect her father from criminal charges, even if it meant killing Cassell. She worked it out so the killing would serve a double purpose—protecting her father and getting her husband elected sheriff."

"What made you suspect her, Doc?" the sheriff asked.

"During our first reenactment, Gallagher asked her to place the revolver on the floor where they found it. She did so, almost exactly, but how could she have known where it was found? She told me the gun had been removed by the time she went to the cabin to retrieve Max. That got me thinking about her, and about why the stopwatch was still running when Gallagher arrived. If Cassell had been tricked into timing something like your arrival, it would explain the phone call. The use of the revolver from your office safe pointed to a past or present employee, in this case a former deputy's wife.

She must have been there with Anders sometime when the safe was open and took the gun without his knowledge."

"Why do you say that?"

"If he knew she had it, he'd have known she was the killer. I don't think he knew that. Remember, he spent Monday night in Shinn Corners, so she was alone at their house."

The news of Jane's arrest was devastating to Anders's campaign. He offered to withdraw, but with the ballots already printed the election went ahead. Sheriff Lens was reelected overwhelmingly. It was the same day that news reached us of Montgomery's victory at El Alamein. The future looked brighter.

THE PROBLEM OF THE BLACK CLOISTER

Less than a week after the 1942 election that insured a seventh and final term for Sheriff Lens, the Allied invasion of French North Africa began. It was a joyous time for everyone, a sign that we had launched a major ground offensive at last. (Dr. Sam Hawthorne paused to refill the glass of his listener.) It was also a time for war-bond rallies in the cities, when celebrities sometimes came to help raise money for the war effort.

Towns like Northmont ordinarily would not have attracted a war-bond rally on any large scale, but as it turned out we had a local celebrity hardly anyone knew about. The November election brought us a new mayor, Cyril Bensmith, a slender, vigorous man of forty, a bit younger than me. I'd hardly known him before he ran for office, and I didn't know him much better now. His family had a small farm over near the town line, almost into the adjoining township of Shinn Corners, which probably explains why I hadn't heard about him or his boyhood chum Rusty Wagner.

Rusty'd been George Snider at the time. He didn't become Rusty till he moved to New York and landed the villain's role in a mildly successful Broadway play. From there he went off to Hollywood and became Paramount's answer to Humphrey Bogart. He was never as big a star as Bogart, but by April of 1943, with the Allies advancing in Tunisia and many of the younger male stars in the service, Rusty Wagner was doing his part by touring the country selling war bonds. Health problems and his age, just turning forty, had kept him out of the army. When Mayor Bensmith heard he'd be at a rally in Boston he invited his old friend to make a side trip to his hometown.

"Did you hear the news?" my nurse April asked that morning. "Rusty Wagner is coming here for the war-bond drive."

"We don't go to many movies," I admitted, though the town boasted a pretty good theater. "I guess I've seen him once or twice."

"I'm going to help out on the drive," she said. April's husband André was away in the service and I could understand her urge to get involved.

"That's good. I'll come and buy a bond from you," I promised.

That night at home I mentioned it to my wife Annabel, who showed a bit more excitement that I had. "That's great news, Sam! Something's finally happening in this town."

I smiled at her remark. "A lot of people think too much happens here already. Our murder rate—"

"I wish you wouldn't blame yourself whenever somebody gets killed in Northmont. I'm sure there were murders here before you ever came to town. I'll have to ask Sheriff Lens when he and his wife come to dinner."

The sheriff had been elected to his first term in 1918, just days before the armistice that ended the war. I hadn't moved to town and set up my practice until a few years later, in January of '22, and for some reason we'd never really talked much about Northmont's past crimes.

We dined with Sheriff Lens and his wife Vera every couple of months, and it was their turn to come to our house two nights later. While Vera helped Annabel with dinner in the kitchen I engaged the sheriff in conversation. "Annabel and I were talking the other night about Northmont's crime rate. How was it before I came here in 'twenty-two? Did you have just as many murders?"

Sheriff Lens chuckled, resting his hand on the glass of sherry my wife had provided. "Can't say that I remember any at all before you came to town, Doc. Guess you brought 'em with you." He took a sip from the glass and added, "There was the fire over at the Black Cloister, of course but no one ever suggested that was murder."

I'd driven past the burnt-out building several times during the past twenty years, wondering why the county didn't just tear it down and sell the land at auction. "Exactly what happened there?" I asked.

"Well, it was in the late summer of 'twenty-one. The place had been built late last century as a sort of farming commune for disenchanted monks and other religious men who'd left their various orders but weren't ready to return to the secular world. Occasionally they took in one or two juvenile offenders if the courts asked them to, on the theory that a hard day's work might set them straight. Nobody paid much attention to them out there, except about once a month when a couple of them came into town for supplies. They called it the Black Cloister, named for the Augustinian monastery in Germany where Martin Luther lived. After the Reformation the monks moved out but Luther continued to live there, offering shelter to former monks and travelers. Upon his marriage in fifteen twenty-five the building was given to him as a wedding gift."

"You know a good deal about it, Sheriff."

"Well, Vera's a Lutheran even though we were married by a Baptist minister. We got talking about the Black Cloister one night and she filled me in on all that history."

"I heard my name mentioned," Vera Lens said as she came in to join us. "Dinner will be ready in three minutes."

"Doc was just wondering about the Black Cloister," the sheriff explained.

"Funny you should mention that, Sam. We're putting together an antique auction for the war-bond rally and someone donated the ornate oak front door from the Black Cloister. You can see it along with the other antiques down at the town hall."

"Maybe I'll take a look. When is this all going to happen?"

"Next Tuesday, the twentieth. That's the day after the Boston rally. They're tying it in with Patriots' Day and the Boston Marathon." Easter Sunday that year was not until April twenty-fifth, the latest it could be.

We took our seats at the table as Annabel came in with our salads. "I was just talking to Vera about the rally," she told me. "I told her I wanted to help out, too."

"A lot of people are. April at my office said she'd help. There's nothing like a movie star to brighten things up."

"Rusty Wagner isn't exactly a heartthrob," Vera remarked, plunging her fork into the salad. "Sometimes his face looks like it went through a meat grinder."

"He makes a perfect villain, though," Annabel said. "I saw a couple of his films before we were married." Turning to me, she said, "Sam, we have to start going to the movies more."

* * *

Somehow the conversation never did get back to the fire at the Black Cloister. It wasn't until Sunday afternoon, two days before the scheduled rally, when I accompanied Annabel to the town hall and stood before the fire-scorched door, that I remembered the burned building. The thick oak door was indeed a thing of beauty, leaning against the wall. Its front showed a bas-relief of a hooded monk kneeling in prayer, and this is what would have greeted visitors to the Cloister.

"You can see the door was badly scorched in the fire," Vera said as she came up to join us. We were in the ornate lobby of the town hall, where a score of items of all shapes and sizes had been assembled for the auction.

I ran my fingers over the bas-relief, admiring the carving. "Looks as if there are a few little wormholes in it, though," Annabel remarked.

There were indeed, toward the sides and top of the door. I pulled it away from the wall, but the back was smooth and unmarked, without a trace of scorching. "What was the story about this fire?" I asked Vera. "It was before I moved here."

"I was pretty young then myself, but I remember the Cloister as some sort of religious community. There was a fire and one young man died. After that the rest of the community just scattered."

"Who owns the property?"

"I have no idea. Felix Pond at the hardware store donated the door. He said it had been in the family for years, but I don't know that they ever owned the place."

"How does this charity auction sell war bonds?" Annabel asked.

Vera Lens explained. "People bid by purchasing the bonds, so it's not really costing them anything. They get their money back when the bonds are redeemed. The items are all donated and I don't imagine they have any great value. But something like this door could be cleaned up and painted and put to good use. Some church might even like it."

I ran my fingers over the wood once more, again impressed by the workmanship. "I wonder who carved this. Was it someone locally, or perhaps one of the residents at the Black Cloister?"

"It's possible Mayor Bensmith might know."

"I think I'll ask him."

Cyril Bensmith had a dairy farm on the North Road. His tall, gaunt frame reminded some of Abraham Lincoln, though he'd never thought of entering politics until his wife died a few years earlier. They had no children, and perhaps in search of a new beginning he'd run for mayor and been elected handily. He still worked his farm every day. Being mayor of Northmont was not a time-consuming occupation.

He had just arrived at the town hall and was greeting people with a handshake when I went up to him. "How are you, Sam? Good to see you here. I think the rally on Tuesday's going to be a big success."

"It should be," I agreed, "especially with Rusty Wagner's appearance."

"Rusty's an old friend. I haven't seen him in years, but we've stayed in touch."

"I was admiring that door from the old Cloister," I explained, gesturing toward it. "Know anything about it?"

"No more than you. Felix Pond at the hardware store donated it."

"I was wondering if the carving was by a local person."

"I couldn't tell you that. If there's an opportunity you might ask Rusty when he's here Tuesday."

"Rusty?"

"He was living at the Black Cloister at the time of the fire."

"How old would he have been at that time?"

"Eighteen, I think. Same age as me. He and another boy, Fritz, were caught stealing a car in Hartford. The judge suggested they could avoid jail by spending the summer doing farm work at the Cloister and they agreed quickly enough. That's how I got to know Rusty. His name was George then, but he never liked it. We saw a lot of each other that one summer, before the fire."

He moved on to greet others, and I was left with unanswered questions.

* * *

On Monday Sheriff Lens stopped by my office in a wing of Pilgrim Memorial Hospital. He was chatting with April as I finished seeing the morning's last patient and I invited him into my examining room. "Everything set for the bond rally tomorrow, Sheriff?"

"I guess so. Vera's had me run ragged, picking up donations for the auction."

"I was talking to our mayor yesterday and he tells me Rusty Wagner was a resident of the Black Cloister. You never did finish about the fire."

"It was so long ago I can barely remember it now. Like I said, it was the summer of 'twenty-one. The Cloister was home to about a dozen men, some from a Trappist monastery that had closed, and others from various Protestant denominations. They were men with problems or at loose ends. There were also those two kids doing farm work to avoid prison. I guess Rusty Wagner was one of them. The other fellow was killed in the fire."

"Tell me about it."

Sheriff Lens sighed. "Don't you have enough mysteries in the present to satisfy you, Doc? This was no impossible crime or anything. No crime at all, as far as I know. The fire started in the kitchen somehow and spread to the rest of the house. It was in the afternoon and the other residents were out in the fields working. Wagner and his other young fellow, whose name I don't recall—"

"The mayor said it was Fritz."

"That's right, Fritz Heck. Anyway, they were preparing the evening meal when it happened. Wagner managed to get out with a few bad burns, but the other boy didn't make it. I suppose that little scarring on Wagner's face didn't hurt when he started playing villain roles."

That was pretty much all he remembered, but I was still interested in tracking down the origin of that door. I drove over to Felix Pond's hardware store on my lunch hour and waited while he took care of a couple of customers. Pond was a bristling, bearded man who seemed strong as an ox, constantly carrying lumber and supplies out to waiting wagons. I was not one of his regular customers, but he knew me by sight. "Dr. Hawthorne! What brings you here? Got a need for a hammer or screwdriver?"

"Curiosity brings me," I told him. "I was admiring that door from the old Cloister and they told me you'd donated it. I wondered how you came by it."

"That's easy," he said with a grin. "I stole it, years ago. The place seemed to be just rotting away after the fire. The residents had all scattered and no one was even sure who owned the property. It was a sin to see that fancy door just sit there and decay like that so I took it home with me. Stored it in my supply shed out back and forgot all about it till somebody asked me about it last year."

"It might be worth some money," I speculated.

"Sure might! It's fine workmanship, made by one of the original residents of the Cloister. But I figured I couldn't really sell it since it wasn't mine to begin with. When someone suggested I donate it for the bond auction it seemed like a good idea."

"I'm sure people will bid on it. I might even do so myself." But then something clicked in my mind. "Tell me, Felix. Did you decide to donate this to the bond auction after you heard Rusty Wagner was going to be here?"

He frowned at my question. "Why would I do that?"

"Someone told me he was living in the Cloister at the time of the fire."

"Really?" He thought about it. "I guess maybe it was after we heard he was coming. Can't remember who suggested it, though."

I left the hardware store, wondering more than ever what was bringing Rusty Wagner back to Northmont.

* * *

Tuesday was sunny and mild, a perfect spring day to greet the crowd that had turned out for the war-bond rally. It was nothing compared to the Boston crowd, of course, but I recognized several people from Shinn Corners and other towns who'd driven over for the event. We'd set up a stage in the town square, with a billowing flag bunting as a backdrop. The auction items were all on view, including the Cloister door standing upright against one of the backdrop supports.

Just before the rally began, Mayor Bensmith made a point of introducing me to the star attraction, Rusty Wagner. He was shorter than I'd expected, and his features were a bit sharper. Close up I could see the scarring on the right side of his face. It appeared that the skin had been burnt, apparently during the Cloister fire. The damaged area was not large and could have been easily covered by makeup if he wished. Accompanying him was his manager, a fellow named Jack Mitchell, looking uncomfortable in a suit already rumpled from their train trip.

"I understand you lived here for a time," I said, shaking Wagner's hand.

He smiled pleasantly. "A long time ago, one summer before I moved to New York City. The town has changed a lot since then."

The mayor rested a hand on his old friend's shoulder. "We're going to start in a few minutes. You'd better get in position on the stage." He turned to me with a wink. "We want to open with a bang, like in Rusty's movies."

For a moment I didn't know what he meant. Then, as Wagner took the stage amidst an outburst of applause, a man in a German officer's uniform suddenly appeared from behind the flag bunting and stood before the Cloister door, taking aim at him with a Luger pistol. There were screams from the spectators as a shot rang out and Rusty Wagner clutched his chest, falling to the floor.

Immediately Mayor Bensmith sprang to the microphone, holding up his arms to calm the audience. "That, folks, is what could happen right here if not enough of us support our government with war bonds! Happily, the German officer is really our own Milt Stern, and Rusty Wagner is alive to fight another day." He motioned to the downed star. "Time to greet your public, Rusty!"

But Wagner remained sprawled on the floor of the stage without moving. I went quickly to his side. There was no blood, no sign of a wound, but I knew at once that he was dead.

* * *

When a well-known movie star dies before hundreds of people at a bond rally, it makes news all over the country. Mayor Bensmith and Sheriff Lens both knew Northmont would be on the front pages the following day and they turned to me for help. I urged them to calm down, reminding them that we didn't yet know the cause of Wagner's death. "One thing we know for sure, whatever killed him, it wasn't a bullet from Milt Stern's gun."

Nevertheless, while the mayor tried to calm the crowd and get on with war-bond auction, Milt was the first person the sheriff and I questioned. He was a ten-year resident of Northmont, in his mid thirties, married with two children. For the past several years he'd worked at the local feed store. "Is Wagner dead?" he asked us at once. "They took him away in the ambulance and somebody said he was breathing."

"He's dead, son," Sheriff Lens told him. "We just didn't want to announce it right away and put a damper on things. After the bond rally's over there'll be an announcement."

Stern passed over the German Luger for our examination. "All I had was one blank cartridge in it." I slid out the clip and confirmed that it was empty. "The mayor got the gun and uniform from a theatrical costume place in Boston."

"It was the mayor's idea?" I asked.

"Well, he was talking about something like that to start things with a bang. I volunteered to play a Nazi and fire a blank at him."

The facts were clear-cut and I would have been awfully surprised if the autopsy showed Rusty Wagner had been poisoned or choked to death. It didn't. By the following morning we knew that he'd died of a heart attack. There was no wound anywhere on his body.

Still, I stopped by the mayor's office to have a talk with him. "Apparently the man had a weak heart," I said. "Maybe that's what kept him out of the army, that and his age."

"It's just a tragedy it had to happen here," Mayor Bensmith said. "He could have dropped dead in Boston just as well."

"Tell me something. Did you explain to Wagner exactly what you had planned, with the Nazi officer and all? Did he know someone would fire a blank cartridge at him?"

"Certainly. I went over every bit of it with him as soon as he arrived. My secretary, Rita, was with us at the time." He called her into the office. "Rita, what did I tell Rusty Wagner when we met him at the station?"

Rita Innes was a prim middle-aged woman who'd worked in Bensmith's office at the farm before his election as mayor. He'd taken her with him to the elective office and she'd settled in well. Now she answered, "You explained about the man dressed as a Nazi who'd fire a blank at him. He'd fall to the stage and you'd tell the audience to buy bonds. He wasn't surprised. He said he'd acted out scenes for audiences in other cities, too."

"The heart attack was just a coincidence, happening when it did," Bensmith decided.

I had to agree with him. From both a medical and legal viewpoint, there'd been no crime.

Wagner's death had completely overshadowed the war-bond auction, and it was a couple of days later before I saw Vera Lens and remembered to ask her about it. "We did well," she reported, "considering everything."

"Who bought that door from the Black Cloister?"

"Funny you should ask. It went to a man named Jack Mitchell. He was Rusty Wagner's manager and was making the tour with him. The door's still here. We're supposed to ship it to him in California."

* * *

On the following Monday, the day after Easter, I was driving past the ruins of the old Cloister and decided to stop. Walking through the high grass to the gaping front entrance, I found a roof partly burned through, and weathered walls still showing scars from the fire. There was evidence of children playing there, and ground into the dirt out back I found a used shotgun shell. Every farm family kept a weapon close at hand. There were always varmints on the prowl.

After lunch I stopped in to see Sheriff Lens at his office. "I drove by the Black Cloister this morning and took a look. Can you tell me any more about the fire and your investigation?"

The sheriff gave one of his familiar sighs. "Doc, there's no crime for you to solve, neither here nor back in nineteen twenty-one. That Rusty Wagner could be killed by a shot from a blank cartridge isn't an impossible crime, it's no crime at all!"

"Let's get back to the Cloister fire for the moment. Tell me about the young man who died there."

He went over to the file and opened the bottom drawer. "I haven't looked at that folder myself in years. Probably should have discarded it after all this time." Opening the slender file, he took out some papers and a few photographs. "The victim's name was Fritz Heck. He was eighteen, same age as Wagner. Nice-looking fellow. That's him on the right in this photo."

"Is this Wagner with him?"

"No, it's Heck's younger brother."

I nodded. "I should have guessed that from the resemblance."

"We got the photo from the family in Hartford, for identification purposes. There was no doubt it was him, though. Heck's fingerprints were on file with the Hartford police. Him and Wagner stole a car but didn't know much about driving it."

'How did the fire start?"

"Wagner told me they were preparing dinner, chatting about a girl they'd met in town, when Heck got careless and some hot grease caught fire. They tossed water on it but that just spread it around. The flames went up along the ceiling and into the living room." He referred to his notes and Wagner's statement. "Heck ran into the living room and tried to beat it out, but it was too late. He was trapped by the fire and smoke, and died inside the front door, trying to get it open."

"Why is the house still standing after all these years?"

Sheriff Lens shrugged. "I heard tell Heck's family bought it, wanted it as a memorial to their son. But they never did anything except pay the taxes."

"Did you ever meet any of them?"

He shook his head. "If they came here I didn't see them. Of course the body was shipped back to Hartford for burial."

"What about Rusty Wagner? What happened to him after the fire?"

"They took him back to Hartford, too, for treatment of his burns. We heard later that he moved to New York and was in a play. Mayor Bensmith was a friend of his and stayed in touch over the years." He squinted at me over the tops of his glasses. "You're tryin' to make something out of all this, aren't you?"

"I'm trying," I agreed with a smile. I picked up the snapshot of Fritz Heck and studied it. "Do you have an autopsy report there?"

"Well, not really. Back in 1921, Northmont's coroner was just a local sawbones eager to make a few extra bucks. He just had to look at the body to know the fire killed Heck. The Hartford police furnished us with medical records on the two boys, though."

He passed them over to me and I glanced quickly through them. There were the usual childhood illnesses, plus a serious bout of influenza for Heck during the nineteen nineteen epidemic. Wagner had suffered from rheumatic fever twice as a child, but had escaped the flu. "What else do you have there?"

"Just Wagner's statement on the fire, which I've told you about. His face was burnt trying to save his friend."

I thought about that. "Do you have a phone number for this manager of his, Jack Mitchell?"

"I think it's here somewhere. Why do you want it?"

"Vera says he was high bidder on that Cloister door. It seems an odd thing to bother about when your client has just died."

I phoned Mitchell's West Coast office and after some delay was put through to him. "Mr. Mitchell, this is Dr. Hawthorne, back in Northmont. We're still investigating Rusty Wagner's unfortunate death."

"Yes," he replied. "I just got in the office. I've been making arrangements for the memorial service. What can I do for you?"

"I'm told that you were high bidder for the door from the Black Cloister, where Rusty lived for a time."

"That's correct. He wanted me to bid on it for him. It seemed very important to him. When the ambulance took him away I was hoping he was still alive. I entered my bid on the door before following him to the hospital."

"What do you plan to do with the door?"

"Do with it?" his voice rasped over the phone. "Nothing. Now that he's dead you can keep the door, auction it off again."

"Did he have any reason for wanting it so badly?"

"None that I know of. He'd lived at that Cloister for one whole summer. I suppose it brought back memories."

"I'm sure it did," I agreed. "His friend died in the fire, and he was badly burned."

"He never went into detail about it. He just asked me to buy the door at the auction."

I thanked him and hung up. Sheriff Lens asked, "Did you learn anything?"

"He doesn't want the door now that Wagner's dead. He said we should keep it and auction it off again."

"I'll tell Vera."

"Where's the door now?"

"Still over at the town hall. In the mayor's office, I think."

"Let's go have another look at it," I suggested.

We walked across the square to the town hall. Mayor Bensmith hadn't yet returned from lunch, but his secretary Rita showed us the door leaning against his office wall. "We're waiting for shipping instructions," she informed us.

"He doesn't want it," I told her. "We'll auction it again."

I moved over to examine the door more closely and asked Rita, "Do you have a pair of tweezers?"

"I think so." She went back to her desk and returned with them.

"What are you after, Doc?" Sheriff Lens wanted to know.

"I'm not sure, but I know Wagner wanted this door, and his statement to you at the time of the fire wasn't completely accurate."

"How's that?"

"He said Fritz Heck died inside the front door, trying to get it open. But look at this door. The scorching is on the outside, while the inside is unmarked by flames. This door had to be open at the time of the fire, and if that was the case how could Heck have been trapped there by the fire and smoke? He could have simply run outside."

"I never thought of that," the sheriff admitted.

I took a penknife from my pocket. "I wish we'd had a more complete autopsy report."

"In those days—"

"I know." I concentrated on one of the wormholes Annabel had noticed earlier, enlarging it a bit with my knife. Then I went to work with the tweezers. After a moment I extracted what I was seeking.

"What is it, Doc?"

"Buckshot. Annabel thought they were wormholes, but I noticed the other side was unmarked. These were worms that went in but didn't come out. Notice the unusual pattern they formed." I pointed out a half-dozen small holes toward the sides and top of the door.

"A buckshot pattern would be more circular," he argued.

"Not if something or someone had been in its way. Don't you see, Sheriff? Fritz Heck was standing by this open door when someone fired a shotgun at him. I know they probably had one on the premises because I found an old shotgun shell in the dirt there. The missing pellets from the pattern are in Heck's body, and judging by the close grouping of these other pellets that shotgun blast was probably enough to kill him."

"Rusty Wagner was the only one in the house at the time."

"Exactly," I told him. "We'll never know now what happened, but Wagner told you they'd been chatting about a girl they met. Maybe it went off accidentally by the front door."

"Then he started the fire deliberately?"

I nodded. "To cover the crime. He probably made a special point of burning the body, to cover up the wounds from the shotgun pellets. When he got too close and burned his own face it added verisimilitude to his story."

"Any coroner today would have found those shotgun pellets."

"Probably. He certainly would have spotted the absence of smoke in the lungs, a sure sign that Heck was already dead when the fire started."

Sheriff Lens sighed. "With Wagner dead there's not much point in exhuming the body now."

"None whatsoever."

"I only wish you'd been around here a year earlier, Doc, and I wouldn't have missed all this. It was a perfect crime."

I shook my head. "No, Sheriff. The perfect crime was the murder of Rusty Wagner in front of this building last Tuesday. And there's not a thing we can do about it."

* * *

As it happened, Annabel and I were dining at Max's Steakhouse, our favorite restaurant, a few nights later when I spotted Milt Stern drinking at the bar. "Excuse me for a few minutes," I told her. "I'm going to talk to him."

"Sam! You said you wouldn't."

But I got up anyway and went over to him. "Got a few minutes, Milt?"

"Sure. What's up?"

"I just want to chat. Over in that empty booth would be best."

He glanced toward Annabel at our table. "You shouldn't leave her alone."

"This won't take long."

He followed me to the booth and slid in the other side. "So what's this all about?"

"Rusty Wagner."

"God, I feel terrible about that! It's as if I'd murdered him."

"You did."

He moistened his lips and gave a half laugh. "Well, not really. The gun had a blank cartridge in it."

"What was it that made you move here, Milt? Did you know your brother had been murdered that day up at the Cloister?"

"He wasn't—"

"Yes he was, Milt. I saw the snapshot of the two of you and even then I noticed the resemblance. Ten years ago you left Hartford and moved here, changing your name from the German Heck to its English meaning, *stern*.

You suspected all along that Wagner had killed your brother. Perhaps he hinted at trouble between them in one of his letters. Once here you settled down and married. Somewhere along the line you saw the Cloister door that Felix Pond had rescued from the place, and recognized those little 'wormholes' for what they were. When you heard that Wagner would be coming here to take part in a war-bond drive, the idea came to you."

"What idea?"

"You would suggest to Pond that he donate that old door for the war-bond auction. Then, when the mayor was discussing a clever way to bring Wagner on stage, you volunteered to dress in a Nazi costume and fire a blank pistol at him. You knew, of course, that he'd had rheumatic fever twice as a child. Perhaps your brother mentioned it or you read it in a movie fan magazine. Such a medical history almost certainly would have left him with a weak heart, probably the reason for his draft deferral."

"He knew in advance I was going to fire a blank pistol at him," Milt Stern said. "That wouldn't have caused a heart attack."

"Perhaps not alone. But when he came onto that stage what he saw was the friend he'd killed twenty-two years ago, aged a bit but still recognizable, standing in front of that same door and pointing a gun at him. In the instant the gun went off, his weak heart failed."

"Do you really expect anyone to believe that?"

"No," I admitted. "Certainly not a jury."

Milt Stern smiled at me. "Then why are you telling me this? Who else have you told?"

"Sheriff Lens knows, and the mayor soon will know. They can't bring any charge against you, but it might be better if you left Northmont, moved back to Hartford."

He studied my face for a long time. "Don't you understand it's something I had to do? Whether he lived or died was out of my hands."

"Whether you stay or go is out of my hands, too," I told him.

"All right," he said at last. "I'll take your advice."

I left the booth and went back to join Annabel. I'd done all that I could.

THE PROBLEM OF THE SECRET PASSAGE

It was Annabel's idea from the beginning (Dr. Sam Hawthorne told his guest over a bit of sherry), and I don't know how I ever let myself get talked into it. The time was early May of 1943, some months after our hard-won victory on Guadalcanal. Axis forces were surrendering in North Africa and there was a tentative air of optimism on the home front for the first time since Pearl Harbor.

Annabel had returned home late from her animal hospital and I'd made a start at preparing dinner. "Out!" she ordered, seizing the skillet from my unresisting hand. "Go read your paper or something!"

"I was only trying to help."

"You'll have plenty of chances for that. I had lunch today with Meg Woolitzer and she's stopping by in an hour. We have to be finished with dinner by then."

Meg Woolitzer was editor of the *Northmont Advertiser*, a weekly paper that appeared each Thursday free of charge. It was delivered to front porches in the town itself, and farmers could pick it up at several area stores. Since buying the paper a year earlier with money from a small family inheritance, she'd been trying to upgrade it into a real newspaper. That was something the town had lacked since the bankruptcy of the *Northmont Blade*. Annabel helped support them with regular ads for her Ark, and she'd become friendly with Meg.

"Let me guess," I said, picking up a copy of the Boston newspaper that I read each evening. "She wants me to take an ad."

"Nooo," Annabel replied with a sly lilt to her voice. "It's something else. Don't worry, it's nothing bad."

"I'll be the judge of that."

Meg Woolitzer was a bright young woman in her early thirties, tall and brown-haired with a take-charge attitude. I sometimes saw her at town meetings, where she always had an opinion and wasn't afraid to voice it. When she arrived at our house that evening she was carrying a briefcase full of newspapers and was accompanied by Penny Hamish, an attractive younger woman who was the paper's assistant editor. "How are you, Sam?" she said, greeting me with a peck on the cheek. That should have warned me there was trouble brewing.

"Fine, Meg. Just the usual round of spring colds. You're looking well, and you too, Penny."

"We've been busy with new ideas for the paper. I was telling Annabel over lunch that it's time Northmont became more involved with the war effort."

"We've sent a great many boys overseas," I pointed out.

"I mean something that everyone can take part in. Something to build community spirit."

"We've had war-bond drives."

"But we haven't had a scrap-metal drive like most other places. Scrap metal is important to the war effort right now. Every family in this town probably has something they could contribute—old radiators, car and truck parts, outmoded farm equipment, lead pipes, and gutters."

"Even metal washboards!" Penny chimed in.

"Meg is going to promote a scrap-metal drive in the *Advertiser,*" Annabel explained. "I think it's a wonderful idea."

Meg Woolitzer dove into her briefcase for some newspapers. "Look here, this is what gave me the idea. A paper in Rochester, New York, runs a weekly feature with a big picture of someone dressed like Sherlock Holmes, with the deerstalker hat, the cape, the pipe, and even a magnifying glass. He goes around the city searching for scrap metal to be donated to the war effort. He even has a name—Unlock Homes! Isn't that clever?"

I studied the pictures and shrugged. "No harm in it if it does some good."

Annabel took over the conversation. "All Meg needs is someone to dress up like this and play Unlock Homes."

"Who—?"

"I told her you'd be glad to do it."

"Me! Is this a joke?"

"Don't you see how perfect you'd be, Sam? You're the best detective in Northmont, and the most famous. Everyone will see the pictures and start searching for scrap metal so you'll come to their house."

"I'm a doctor," I tried to remind them. "Sheriff Lens handles crime."

"But this isn't crime," Meg pleaded. "It's for the war effort. You'd make a perfect scrap-metal Sherlock! Your initials are even the same—S. H."

It took a half-hour for them to wear me down, but finally they succeeded. Meg promised to come up with the costume and props, and I agreed to try it at least once. "After that you can get someone else and not show his face. Your readers will think it's still me."

"We'll see," she replied. "I'll try to line everything up for this Saturday. That way we can run the first picture in next week's edition."

And that's how I contributed to the war effort.

* * *

Saturday morning a dense, chilly mist hung over the fields. Until spring arrived in earnest the local farmers had little to do, churning the meager milk supply into butter and making sure the cows had enough to eat. Even the town's single school bus sat idle on Saturday, and as we passed Seth Grey's house I saw him working on something under its hood. Meg gave him a beep of her horn and he glanced up, grinning. Annabel and I occasionally saw them together at Max's Steakhouse.

"We're going to the Cartwright place," Meg Woolitzer said as we'd started out. "It's pretty far out but the old man told me he has lots of scrap metal for us."

Annabel wanted to check in at the Ark first, to see how a sick parrot was doing, but promised to meet us at the Cartwright house in an hour. "Don't worry," she assured me. "I won't miss the debut of Unlock Homes." I growled something in return, still wondering how I'd been talked into a stunt like this.

There was a small panel truck in the Cartwright driveway when we arrived, with a sign on its door that read Gardenware Sales. It was the time of year when the traveling salesmen made their rounds and I knew old Cartwright prided himself on his garden. He was probably a regular customer of theirs. The house itself resembled something out of Nathaniel Hawthorne, with three floors and a great gabled roof. It could have used a coat of paint, but otherwise seemed in good shape.

"Has he ever shown you the secret passage?" Meg asked as we walked up the front steps.

I shook my head. "He's never been a patient of mine, claims he doesn't believe in doctors. Except for his hearing, he's been healthy for nearly eighty years so I can't argue with that."

"I did a story on his garden last summer and he showed me around outside. He's a nice old man."

"That he is," I agreed as the front door swung open in response to our ring. Cartwright's one employee was a middle-aged man I knew only as George, who lived there with him and assumed the combined duties of butler, cook, and gardener.

"Come right in," he told us. "Mr. Cartwright is expecting you."

I'd donned the deerstalker and cape in the car, but if he thought my costume was odd, he said nothing. Perhaps he believed I was only trying to keep warm, though it certainly wasn't chilly inside the oak-paneled foyer. We followed him into the library, Meg lugging her bulky Speed Graphic because she had no budget for a photographer. "I'll have to train Penny to do this," she said.

Aaron Cartwright, whose hearing was now so bad that he used an ear trumpet, sat in an overstuffed chair against a wall of books. His visitor, a balding man in a gray suit, was brandishing a molded clay object about nine inches high that looked for all the world like a birdbath for crickets. "This is our Empire model. Notice the intricate design around the base."

"Come in, come in!" Cartwright said, putting down the ear trumpet so he could offer both hands to Meg Woolitzer. "It's a pleasure to see you again, Meg. Sit right down!"

"I hope we're not interrupting anything."

"Of course not! Mr. Snyder here was just leaving."

Snyder put down the miniature birdbath and took an order pad from his briefcase. "Should I put you down for two of our Empire models, Mr. Cartwright?"

"Certainly, certainly!"

"What will you do with birdbaths that small?" Meg asked him.

Cartwright put the trumpet to his ear. "Speak louder, dear," he requested, and she repeated her question. He laughed. "No, no! This is only a miniature that the salesmen carry with them as samples. The ones I'm buying will be full-sized."

"You'll have delivery in about three weeks," Snyder promised, reaching for his sample.

But Aaron Cartwright was faster, batting away his hand with the ear trumpet. "Let me keep it for now, while I plan the rest of my garden. You can pick it up next time."

The salesman agreed but looked unhappy. Obviously the old man was a good customer. "When I return, I'll have a full selection of annuals and shrubs for you, too," he promised. "Will you be going away this summer?"

Cartwright laughed. "Where would I go? Over to fight the Nazis? I'll be right here with George."

The servant showed him out and I picked up the miniature birdbath to admire it, surprised by its weight. "This must weigh three or four pounds."

"That's natural-deposit Ohio clay; they use authentic molds from early in the century."

"His garden is a thing of beauty," Meg told me.

"Who are you, fella?" Cartwright asked, glaring at me. Though we'd met before, he didn't recognize me in my costume.

Meg answered for me. "This is Dr. Sam Hawthorne."

"Doctors! Don't have anything to do with doctors! My health is fine."

She smiled. "He's not here about your health. I'm going to use him in a photograph for the newspaper. You've heard of Sherlock Holmes?"

"Used to read about him all the time."

"Well, Sam here is Unlock Homes. He's going to uncover scrap metal to help the war effort. You told me on the phone you had some old radiators and other things. I want to run a picture of Sam, dressed as Sherlock Holmes, uncovering these things."

Aaron Cartwright snorted. "Nothing to uncover. It's all back in the barn. George can show you. But wouldn't you rather take a picture of my secret passage? That's the sort of thing Holmes would find."

"He's right about that," I agreed.

"Well, we can take a look at it," Meg said with some hesitation.

Cartwright grinned, showing off a row of yellow teeth. "My father had it put in when he built the place, back in 'ninety-seven," he told us, rising from the chair with some difficulty. "My wife was still alive then, and I didn't move here till she died twenty years ago. I hated to see this place just standing empty. That's when I put in forced-air heating and took out the radiators and bought the old Hamish farm to add to my acreage."

"Where is this secret passage?" I asked.

"Right in front of you."

"The bookcases?" I knew that English mansions sometimes covered doors with bookshelves, but I hadn't encountered anything like that in Northmont until now. He gripped one of the bookcases and swung it out from the wall, revealing a dark staircase leading up.

He turned a switch just inside the passage and a light went on above us. "This is neat!" Meg decided. "Sam, take out your magnifying glass and I'll get a picture."

I kept telling myself I was doing it for the war effort as I assumed the pose at her direction. She lifted the Speed Graphic and the flashbulb momentarily blinded me. "Where does it lead?" I asked Cartwright.

"Up to my bedroom. I keep the other end locked so no one can sneak in on me at night. Combination lock that only I can open. My father was a poor sleeper and he liked the idea of coming down here to work or read without disturbing the household. Come along and I'll show you." We followed him to the top where a plain metal door without even a knob blocked our passage. "You see? My bedroom is on the other side." We went back down the stairs and found George waiting at the bottom. "But it's the barn you want to see. George, show them our scrap metal and make any arrangements Miss Woolitzer wishes. I'm pleased to be rid of it."

"You're not joining us?" she asked.

He shook his head. "Can't take the cold air anymore. Bad for my lungs."

We followed George out the back door and across the damp grass to the old barn, probably unused for decades. "How long have you been with Mr. Cartwright?" I asked, making conversation. He was a familiar figure in Northmont, but I didn't even know his last name.

"Ten years now. I'm his nephew, George Chabber. You've probably seen me around town."

"Glad to meet you formally," I said, half turning to shake hands. "Your uncle is doing pretty well for his age."

"He gets by. I'm a light sleeper and if he needs me I'm right there."

We heard a horn honking behind us and turned to see Annabel pulling up behind Meg's vehicle in the driveway. "I see I'm just in time," she called out, hurrying to catch up.

George Chabber unlocked the barn door and ushered us into a dismal, cobwebby area filled with a lifetime's treasures. I recognized an old buggy, half hidden behind rotting bales of hay, a china cabinet with a broken glass door, a sofa with the stuffing pulled apart by rats. "Here are the radiators," George said, yanking away an old horse blanket to reveal them. "Don't know why he kept them all these years."

"This'll make a great picture," Meg decided. "Sam, if you could just get over here with your magnifying glass—"

"Do I have to?"

"You do! It's your contribution to the war effort," Annabel reminded me.

And so it was. The picture appeared on page one of the following Thursday's paper, showing me in costume standing by the china cabinet and peering through my magnifying glass at the uncovered radiators. Meg Woolitzer's scrap-metal campaign was launched. All that morning I had people calling me Unlock, starting with my nurse April. It didn't last too long, though, because that was the day we found Aaron Cartwright murdered.

* * *

The call came in to my office just before ten. "Agitated male," April said, covering the phone's mouthpiece. "Says he needs the detective. Think he's calling for Unlock Homes?"

I made a face and reached for the phone. "Dr. Hawthorne here. What can I do for you?"

"Doc, it's George Chabber, out at the Cartwright place. I think something's happened to my uncle. I think he's badly injured or dead."

"What happened?"

"He went to bed at his usual time, a little after ten, but he wasn't up before six like he usually is. I waited till nine o'clock and then went into his room. His bed had been slept in, but he wasn't there. I went down to the library and tried the door, but it was bolted from the inside. He did that occasionally when he didn't want to be disturbed. I knocked on the door but he didn't answer, so I went away. I started making breakfast, knowing the aroma of coffee usually attracted him. But this time it didn't. Finally I looked in the keyhole and saw him on the floor, all bloody. I called the sheriff and thought I should call you, too."

"I'll be out as soon as I can," I promised. I hung up and turned to April. "Something's happened to old man Cartwright. George wants me out there."

"You have an eleven o'clock with Mrs. Hennisey," she reminded me.

"Try to shift her to tomorrow. If she needs someone today, maybe Lincoln Jones can see her." Lincoln, Northmont's first black doctor, had recently gone into private practice and we sometimes helped with each other's patients.

"I'll call her."

I grabbed my black bag, aware that Aaron Cartwright might still be alive behind his library door, and hurried out to my Buick. It was a few years old now, suffering badly on our bumpy country roads, but I knew there was no chance of getting a new car until the war ended. At least my status as a physician earned me extra gasoline under the government's rationing system.

It had been raining off and on all morning and my wipers were going. Sheriff Lens's car pulled into the Cartwright driveway just ahead of mine and it took me a moment to notice that a familiar truck was already there. It was

Snyder's Gardenware Sales vehicle that I'd seen on my earlier visit, and I saw that Snyder himself was at the door speaking with George Chabber.

"You got a call, too?" Sheriff Lens asked me, trying to dodge the raindrops as he hurried toward the porch.

I nodded. "George phoned me. I brought my bag in case Cartwright's still alive."

"This way," George said, motioning us to follow him inside. Snyder started to say something, but thought better of it, remaining on the porch.

"What did Snyder want?" I asked.

"To see Mr. Cartwright. I said he was indisposed."

The library door was solid oak. It would have taken a truck to get through it. I dropped to my knees and peered through the keyhole. Cartwright's body was visible, as George had said. It was on the floor near his desk, with a great deal of blood. "We have to get in there," I said. "What about the windows?"

"All the ground-floor windows are barred. Cartwright's father built it like that to protect his valuable antiques."

"The volunteers have a battering ram at the firehouse," Sheriff Lens said.

"There must be another way." I turned to George. "What about the secret passage from his bedroom?"

"He kept it locked at all times, and only he had the combination."

"Let's go upstairs and have a look."

George led the way to a closed door at the top of the stairs. "That's my room across the hall. I sleep with the door open in case he needs something at night."

He led us into the old man's bedroom. The rumpled sheets gave evidence that he'd slept at least part of the night. There was a telephone next to the bed, and a small radio. However, I was more interested in the bookcase built into the wall opposite the foot of the bed. If I had my bearings right, it would hide the entrance to the secret passage. The bookcase pulled easily away from the wall on oiled hinges, but it revealed only a solid metal door with a combination lock.

"You don't know the combination?" I asked George.

"No idea. He told me once that he was the only one who ever used the passage, so no one else needed to know it."

The sheriff peered over my shoulder and gave a snort. "You won't be getting in there without a combination. The man really wanted his privacy."

"Let's go back downstairs and put some muscle into that door," I suggested.

It took the combined strength of Chabber, Sheriff Lens, and myself to splinter it after several tries. "It was bolted, all right," the sheriff said, examining the mechanism dangling from the splintered wood. "Looks like you've got another locked room on your hands, Doc."

I hurried to the body, but one look at his crushed skull told me Aaron Cartwright had died instantly. He was crumpled on the rug, fully dressed, and the weapon was not far away. The miniature birdbath lay there, caked with blood and hair. George Chabber's face had gone white at the sight of it. "How could this have happened? I never heard a thing."

"You'd better get that salesman in here from the front porch," I told him.

"How long do you think he's been dead, Doc?" the sheriff asked.

"A few hours, at least. This blood has dried."

Then I saw something else on his desk. It was that morning's copy of the *Northmont Advertiser,* unfolded to show my front-page picture as Unlock Homes.

* * *

I glanced around at the walls of the library, feeling that someone might be watching us. After the sheriff finished calling his office for help, I suggested he search the room for a possible hiding place. "The killer may still be here."

He did as I said, with one hand resting on his service revolver. "No one's hiding here," he reported.

"Try pulling those other bookcases." He did, but none of them moved. I sighed and said, "Then there's only one place he could be hiding—in the secret passage."

"How could that be, Doc?"

"It's the only possibility. The killer had to be in this room to swing that clay birdbath at Cartwright's head. This door was solidly bolted from the inside, and no one is hiding in the room." I carefully swung open the bookcase, revealing the secret passage. "We know there's a locked steel door at the top, without even a knob on this side. The killer has to be trapped on this stairway." I snapped on the light, as Cartwright had done on my previous visit.

"Come out of there!" Sheriff Lens ordered, raising his revolver.

There was nothing but silence from above. We moved slowly up the wooden staircase, the single bulb above casting an eerie glow on our path. When we reached the top, it was as it had been before, a solid steel door without a knob, like the inside of a safe. I pushed on it but it didn't budge. The passage was empty.

A secret passage leading off of the secret passage? Nothing was beyond imagining. The sheriff and I went over every inch of the stairs and wall and ceiling, but there was no other passage. I'd run out of ideas.

We went back down to the library and I saw that Meg's assistant, Penny Hamish, had arrived. "What's happened here?" she asked me. "I saw the sheriff's car and now—" She glanced in at the body on the library floor and then looked away.

"Aaron Cartwright's been killed," I told her. "You'd better phone Meg with your scoop."

"Not much of a scoop when it's a weekly paper," she complained. "It'll be old news by next Thursday." But she spotted the telephone on a side table beneath a banjo clock and gave the number to the operator.

I turned my attention to Mr. Snyder, the birdbath salesman. He looked rumpled and unhappy, no doubt regretting he'd chosen this morning to return. "What brought you back here?" I asked.

"I needed my sample, so I brought him a picture of it, hoping that would satisfy him till the real birdbaths arrived."

Sheriff Lens grunted. "You won't be getting it for a while now. It's a murder weapon and we'll need it as evidence."

Snyder started to protest, but saw that it was useless. Penny hung up the phone and told us Meg Woolitzer was on her way. "She's bringing her camera."

"No shots of the body," the sheriff said. "She knows better than that."

Snyder was growing restless. "Can I go now?"

"I'd like to ask you some questions first," I told him. "What time did you arrive here?"

"Just after ten o'clock. I didn't come earlier in case he was a late sleeper."

"Mr. Cartwright was usually up before six," George told us again. "That's why I was so surprised when he didn't appear for breakfast."

"You heard nothing in the night?" I asked. "No sounds of a struggle?"

"Nothing." He hesitated and then added, "Once, toward morning, I thought I heard the phone ring, but I may have been dreaming. It didn't ring a second time."

Sheriff Lens took me aside and said, "Doc, this Chabber guy has got to be involved. He was alone in the house with Cartwright when the killing took place."

"What about the locked room?"

"He had three or four hours to figure out a gimmick before he called you and me."

I sighed. "Don't you see, Sheriff, that being alone in the house with Cartwright is enough to point to his innocence? Since the killing couldn't have been suicide, it would have been to George's advantage to suggest an intruder by leaving the front door ajar. Alternatively, he could have used those hours to dispose of the body, hiding or burying it. Creating the illusion of a locked room is the last thing he would have done."

"This locked room is no illusion, Doc."

"I know."

The sheriff's deputies and a photographer had arrived, along with the coroner. The birdbath weapon was being checked for fingerprints, though I was pretty certain they'd find none. Before long Meg Woolitzer arrived, accompanied by Seth Grey. That was a surprise, though I knew she and the school-bus driver were seeing each other. "What happened here?" he asked me.

"Somebody killed Aaron Cartwright," I said, gesturing toward the library where the coroner was making it official.

"I was at Seth's house when Penny phoned me," Meg explained, not bothering to say how her assistant knew where to find her. "He gave me a ride over."

"Your newspaper was on his desk, with my picture on the front page. The doors were locked and the windows barred."

"Do you think the killer was taunting you, challenging you to solve another locked-room murder?"

"I don't know. It's a possibility. But we have to remember the murder weapon, that miniature birdbath, was in the room already. It was nothing the killer brought along. That implies the killing might have happened on the spur of the moment rather than with premeditation."

"What time was he killed?"

"I'd guess about three or four hours before we found him. No later than seven o'clock."

She glanced over at the body and then quickly away. "But he's dressed. He's not wearing nightclothes."

"George says he was an early riser. There also might have been a phone call from someone. He could have been expecting a visitor."

"But who? And why?"

"You were the one who chose this place for launching your scrap-metal drive. I hate to ask you this, Meg, but where were you around six this morning?"

She flushed a bit and answered, "I spent the night with Seth. I was at his house. I like to relax on Wednesday nights after the paper goes to press. We had a few drinks and I got sleepy. I guess Wednesday nights are my weekend."

"Penny knew you were there? That's where she phoned you."

"Penny knows my habits."

I glanced at Seth Grey, standing off to one side. He answered my unspoken question. "She was at my house all night. I can tell you she didn't have anything to do with this business."

"All right." Penny Hamish had come up to join us and I left them. Sheriff Lens was in the front hall with Snyder. The salesman was anxious to be out of there, pleading that he had other calls to make.

The sheriff took me aside. "What do you think about this Snyder fellow, Doc? It's quite a coincidence he turned up here just as Cartwright was being killed."

"But what motive could he have to kill a good customer? Would he have used the miniature birdbath, the very object he came to retrieve, as a murder weapon?"

"I don't know, Doc, but what other explanation is there? Do you think Cartwright heard a prowler and came down to look around?"

"I think he'd have sent George down to investigate a prowler."

"Then where are we?"

"Let me think about it, Sheriff. There's something here we're not seeing."

I went out to my car, maneuvering it around a lineup that now included Snyder's truck, Sheriff Lens's car, vehicles for his deputies and the coroner, and Seth Grey's car. Aaron Cartwright had probably not had that many visitors at once in his lifetime.

* * *

Annabel came home early from the Ark when I told her what had happened. She could see that I was troubled, believing somehow that my photograph in the *Advertiser* had caused Cartwright's death. "You can't blame yourself, Sam. And you can't blame Meg for running that picture. The idea that someone killed him in a locked room as a challenge to you is ridiculous."

"Then why was the paper left there, unfolded to show my picture on the front page?"

She couldn't answer, but told me, "Think it through, Sam. Put yourself in the killer's position, inside his skin. That's what I try to do sometimes with my sick animals."

I smiled at her. "Does it help?"

"Once in a while it does."

"All right. Taking all the facts as we know them, someone might have phoned Cartwright in the early morning. That someone could have been the killer. Cartwright let them into the house and library, perhaps bolting the door so George wouldn't disturb them."

"What time would this have been?"

"Somewhere around six, probably. No earlier, or he'd have turned on the library lights. But it's full daylight by six this time of year. It couldn't have been much later than that because of the dried blood and condition of the body."

"This birdbath weapon was in the room, so the killing probably wasn't premeditated. Someone called him, they met in the library, and the killer bashed his skull in."

"Then what?" I asked. "The windows were barred, the door was bolted on the inside, and the secret passage—even if the killer knew about it—led only to a solid steel door without a knob."

And even as I said the words the whole thing clicked into place. I knew how the killer escaped from the room, and I knew who it had to be. I even had a pretty good idea of the motive.

"I'm going out for a while," I told Annabel.

"Don't do anything foolish, Sam."

"I'll try not to."

I drove over to Meg Woolitzer's office, a storefront near the town square that served as the paper's editorial office. Though it was late afternoon of her publication day, I was pretty sure she'd be at work, preparing a story on Aaron Cartwright's murder. She looked up as I entered, a trace of sadness in her smile. I could see Penny at work in the back office.

"Hello, Sam. I'm sorry about what happened. I'd hate to think your Unlock Homes photo had anything to do with it."

I pulled out a chair and sat down opposite her desk. "I'm afraid it had everything to do with it, Meg. I thought I should come over and tell you about it."

"You know how the killer got out of that room?"

"I do. More important, I know how that copy of the *Advertiser* got into the room."

"What?"

"No one thought to question how your paper could have been on Cartwright's desk as early as six in the morning. It's only delivered to houses in town, not as far out as his place. And even the town copies probably aren't delivered that early. I questioned your whereabouts this morning because it occurred to me that the only way the *Advertiser* could have gotten into that house by six A.M. was if the murderer brought it."

"You're saying I killed him?"

I looked beyond her at Penny Hamish, who'd come to the door to listen. "No, Meg. I'm saying that Penny killed him."

* * *

She stepped into the room to face me. "Because of the newspaper? Because I would have had an early copy of it?"

"Partly that, yes. But if the killer brought the paper along and unfolded it to show Cartwright that picture, it was to confront him with it. You weren't along when Meg took the picture, but when you saw it you noticed something familiar, didn't you? Not the stack of old radiators Unlock Homes had uncovered, but what was just behind me in the photo—an antique china cabinet with a cracked glass door. I remembered that Cartwright bought the old Hamish farm some years back to add to his property. That was your family's place, wasn't it? And I suspect the familiar china cabinet came from there. Whatever you thought happened to it, you had no idea it was rotting away in Aaron Cartwright's barn. You may have seen the photo in the office earlier, but you didn't recognize the china cabinet until you saw it in print. You phoned Cartwright early this morning and demanded to see him. He was fully dressed—a hint that he was receiving a woman visitor—and let you in himself, taking you into the library and bolting the door so George wouldn't interrupt. Then you argued, and in a fury you grabbed that miniature birdbath and hit him with it."

Penny Hamish wet her lips nervously and I knew that my reconstruction was mostly accurate so far. "If I killed him, how did I get out of that locked room?" She was challenging me, but I was ready for her.

"The room wasn't locked," I said simply. "Not then."

"Not locked?" Meg repeated.

"With a female guest arriving at six in the morning to see him, old Aaron didn't want to leave his room and walk past George's open bedroom door. Surely the young man would have awakened from his light sleep. Aaron used the combination only he knew to open the steel door to the secret passage. He descended to the library that way and watched for your arrival. Since there was no knob or combination dial on the interior, he had to leave the door open. No doubt the bookcase door downstairs was left ajar, too. After you killed him—"

"He told me he'd return the cabinet if I—if I had sex with him. He put his clammy hand on my arm and that's when I hit him."

"Penny!" Meg went to her then, wrapping protective arms around the young woman.

"You feared that George might have been attracted by the noise, so you couldn't unbolt the door and go out that way. Instead, you went up through the secret passage to his bedroom, closed the metal door behind you, and hid there, perhaps under the bed."

"Yes," she muttered.

"After George checked the room and went downstairs to phone the sheriff and me, it was easy for you to sneak out and remain hidden upstairs until the rest of us arrived later. Then you acted as if you'd just come in, and phoned Meg to report the killing. But when I left, I noticed all the cars in the driveway, and there wasn't one for you. Where did you park it, Penny?"

"Down the road behind some bushes. I didn't want people to see my car in his driveway at six in the morning."

"He'd made advances to you before?" Meg asked.

"God, he was old enough to be my grandfather!" She turned to stare me down. "That's the one thing you got a bit wrong, Dr. Hawthorne. He bolted the library door so George wouldn't interrupt while he tried to seduce me."

Meg shook her head. "You were a fool to go there alone, Penny."

"When I recognized our china cabinet in that picture I was just so furious! He claimed someone broke in and stole it from our old house, and there it was, all the time."

"What do we do now?" Meg Woolitzer asked me.

Before I could speak, Penny answered for me. "Call Sheriff Lens. And then go to press with an extra edition, Meg. I'll give you an interview for the front page. That should be enough to make the *Advertiser* into a real paper!"

THE PROBLEM OF THE DEVIL'S ORCHARD

Labor Day weekend of 1943 was a memorable time for us all. (Dr. Sam Hawthorne began when his guest was settled in a comfortable chair with his drink). It was a turning point on the war front. British troops invaded the Italian mainland on Friday, the 3rd of September. American troops followed six days later, and Italy quickly surrendered. But in Northmont, it wasn't only the war we had on our mind that holiday weekend. A young man ran into Desmond's Orchard—the Devil's orchard, some called it—and vanished almost before our eyes.

But I'm getting ahead of myself here. First I'd better tell you about Phil Fitzhugh. He was a handsome young fellow just past his nineteenth birthday who'd worked in his family's feed store since graduating from high school. His girlfriend's name was Lisa Smith and they'd been dating since they co-starred in a senior-class production of *Our Town*. My wife Annabel had hired Lisa to help out at her animal hospital that summer, after graduation, so we'd gotten to know her quite well.

It was Friday night, the start of the Labor Day weekend, and the setting sun had finally broken through the clouds after two days of rain. I was on my way home from my office at the hospital. Annabel had phoned to ask that I pick up some snacks because Sheriff Lens and his wife were joining us for a backyard picnic on Sunday afternoon. I pulled my Buick in at Desmond's General Store on the town square and went inside. It no longer boasted the cracker barrel and wheel of cheese I remembered from fifteen years earlier when Max Harkner owned the place, but it was still one of the favorite hangouts for the town's youth. Three pinball machines near the front door were usually occupied, adding their din to the usual conversation.

Desmond's General Store was owned by Carter Desmond and his wife Phyllis, but this time of the year she was usually in charge while Carter remained back at their hundred-acre apple orchard preparing for the harvest. The orchard had acquired a reputation for being haunted, possessed by Satan in much the same way the serpent had besotted the Garden of Eden. Most residents of Northmont snickered at the stories, especially when the Desmonds were heard to tell larcenous children it was the Devil's orchard.

They'd erected an ugly chain-link fence on two sides to further protect their apples from theft.

"Hello, Phyllis," I said, bringing my few purchases to the cash register. "Has Carter started the apple harvest yet?"

"Tomorrow morning. He's hiring, if you know anyone who needs work. Most of the young men are in the army." She brushed a loose hair from her eyes and gave me a smile.

I happened to glance out the front window while she was ringing up my purchases. A bald man with a goatee, wearing an earring, was walking by. "Who's that fellow? He looks like he might need a job picking apples."

"Don't know. I think he's a gypsy or something. He took a room at Mrs. Dobbs's place a couple of weeks ago, but she says he's hardly ever there."

On my way to the car with my bag I called out to him. "Hey, mister— looking for work?"

He glanced in my direction and then looked away. "No," he muttered half audibly, and kept on walking.

When I reached home I saw an unfamiliar blue Ford parked in our driveway. I was surprised to find Lisa Smith in the kitchen with Annabel. The girl's eyes were red and I suspected she'd been crying. "Is this all girl-talk?" I asked, not wanting to interrupt.

"Sit down, Sam," Annabel urged. "Lisa has a problem."

She was a pretty girl with shoulder-length brown hair and glistening blue eyes. I knew Annabel was pleased with the work she'd done over the summer at the Ark. But now she kept her eyes downcast as she spoke to me. "Phil and I want to get married and my folks won't hear of it. They say I'm too young. They want me to date other boys."

"I guess you're not the first person to have problems like that," I told her. "Time is a great healer. A year from now, when you're both older, I'm sure they'll welcome him into the family."

"You don't understand!" Her voice broke into a sob. "He's being drafted. He has to report for his physical right after Labor Day!"

"What does his family say about it?"

"His father's dead and he hasn't told his mother or brother about our plans yet. I don't know what we're going to do."

I exchanged a glance with Annabel and she took over. "Lisa, maybe we should talk with you and Phil together. Where is he tonight?"

"Out drinking, I suppose. He's terribly upset."

"Does he have a favorite place?"

She mentioned a couple of local bars but added that he might be at some friend's apartment. I went to the telephone and called the bars, but Phil Fitzhugh wasn't at either one. Then I called his home, but Mrs. Fitzhugh said simply that he was out. I thought of Sheriff Lens. I knew he often patrolled the town on Friday nights, especially at the beginning of a holiday weekend. When I reached him I said, "This is nothing urgent, Sheriff, but I'm trying to locate Phil Fitzhugh. If you see him around anywhere tonight, could you give me a call at home?"

"Sure will, Doc," he responded. "It's been a quiet night so far. I'm going to swing by Max's Steakhouse. If I see him around there I'll give you a call."

I doubted if he'd find Phil at Max's, a pretty fancy place by Northmont standards, where Annabel and I had held our wedding reception. But twenty minutes later, as we were finally persuading Lisa to return home, he called back. "Doc, I'm over at Max's. Our friend Fitzhugh is at the bar, acting a bit unsteady. I don't think he should drive home by himself, but he won't come with me and I don't want to arrest him or anything. Could you come get him?"

"I'll be there in ten minutes. I'll bring Lisa Smith along."

Sheriff Lens hesitated, then said, "You'd better come alone, Doc."

I told Annabel and Lisa where I was going, but urged Lisa to stay at our place. "I think he's had a few drinks. if he's not too bad I'll bring him back here. Otherwise I might drive him straight home."

"I hate to see him like that," she admitted.

At that time the drinking age in our state was eighteen, so I doubted that Max's bartender had broken any law by serving him. Still, I felt a certain responsibility for his well-being. I left them at the house and drove to Max's Steakhouse. The sheriff's car was parked across the street and I saw Deputy Joe Hauser behind the wheel, waiting for his boss's return. I went into Max's and immediately spotted Sheriff Lens at the bar with Phil Fitzhugh.

Phil was a handsome kid whose thin face was topped by a bush of sandy hair, worn a bit longer than most of the other kids back then. I couldn't help thinking that the army would make short work of that. He was wearing blue jeans and white T-shirt with the name *Fitzhugh's Grain & Feed* stenciled across the back. I saw at once why the sheriff wanted me to come alone. Phil was conversing with a dark-haired young woman seated next to him on a barstool.

"Hello, Doc," Sheriff Lens said, shaking my hands as though he hadn't expected to see me there. "Look, Phil, here's Doc Hawthorne."

Phil Fitzhugh turned toward me and gave a half smile. "I'm not feeling so good," he muttered. Then, turning back toward the dark-haired woman, he asked, "How you feeling, Ellen?"

"I'm fine, Phil." She was obviously in a more sober state than he was, and also some years older. I'd seen her around town but didn't really know her. "But maybe you should go on home."

"I can give you a ride," I offered.

"Got my car," he slurred, dipping his head. "One more drink and I'm on my way."

"No more tonight," I said calmly. "Come on, Phil. I'll give you a ride."

But it wasn't to be that easy. "I'm getting drafted next week. This is my last weekend of freedom and I'm making the most of it." He started off the barstool and his legs seemed to collapse under him. Luckily Sheriff Lens caught him by the arm and I helped steady him.

"Does he owe you anything?" I asked the bartender.

"All settled."

Ellen watched all this with a mixture of guilt and trepidation. "You'd better get him home," she agreed.

Once we had him outside I said, "We'll take my car. I don't want the sheriff bringing him home to his mother."

But Phil Fitzhugh was still scuffling with me, trying to break away. "You'll never manage him alone, Doc, not while you're driving the car. I'll come with you and Joe Hauser can follow after us and pick me up at the Fitzhugh home."

So they got in the backseat and we started off. The shortest distance out to the Fitzhugh house was along Mill Road, running behind the apple orchards of Carter Desmond and his neighbors. Even in the dark I knew when we'd reached this stretch because an old stone wall ran along the road by the orchards. The Desmonds had caused a rumpus a few years back when they put up two eight-foot chain-link fences along the sides of their property, complete with a strand of barbed wire at the top. The town council had sent our official fence-viewer out to inspect the situation and plead for traditional New England stone walls, but Carter Desmond said he couldn't afford them for a such a long stretch, almost a mile along each side, and he had to do something to keep kids (and neighbors) from stealing his apples.

It was hard for me to concentrate on the road with Phil and the sheriff tussling the backseat. "Let me out," Phil insisted. "I'm not ready to go home yet."

"Just calm down, son," the sheriff growled. "Don't make me cuff you."

Then, before I knew what was happening, Phil had wrenched open the back door and jumped from the moving car. The stone wall was on our right, and I could see the chain-link fence running from it to mark the boundary of Desmond's property. "It's the Devil's orchard!" Phil Fitzhugh shouted with drunken glee. "Don't try to follow me!"

He ran down past the chain-link fence and clambered over the stone wall. I'd pulled my car to a stop and the sheriff and I were out and running. But once he was over the low wall he quickly disappeared among the rows of apple trees, their branches hanging low with ripe fruit.

"We'll never find him in the dark," I said. "I'll drive around to the Desmond house on the other side. You stay here with your deputy in case he doubles back." Behind us I could see the lights of the approaching sheriff's car being driven by Joe Hauser.

"I hope the damn fool doesn't hurt himself," Sheriff Lens grumbled.

I hurried back to my car. We were closer to the next corner than I'd thought, but it was still nearly a mile down to Desmond Road and their family homestead. Finally I turned onto it, watching the right side even though I knew no one could have run that distance, day or night, in the three minutes it took me to drive around the block. There was a matching stone wall on this side, broken only by the driveway up to the Desmond house.

The place was ablaze with lights and Carter and Phyllis themselves were enjoying the night air on their front porch. "Hello there, Sam," he called to me. "You making house calls?" Carter Desmond wasn't the friendliest man in Northmont, and the business with the fences had turned a lot of people against him. Simon Faulks, with the adjoining orchard, had taken the fence as a personal affront to his integrity. Phyllis was just a big friendlier, and she immediately invited me up on the porch for some lemonade.

"Can't right now, Phyllis. We were driving young Phil Fitzhugh home and he jumped out of my car over on Mill Road. He went over the wall and ran into your orchard. We're trying to find him before he hurts himself."

"He hasn't come out this side," Desmond assured me. "We've been sitting out here all evening with the lights on. We can see along the wall in both directions to the fences."

"He's only had five or six minutes. It's a bit soon for him yet."

Phyllis Desmond poured me a glass of lemonade and I sat down to wait for him. I'd been waiting a full hour when their phone rang. It was Sheriff

Lens, his call relayed to me from the police radio in his car. "No sign of him here, Doc. How about you?"

"Nothing, Sheriff. I'm beginning to think he just collapsed and fell asleep, but it would be tough finding him in the dark."

Carter Desmond interrupted. "I'll have fifty workers here at dawn to start the harvest," he said. "We can search every inch of the orchard."

I relayed that news to Sheriff Lens. "Maybe you and I should go home and get some sleep, Sheriff. Can you assign deputies to watch both sides of the orchard, on Mill Road and Desmond Road, in case he wakes up and staggers out?"

"I can do that," he agreed, "unless we get a sudden crime wave in the middle of the night."

"That's not too likely. I'll see you back here in the morning, then."

I said goodnight to the Desmonds and waited out in my car till one of the sheriff's cars arrived to take up the watch, then drove home to tell Annabel about it. Lisa Smith had already gone home, but my wife was still awake and eager to talk about it.

"That girl is a wreck," she told me. "She's worried sick."

"There's a war on. A lot of young people have had to put off their wedding plans."

Annabel took a deep breath. "Her father said he'd kill Phil Fitzhugh if he ever got Lisa pregnant."

"And?"

"She's pregnant."

* * *

I pulled up at the Desmond orchard shortly after seven on Saturday morning, when Carter was already giving instructions to a ragged line of apple pickers. "Morning, Sam," he greeted me. "The deputies report that Fitzhugh hasn't shown up at either end of the orchard so he must be still in here someplace. I've instructed my pickers to walk through a solid line and give a yell when they find him."

I noticed Phyllis watching from the porch, a cup of steaming coffee in her hand, as the men started walking. All of them had burlap sacks thrown over their shoulders and I imagined they would start picking apples as soon as the wayward young man was found. It was about ten minutes later that we heard a shout from deep within the orchard. Desmond and I ran toward it together.

The line of searchers had halted and a few of them were grouped around something on the ground near one of the chain-link fences. Whatever they'd found, it seemed too small to be a body and it wasn't. "Don't touch it," Carter Desmond ordered as we approached. Now I could see that it was Fitzhugh's T-shirt with its black lettering, held down by a stone as if to keep it from blowing away. There were spots that looked like blood and they hadn't been there before. "Keep walking," Desmond ordered his men. "He's hurt and we have to find him."

"What do you think happened?" I asked.

"Damn fool must have tried climbing the fence and cut himself on the barbed wire."

"It's eight feet tall."

"He's young and strong. He might have been able to do it if it wasn't for the barbed wire."

I'd walked over to the nearby fence and noticed there was no grass over the last couple of feet. "This ground is still soft and muddy from all the rain," I pointed out.

"We keep the grass away from the fence so it's easier to mow," he explained.

"But there are no shoeprints, at least in this portion. He couldn't have tried to climb the fence without leaving marks in the damp soil." We checked the rest of the fence together but the dirt along it was undisturbed. As we crossed to the other side of the orchard the apple pickers began drifting back to their assigned sections. They'd reached Mill Road and the deputy who was stationed there.

Phil Fitzhugh was nowhere to be found. He'd left his bloody T-shirt and vanished without a trace. Perhaps there really was a devil in Carter Desmond's orchard.

The first thing we did was to check the blood on Fitzhugh's T-shirt. It was his blood type, recorded at Pilgrim Memorial Hospital when he'd had his tonsils removed years earlier. While this was being done, deputies examined every inch of the fence on both sides of the orchard. There were no footprints in the damp soil, and as near they could tell, no indication of blood on the strand of barbed wire at the top of the fence.

"He might have used one of them pole-vaulting things," the sheriff speculated.

"Then where's the pole? It would still be on Desmond's side of the fence."

"Yeah, I guess so," he glumly agreed.

We walked back toward the Desmond house. All around us the harvesters were filling their sacks with shiny apples. Phyllis Desmond walked among them, issuing brief instructions from time to time. I watched them work for a while and when we reached the house I asked her, "How many workers are here today?"

"Forty-nine. My husband signed up fifty, but one man didn't show up this morning. Probably hungover. These migrants aren't the most reliable of workers, but we have little choice with so many local boys away at war."

"Do you pay them at the end of each day's work?"

"Of course. We pay so much for every sack of apples."

"Let me know how many workers you have at the end of the day."

She was puzzled by my request. "There'll be forty-nine. You can come back and count them yourself if you wish."

I told her I just might do that. "What are you thinkin', Doc?" Sheriff Lens asked. "That Fitzhugh mixed in with the workers while they were searching the orchard this morning?"

"It's a possibility, though a slim one. They were walking along in a straight line. Still, after they found his bloody shirt there might have been an opportunity for someone to slip in and join them. That's why I want a count when they finish up."

The sheriff and I went next-door to talk with Simon Faulks, who owned the adjoining orchard. He was a bearded man who walked with a decided stoop, a Northmont resident for as long as I could remember.

"What's going on over there?" he demanded, as irritable as I remembered him being. "Not enough that the damned Desmonds put up their damned fence, now they keep me awake half the night with sheriff's cars!"

"We're looking for a missing man," I explained. "Phil Fitzhugh. He'd had a bit too much to drink and jumped out of my car last night. He ran into the Desmonds' orchard and never came out. This morning we found his bloody shirt."

"Devil's orchard," Faulks muttered. "Always knew it. Killed a snake on my land last year, knew it came over from over there."

"Could we take a look along the fence on your side?" Sheriff Lens asked. "See if there's any clue to where he went?"

"Go ahead. Don't go taking any of my apples, though. I've got a crew coming after Labor Day to pick them."

The sheriff and I walked the entire stretch of fence on Faulks's side, but found nothing. The damp earth was undisturbed. "Now what?" he asked.

I glanced at my watch. "It's time we called on the parents."

Phil Fitzhugh's home was beyond Mill Road, a small, neat house where his mother and younger brother lived. "Is he dead?" Mrs. Fitzhugh asked, her face frozen with fear when we appeared at the door.

"We don't know," I answered honestly. "We were wondering if you could tell us anything. I understand he was unhappy about going into the army."

She was a neat woman in her forties who went well with the house. I wished I could give her some reason to hope. "I don't know what came over him these last weeks," she told us. "He was frantic when he received his draft notice."

"What about the Smith girl?" Sheriff Lens asked.

"I guess it was getting pretty serious," she admitted. "I just wanted them to wait until after his army service."

"Sometimes young people don't like to wait," I said. "Could we take a look at his room?"

"I suppose so, if it'll help. Follow me."

Like the rest of the house, the upstairs room was fairly neat, with a photo of the missing youth and Lisa Smith next to the bed. The walls were decorated with a high-school banner, a poster for the school production of *Our Town*, and a map of the world on which he'd carefully noted the progress of the Allied advance. I looked it all over and asked, "Did Phil have any enemies, anyone who'd want to harm him?"

"No one I know of. You can't really think he's dead, can you?"

"We just don't know, ma'am," the sheriff told her. "We're following up every possibility."

Back in the car, headed for Lisa Smith's home, Sheriff Lens was less uncertain. "There's no way he could have left that orchard alive, Doc. We both know that."

"There's no way he could have left it dead, either. Let's wait till we have a count on those workers this afternoon."

"You know, if someone killed him it might have been over that Smith girl. Maybe she had another boyfriend."

"Did you ever see her talking with anyone else?" I asked.

"Not really. The other day I saw that bald gypsy guy say something to her outside the drugstore, but she just kept walking."

Lisa's father Harold was a stout man with thinning hair and glasses who worked at the Northmont Trust Company. The bank would have closed at noon on Saturday and he'd removed his suit coat and tie, along with the detachable collar that many bankers and businessmen still wore. "Is there any news about that Fitzhugh fellow?" he asked. Lisa had come down from upstairs to join us.

"Nothing so far," the sheriff said.

"Do you have any idea what might have happened to him?" I asked, directing my question at both of them.

"I hardly know him," Harold Smith replied. "I only know he's been seeing too much of my daughter to be healthy."

"We want to get married, Daddy," she said in a soft voice.

"Let's see how he does in the service first. Plenty of time for marriage after the war." He returned to the living room where he'd been reading the newspaper.

"Could I speak to you for a few minutes in private?" I asked Lisa.

"I . . . I guess so." She led the way into the kitchen while Sheriff Lens followed her father into the living room. "Mom's out grocery shopping. I can't tell you much of anything, though."

I held out my hand to grasp Lisa's. "Annabel told me about your condition," I said softly.

She yanked her hand away. "I didn't want—"

"I'm a doctor, Lisa. Is it possible someone might have attacked him because of that condition?"

She looked away. "I don't know what my dad might have done if he knew about it."

"Anyone else? A jealous boyfriend, perhaps?"

She shook her head. "There's no one but Phil."

"The sheriff saw that gypsy fellow talk to you the other day."

"He wanted to buy me a drink. I just kept on walking."

"Was that the only time he approached you?"

"Yes. I don't know him. I don't even know his name."

"Someone said it was Howie Newsome. He has a room at Mrs. Dobb's place."

Sheriff Lens came in to join us. "He denies knowing anything about the boy's disappearance, Doc. What's next?"

"Time to go back to Desmond's Orchard."

* * *

We sat on the porch and watched while Phyllis Desmond paid each of the apple pickers. "Forty-nine," her husband said, checking off his list. "The missing man's brother says he sprained his ankle and couldn't pick today. Everyone's accounted for, and there are no extras."

Sheriff Lens looked unhappy. "Where does that leave us, Doc?"

"I'm going to try analyzing this whole thing." I took a pad of notepaper Phyllis had been using and drew up a list of possibilities. "There's no doubt he went into the orchard. We saw that ourselves. I was at this end with the Desmonds. He didn't come out while we were here. Can you trust your deputies who stood guard overnight?"

"Joe Hauser is the best man I have, you know that. And the others are just as good. He couldn't have left the orchard during the night unless he went over one of the fences."

I ruled that out. "That strip along the fences on both sides is soft enough to show footprints, and despite the blood on his shirt there's no indication he cut himself on the barbed wire. I think we've already ruled out any sort of pole vault."

"Then he was still here at daylight."

"He had to be," I agreed. "But every inch of the orchard was searched, and the only people who left here were the apple pickers who are all accounted for."

"Then there's no possibility, Doc."

"There's one we haven't considered. Phil Fitzhugh is still in there, unseen by us."

"Unseen? You mean invisible?'

I turned to Carter Desmond. "Was there ever a well on this property?"

He thought about that. "Phyllis, remember that well we covered over? Was that in the orchard?"

"Sure, it must have been ten, fifteen years ago. I don't even remember where it was."

"Do you have an old map or land survey that might show it?"

He disappeared into his little office and returned after a few moments, unrolling a survey map. "Here it is."

We peered over his shoulder and saw the rows of apple trees, each indicated by a circle. Perhaps a hundred feet back from the house, within the area of the stone wall and fences, there was a smaller circle with the letter "W" on it. "This was the well," he said. "We covered it over and planted grass there."

"Let's go look," I suggested.

We found the location by counting the rows of trees, but there was no sign, the ground had been dug up or tampered with. "It's pretty solid," Desmond told us. There's no possibility he could have fallen into the well, if that's what you're thinking."

I had to admit he was right. It was another dead end.

* * *

What with gas rationing, there were no long drives over holiday weekends. Folks stayed close to home for family gatherings. We'd invited Sheriff Lens and Vera over for a Sunday picnic in our backyard, but he spent much of the afternoon by the phone. "My deputy Joe Hauser, spotted that gypsy Newsome following Lisa Smith home from church this morning. I'm thinking we should pull him in for questioning."

"There's no proof yet that a crime was committed."

"Fitzhugh's blood on his shirt is proof enough for me."

"Let's wait awhile," I urged.

"Suppose the gypsy followed him into the orchard, or just came upon him there. He might have killed the boy and buried his body along that bare strip by the fence, smoothing the ground over to hide the traces."

"How could he follow him into the orchard without being seen? What would he use for a shovel? And how would he leave the orchard without being seen?"

"I don't know, Doc," he admitted. "But people don't just disappear."

As we finished our picnic lunch and Vera was helping Annabel clean up, I was aware that Sheriff Lens was still uneasy. "This Newsome fellow is staying at Mrs. Dobb's boarding house. Let's take a drive up there and talk to him," I suggested.

"You're working on a holiday weekend?" Vera complained to her husband.

"We won't be long," I promised.

We took the sheriff's car, and with him driving we were at Mrs. Dobb's house within ten minutes. She was a kindly widow who'd rented out rooms after her husband died and her children moved away. We found her on the front porch in a rocking chair, chatting with a neighbor.

"We'd like to talk with one of your boarders, Howie Newsome," the sheriff said. "Is he in?"

"The bald one? You just missed him. He packed his suitcase and left about an hour ago. Said he was catching a train to New York. He slept here the last two nights, but he seemed upset when I told him a deputy had been asking about him."

Sheriff Lens started to curse, then caught himself. "He knows we're on to him, Doc!"

"What time's the next New York train on Sunday?"

"Four-thirty, I think. We've got fifteen minutes. Maybe we can still catch him." Back in the car he reached Deputy Hauser on the police radio. "Joe, this is the sheriff. We're at the Dobbs place but Newsome has flown the coop. We think he's trying for the next train to New York."

"See you at the station," he said at once and signed off.

We pulled into the station parking lot just as Hauser arrived in the other car. There was no sign of the bald gypsy among the few people waiting on the platform. "He might have lied to Mrs. Dobbs about his plans," I said. "You and Hauser can check inside. I'll go down to the far end of the platform."

Already we could hear the approaching train, and in a moment the Boston & Maine locomotive rounded the bend to come into view. The short train slowed to a stop and the conductor helped a passenger off, then shouted his traditional "All aboard!" The waiting passengers climbed on and he followed them.

That was when I spotted Howie Newsome break from the cover of some trees and run toward the last car of the train, carrying his suitcase. "Sheriff!" I yelled.

Lens and his deputy spotted him in the same instant. "Stop!" the sheriff shouted, but Newsome paid him no heed. It was Deputy Hauser who broke into a run and tried to head him off. He was almost upon the fleeing man when Newsome paused to swing his suitcase at Hauser's head. The deputy ducked and came in low to tackle Newsome around the hips. They went down together as Sheriff Lens came running up to help in the capture.

I kept my distance while they cuffed him and searched his pockets. After a moment the sheriff walked over to me. "We've got our man, Doc. He had Phil Fitzhugh's wallet in his pocket. I'm holding him on suspicion of murder."

"Wait," I said. "You can't do that."

He gave me a puzzled look. "Why not?"

"Newsome couldn't have killed Phil Fitzhugh because Newsome *is* Phil Fitzhugh."

* * *

Of all the cases I'd helped to solve during my years in Northmont, none could compare with the Devil's Orchard affair, as I pointed out to Sheriff

Lens later that day. "There was no murder here, Sheriff. The only crime I can see is attempting to dodge the draft, but he wasn't due to report till next week anyway. He simply couldn't go off and leave Lisa pregnant, living with a father who'd threatened to kill him if that ever happened. Once they saw that a quick marriage was impossible, Phil Fitzhugh came up with a bizarre plan. Rather than report for the draft he'd simply disappear, assuming another identity so he could remain in Northmont to watch over Lisa during her pregnancy."

"But Newsome was bald, with chin whiskers, Doc."

"When he decided on this scheme he shaved his head and glued on false whiskers. He and Lisa met when they were in the high-school cast of *Our Town*, remember. He even had the play's poster on his bedroom wall. It's amazing how the absence of hair and the presence of a goatee changed his appearance so completely. Though the only time I met him as Newsome he turned away from me before I could get a good look at his face. He put some clothes in a suitcase and took a room at Mrs. Dobbs's house, establishing a second identity. That school play did more than teach him about makeup and acting. The name he used, Howie Newsome, is a character in *Our Town*."

"We saw him with his own hair after Newsome appeared in town," the sheriff argued.

I shook my head. "That was a wig, with hair worn just long enough to hide the pierced ear for the earring he wore as Newsome. It struck me as odd when Mrs. Dobbs told someone her new tenant rarely slept there—and odder still when she told us he had slept there on Friday and Saturday night. Of course he was sleeping at home before Friday, but after his disappearance he had to stay with Mrs. Dobbs in his new identity."

"What about that disappearance, Doc? You still haven't explained how he could have gotten out of Desmond's Orchard."

"He didn't need to get of it because he was never in it, Sheriff. He was only acting drunk on Friday night, looking for an opportunity to escape from us and disappear. He couldn't have planned it the way it happened, but when he saw my eyes were off the road while you two were tussling in the backseat, he jumped out, saying he was running into the Devil's orchard. Actually we'd already passed the first chain-link fence, unnoticed by me in the dark. When the second fence came into view, he leaped from the car and went over the low wall just beyond it, not onto Desmond's property but next-door into Simon Faulks' orchard. When I drove around to the other side I remember noticing I was closer to the corner than I'd thought."

"I'll be damned! But we were watching that whole stretch of wall. We'd have seen him if he came back."

"He didn't come back, Sheriff. He simply walked through the Faulks' orchard and came out on Desmond Road, next to the Desmond property."

"You forget we found his bloody shirt, Doc. That was in the Desmond orchard."

"And you forget the stone it was wrapped around Fitzhugh inflicted a superficial cut on his arm or leg, enough to spread blood on his T-shirt. Then he simply wrapped it around a stone, whirled it around over his head, and sent it sailing over the fence to land in Desmond's Orchard, hoping to confuse us as to his fate. We thought the stone was placed there to hold the shirt down, but actually it had carried the shirt there from over the fence."

"Why didn't I see all that?" he asked.

"You saw it all and drew the wrong conclusion. Newsome was seen speaking to Lisa, he followed her after church, he tried to escape when we started asking questions, and he was carrying Fitzhugh's wallet. You saw it as proof of a crime, I saw it as proof of love."

This was one mystery that had a happy ending for all concerned. Phil Fitzhugh reported for his army service the following week, and went to Fort Dix for basic training. After the baby was born, Lisa joined him and they were married there, with her father's reluctant blessing. Phil was sent overseas only toward the end of the war, and returned to a long and happy life with Lisa and their children. Sometimes I wish they could all end that way.

THE PROBLEM OF THE SHEPHERD'S RING

It was in early December of 1943, just two years after our marriage, that Annabel told me she was pregnant (Old Dr. Sam Hawthorne paused to refill his visitor's glass before continuing his story.) Of course, I was overjoyed by the news, even though it meant bringing a child into a world ravaged by war. Churchill, Roosevelt, and Stalin had just met for the first time in Teheran, agreeing on a plan for the invasion of western Europe during the coming year, and we hoped the worst might soon be over.

Our good friend and Northmont's first black doctor, Lincoln Jones, had gone into obstetrics and opened his own office. He'd been slow in building a practice, but Annabel and I quickly agreed there was no one we'd trust more to deliver our first baby. Lincoln examined Annabel on Monday morning, our wedding anniversary, and estimated that the baby was due toward the end of July. She was already making plans for her assistant to take over the veterinary practice at Annabel's Ark during her confinement. I'd be forty-seven years old when my child was born, but Annabel was ten years younger, still a beauty with her blond hair and hazel eyes.

"I'll need you, Sam," she told me. "When it gets closer you'll have to cut back on your detective work."

I assured her I'd be happy to abandon it completely if Northmont would only settle down to being a quiet New England town. But that wasn't about to happen right away.

I arrived at my office the following morning, another anniversary day, but this one far from joyous. It was two years since the attack on Pearl Harbor, and I knew my nurse April would be thinking of her husband André, still fighting the war in the Pacific. I couldn't resist telling her the good news about Annabel's pregnancy and she was overjoyed. I was the godfather of her son Sam, named for me and now a seven-year-old second-grader, living here with his mother while they awaited his father's return from the war. When I'd finished with my news she told me Sheriff Lens was coming in to see me. I knew it wouldn't be just a social visit.

"How's it going, Doc?" he asked as he came through the door a bit after ten.

"Just fine, Sheriff. Annabel and I were out to see Lincoln Jones yesterday."

"Oh? How's he doing with his practice?"

"It's growing. We brought him some new business."

"Who–?" he started to ask, and then understood what I was telling him. "You and Annabel are expecting?"

"Well, just Annabel actually."

"Doc, that's a great news. Wait till I tell Vera! When's she due?"

"Late July, near as we can tell."

"Maybe by then the war will be over. The invasion's getting closer."

I shook my head. "I hate to think of all the boys who'll die over there. But what can I do for you, Sheriff?"

"You've got a patient named Julius Finesaw?"

I gave a silent groan. "I suppose you could call him my patient. I set his broken leg a few weeks ago when his tractor rolled over. But the man needs more help than I can give him. He needs a psychiatrist."

"Don't have any of them in Northmont," the sheriff pointed out.

"I know."

"So you think he's crazy?"

I shrugged. "Deranged, certainly."

"Same thing, isn't it?"

"I suppose so. What's he done now?"

"Says he's going to kill Ralph Cedric for selling him that defective tractor. His wife Millie was so upset she called me out to talk to him."

"Did you convince him to behave himself?"

"Far from it. Says we can't stop him, that he can make himself invisible and walk down the road to Cedric's place."

"He's not likely to do it with a broken leg, invisible or not." I glanced at the day's schedule. "Tell you what–I've got a house call this afternoon out at the McGregor farm. One of their kids is in bed with chicken pox. On my way back I'll stop at Finesaw's place. I should check on that cast anyway, make sure there's no swelling."

"Maybe you can talk some sense into him, Doc."

* * *

The McGregor lad was coming along fine as the chicken pox ran its course. When I'd finished with him I cut across to Chestnut Hill Road. The old Buick was still running pretty well, and I hoped it would last till the war ended. I pulled into the driveway at the Finesaw farm, once more admiring the main house, even though it was an old place dating from the last century and badly in need of a paint job. As I left my car I saw Millie Finesaw come to the door. She was a petite blonde a bit younger than I was who had never seemed the right match for the tall, brooding Julius. Their son had fled home as soon as possible, joining the army when he turned eighteen. He was somewhere in Italy at that time.

"Hello, Millie. I was over at the McGregors and thought I'd stop by to see how Julius's leg is coming along."

"I'm concerned about him, Dr. Hawthorne. He's been acting even crazier than usual. I had Sheriff Lens come out and talk to him yesterday." I followed her into a living room cluttered with tables and bookshelves lined with plants and china figurines. "I've been giving him the painkillers you prescribed and they make him dopey at night, but during the day he just rants and raves."

"I'll see if I can do anything for him."

She led the way up the creaking staircase to the second floor. He'd stayed up there to be near the bathroom, though I was glad to see he was seated in an armchair by the window, his immobilized leg supported by a footstool. A bare right foot stuck out from the bottom of his cast. The room was sparsely furnished, with not even a bookshelf in sight. A Sears catalogue on one table seemed to be his only reading matter.

"How are you feeling, Julius?" I asked, opening my black bag.

"I'll feel a lot better after I've killed that bastard Cedric. He sold me a tractor damn near killed me, and now he says it was my own fault."

"You two have been feuding for as long as I can remember. Isn't it time you called a truce?"

"When he's dead."

"And when will that be?" I asked to humor him.

"Tomorrow midnight."

"You can't do that, Julius. You've got your right leg in a cast."

"That won't stop me."

"Do I have to get a sheriff's deputy to park outside your house all night?"

He gave a sly, twisted smile. "Wouldn't matter. I can be invisible."

I sighed. "Julius, you need to see someone who can help you. I'm just a general practitioner."

"Don't believe me, do you?" He held up his right hand, showing me a gold ring with a gem of some sort in it. "This is a genuine shepherd's ring, described in Book Two of Plato's *Republic*. It was found by Gyges, a shepherd in the service of the king of Lydia. If I turn it so the stone is inside my hand, I become invisible."

"I'd like to see that," I told him, playing along.

"Not now. Tomorrow midnight, when I kill Ralph Cedric."

"Where'd you get the ring? Something like that must be valuable."

"It was a gift," was all he'd say.

"Julius, suppose I bring Ralph Cedric over here in the morning, so the two of you can straighten this out like civilized people."

"Bring him here and I'll kill him. Save me having to walk over there." He emphasized his words by lifting a gnarled walking stick leaning against his bed.

I glanced at Millie and saw that she was beyond dealing with him, her face frozen into a helpless mask. I dropped the subject and went about examining his cast and leg. "You're coming along pretty well," I told him. "Another few weeks and the cast can come off."

He raised his eyes to mine, and in that instant I had no doubt that he was mentally ill. If it was physically possible, he would indeed walk down that road tomorrow midnight and kill Ralph Cedric. "See my ring, Doc? Pretty, isn't it? Going to make me invisible."

* * *

I stopped by the sheriff's office on my way back, giving my opinion. "The man's deranged, Sheriff. He may not be capable of making himself invisible, but he's certainly capable of bashing Cedric's head in if he gets close enough."

Sheriff Lens grunted. "Doesn't really need to get close, does he? Every farmer on Chestnut Hill Road owns a hunting rifle. How far is it—about a hundred yards or so?—between the houses. He could sit in his bedroom window and pick off Ralph Cedric when he comes out the door."

"His window's on the other side," I pointed out.

"He could crawl to the other side of the house, or limp over with his walking stick and rifle."

"You can't arrest a man for making crazy threats, Sheriff, especially not if he's crazy to start with."

"I'll have a deputy check the area tonight, in case he decides to go a day early."

I nodded. "And I'll find some excuse to call on Cedric and his wife tomorrow. Whatever happens, Julius Finesaw isn't going to become invisible and kill anyone."

* * *

The following morning was exceedingly mild for the eighth of December and I was beginning to wonder if we'd have a white Christmas. I parked in front of Ralph Cedric's house and rang the bell. His wife June came to the door and greeted me with a smile. She was a tall, attractive woman in her thirties, with only a few gray hairs showing among the waves of brown.

"Dr. Hawthorne! What bring you to our doorstep? Are you giving free samples today?"

"Afraid not, June. I'm helping your neighbor Finesaw with an insurance claim for his busted leg. I was thinking Ralph could give me some information about that tractor."

June bristled a bit. "It wasn't the tractor caused that accident! Any sane person knows you don't run a tractor along the side of a hill that steep. The man is crazy."

"Is Ralph around? I see his car's in the driveway."

Ralph Cedric appeared from the kitchen holding a cup of coffee. He was a stocky bald man somewhat older than his wife. He'd been running Cedric Tractor Sales for the past ten years and doing pretty well until the war made new farm equipment almost as hard to come by as new cars. Still, farming was necessary to the war effort and he was in business on a limited scale, even though his main supplier was now building tanks. "You want me, Doc?"

"Just what happened with that tractor and Finesaw's broken leg? I set it for him at the time but he was next to incoherent about how it happened. He seemed to blame the tractor you sold him."

Cedric leaned against a bookcase, sipping his coffee. "I can't imagine how Millie stays married to him. That man's impossible. The tractor wasn't new, but it was the best I could get secondhand. I warned him that he should stay on relatively flat fields with it. He hadn't had it a week when he tried to plow the side of a hill. It's a wonder his leg was the only thing got broken."

June interrupted then, taking up the battle. "He told Millie he was going to kill Ralph as soon as he could get over here. Said he could make himself invisible. Isn't that enough to get him committed?"

"He hasn't done anything yet," I pointed out. "But I've asked Sheriff Lens to keep an eye on the place."

"What's this coming up the front walk?" Cedric asked, glancing out the window. "Is that Millie carrying a snowman?"

It was indeed. Millie Finesaw was bearing down on us with a three-foot-tall snowman made of giant cotton balls with a carrot nose and coal for eyes, a corn-cob pipe and a little top hat. June greeted her at the door. "Millie—what have you done?"

"I made this as a peace offering. There's no snow yet, but you can have a cotton snowman in your yard, or even in your living room if you want."

June took it from her and invited her in. "This had to be a lot of work, Millie." She placed it on the floor near the fireplace.

"It was nothing. I love fiddling around with things like this. Takes my mind off—" She stopped short, with a pained expression we could all read.

It was my job to ask the question, so I did. "How is Julius today?"

"All right, sleeping mostly. I think those pain pills really numb the brain. He just hasn't been himself lately."

I nodded. "It's best he sleep as much as possible. I have to be getting along now. I'll let you people visit."

Somehow Millie's visit seemed to relieve the tension all around. I left them with a good feeling that, shepherd's ring or not, her husband was not about to transmogrify into an invisible murderer at midnight.

* * *

Annabel and I had dinner that night at our favorite restaurant, Max's Steakhouse, so we could tell him our good news. We'd held our wedding reception there and Max Fortesque was like one of the family. "That's great news!" he told us, ordering a bottle of wine for our table. "It means one more customer."

"Not for a few years," Annabel told him with a smile.

Sheriff Lens came in then, perhaps hoping to find me there, and joined us at our table. "Vera and I are delighted about the baby," he told her at once. "I guess I'm too old to be godfather but we'll love it like our own. Vera's already planning to knit some bootees."

"Thanks, Sheriff."

We invited him to join us and he agreed to a glass of wine. Annabel was careful to take only a few sips for herself. I told him about Millie's gift of a homemade snowman for the Cedrics and he agreed it sounded as if things were under control. "But I think I'll manage to be out on Chestnut Hill Road around midnight, just in case."

"That's good," Annabel agreed, "because Sam will be home in bed." She said it with a smile, but I knew she meant it. She was never happy when I went chasing off after dark.

Although I usually tried to be in bed by eleven, I found excuses that night to stay up later near the telephone, even as my wife was calling to me from upstairs. "I'll be up in a few minutes," I told her, knowing that Sheriff Lens would radio in to his office if anything happened.

I was about to call it quits and go to bed when the phone rang. It was one of Lens's deputies. The sheriff had called for assistance at Ralph Cedric's home, and he wanted me there, too. I quickly explained the situation to my unhappy wife and slipped into a coat as I hurried to the car. On the deserted midnight roads it took me only ten minutes to reach Chestnut Hill Road and the flashing lights of three sheriff's cars.

Sheriff Lens was waiting for me out front. Even in the dim light from the house windows I could see he was distraught. "Sheriff—"

"It was Finesaw," he told me. "I was watching the street all the time. He never crossed it, yet the next instant he was there by the front of the house. He smashed the door glass with his walking stick and unlocked the door. As soon as he was inside June ran out screaming and wailing. My God, Sam—"

I followed him into the house. The destruction seemed to be everywhere. Even the cotton snowman had been trampled and pulled apart, a lamp broken, books pulled from their shelves, clothes scattered. Ralph Cedric lay in a pool of blood on the kitchen floor, his skull battered by Finesaw's gnarled walking stick, which lay at his side.

"Is he still here?" I asked.

The sheriff shook his head. "We've searched every inch of the house. I've got a couple of men watching Finesaw's place but we haven't gone in yet."

I could hear sobbing from the dining room. "What about June?"

"She's in bad shape, Doc. Maybe you could give her something."

I went into the next room, where a deputy was trying to comfort her. "Is there any family we could call?" he was asking, but she only shook her head.

"Give me a few minutes alone with her," I told the deputy, then sat down at the table. "Tell me about it, June. How did it happen?"

"He—he smashed in the door with his cane. Then he just started breaking everything."

"It was Julius Finesaw?"

She nodded. "He had a hooded jacket on but I knew him. He walked stiffly because of the cast on his leg. Ralph came running out of the kitchen. I told him to go back, but Finesaw was already on him with that cane. I ran to the door and started screaming. The sheriff came running but by that time it was too late. Ralph was dead."

"And Finesaw?"

"He was just . . . gone."

I turned back to Sheriff Lens. "What did you see?"

"Like I said. All of a sudden he was on the front walk, heading for the door. When he smashed the glass I jumped out and ran toward the house. If I'd been parked a little closer I might have gotten here in time to save Ralph's life."

"We'd better see about Finesaw," I said grimly. "And Millie."

I think we were both a bit fearful of what we would find at the Finesaw house, but after a couple of rings of the doorbell Millie appeared in her robe and slippers. "What is it?" she asked. "What's happened?"

"Is Julius here?" Sheriff Lens asked, delaying an answer to her question.

"Why . . . I think he's sleeping. I gave him another pain pill."

She led the way up to his room, and I noticed the sheriff surreptitiously slip the gun from his holster, holding it out of sight against his leg. She opened the door to her husband's room and turned on the light. He was lying there in bed, his cast-bound leg up on pillows, and his eyes opened at once. When he saw me he smiled and said, "I've done it just as I promised. I've killed Ralph Cedric."

* * *

Impossible as it seemed, there was evidence to bear out his words. The gnarled walking stick that had leaned against his bed on my previous visit was now blood-stained murder weapon in Ralph Cedric's kitchen. The slippers next to the bed showed traces of dirt on their bottoms, and a hooded jacket lay on the floor nearby.

"Let me take your pulse," I said, gripping his right wrist. It was racing a bit, though I couldn't attribute that to any recent physical activity. The sight of us invading his bedroom in the middle of the night might have accounted for it.

"You weren't sleeping with him?" the sheriff asked Millie.

"Not since the accident. With the cast and all I knew he'd be more comfortable with the entire bed. I've been using the extra room." She took a deep breath. "Tell me what happened to Ralph Cedric."

"He's dead, Millie. June and I both saw a figure that looked like Julius entering their house."

I was more interested in hearing what Finesaw had to say. "Tell us how you did it," I urged.

His smile was sly as a tiger's, a mixture of pure evil and insanity. "Millie was in her room. When it got near midnight I got out of bed with my cane, put on my slippers and jacket, and made myself invisible."

"Show us that," I suggested, as I had the previous day.

"No, no! I can't overuse the power."

"How did you kill Cedric?" Sheriff Lens asked.

"When I reached his door I became visible again. I wanted him to see who was killing him. I smashed the glass and opened the door, then swung my stick around at things. June was screaming. I felt sorry for her. Then Cedric appeared and I clubbed him with my stick."

"You left it there," I said. "How did you get back without it?"

The sly smile again. "I don't need the stick when I'm invisible. My body has no weight and I can float."

"If you admit to killing him, I'm going to have to arrest you," the sheriff said.

"Of course. I don't expect you'll be able to hold an invisible man in prison very long, though."

"We'll see to that," I said. Before he knew what was happening I gripped his wrist and pulled the shepherd's ring from his finger.

"*No!*" he screamed, but it was already off.

"Now you're just a human like the rest of us." I handed the ring to Sheriff Lens. "Keep this in a safe place."

Finesaw was thrashing in the bed. "Millie!" he shouted. "They've taken the ring!"

She stood in the doorway shaking her head, close to tears. "We'll have to take him away," the sheriff told her. "I'm sorry."

He called for an ambulance and stretcher, and when Finesaw tried to resist I had to sedate him. There was no doubt that the man was mentally incompetent, but that still didn't explain—in a rational world—how he'd killed Ralph Cedric.

* * *

Finesaw was hospitalized under guard, and a grand jury quickly indicted him for murder. In his testimony Sheriff Lens admitted he might not have seen the man approaching the house because the light was poor. "What else could I say, Doc?" he told me later. "They'd never buy an invisible man. Finesaw admits to the killing and has even described how he did it. Except for the invisibility part it makes perfect sense."

"Except for the invisibility part. Don't you see, Sheriff, that's the most important element."

"There are no streetlights on Chestnut Hill Road. Maybe I didn't see Finesaw until he was in the light from Cedric's house."

I shook my head. "Even without the invisibility I doubt Finesaw could have hobbled over a hundred yards with his cane. He certainly couldn't have gotten back to his bed without the cane."

"What other possibility is there?" he asked.

"Cedric's wife."

"June? That couldn't be. She ran out screaming before I even reached the house. There was no time for her to have done it. Besides, if she killed her husband how could Julius know exactly what happened?"

"You're right," I admitted, but I still didn't like it.

The case dragged on through the Christmas holidays and into January. The war news was mainly about the Russian advances, recapturing much of the land Hitler's legions had overrun the previous year. With the war and Annabel's pregnancy always in my thoughts, I had little time for Julius Finesaw's situation.

That was why the phone call from Millie in mid January came as a surprise.

"Dr. Hawthorne? This is Millie Finesaw. I've engaged a lawyer from Shinn Corners to defend my husband and he needs to speak to you. I was wondering if you could meet with us one day this week."

I glanced at my appointment calendar. "I have some free time tomorrow afternoon, around two. How would that be?"

"Fine. At your office?"

"I'll be expecting you."

They arrived right on time, Millie wearing a fur jacket against the winder winds and Terrance Mellnap dressed in a ski parka and boots. He shook hands and gave me his card. "We've got more snow in Shinn Corners than you have," he said, perhaps as an excuse for his foul-weather gear. Then he added, "It's a pleasure to meet you, Dr. Hawthorne. I've heard a great deal about you over the years."

"All good, I hope."

"Certainly." He opened his briefcase. "There's a preliminary hearing next week. Naturally we'll be pleading not guilty by reason of insanity."

"Of course." I glanced over at Millie.

"Since he was never examined by a psychiatrist, we'd like your testimony as to his mental condition. That should persuade the judge to order a mental examination."

"I can testify as to what I know. Tell me, Millie, what is his present condition?"

"He's depressed. He keeps telling me he wants his ring back."

I shook my head. "That's not going to happen. It's part of his obsession."

"What harm would it do?" Mellnap asked. "Surely you don't believe this invisibility business."

"Of course not, but my point is that he still does. Give him the ring and he might think he's invisible and try to escape when they're bringing him to court."

The attorney nodded in agreement. "You have a point there."

* * *

The following Monday I testified at the preliminary hearing and the judge ordered a psychiatric examination for the defendant. I doubted if the case would ever come to trial with the shape Finesaw was in. After the court session I had lunch with Sheriff Lens at the counter in the drugstore across from the courthouse.

"How's Annabel doing?" he asked.

"Fine. She's seeing Lincoln Jones for her regular checkup next week."

"July will be here before you know it."

"I hope so."

"What's the matter, Doc?"

I shook my head. "It's this Finesaw case. Nothing about it satisfies me."

"What do you mean?"

"Since Finesaw couldn't have become invisible there has to be some other explanation. You might have missed him hobbling down the street in the dark, but he still had no way to get back. The person who killed Ralph Cedric must have gone out the back door of the house and run through the field in the dark."

"But in his confession Finesaw described the crime in detail. If he didn't do it, how did he know about it?"

"Exactly, Sheriff. And there's only one explanation for that. It was Millie who crossed that road in the hooded jacket, Millie who killed Cedric and escaped through the back door to tell her husband exactly what she'd done."

It was a good idea but Sheriff Lens shot it down at once. "Couldn't be, Doc. For one thing, Millie is a full head shorter than her husband. I could never mistake her for him, not even in dim light. And I had a deputy there within minutes, watching Finesaw's house to catch him returning. He was shining a spotlight around the place and saw nothing."

I thought about that but I didn't like it. "It couldn't have been Julius unless he really was invisible. It couldn't have been June Cedric because there was no time for her to do it, and she couldn't have told Julius what she did. It couldn't have been Millie because she's too short and would have been seen returning to her house. Where does that leave us?"

The sheriff shrugged. "A passing hobo, looking for a house to rob?"

"You forget the murder weapon was Julius Finesaw's walking stick, which I saw in his house just a day earlier."

"Then it has to be Finesaw, Doc. However he did it, he's got to be guilty. What difference does it make? He belongs in a mental hospital anyway, and that's where he'll go."

I felt as if the spirit had drained out of me. "And for the first time since coming to Northmont I've got a mystery I can't explain."

It nagged at me, in the office and at home with Annabel. "You've got to get it off your mind, Sam," she told me a few days later. "Think about becoming a father."

She was right, of course, but the following morning I decided on one more visit to the sheriff's office. "What's up, Doc? he asked, imitating a popular movie cartoon character.

"Please, Sheriff."

"Just joking a bit. What can I do for you?"

"Do you still have Julius Finesaw's ring, the one that makes him invisible?"

"Sure do. If the case goes to trial, the district attorney might need it, but for now it's still in my file."

He slid it from an envelope onto his desk and I studied it carefully. "It doesn't look particularly ancient or valuable."

"It's not. They sell ones like it at Ross Jewelers for nineteen ninety-five. I checked."

"And yet something convinced him it was like the shepherd's ring of Gyges, described in Book Two of Plato's—" I froze in mid sentence.

"What is it, Doc?"

"That's it, Sheriff! That's the answer! Come on, I'll explain on the way."

* * *

We took the sheriff's car and as he drove I talked. "Where would a man like Julius Finesaw, a farmer with mental problems, who didn't know enough to keep a tractor off a steep hillside, come across a book like Plato's *Republic*? Certainly not in his house, where the bookshelves were filled with plants and china figurines, and the only reading matter in his bedroom was a Sears catalogue."

"What are you saying, Doc?"

"The books were down the road in the other house, Ralph Cedric's house. Remember how some of them were pulled from their shelves during the killing?"

We turned onto Chestnut Hill Road. "Is that where we're going now?"

"No. We'll stop first at the Finesaw house."

It was a lucky choice. Millie and June were having morning coffee together. "What is it?" Millie asked, meeting us at the door with a cup of coffee in her hand.

"There's been a new development," I said.

"Join us. I'll get two more cups."

"What is it?" June Cedric asked. "Bad news?"

"In a way. I want to tell you both a story. It's about two women, neighbors, who desperately wanted to get rid of their husbands."

The coffee cup slipped from Millie's hand. "Oh my God!"

"Don't say anything," June warned her.

"She doesn't have to," I told them. "I'll do the talking. The idea probably came to you when Julius broke his leg in the tractor accident and threatened to kill Ralph for selling him a defective machine. Over coffee one morning you must have decided that would be the perfect solution to your problems—if Julius killed Ralph and ended up in a mental hospital. Julius's mental condition was already so bad that you thought he could be goaded into making good on his threat. It must have been you, June, who remembered reading about the shepherd's ring and its powers of invisibility. You even found a ring that Millie could use to convince him of its power."

"How could I ever convince him of that?" Millie asked.

"He was taking painkillers for his leg and they left him muddled. Added to his existing mental problems, it wasn't hard to convince him he was invisible when he turned the ring a certain way. The killing was set for that certain midnight, only when the time neared it became clear Julius might have been mentally willing to commit murder but wasn't physically able. You switched to plan two. While Julius stayed in bed with an extra dose of mind-numbing painkillers, June did the job for him and bludgeoned her husband to death."

"Wait a second, Doc," the sheriff interrupted. "You're forgetting he was killed with Finesaw's walking stick. How did it get over there?"

"We witnessed its arrival, Sheriff, in that cotton-ball snowman Millie made. It was about the same height as the walking stick, which must have served as the anchor for those big balls of cotton. That was why the snowman had to be ripped apart, and why the other damage was done, to make it less obvious."

"You're saying it was June that I saw entering her own house?"

"It had to be, Sheriff. Millie was too short to pass for her husband, but June was taller. She wore the hooded jacket, a duplicate of Julius's own coat, wrapped a piece of white paper around her leg to pass for a cast, and limped along on the cane. She'd gone out the back door of the house and walked around the far side to the front, which was why the figure seemed to appear out of nowhere in front of the house."

But the sheriff had another objection. "I thought we ruled that our earlier, Doc. She wouldn't have had time to kill him, bust up the place, and appear in the doorway almost instantly."

"She killed him first, Sheriff. She did it all first. When she approached her front door and smashed the glass, he was already dead on the kitchen floor. She only had to toss the jacket and paper into the mess, drop the cane near his body, and return screaming to the front door."

"What was Millie doing all this time?"

"Talking to Julius in his crazy drugged state, telling him exactly what he'd done, how he'd become invisible, crossed the street, broken the glass, and killed Cedric with his walking stick. She even dirtied the bottoms of his slippers to add to the story. Ralph Cedric was dead and Julius Finesaw admitted to killing him. You had witnessed part of it yourself, Sheriff. It had to be true, only when they changed their plan June and Millie here neglected to work out a way in which Julius could have returned home. It left the invisibility part in place without any alternative."

They were both held on suspicion of murder, and it only took a day before Millie cracked and confirmed everything I'd said. It was sometime later that Sheriff Lens said to me, "You know, Doc, maybe the ring could have made him invisible. Did you ever consider that?"

"We live in a rational world, but there are times when even I must consider the irrational. Remember when I checked the pulse on Finesaw's right wrist? I twisted the ring so the stone was inside. It didn't make him invisible.

THE PROBLEM OF SUICIDE COTTAGE

It was a sunny day in 1976 and plans were well under way for Dr. Sam Hawthorne's eightieth birthday party. He'd grumbled about all the fuss, preferring to spend the day quietly, but that was not to be. His visitor was a familiar one, always a joy to see. "You tell stories to old friends but never to me. Now it's my turn. You promised me one for your eightieth birthday and this is it. I want to know about that summer of nineteen forty-four."

He smiled and said, "I usually supply a bit of libation to go with my stories. How about a glass of sherry?"

"I'd prefer scotch if you don't mind. Scotch and water would be fine."

* * *

It was an exciting summer (Dr. Sam began, after he'd supplied the refreshments). The Allies had stormed the French beaches on June 6th, landing in Normandy at dawn following an airborne attack further inland. Despite heavy casualties, the landings were successful and a second wave of troops quickly followed. Back home in Northmont things were relatively quiet as I awaited the birth of our first child. Annabel's baby was due in late July and she'd already decided if it was a boy it should be called Sam Junior. I wasn't too happy with the idea and it was still under discussion.

Annabel had turned over the daily routine at the Ark to her assistant when her pregnancy reached the eight-month mark in late June, though she insisted on remaining on call for any unusual veterinary problems. I readily agreed with her suggestion that we wait out the final month at a cottage on Chester Lake just a few miles from town. It was peaceful there, though I still made a few house calls and my nurse April knew how to reach me in an emergency.

Chester Lake was a placid body of water about a mile wide and five miles long, named after an early landowner in the area. I'd spent a summer there in 1929 when I'd solved a mystery involving some people vanished from a houseboat and it was there, at the age of 33, that I'd fallen in love for the first time. Her name was Miranda Grey and I often wondered what became of her.

We'd barely unloaded the car for our month-long stay before Annabel started kidding me about her. "Too bad we couldn't have rented the cottage where Miranda Grey stayed with her aunt and uncle. I'll bet it would have brought back fond memories."

All I could give her was a sigh. "I should have known better than to tell you about Miranda Grey. It only lasted a few months."

All the small one-story cottages at Chester Lake were similar, and soon as I entered the one we'd rented I was transported back to 1929. The entire front half of the house was given over to the living room with a small fireplace. There was a single bedroom in the left rear. The kitchen and bathroom occupied the right rear, with a back door leading out to the gravel driveway. If there were more than two people staying overnight someone had to sleep on a foldaway bed in the living room. It was a perfect place for the two of us since it discouraged unwanted visitors.

"I guess it's like a second honeymoon," Annabel said, settling in. "Or it would be if it weren't for this bump." She patted her stomach fondly and gazed up at the living room ceiling. "I wonder what that hook is for."

"Probably a hanging plant. I doubt it's for any erotic activity."

"Sheriff Lens mentioned there'd been some burglaries up here last summer. If we catch a thief we can hang him by his wrists."

"You should be thinking only nice thoughts these days," I suggested.

"Yes, Doctor."

"And the sheriff did tell us they'd installed new locks on all the cottage doors this season."

That was when we heard a knocking on the screen door and I went to answer it. A smiling man of about my age stood there, wearing bathing trunks and an undershirt. "Dr. Hawthorne, you probably don't remember me."

"Well, I—"

"Raspin, Jerry Raspin. I was one of the trustees at Pilgrim Memorial Hospital a few years back."

"Of course!" I told him, because I did remember him then. He had a real-estate business that had been fairly profitable before the war.

"Probably didn't recognize me without my suit on. I have the cottage next-door."

"Come in," I urged, trying to make amends for any hesitation.

He followed me in, as Annabel hurriedly wrapped a robe around her bulging belly. "I hope I'm not intruding, Mrs. Hawthorne," he said. "I'm your neighbor for the month of July. The wife and I have the next cottage."

"How nice," Annabel said.

"We may not be here the entire month," I explained. "My wife is expecting our first child in a few weeks."

"Well, congratulations! That's great news." He helped himself to a seat on our sofa.

"Do you take a cottage here each summer?" Annabel asked.

Jerry Raspin nodded. "The wife likes it, and there's nowhere else to go with this gas rationing. I sure hope the war ends soon. My old clunker of a car won't last much longer."

"The news is pretty good," I told him. "The Allies are advancing on all fronts."

Raspin nodded. "We have a son who just got drafted. I'm hoping the war ends about the time he finishes his basic training."

Annabel glanced out the side window. "Your cottage looks pretty much like ours."

"They're all about the same on this side of the lake. Yours has one distinction, though. The regulars here call it suicide cottage."

"Why, for heaven's sake?"

"Each of the last two summers there's been a suicide here. In 'forty-two it was an elderly man and last year it was a young woman whose husband had been killed by the Japanese in the Solomon Islands. A terrible tragedy!"

"I remember both of them," I said, "but I hadn't realized they were both in this same cottage."

"I'm sure you two will break the jinx," he replied with a smile, trying to make light of it.

Annabel snorted. "Two instances hardly qualify as a jinx, Mr. Raspin. I'd call it a coincidence."

About that time he must have decided that his visit had been ill-timed. "I'd better be getting back. We'll talk again."

I saw him to the door and then returned to Annabel. "Can we stand a month of him in the next cottage?" she asked. "I remember that his wife was nice. I met her once at a hospital function when he was a trustee."

"All this talk of suicide–"

"There'll be none here this month. I promise you that."

* * *

On the night of July 4th the Chester Lake residents marked the occasion with a display of railroad flares that ringed the shoreline. A few cottages even fired skyrockets and small firecrackers, but these were hard to come by in our area. The following morning was a Wednesday that year, and the day dawned bright and sunny. Already before breakfast there were children splashing in the water. Annabel watched them fondly from our porch.

"One of those could be our Sam a few years from now. We'll have to come back here again." Later in the morning she even went wading herself, with me standing nervously behind her in case she started to fall.

We had a telephone in the kitchen and every morning I checked in with April at my office. But it was a quiet July and the most serious case she had to report was one of the Walker boys being stung by wasps. He was one of those kids who were always getting into trouble and I remembered last summer when he'd gone missing from his parents' cottage and been feared drowned at Chester Lake. After a day of dragging the lake they'd found him hiding in a tiny crawlspace behind the kitchen sink.

The following Monday I drove Annabel in to see her obstetrician, our old friend Lincoln Jones, and he reported that all seemed to be going well. "Another two weeks at most," he predicted.

Back at the cottage we became acquainted with another of our neighbors. Mrs. Spring was a petite woman in her late forties who'd been a nurse in Boston. She lived two doors down from us, in the opposite direction from Jerry Raspin and his wife. "I'm right next to Judge Hastings," she told us, pausing in her stroll along the water's edge to chat. "You know the judge, don't you?"

I did know Hastings, a popular man around town, but hadn't realized his cottage was next to ours. I'd seen no activity there since we arrived. After Mrs. Spring had continued on her walk, I said to Annabel, "If the judge is really next-door I should call on him to say hello. I'll take a walk over there."

At first I thought my knocking at the door would be met only by silence, but after the second knock I saw movement behind the curtains and Judge Hastings himself opened the door, as tall and formidable as he appeared on the bench. "Well, Sam Hawthorne! What brings you here?"

"Annabel and I have had the cottage next-door since the first of the month and I only now found out you were here. I didn't see anyone around and assumed it was empty."

He seemed hesitant about inviting me in, and finally compromised by motioning toward the porch chairs. "Maud hasn't been feeling well," he explained. "That's why you haven't seen us out."

I chose one of the two Adirondack chairs and settled into it. "I hope it's nothing serious. If she needs a physician, I'm right next-door."

"No, no." He rejected the possibility with a wave of his hand. "It's not serious. Is this your first summer here?"

"The first since our marriage. I visited here years ago, but somehow with my practice I never had time for a real vacation till now. Annabel's expecting our first child this month and I wanted to be with her as much as possible."

"There's nothing like a first child, Sam. I can still remember when Rory was born, though it's close to thirty years ago now."

"How's he doing?"

"Air Force lieutenant. We're very proud of him."

"You should be. He's helping to win this war for us."

The door opened, surprisingly, and Maud Hastings came out to join us. She was a decade younger than the judge, but just then she seemed older. She wore no makeup and she'd put on weight since I last saw her. I suspected her problems were more emotional than physical. "Hello, Doctor," she addressed me with some formality. Perhaps she thought her husband had summoned me in my professional capacity.

"How've you been Maud?"

"Better. I'm on my feet again, at least."

Judge Hastings seemed as surprised as I was by her unexpected appearance. "Shouldn't you be resting, dear?"

"I've had enough resting to last through the summer. I want to see what's going on out here."

"Nothing much. Sam and his wife have the next cabin."

She glanced over at it. "Suicide cabin."

"Didn't know that when we rented it," I told her.

Judge Hastings cleared his throat. "We were here last summer when that young woman took an overdose of sleeping pills. She couldn't go on after her husband was killed."

"How'd the first one die?" I asked. "The old man."

"Shot himself. The place was a mess after that. Owner had to hire people to wash away the blood and repaint the living room."

"Any doubt about either of them?" I asked, because that was the sort of question I always asked.

"Sheriff Lens was called out both times, but the cottage doors were locked and bolted from the inside."

"Windows?"

"Those too, Sam. Don't worry, you'd have heard about it if there was anything suspicious."

About then I saw a familiar figure strolling along the rocky shoreline. It was Jerry Raspin, my new friend from the previous week, and I assumed the woman with him was his wife. When he saw us on the porch he changed his route and walked over. He nodded to me and then addressed the judge's wife. "Good to see you up and about again, Maud. Feeling better?"

"Very much better, thank you."

"This weather would make anyone feel better." He turned to me. "Dr. Hawthorne, this is my wife, Susan."

I smiled and shook her hand. "I believe we met at one of the hospital functions some years ago." She was a large woman, about her husband's size, and I imagined they made a matching set on the local social scene, where Annabel and I rarely ventured.

Our mailman, a little fellow named Cally Forbes, had appeared at the next cottage, the one rented by Mrs. Spring. Since the cottage mail in this section was usually left in a row of boxes on the street, I assumed he must have some sort of special-delivery item for her. "I'd better go see what Cally wants," I decided, when his knocking on the door yielded no response.

He turned as I approached. "I have a special delivery for Mrs. Spring. Do you know if she's around?"

"I was talking to her earlier, Cally. She probably just drove into town. Is it something you can leave with me?"

"No, she has to sign for it. Thanks anyway, Dr. Hawthorne. I'll try again later."

"I saw her yesterday," Susan Raspin volunteered when I returned to the porch, "but not to talk to. She was going somewhere in her car. I think she has problems."

After a bit more chatting about the weather and the beauties of Chester Lake, Raspin and his wife moved on and I returned home too. Whatever the cause of Maud Hastings's illness, she seemed to have recovered now.

* * *

The following day, Tuesday, President Roosevelt announced he would run for a fourth term, bringing further grumbles from those who felt there should be term limits for the President. But the nation was behind him and few thought New York's Governor Dewey would be able to defeat him.

Annabel's assistant had phoned earlier with an emergency involving a dozen undernourished cats being kept by an elderly widow. "I have to go in to help her for an hour or two," she told me as she grabbed the key to our old Buick. "I'll be back as soon as I can."

"You'd better be! I don't want my son delivered at Annabel's Ark."

It was early afternoon when Mrs. Spring appeared at our door, wondering if anyone was home. "I'm right here," I called out, going to greet her. "My wife had to go in to the Ark."

"Was the mailman looking for me?" she asked.

"Cally Forbes? He had something yesterday you had to sign for. Said he'd be back later and try again."

"I must have been at the grocery store and missed him."

"Maybe he'll try again today. I haven't seen him yet this afternoon." I invited her in and offered her a cup of tea, which she accepted.

"That's very kind of you," she told me as I poured hot water over the tea bag. "Please call me Grace. I feel like an old lady having tea in the afternoon. Because I'm a widow, everyone feels sorry for me."

"Did your husband die in the war?"

"Nothing so dramatic. He died of cancer in prison. He'd been drinking and he killed a teenage girl with his car."

"I'm sorry."

"Don't worry. I'm not going to kill myself like last year's widow."

"I hope not."

"This tea tastes good."

I smiled and said, "I should have offered you a beer, but I'm not sure we have any."

I told her about my visit to Judge Hastings the previous day. "Apparently his wife had been ill, but she's better now. She came out on the porch and talked a bit."

"Maud imagines all sorts of things. She's no sicker than you or me. She's just looking for pity from her husband." She hesitated and then continued, "One night I caught her peering in the window of my cottage."

"Why would she do that?"

Grace Spring sighed. "Perhaps she thought I was entertaining the judge."

"Oh."

"I wasn't. I'd never do anything like that."

"I believe you."

Just then the telephone in the kitchen rang and I went to answer it. Annabel was on the phone, saying she'd be another hour at the Ark. "Are you all right?" I asked.

"Fine. I'll be home in an hour."

"Okay. Maybe we'll go out for dinner."

We chatted a few minutes longer and I heard Grace Spring call out, "I have to go now. Thanks for the tea." The screen door opened and closed before I could say goodbye.

Annabel came home shortly after five and I could see she was a bit tired. "Do you want to just rest?" I asked.

"No. I'm hungry. I just don't have the energy to make dinner for us."

"That's easily solved. We'll drive in to Max's Steakhouse. We haven't seen him in a few weeks anyway."

"Sounds good to me. He always has something I can eat. Call him and make sure he's got a table.

The night had grown and cooler and I decided to wear a jacket. While Annabel changed her clothes I locked and bolted the front door and made sure all the windows were latched, remembering Sheriff Lens's warning about burglaries. As we were exiting out the back door she spied the teacup and saucer I'd put in the sink. "What's this? Have you become a secret tea drinker?"

I chuckled. "Forgot to tell you, Grace Spring stopped by and I gave her some tea. She's had a hard life." I locked the back door as we left and I told her about Grace's visit as we drove into town.

"You're on a first-name basis with her now, I see."

"Yeah, Grace Spring is my secret lover."

"You never know. Things happen at summer cottages."

"They sure happen at ours. People commit suicide."

I swung into the Steakhouse parking lot. Max was glad to see us, as always, and asked if he could send over his usual bottle of wine. Annabel demurred and I settled for just one glass. It was a pleasant meal, and only Annabel's condition had us leaving earlier than usual. We drove by our house and stopped to pick up any mail that hadn't been forwarded to the cottage. It had just gotten dark by the time we returned to Chester Lake. I pulled up and parked behind the cottage, then helped Annabel out of the car and slid my key into the lock. It turned, but the door didn't open.

"What's the matter with this?" I asked.

"The inside bolt must be on."

"How could that be unless there's someone inside?"

We went around to the front door with the same results. "I threw the bolt on that myself," I said, "but the back door couldn't be bolted. The cottage was empty when we left."

There were no lights on and we could see nothing inside the darkened cottage. I went back to the car, took the flashlight I carried in the glove compartment, and shone it through the glass in the kitchen door. I could see nothing unusual and went around to one of the living room windows. Annabel started to follow me but I made her get back in the car and lock the doors. I didn't like the looks of this at all.

I took a moment to peer into the living room by the flashlight's glow, then shut it off and walked quickly next-door to Jerry Raspin's cottage, where a light was burning. "May I use your phone?" I asked Susan when she came to the door. "It's an emergency."

"Of course," she said, looking puzzled.

"What is it?" Jerry asked, but I didn't answer.

I gave the operator the sheriff's number and when he answered I spoke quickly. "I'm at our cottage. You'd better come out right away. It's locked but I looked through the window and I can see Grace Spring's body hanging from a hook in our ceiling."

Behind me, Susan Raspin screamed.

* * *

Sheriff Lens arrived with two deputies within fifteen minutes. "What is it, Doc?" He asked grimly.

"I've checked both doors and all the windows. They're all locked from the inside. I wanted you here to do the break-in. I could see from the angle of her neck that she's dead."

"Another suicide in this cabin?"

"That's what we're meant to think. But how did she get in?"

The sheriff smashed the glass in the kitchen door and pulled open the bolt so I could unlock the door with my key. Annabel was out of the car now, standing by my side, but I wouldn't allow her into the house. Once inside, I turned on the lights and confirmed that Mrs. Spring was dead. "Probably more than an hour ago," I guessed. I gave the sheriff a timetable of when we'd left for dinner and returned, then told him about the dead woman's visit that afternoon. Her teacup still sat in the sink.

"Nobody here," one of the deputies reported, finishing his search of the cottage. He even glanced in the tiny crawlspace behind the kitchen sink, removing a little stepladder I stored there.

Sheriff Lens looked over the scene, examining a footstool placed some three inches below her dangling feet. "Get some pictures of this before we cut her down. And fingerprints of the doorknobs and bolts, if I didn't smudge them too badly." He turned to me. "What do you think, Doc?"

"It's a poor attempt to make it look like suicide. The rope was one I had in the kitchen. She's too short to have stood on that stool and put the noose around her neck. Besides which, she assured me just this afternoon that she wasn't going to kill herself like last year's widow in this cottage."

"But how did she get in with the doors and windows locked, and if it's murder how did her killer get out?"

"I assume there are no tunnels in the basement," I replied.

"Heck, Doc, these cottages don't even have basements!"

I went over the locks carefully. They were the latest Yale models, each with individual keys, and Sheriff Lens assured me there was no chances of someone else's key opening my doors. Likewise, a careful inspection of all the windows showed no cracks or defective locks. I turned my attention briefly to the fireplace, but the flue was barely large enough for a squirrel. I know of trickery involving thread or fishing lines used to pull bolts shut from outside the room, but there was no space around the tight-fitting doors to allow such a stunt. I even considered the remote possibility that the hanging body itself might have been used to pull a string and slide a bolt closed, but there was no string in evidence and those door bolts didn't slide easily.

"I'm stumped," I admitted.

"Come on, Doc," the sheriff chided me. "You've solved cases a lot tougher than this one."

"Maybe it'll look better by daylight."

I watched while Grace Spring's body was cut down and removed for the autopsy. Only after the sheriff and his men had departed did I call next-door and allow Annabel to return from her safe haven at the Raspin's cottage. "Is it all right to stay here tonight?" I asked. "Or would you rather go back home?"

"I'll be fine here."

"When I phoned the sheriff to tell him about Grace's body, Susan Raspin screamed. She seemed to take the news very hard."

Annabel nodded. "She was still pretty shook up. Apparently she was close to Grace Spring. She said someone had been sending Grace threatening letters, almost like blackmail letters."

"Interesting." I thought about that bit of information. "But as the mystery writer Raymond Chandler once noted, blackmailers don't shoot. They have nothing to gain from killing off a source of income."

"What could a woman like Mrs. Spring have done that would cause her to be blackmailed?"

"Almost anything, I suppose. She told me her husband died in prison after a drunk-driving accident."

I checked all the doors and windows again, making certain they were locked and bolted before we went to bed. But sleeping wasn't easy. I kept thinking of Annabel at my side, only a week or so away from giving birth. Perhaps suicide cottage wasn't the best place for either of us.

* * *

I was up before eight, wandering around the little cottage, going through the kitchen to use the bathroom, and Annabel joined me a short time later. As I fixed breakfast for us, she remarked, "Maybe we should have slept at home. All I could think of was that woman hanging there, even though you wouldn't let me see her. I guess this really is the suicide cottage."

"That wasn't suicide. Someone killed her."

"Even with all the doors and windows locked?"

"She got in here somehow, and if she could get in, the killer could get out."

Sheriff Lens arrived a bit after nine o'clock looking as if he'd been up most of the night. "We have a preliminary autopsy report. Doc's still working on it, but there are finger marks on her throat. She was strangled before she was hanged."

"How terrible!" Annabel said with a compassionate tremor in her voice. "But why pick this cottage? Just because of its reputation for suicides?"

"Apparently." I told the sheriff, "Susan Raspin in the next cottage thinks Grace was being blackmailed."

"Her husband was convicted of drunk driving a few years back, but some folks thought he took the blame for her. Then he died in prison."

"She mentioned her husband when she was here yesterday, and apparently she told Susan Raspin she'd been threatened."

"I'll dig out the records and look into it. Are you two staying around here, Doc?"

"For now."

He left us then and I saw Judge Hastings coming over from his place. "Did he have any new information, Sam?"

"Not much. She was strangled before the killer hanged her, so it certainly wasn't suicide."

We sat on the porch for a bit discussing it while Annabel remained inside. "If there's a killer on the prowl, none of us are safe," he told me.

"Do you have any idea why someone might have been blackmailing Grace Spring? Maybe something about her husband's accident?"

He thought about it, rubbing his lean jaw. "I heard that case in my courtroom. There was a suspicion she'd been driving, but he took the blame and we had to accept that. A girl was killed and I had to give him prison time. We discovered later he knew he was dying of cancer and maybe that's why he was willing to take the blame."

A mailman came by carrying a leather sack. "Does your mail get delivered right to the cottages?" he asked us.

The judge shook his head. "There's a line of boxes across the road. You must be new to this route. Where's Cally Forbes?"

"He called in sick this morning. Long as I'm here I might as well give you the mail."

Judge Hastings accepted a couple of letters but the only thing for Annabel and me was a doctor's bill that I'd told Lincoln Jones to send us. "I'd better be getting back to Maud," the judge decided. "She's having a bad day."

"Anything I can help out with?"

"No, no. It's just—"

"Change of life?"

"Yes. Some women like Maud really suffer through it."

"There's a new medication that might help. Ask her to make an appointment with April at my office. I'd be happy to come in and examine her any time she wants."

"Thank you, Sam."

After he'd left I went back inside. Annabel was resting in one of the easy chairs when the phone rang. The cord was twisted awkwardly and it took me a moment to unwind it. Sheriff Lens was on the other end. "I don't have much on Grace Spring, Doc. I tried to track the parents of the girl who was killed in that accident but they live in Chicago. They were just here visiting the wife's brother when it happened."

I barely heard his words. I was staring at the telephone cord, trying to remember the last time we'd used it. I thought it was last night when I phoned Max's Steakhouse for a table. "Sheriff," I said quietly, "I think you'd better come over here."

"Who was that?" Annabel wondered, following me outside when I returned to the porch.

"Just Sheriff Lens. He had some new information about the dead woman. I suggested he take a ride over here."

"Are you getting anywhere with this?" she asked.

"Maybe."

I shifted the conversation to the weather, commenting on the cloudless blue sky and the comfortable temperature. She was so close to delivery that I didn't want to upset or frighten her in any way. When I saw the sheriff's car pull up behind the cottage I suggested she might go over to visit Susan Raspin, who'd come out onto her porch.

"What is it, Sam?" my wife asked. "Why don't you want me here?"

"I just thought you'd be more comfortable there."

"I'm staying," she said firmly. Annabel could be stubborn at times.

Sheriff Lens entered through the kitchen door, an expectant look on his face. "You've figured it out, haven't you, Doc?"

"I think so."

"Well, tell us!" my wife demanded. "Why are you so nervous about it?"

"All right," I said. "I think we've shown that Grace Spring couldn't have killed herself. And we've also shown that her killer couldn't possibly have left this cottage after he killed her. I think it was Sherlock Homes who once remarked that when you've excluded the impossible, whatever remains, however improbable, must be the truth."

"What are you saying, Doc?"

"The killer was here, and couldn't have left through the locked doors or windows. Therefore, the killer is still here."

The sheriff's hand dropped instinctively to the butt of his holstered revolver. "That's impossible."

"Is it? My first problem was how Grace Spring got in here in the first place. And why. I thought I'd heard her leave yesterday afternoon while I was on the phone with Annabel. She'd been drinking a cup of tea, but she called out she was leaving and I heard the screen door open and close. I noticed this morning that our phone cord was oddly twisted. Someone other than Annabel or me had used the phone after we left. That's when I started suspecting that Grace hadn't left at all. She'd hidden here and phoned her killer after we left for dinner. She'd heard me tell Annabel we'd probably go out for dinner and realized suicide cottage was the perfect setting for what she had in mind."

"And what was that?"

"She was going to kill her blackmailer and make it look like one more suicide."

"But where could she have hidden?" my wife asked. "This place isn't that big. Even the crawlspace behind the sink was too crowded with that ladder in it."

"She was a small woman. It only took her a moment while I was on the phone to partly open the foldaway bed in the living room and slip inside." Their eyes went to the sofa and I kept on talking. "Once we were gone she came out and phoned her blackmailer, arranging for him to meet her here on some pretext, probably promising him money. While she waited, she may have slipped out the back door and gone over to her cottage for a weapon. She was ready when he arrived, probably with a gun. That would be the most likely weapon to fake a suicide."

"You're saying the blackmailer killed her?" Sheriff Lens asked. "But if she had a gun why didn't she shoot him?"

"They must have struggled over it and he choked her to death. Once he'd done that, he strung her up to the ceiling hook in hopes we'd miss the finger marks on her throat. It would have been one more death in suicide cottage."

"Are you telling me that the killer took her place in the foldaway bed, that he's still there now?"

"That's just what I'm telling you. He figured we'd never spend the night here after finding the body, and once it was established as a suicide he'd simply walk out the back door. Only we stayed and he was trapped here."

That was when Sheriff Lens walked over and lifted the sofa seat to check inside. Maybe he thought my idea was too crazy to be true. Maybe it didn't occur to him that if I was right the killer might be in there with Grace's gun. As the foldaway bed opened and he came into view, he pointed the gun at me and Annabel did the craziest thing she'd ever done. She launched herself at him like a fury, baby and all. . . .

* * *

Old Dr. Sam finished his story and his drink. Looking into his listener's eyes, he said, "You were born that night, Samantha, one week early."

"And the killer was . . .?"

"Our postman, Cally Forbes, of course. He was small like Grace Spring and able to hide in there easily. He'd even gotten out of bed early that morning to use our phone and call in sick. He couldn't just leave, though, because we'd have discovered the unbolted door and known he'd been hiding. He was the uncle of the girl killed in the accident, and he was convinced Grace had been driving. She started paying him money, maybe out of a guilty conscience, but finally she decided she'd have to kill him. She lured him here after we went to dinner and was waiting with the gun. Most postmen have strong arms and he got the gun away from her, strangling her in the process. Then he found the rope, tied it around her throat to cover the bruises, and lifted her up to that hook with the aid of my stepladder. He put that away and only realized at the last minute she'd have needed something to stand on. He placed the stool there, not realizing in the near-darkness that it was too low."

Samantha shook her head in wonder. "Mom could have killed herself jumping at him like that. She could have killed me!"

"I guess that's why we never told you about it till now. You want another scotch?"

She pushed the long dark hair from her beautiful eyes and smiled. "No, let's go join Mom and the grandkids."

THE PROBLEM OF THE SUMMER SNOWMAN

Our new daughter Samantha was only seven weeks old (Dr. Sam Hawthorne was telling his visitor) when Northmont was hit with one of the most baffling murders I'd ever been called upon to solve. And in a way it was never solved. If you'll let me pour you a small libation, I'd be happy to tell you about it.

It was late August of 1944 and the war was going well on all fronts. Allied troops were on the outskirts of Paris, with the city expected to fall within days. Some of our local boys were even coming home on leave and I'd seen them around town. Annabel was back to work at the Ark, taking our daughter with her each day in a wicker basket. I couldn't imagine how she'd grow up after spending her early days in a veterinary hospital, but I knew with Annabel as her mother nothing dangerous would occur. We were already looking for someone to take care of her when she reached the toddler stage.

It was Annabel who mentioned Scott Grossman to me one night over dinner. With most young men off in the military, he was one of our town's few eligible bachelors. "We should find a nice young woman for him," she decided one evening after he'd brought his cat in for some minor ailment.

"What's the matter with him? How did he avoid the draft?"

"Some medical condition, I suppose. You don't ask questions like that, Sam. Any number of things might keep him out of the army, all the way from a punctured eardrum to homosexuality."

"If it's the latter, he doesn't need a nice young woman," I pointed out.

"Sam!"

Grossman was in his late thirties and lived alone with his cat, though he had a married brother and sister, both with families. He wasn't one of my patients, but in a town the size of Northmont we all pretty well knew each other. "What makes you so interested him all of a sudden?" I asked her.

"I don't know, he just seems like a nice guy. He told me he's planning a birthday party for his eight-year-old nephew on Saturday. Another nephew is home on leave from the navy."

"He'll be going back," I predicted. "The war's not over yet."

"They say once Paris falls, the German army will fall apart."

"I doubt that. They'll protect the fatherland at all costs."

I thought no more about Grossman until Saturday, when the radio news reported that Paris had fallen and American troops were marching up the Champs-Élysées. It was a great day, made even finer by a late-summer warmth that covered the area. I was relaxing on the porch while Annabel fed our daughter, and I thought nothing of it when Sheriff Lens pulled up in front in his patrol car.

"Enjoying the weather?" I called out to him.

"I was until a half-hour ago. Something's happened out at Scott Grossman's house, and I may need you if you're free."

"What is it, a medical problem?"

"Don't know. Some family members arrived for a birthday party and the house is locked up. They think they see someone on the floor through the kitchen curtains."

I told Annabel I was going with the sheriff, which prompted her to reply, "Please, no more locked rooms!"

We arrived at Grossman's small house on Dakota Street about ten minutes later to find a group of people standing out in front, all arrivals for the birthday party. Eight-year-old Todd was the star, restlessly waiting for the party to begin. His older brother Mitch, on leave from the navy but wearing civilian clothes, was trying to keep the birthday boy in tow. Young Todd's parents, Hugh and Vicky Grossman, looked increasingly concerned, and Grossman's sister Ethel was positively frantic. As I stepped from the sheriff's car she came running up to me, dragging along a small girl with blond curls who couldn't have been more than five years old.

"Dr. Sam, this is Amy Feathers. She lives two doors away in that green house. Tell the doctor what you saw, Amy."

The little girl looked up at me with wide blue eyes. "I saw a snowman," she said, "just for a second. He went into Mr. Grossman's house."

* * *

We broke the glass in the kitchen door and Mitch Grossman reached in to unlock the bolt. When we entered we found Scott's body on the kitchen floor, just inside the doorway to the living room. "Looks like a wound to the heart," I said. "Too big for a bullet. Probably a knife."

The children were kept outside in the care of Vicky Grossman while Sheriff Lens and I investigated. "Front and back doors both locked and bolted from the inside," the sheriff told me. "One side window open for some fresh air, but the screen is securely latched from the inside. No one went out that way."

"The neighbor girl says she saw a snowman go in."

"Sure, in August!"

"You may not like it, but she's our only witness."

"She might as well have said Santa Claus killed him. Any chance he lived long enough to bolt the door after his assailant left?"

I shook my head. "He was probably killed instantly. The autopsy should show a wound directly to the heart. Any sign of the weapon?"

Sheriff Lens shook his head. "Killer must have taken it with him."

I walked around the small living room, noting a few paperback western novels and an inexpensive chess set. A 12-inch world globe shared an end table with a crystal lamp that looked like an antique. I tried to think of what was missing, and then it came to me. "Where's the cat?" I asked.

"What?"

"Scott's cat. Annabel just treated it for an infection or something."

We searched around without luck, and finally I went upstairs to the tiny bedroom under the rafters. "Here she is," I called out as I opened the door and the cat came running to greet me. "I'm surprised he kept it up here." I bent to pet her a bit and then closed the door. It wouldn't do to have her down by the body. While I was upstairs I checked a small storage area, but there was no place big enough to hide even a midget. There was no sofa or fold-out bed that might have concealed the killer, and the house had no basement.

Sheriff Lens had noticed something on the living room carpet and was on his knees when I went back downstairs. "Look here, Doc. This big portion of the carpet is soaking wet. What do you make of that?"

I hated to say it, but I had no choice. "It's where the snowman melted, Sheriff. And probably the weapon too, if it was an icicle."

* * *

The family had gone home to celebrate Todd's birthday at his own house. "We can't let his uncle's death ruin his birthday," Vicky Grossman said, seemingly unmoved by her brother-in-law's murder. I promised to come over later, if only to cheer them up on this bleak day, but first I wanted to speak with the parents of little Amy Feathers. Her mother, Jeanette, was at home, and she let me in at once, wondering just what had happened two doors away.

"I'm afraid your neighbor has been killed," I told her.

She was a large woman, tending to overweight, and I hoped her daughter wouldn't grow up the same way. "Mr. Grossman? That's what Amy said, but I couldn't believe it."

I glanced through the parlor at the little girl playing with one of her dolls. "Does she often make up stories, Mrs. Feathers?"

"Amy? Not really. Sometimes when she's playing with her dolls she invents a little tale, like most girls her age, but she never lies to me."

"She said she saw a snowman going into the Grossman house."

"I know. I've tried to reason with her about that, telling her snowmen don't come out in the summer, but she insists that's what she saw."

"Could we take her out in the yard for a moment so she can show me where she was standing?"

"Certainly." She called her daughter, who came running, ready for a new adventure. Outside, she pointed across the adjoining yard toward Scott Grossman's house. "I was right here when I saw the snowman."

"There's a hedge in-between," I said. "You couldn't have seen his feet."

"No, but I saw the rest of him, especially his head."

"Could you draw us a picture of what you saw?"

"Sure," she agreed, eager to oblige. We went back in the house and she quickly drew a figure in white passing behind the hedge, with a big round head that could only have belonged to a snowman.

"Did he have eyes and a nose?" I asked.

She thought about that. "I didn't see any."

"Thank you, Amy. You've been a big help. And you too, Mrs. Feathers."

When we were out of Amy's earshot she asked quietly, "Was it a robbery?"

"At this point we don't know what it was. Did you happen to see anyone leaving his house?"

"No, but I wasn't looking that way. Out back I saw one of the high-school boys was running in his shorts and undershirt, and the woman down the street was walking her beagle. The local rubbish men were doing their usual Saturday pickup, and I pretty much keep my eye on Amy when she's in the yard alone."

"So you didn't happen to see a snowman."

She smiled. "I think you have to be a five-year-old to see one in this heat."

I left them and drove over to Hugh Grossman's house. He was on the phone, notifying friends and family of Scott's death. In the living room, his wife Vicky was doing her best to ensure that young Todd's birthday party wouldn't be completely ruined. Grossman's sister Ethel had been joined by her husband Pete Norris, a truck driver who'd parked his rig in front of the house.

"Has Sheriff Lens been here?" I asked Vicky.

"Not yet. He said he was coming as soon as they finished at the crime scene."The fact of Scott's death was finally getting through to her and I could see she was close to tears.

When I noticed Hugh was off the phone I went to speak with him. "Any idea who could have done this to your brother?"

"None at all. Most everyone in town liked Scott."

"Did he always keep his house locked up like that?"

"Not in this hot weather. Whoever killed him must have been afraid of being interrupted."

"Everyone has enemies, Hugh. Your brother must have had some too."

"Not outside the family."

I perked up. "What's that supposed to mean?"

Before he could answer, Sheriff Lens arrived with one of his deputies. Vicky hurried to intercept him, lest he dampen the celebration. Todd was busy playing a new game with his brother and seemed to take no notice of the sheriff.

"Am I in time for the birthday cake?" the sheriff asked Hugh.

Grossman smiled. "We'll always have a piece for you. Any news?"

"Nothing. The doorknobs and other likely surfaces were all wiped clean of prints."

Ethel Norris came over to join us. She was a slender woman who looked a bit like her brothers. "I don't know what you've been hearing, Sheriff, but I want you to know my husband wasn't even in town when Scott would have been killed. He just pulled in with his truck about a half-hour ago."

I remembered Hugh's remark of a moment earlier. "Was there trouble between them?"

She tossed her head as if dismissing my question, but then decided to answer it. "Pete's a truck driver. He's got a bum leg that kept him out of the service. Scott was always riding him about it, even though he'd never been in the army himself. It was such a little thing, but somehow it grew into a big thing."

"Not big enough for murder, surely."

"Of course not! I just wanted the sheriff to know."

She walked away and was immediately replaced by Vicky Grossman. "It's my son's eighth birthday, Sheriff, and it's been bad for everyone. Can't you save the questions till tomorrow?"

"All right," he agreed.

I followed him outside and we sat in his car for a while, talking about the case. "Any ideas?" I asked.

"Not a one. A snowman, or someone dressed as a snowman, entered Scott Grossman's house and stabbed him, then just melted away, leaving both doors bolted from the inside and a window screen latched from inside."

"Maybe the snowman didn't kill him," I suggested. "Maybe the snowman was Grossman himself."

"A suicide?"

"Well . . . then we'd have to explain the missing weapon. And what happened to the snowman costume? And why didn't anyone but that little girl notice a snowman?"

"You always make everything so difficult, Doc."

"I merely smiled. "Guess I'll head home and see how Samantha's doing."

"That's a wonderful name. It makes me smile when I say it."

"Me too."

* * *

In the morning Annabel insisted we go to church. I'd never been a regular Sunday churchgoer, but since our marriage I've gone with her more frequently. "We have to think about the baptism," she said. "And godparents."

"I'd want my nurse April as godmother," I decided. "I'm godfather to her son, whom she named after me."

"Fine. How about Max for godfather?" Max Fortesque was our favorite restaurateur, owner of Max's Steakhouse, where we'd held our wedding reception.

I smiled. "That was quickly settled. If the minister's around maybe we can set the date."

"What about Scott Grossman's murder? Any leads?"

"Sure. It was supposed to be his nephew Todd's eighth birthday party. A neighbor girl thought she saw a snowman entering the house. Of course she didn't, but what did she see? Someone in a snowman costume that no one else noticed? And how'd the killer get out of the house?" I ran over what few details we knew.

"No one else was there?"

"No one except the cat in an upstairs bedroom. I don't know why Scott put her up there."

"I can answer that," Annabel said. "You said he was having a party for young Todd. Scott mentioned once that Todd's allergic to cats. It's something that runs in that branch of the family."

"Do you know anything about Ethel's husband, the truck driver?"

"Pete Norris? I've never really met him, but I see him around. Sort of a loudmouth at times. I heard he and Scott had a skirmish at a family picnic last month."

"Anyone else who might have had reason to kill Scott?"

"No. Far as I know he didn't have any girlfriends who could feel jealous or jilted. If he did, he certainly kept it quiet."

After the service we spoke to Reverend Charters about the baptism and arranged a date for it. As we were about to leave he asked me, "Are you helping Sheriff Lens with the Grossman killing?"

"We talked about it," I admitted. "Did you know Scott?"

"I know the whole family. I'll be doing the funeral service on Wednesday. Hugh and Vicky are parishioners, though I don't see them too often."

When we returned home I phoned the sheriff and learned that the autopsy was complete and Scott's body had been released to the funeral parlor. "It was a wide blade," he told me. "Most likely one of the kitchen knives, but we haven't found it yet. Went right to the heart. He'd been dead about two hours when we found him."

"I'd better go over and see the family," I decided.

It was a glum gathering at Hugh and Vicky's house as they waited for the visiting hours that evening. Mitch was doing his best to keep the conversation going with stories about the war in the Pacific. Young Todd was all ears, asking him about the naval battles he'd seen. Mitch was a handsome lad, looking as if he should still be in school rather than fighting a war half a world away. "In June I was on an escort carrier off Saipan," he told us. "When my leave is over I have to go back to San Diego for a new assignment."

Too old for the draft, and never having served in the military, it was difficult for me to imagine what it must be like. The constant stress of warfare, with enemy planes and submarines on the prowl, would have to be unnerving even on shipboard where one was never face to face with the enemy.

"I hope the war is still on when I'm old enough to fight," Todd told them after listening to his brother's adventures.

I prayed he'd never know what war was really like.

* * *

Annabel and I went to the funeral parlor that evening. In those days it was common for the deceased to be laid out for viewing two or three days before the funeral. On our way out, Vicky who spoke to my wife about the dead man's cat. "Her name is just Meow," she said. "Do you know a family that might like her? We'd take her ourselves, but with the boys' allergies—"

Annabel glanced at me. "We could take her for a time, until I hear of a family that would like a cat. She's a beauty."

I feared this might be the beginning of a permanent relationship, especially when Samantha grew a bit older, but I readily agreed.

"We'll be glad to take her. Where is she now?"

Vicky called to her sister-in-law. "Ethel, you have Meow, don't you?"

Ethel Norris joined us. "Sure. Have you found a home for her?"

"Dr. Sam and Annabel will take her for now."

"That's great. She's at our house. We'll be out of here at nine and you can come pick her up then if you'd like."

It was only twenty-five minutes, so we decided to wait. The Reverend Charters came by to lead a few prayers, and just before nine Jeanette Feathers slipped in. "Amy's home with her father," she told us, "but I thought I should pay my respects. Scott was a good neighbor."

"Did he ever have Amy over to his house?"

"Oh no, I don't allow her to go in neighbors' houses unless I'm along. But he was always pleasant when he saw her playing in our yard."

Todd had been spared the rigors of the funeral home, but his brother Mitch was there in his blue uniform, helping to greet the mourners. "When do you go back?" I asked him.

"After the funeral. The escort carrier I've been assigned to will be sailing from San Diego next week." He grinned. "But I probably shouldn't be telling you that. Military secret."

"It's safe with me," I assured him.

His father, Hugh, came over to join us. "Doesn't he look great in his uniform? His mother and I are so proud of him. It's too bad this terrible tragedy had to spoil his leave time."

"Any idea what might have happened to your brother?" I asked Hugh.

"I suppose it was a robbery. He didn't have an enemy in the world."

"The doors were all locked from the inside, and the window screen was fastened from inside, too. He may have let the killer in, but there was no way for him to get out." I thought it best not to mention the snowman at this point.

"I hate to suggest it, but might he have committed suicide?"

"Had he ever hinted at it?"

"No, but sometimes he was depressed."

"What does your sister think?"

He snorted. "Ethel is just anxious to tell everyone that Pete was out of town when it happened."

"We're going over there now to pick up Scott's cat. Annabel and I will take care of it till we find it a proper home."

"That's good of you. Meow was Scott's only companion."

We followed Ethel and Pete from the funeral parlor to their modest home on the north side of town. "The rest of the family is coming over for a short while too," she told us. "Vicky just has to pick up Todd at a neighbor's house."

When the family was assembled and Annabel was renewing her acquaintance with Meow, I went over to talk with young Todd.

"How was your birthday party?" I asked casually.

"Good, I guess. But I was sad for Uncle Scott."

"Did you see him often?"

"Sure. Sometimes he took care of me when Mom and Dad went out somewhere."

"Did you like him?"

He nodded. "We played games together."

"Did you get lots of good gifts for your birthday?"

"Mom and Dad gave me a bike, and Aunt Ethel and Uncle Pete gave me an Erector Set."

"Do you like to build snowmen in the winter?"

He grinned. "Sure, when there's enough snow."

"Did you ever see a snowman in the summertime?" I asked.

"Of course not! They'd melt!"

"Do you know that little girl, Amy, who lives near your uncle Scott?"

"I don't have much to do with girls," he told me. "I see her playing sometimes when I'm over there."

Annabel and I left a short time later with Meow. "She's a cute little thing," my wife said, holding the cat up for a closer look. "But maybe we'll come up with a better name for her."

* * *

On Monday, our good weather gave way to an overcast day with a threat of rain. I'd awakened that morning with an idea about the snowman murder, as I thought of it, and all through breakfast the idea gnawed at me. I phoned the office and told April I might be a bit late coming in.

Annabel and little Samantha had already left for the Ark when I drove over to Dakota Street once more. This time I wasn't interested in Scott Grossman's house so much as the contents of the backyard rubbish cans belonging to his neighbors. I'd checked a half-dozen of the closest ones when Jeanette Feathers appeared on the scene.

"Oh, it's you, Dr. Hawthorne. I saw someone looking through the rubbish and wondered what was going on."

"Pardon me, Jeanette. I should have asked you first. But the rubbish cans all seem to be empty."

"Sure. They pick it up here on Saturday afternoons."

"Of course. I should have remembered that."

"Want to come in for a cup of coffee?"

"Afraid I'm too busy for that today, but thanks for the invitation."

I headed out to the town dump, knowing it was a hopeless task. My Buick was beginning to sputter a bit and I only hoped it would last through another year. As a physician I had a high priority for a new car when one was available, but I hated to take one away from someone with an even greater need.

At the dump I asked the workers where I might find Saturday's rubbish. "You lose something?" one of them asked. "Hard to find anything in this mess."

"It would be a flat parcel, not too large, wrapped in white paper."

"What part of town did it come from?"

"Around Dakota Street."

"Saturday, you say?"

"That's right."

He led me over to the right side of the dump. "It would probably be somewhere in here. Nothing got picked up yesterday so it should be near the top."

I pawed through the mess for about fifteen minutes, pretty much convinced that I wouldn't find a thing. Then I spotted a bit of white paper such as butchers might use to wrap meat. I held my breath and tugged at it.

"Find what you're looking for?" the workman asked as I carefully unwrapped the paper.

"Yes," I said, barely able to speak. "This is it. Thanks for your help."

* * *

Late that afternoon, Sheriff Lens and I paid another visit to the funeral parlor. A restful smoking room was provided downstairs for family members and friends to take a breather from the upstairs commotion, and it was here that we found Mitch Grossman in his navy uniform. His face buried in his hands, and I knew at once that this most baffling of mysteries had reached its conclusion.

"Do you want to tell us about it, Mitch?" I asked quietly, sitting down beside him.

"What, Doc?"

I opened my medical bag and took out the parcel wrapped in white paper. "We have this," I said. "Do you want to tell us what happened?"

He was aghast at the sight of it, throwing up his hands as if to ward off some unspeakable horror. "How could you have that? How?"

"I dug around at the town dump until I found it." I unfolded the white paper and showed him the white summer uniform he'd been wearing on Saturday. Across the front was a telltale splatter of dried blood. "Why did you kill your uncle, Mitch?"

"God help me, I had no other choice."

"Tell us about it," Sheriff Lens urged.

"From the time I was eleven or twelve, he'd been—I don't know, putting his hands on me, things like that. He wanted me to do things."

"Did you tell your parents?" the sheriff asked.

"How could I? He was my father's brother. They'd have said I was imagining it."

"What happened Saturday?"

"He was having the birthday party for Todd and he suggested I come by early, before the party, so we could chat. I should have known what he wanted, but I'd been away. I thought he was over that. I arrived with my birthday gift for Todd, and he started in again, like I'd never been away. I told him to stop it. We were standing in the kitchen doorway and he said something about Todd, how in a few more years Todd would be old enough. I—I just went crazy. I grabbed up one of the kitchen knives and drove it into his chest."

That was all. He started sobbing and I knew the rest of the story would be up to me. "Tell us how you knew, Doc," the sheriff said.

"There were two things, the killer's entrance and his exit. The entrance, apparently, was observed by five-year-old Amy Feathers down the street. She had only an instant's glimpse, but she thought she saw a snowman. She even drew us a picture of his big round head. Of course it was no snowman in August, so I asked myself what it might have been. Could one of the birthday guests have arrived early with a gift? There were no white spheres in evidence in Scott's house, but there was twelve-inch globe, positioned rather awkwardly on an end table with an antique lamp. It seemed the perfect gift to an eight-year-old boy from his brother in the navy far away."

"You mean Mitch arrived with the globe on his head?"

"On his shoulder, actually. Right, Mitch? it was large enough to block out your head when seen from the side, wrapped in white paper. Little Amy's quick glimpse saw a figure in white with a globular white head. A snowman, of course, to someone with her limited experience."

"But why did he unwrap the birthday gift?" Sheriff Lens wanted to know. "He didn't need that globe for anything.."

"He didn't need the globe, but he needed the paper." I gestured toward the parcel in front of me. "Scott's blood splattered on his white uniform, and he couldn't leave the house wearing it. In those moments after the killing he was still hoping to cover up the crime and hide the body."

"What about the large area of wet carpet?"

I smiled slightly. "Where you thought the snowman melted? He was merely washing the blood from the carpet. Maybe he had some crazy idea of getting the body out of there before it was found. That was impossible, of course. He dragged the body into the kitchen, washed off the knife, washed the blood from the carpet, and took off his uniform."

"What? Are you telling me he left the house naked?"

"Of course not. He wrapped the bloody uniform in that white paper and ran out the back door, depositing it in one of the rubbish cans waiting to be empties. Then he simply kept running home in his shorts and undershirt. With his boyish face, at least one neighbor mistook him for a high-school boy, perhaps practicing for the track team."

"That back door was bolted from the inside," Sheriff Lens reminded me.

"Not when he left, it wasn't. You're forgetting it was Mitch who reached through the broken glass in the door, supposedly to unbolt it. He covered the fact that it was unbolted all along, and provided us with a seemingly impossible murder. He was the only one who could have faked it, and once I realized that the rest of it started falling in place. Another element was the cat. Why did Scott have to lock it away two hours or more before young Todd would arrive? Because his brother Mitch was allergic too, and he was arriving earlier."

Sheriff Lens took a deep breath. "I'm sorry, Mitch, but I'm going to have to arrest you."

I saw the anguish in his face, an anguish the sheriff and I both felt too. "Couldn't it have been suicide after all, Sheriff?" I asked. "Will this make it any easier on the family if his motive comes out?"

"What about the weapon?"

"We found it under the stove."

"But I searched—" Then he stopped and peered at the young man, still so close to being a boy. "When did you say you were due back?"

"I'm supposed to leave right after the funeral on Wednesday."

Sheriff Lens glanced in my direction. "You're getting a second chance, son," he told Mitch Grossman. "Make good use of it."

To the people of Northmont, the death of Scott Grossman became a suicide. But the ways of the gods are strange at times. Two months later, on October 26th, Mitch Grossman was killed in action when one of the first Kamikaze suicide flights hit his escort carrier in the sea off the Philippines.

THE PROBLEM OF THE SECRET PATIENT

In Northmont, we'd felt the effects of the war from the beginning, through the lives of our half-dozen brave local boys who'd died in combat (Dr. Sam Hawthorne was telling his visitor as he poured a small libation for them both), but it was in October of 'forty-four that the war really came home to our town, in a strange way that's been kept secret for all these years.

It started for me when I was visited at my office one gloomy October Monday by a well-dressed young man with chiseled features who introduced himself as Robert Barnovich. He was probably in his thirties and I wondered why he wasn't in the service. "What seems to be your problem?" I asked. He didn't look or dress like a local and my first thought was that he'd been stricken ill while on the road.

"No health problem, Dr. Hawthorne." He flipped open a card case and showed me a badge and photo ID. "Special Agent Barnovich of the FBI."

"Well!" was all I could think to say.

He smiled. "Don't worry, you're not under arrest. I've been sent to discuss a situation that will be arising here in two days' time. You understand this is top secret. The hospital administration knows, of course, and I'm telling you because your office is here at Pilgrim Memorial and you're likely to be consulted on the case. Also, you've been cleared through a background check. We're bringing in a secret patient from overseas. He's had certain injuries that are not believed to be life-threatening. He'll arrive here with his head and face bandaged, partly because of the injuries but also to keep his identity secret."

"Is it Hitler?" I asked with a smile.

The FBI man's face remained grim. "It is not Hitler, but that's all I can say. He'll be well guarded during his stay, but not a word of this is to leak out. Is that understood?"

"I suppose so. But why in heaven's name are you bringing him to Pilgrim Memorial rather than one of the big government hospitals?"

"The decision was made after careful study. The government wanted an East Coast hospital that was easier to reach from Europe. And they wanted a first-rate small-town hospital where a secret patient wasn't likely to attract the attention of the media. I told the Surgeon General I considered the attributes of ten small East Coast hospitals before settling on Pilgrim Memorial."

"I suppose we should be honored at that. Tell me one thing. Does this patient speak and understand English?"

"To some extent, yes. That's all I can say."

"And he'll arrive on Wednesday the eighteenth?"

"That's correct."

"Will you be here?"

He gave a brief nod. "I'll be here with my men as long as he is."

* * *

That night over dinner I told Annabel about it. Samantha was three months old now and Annabel was back to work at the Ark a few hours a day, taking our daughter with her. Soon she hoped to be back full time, and we'd need someone to take care of Samantha. But not yet.

"What does it mean, Sam? A captured Nazi that they're flying over here?"

"I don't know. It's someone important, with the FBI involved."

"I'm glad to know you passed the background check. They probably don't know you tell your wife everything."

"You needed to know," I answered defensively. "I might have to work overtime some nights."

The war news that weekend had reported the death of Field Marshal Erwin Rommel three months after his supposed injury in an auto accident. We'd known for some time that his head injuries were actually caused by Allied planes strafing his staff car in July. Rommel had been friendly with the generals behind the failed plot to assassinate Hitler, and some rumors even had him taking command of the country if the plot had succeeded. But now, with his death, a state funeral was planned.

"Would it have made any difference if Hitler had been killed?" Annabel had wondered back in July when the news broke.

"Germany might have surrendered rather than fight to the death as they're doing now." With the conspirators dead and a half-crazed Hitler still in control, the inevitable Allied victory stretched further into the future.

Tuesday morning was a quiet day at the hospital, but from my office wing I could detect preparations being made for the new arrival. Lincoln Jones, the black doctor who'd delivered our baby, stopped by the office to ask how Samantha was doing. After I told him all was well and Samantha was even accompanying my wife to work a few hours each day, Lincoln asked, "What's going on at the hospital? They've closed off several rooms at the end of the south corridor and are moving in some equipment."

"It's all very hush-hush," I confirmed. "Some sort of secret patient is arriving tomorrow. The FBI's in charge."

"Why here?"

"They wanted a good small hospital on the East Coast. I suppose we should consider it a compliment."

"Are you involved, Sam?"

I was told they might call on me."

"Who do you think it is?"

"I've a hunch it might be some top Nazi prisoner, but the FBI assured me it's not Hitler."

Lincoln Jones gave a familiar grunt. "And what will your job be? To cure him or kill him?"

* * *

It was Dr. Dwight Pryor, the hospital administrator, who came to my office on Wednesday morning. He was a gaunt, well-dressed man with glasses and a moustache, who rarely wore the white jacket that was the uniform of other staff physicians. I barely knew the man, and his only other visit to my office had come when he first took over as administrator and visited all the doctors with offices in the building.

"Dr. Pryor," I said, rising to shake his hand. "You're a rare visitor to our wing of the building."

He sat down without being asked. "You and Dr. Jones have your own practices; you're not part of the hospital's staff. But with this new situation I thought I should speak with you. I understand Special Agent Barnovich has already filled you in on the basics."

"Somewhat. I know we're receiving some sort of secret patient today."

"Correct, and that's about all I know, too. He's going to be under close supervision during his stay here, which I understand will be only a matter of a few days. If his health is satisfactory he'll be transferred elsewhere."

"Is there anything I can do to help?"

"Dr. Francis will be examining him, and he will call on you if needed. While the patient is at Pilgrim Memorial he will be known as Mr. Fuchs."

"A German name."

"Yes, but that means nothing."

After he left I called my nurse April into my office and told her what little I knew. With her husband still away in the service, she was anxious to help in any way she could. "I just want to get André back home in one piece," she told me. "Do you think this might be some important Nazi who will reveal information?"

"I have no idea," I answered honestly. "But while he's here I want you to be able to reach me at all times. Whenever I'm out of the office you'll have a phone number where I can be contacted."

She glanced out my window. "It looks as if the mystery man is arriving now."

Sure enough, an ambulance had pulled up to the hospital's emergency entrance and a patient on a stretcher was being removed. I could see his bandaged head, and a couple of men in suits accompanying him. I recognized one as Agent Barnovich. "I'd better go out to greet them," I said.

Dr. Pryor was there too, and Judd Francis, the primary physician on the case. I knew him socially, and he'd treated a couple of my patients with head injuries, his specialty. "What's up, Judd?" I asked him. "Your mysterious patient arriving?"

"Hello, Sam. Yeah, he's here. I'll probably be calling on you to check his vital signs. I'll be examining his head injury to see how it's healing. I've got some free time now if you want to get started."

He nodded. "Let's do it. The faster we give him a clean bill the sooner he'll be out of here, along with his keepers." He nodded toward the FBI agents.

"Any idea who he is?"

He shook his head. "He's just a patient. I don't ask questions. Come in with me while we take off the bandages. Then you'll know as much as I do."

Special Agent Barnovich and his team were careful to search everyone entering the patient's room and to check all food, water, and medication. It seemed they feared someone might try to kill him.

After we'd passed inspection, I stood by the bed while the patient had his head bandages carefully removed by Dr. Francis. One of the FBI men was at the door, his back to us. The face that came into view was that of a ruggedly handsome man in his fifties with his head shaved for treatment of wounds. The man opened his eyes and Judd Francis asked, "Do you understand English?"

"Some," the man answered, shifting slightly in his bed. "Where am I?"

"You're in America, in a place called Northmont. They brought you here for a medical checkup before you move on."

"I see," he muttered and closed his eyes. I wondered if he'd been drugged.

"I'm Dr. Francis and this is Dr. Hawthorne. We'll be examining you for the next few days. My nurse, Marcia O'Toole, will be looking after you, too. What can you tell me about these head wounds, Mr. Fuchs?" It was the first time he'd used the patient's supposed name.

"Fuchs?" the man repeated with a half chuckle. "Is that the name they gave me?"

"Yes."

"It is as good as any, I suppose. The head wounds came about three months ago when my car was strafed by an enemy plane."

"I see. They seem to have healed well."

"I still have frequent headaches."

"How frequent?"

"A few times a week."

"That's probably normal, but we'll X-ray you. I'm the head man around here." It was a line he loved to use. "Dr. Hawthorne will handle the rest of your body."

The jokes were lost on Fuchs, who remained silent. It was a good time for me to escape. "I'll be in to see you later," I promised the patient.

On the way out I stopped to see Marcia O'Toole, the nurse who'd been assigned to him. She was an attractive young woman in her mid-twenties who'd lost an older brother to the war in North Africa. I didn't know her well, but we'd chatted a few times. "I understand you'll be helping with our new patient," I said.

"That's what I hear. I've already got that G-man Barnovich breathing down my neck."

"Don't mind him. He's just doing his job."

She laughed. "He's doing more than his job. He asked me for a date."

* * *

That night at home Annabel quizzed me about Fuchs. "Who is he?" she wanted to know. "A German prisoner?"

"Perhaps. He spoke his few words of English with a German accent. They must think he has important information if the FBI is guarding him so carefully."

"You said Judd Francis is the attending physician?"

I nodded. "Because of the head injury, which is pretty well healed now. Judd did a thorough examination of his head and neck. At first I was only going to be on call if they needed me, but somehow I've gotten the job of giving him a complete physical."

My wife smiled. "The FBI checked you out and decided you were trustworthy."

"That may be the answer. I'll be examining him in the morning and maybe I'll learn something."

I stopped at my office the following morning to tell April I'd be in the hospital examining Mr. Fuchs for the next few hours. When I entered his room Marcia O'Toole was washing him and brushing his teeth. "He's still weak but he's coming along, aren't you, Mr. Fuchs?"

"Ah . . . yes," he managed between brushings, still a bit dazed from his medication.

"The sun's out today. Maybe later I can wheel you outside for a bit," Nurse O'Toole said, flipping her brown hair as she spoke, almost as if she was flirting with him. But I'd seen her do the same thing with doctors and other patients.

When she'd finished the clean-up I took over, checking his pulse and temperature and blood pressure, asking him all the routine questions about his health. He told me his age was fifty-two, that he'd be fifty-three the following month. We talked a bit, and though he admitted to being German he said nothing about the circumstances that had brought him here under FBI guard. Once he asked me, "What day is this?"

"Thursday, October nineteenth," I replied.

"Is that all? It seems it should be so much later." The more he spoke the easier it was for me to understand his accent.

"You seem in pretty good shape. I think we'll be able to send you on your way soon."

"To where?"

"That's not for me to say."

The following day, when we were alone, he engaged me in further conversation. "How long will I be here?" he asked after I'd checked his temperature and the usual vital signs.

"Perhaps only another day. Dr. Pryor, the hospital administrator, is anxious to get things back to normal."

"I am disrupting your routine?"

"Not you, but the FBI certainly is."

"For that I regret."

"You're an important person. They must guard you well."

"I am not important," he said quietly. "I am dead."

Before I could ask him what he meant, we were interrupted by Barnovich, the FBI man. "You about done in there, Doc? I have to speak with Mr. Fuchs."

"Just finishing up," I said, and retreated from the room.

Dr. Pryor visited my office after lunch to see how things were going. "Have you completed your examinations, Sam?"

"All but the blood tests. I'll have those results in the morning."

"Good! Judd Francis has cleared him as far as the head wounds are concerned."

"Where will he be going next?"

Pryor lowered his voice. "The rumor is that he'll be taken to Shangri-La to meet with the President."

"Where?"

"It's a secret camp somewhere in the Maryland hills where FDR goes to get away from Washington."

"He's that important a person?"

"Apparently."

"I'll have the blood results in the morning," I assured him. Saturday morning was my last opportunity to speak with the patient, and I took advantage of it. Barnovich was on duty at the door, but he seemed more interested in flirting with Nurse O'Toole than in paying attention to what we were talking about.

"Tell me what happened to you," I urged my patient. "You'll probably be gone by the end of the day and we'll never see each other again. The rumor is that you're on your way to meet our President."

Fuchs gazed at me sadly. "You are a good doctor. You treat me well. What is today? Saturday? I will tell you what happened. They came to my house a week ago today, men whom I thought to be my friends. After the unsuccessful plot to kill the *Führer* in July, many of us were suspect. Because of my wounds they left me alone for a time, but then last week they came. I was never part of the plot, but I did know about it in advance. That was enough to condemn me. I was given a choice–a tiny cyanide capsule that would kill me in three seconds, or a trial for treason that would ruin my family. The cyanide was my only true choice. I went off with them in a car to the place where I would swallow the capsule. All left me except one man who had been my friend. I held the tiny capsule in my hand."

"But how did you–?"

"Escape? If that is what this is. The man was still my friend. He drove me over a dirt road to a field where a small unmarked plane was waiting. What he did may have cost him his life, but I am eternally grateful. Of course the government could not report my defection to the Allied side. They announced that I had finally died from my accident injuries, and a state funeral was planned." He smiled sadly.

"A funeral without a corpse."

"Tell me who you are."

He shook his head. "Call me Fuchs. My real name is unimportant."

I held out my hand to shake his. "Good luck, wherever they take you."

"I will remember your kindness, Dr. Hawthorne. We are all on this earth together. It is only politics that sometimes makes enemies of us."

Those were the last words our secret patient ever spoke to me. I was awakened during the night with news that he was dead.

* * *

It was not yet dawn when I reached the hospital, but already Sheriff Lens was on the scene. I hadn't been told the cause of death, and his presence alarmed me. "Are you here about the death of a man named Fuchs?" I asked.

"Guess so, Doc. The boss, Dr. Pryor, reported it as a possible poisoning."

"I can't imagine that. He was being guarded by a team of FBI agents."

"We'll see."

The first person we encountered inside the hospital was Agent Barnovich, looking flustered and frightened. "It couldn't have happened," he told us. "No one could have poisoned him. We tested every bit of food and drink that went into that room."

"We'll want to talk with Dr. Pryor first," Sheriff Lens told him. We found the hospital administrator breathless in the corridor outside the room occupied by Fuchs. "What happened?" I asked.

"We don't know. Dr. Francis was in the emergency room with an accident victim a little after three o'clock. He decided to stop in and see if Fuchs was sleeping well. Barnovich was outside by the door and they checked him together. They found him dead. There was an odor of bitter almonds—"

"Cyanide?"

"We're doing an immediate autopsy. That's what we suspect."

Sheriff Lens turned to me. "What do you think, Doc?"

I turned to Agent Barnovich. "Were you on duty here all night?"

"I was."

"Did you keep a log of everyone who entered the patient's room?"

"Of course."

"We'd better take a look at that."

Dr. Pryor interrupted. "I want it known that no cyanide in any form is kept at Pilgrim Memorial. We have no medical need for it here. If someone killed Fuchs, he brought the poison in with him."

"Let's go in your office and talk this over," I suggested. Pryor led the way to his office with Barnovich, the sheriff, and me following.

Within minutes Judd Francis joined us. "I can't believe this could happen," he said as he took a chair in the administrator's office.

"Who even knew he was here?"

"We're working on that," Sheriff Lens told him. "First I'd better know the identity of this mystery patient."

"We don't know," Dr. Pryor insisted. "You'd better ask the FBI that question."

The sheriff turned to Agent Barnovich, who held up his hands. "I only know he was an important German, flown out of there last Saturday night. Maybe he was a defector, like Rudolph Hess."

"But no name?"

"No name, only Mr. Fuchs."

"Have you notified Washington of his death?"

"Of course. They're awaiting further news."

"What sort of news?" I asked.

"I haven't told them he may have been poisoned. I wanted to be sure of it first."

He handed me the FBI log and I ran my finger down the list of everyone who'd visited the patient after I'd left. Dr. Pryor had been in to see him at a few minutes before six. "I wanted him gone from here as soon as possible," the administrator told us. "His presence was disrupting the hospital routine, and since the entire matter was top secret we couldn't even profit from the publicity."

"Were you searched when you came to visit him?" I wondered, remembering the cursory inspection I'd received from the government agents.

"I was," Pryor acknowledged.

"So was I," Judd Francis told us. "I came by around eight o'clock and our patient seemed to be resting comfortably. His throat was dry and I had Nurse O'Toole bring him some ice water."

Sheriff Lens raised his eyebrows but Barnovich quickly said, "I tasted it, just like we tasted every scrap of food and drink that he had. And after I tasted it he took a couple of swallows himself. Nothing but water."

"No one else visited him?"

"The nurse came back to check his blood pressure around midnight but I was with her. He was half asleep then, and only wanted to know when he'd be out of here. I told him soon."

"Did you kill him?" Sheriff Lens asked the FBI man.

"Me? Of course not! What motive would I have?"

"He was an enemy. A German."

"But he was over here now. He'd left Germany."

"Perhaps that's why he was killed," Dr. Pryor speculated. "To keep him from revealing Nazi secrets to our side."

I smiled at the suggestion. "Do you think there's a Nazi agent at Pilgrim Memorial Hospital?"

"Well, somebody killed him."

I turned back to Barnovich. "Let's go over this again, step by step. I assume Fuchs was carefully searched when he arrived here."

"Right down to the skin," the FBI man said. "They put their own hospital garments on him here. And he had no possessions at all with him. His own clothes had been taken away in England, before he was flown here, to avoid any trace of his identity."

"And no one at Pilgrim Memorial had access to cyanide?"

"No one," Dr. Pryor insisted. "Of course, cyanide is a gas. The solid state is usually potassium cyanide. It can kill almost instantly if swallowed on an empty stomach, where the stomach acids quickly turn it back into a gas."

"Three seconds," I murmured, remembering what Fuchs had told me. "And no one was in the room when he died?"

Barnovich shook his head. "I was on a chair right outside his door. No one entered the room after my midnight visit. I went back outside and partly closed the door to his room."

"There are no other exit doors, of course, and no one was in the bathroom," Judd Francis said. "Before I realized he was dead I took his water glass to the sink to refill it. The bathroom was empty."

"We need to pin down the time of his death," I decided. "That might help."

Pryor nodded. "We'll have the preliminary autopsy report by morning."

* * *

Annabel was up with Samantha when I returned home and I told her what had happened. "Who do you think he was, Sam? Someone important enough he had to be murdered?"

"I have to see the autopsy report this morning and talk to some more of the staff."

"How could anyone have gotten into the room to poison him, and why would they want to?"

"That's what I need to find out."

"Why you, Sam? The FBI is on the case."

"The FBI is one of the suspects."

I tried to get a couple of hours' sleep, but I was up before eight and on my way back to Pilgrim Memorial. Judd Francis was waiting at my office with the autopsy results. "These are just preliminary, Sam, but it was cyanide as we suspected. He'd been dead about three to four hours when the coroner examined the body around five, which means he died somewhere between one and two, near as we can tell."

"Thanks, Judd." I glanced through the report and handed it back. "So the last people to enter his room were Agent Barnovich and Nurse O'Toole around midnight. I'll have to talk with them."

"Marcia doesn't come back on duty until noon, and the FBI is calling back its guard detail now that Fuchs is dead."

"I'd better try to catch Barnovich, then."

He was indeed preparing to leave. "No reason to stay," he told me.

"Isn't solving this murder reason enough?"

He sighed. "Look, Dr. Hawthorne, guarding this man was an FBI assignment. Solving his murder is something for the local police, unless you can show me that a federal law was violated."

He had me there. "Tell me about your midnight visit to the patient's bedside."

"Nurse O'Toole wanted to check his blood pressure and pulse before she went off duty. I guess that's the standard procedure here. I went in with her and stood by the bedside. She asked if he needed anything and he said no."

"He didn't request a sleeping pill or anything like that?"

"No, and she gave him nothing. We were only in there about two minutes and we left nothing behind. I said good night to her and went back to my chair."

"When were you due to be relieved?"

"Not till six A.M. I had the night shift."

"Will you be leaving today?"

He nodded. "Most of my men have already departed. I want to get some sleep first before I drive up to Boston."

"I'll see you before you go," I told him.

It was Sunday and I had no patients to see. By noon I arranged to be on Marcia O'Toole's floor when she came on duty. "I just heard what happened to Mr. Fuchs," she said when she saw me.

"That FBI man, Barnovich, says you two went in there at midnight and he was still alive."

She nodded, her brown hair bobbing. "I checked his signs and asked if he needed more water but he said he was fine. I expected he'd be gone by today, but not like this."

"Did Barnovich touch him or move him in any way?"

"Not while I was there. Why would an FBI agent want to kill him?"

"He probably wouldn't," I agreed, "but somehow he was poisoned, and I need to find out how."

I decided I had to read up on cyanide in the hospital's medical library, and I spent much of the afternoon there. Finally I knew what I had to do. I phoned Dr. Pryor and Sheriff Lens and asked them to gather the others in Pryor's office at five.

Judd Francis and Nurse O'Toole were there when I arrived, and Sheriff Lens soon entered with Agent Barnovich. "I have to get back to Boston," the agent told us, but I quieted him down.

"This will only take a few minutes, and I think you'll want it to complete your report."

"Go on," Dr. Pryor told me.

"Well, this was an especially baffling locked-room problem for me, because the room wasn't locked at all. The door to a hospital room is always unlocked, often open. The only question was how our mysterious patient obtained the poison that killed him. No cyanide or cyanide compounds are kept at the hospital, all food and drink was tasted before it entered the room, and by Agent Barnovich's testimony the patient was absolutely alone for an hour or two before he was poisoned. My first suspicion, of course, was that he might have lied. But even though Miss O'Toole had gone off duty there were other nurses on the floor. If he had left his chair and entered the room after midnight, someone might have noticed and reported it after the body was discovered."

"Thanks for believing me," Barnovich said with a trace of sarcasm.

"Dr. Pryor and Judd Francis both visited the patient, as did Nurse O'Toole. Could they have poisoned him during their examinations, perhaps with the tip of a thermometer inserted into his mouth to take his temperature? No, because cyanide, you'll remember, kills instantly. And none of them visited him after midnight, when Barnovich and O'Toole both swear the patient was alive and talking. Where does that leave us? Is there anyone who was in that room between the hours of one and two when Fuchs died instantly from cyanide poisoning? Most especially, was anyone in there who had access to the poison? I asked myself that, and I saw the only possible answer. The victim himself!"

"He had no cyanide," Barnovich insisted.

"But he did at one point. I spoke to him yesterday about how he got here. He wouldn't reveal his name, but he'd fallen out of favor with Hitler, who gave him two choices—a trial for treason or a cyanide capsule and a hero's funeral. He chose cyanide and had the capsule in his hand when a friend whisked him away to a waiting aircraft. He had the tiny capsule in his hand!"

"Not when he arrived here," Barnovich insisted. "And he sure didn't swallow it or he'd have been dead."

"I spent the afternoon at the library, reading books about cyanide poisoning. There were accounts of spies and high-ranking military officials who preferred suicide to capture and torture. One method was to carry a small cyanide capsule inside a hollow false tooth. Even if fettered, the prisoner could work the capsule free with his tongue and bite or swallow it."

Barnovich's mouth dropped open. "Do you think that's what happened?"

"There's no other explanation. He had the cyanide and he brought it with him. The man named Fuchs killed himself."

"If Doc says it, I'm satisfied," Sheriff Lens decided. "Far as I'm concerned, the case is closed." Dr. Pryor nodded. "I agree."

I went back to my office and phoned April at home to tell her it was over. "That's good," she said. "With this damp weather we're bound to start getting some flu cases."

"I'll be in tomorrow morning for the entire day."

But there was one thing I had to do first. I went back into the hospital and sought out Marcia O'Toole. I found her without difficulty, caring for an elderly patient. She smiled when she saw me. "I'm so glad you were able to wind that business up. This place hadn't been the same since he arrived."

"Is there someplace we can talk, Marcia?"

"Why—I guess we could use the nurses' lounge for a few minutes. What is it?"

I waited till we were alone before I answered. Then I looked her in the eye and asked, "Why did you poison Fuchs?"

For a moment she didn't answer. Perhaps she was weighing her options. Then she said, quite softly, "Because my brother was killed in North Africa." There were tears in her eyes. "How did you know?"

"There was no cyanide here at the hospital. It had to come from outside, and my explanation of the false tooth seemed the most likely. Fuchs couldn't have known what sort of welcome awaited him here, so he kept the cyanide capsule and secreted it in a hollow tooth he wore for just that purpose. If we'd charged him with being a war criminal he'd have had a way out."

"But he wasn't charged with anything! The rumor was he'd be meeting the President, to be treated as some sort of hero."

"Hardly! I'm sure he would have been held as a prisoner of war."

"And then released at the end of the war! I wanted someone to pay for my brother. I wanted him to pay. The man I killed was Field Marshal Erwin Rommel, commander of the Afrika Korps."

"I know. I think others in the hospital must have known too. The code name they gave him was Fuchs, the German word for Fox. Rommel was well known in North Africa as the Desert Fox." Remembering my conversation with him, I added, "I think he found a bit of humor in the code name."

"How did you know it was me?" she asked again.

"I came in to see him the other day and you were washing him and brushing his teeth. That was when you found the hidden capsule. You must have guessed what it was and you kept it. He was still a bit drowsy then and probably didn't even realize you'd taken it. Once I suspected you of having the cyanide, I only had to determine how you could have managed to kill him with it. Then I remembered that Judd Francis asked you to bring him a glass of ice water last evening."

"Agent Barnovich tasted it as he always did. And Fuchs drank some right away."

"They tasted the water but not the ice cubes. You'd frozen that tiny capsule inside a cube of ice. When the ice melted during the night, the capsule was left floating there. Fuchs drank the rest of the water during the night and probably never noticed the capsule in the dark. By the time he realized it he was seconds from death."

"What will you do now?" she asked. Her breath was coming fast.

"I don't know," I admitted. "If it was Rommel, in a sense he was a casualty of the African campaign. It was as if your brother had shot him dead. Deaths in battle are not considered murder—though sometimes I think they should be."

Within a month Marcia O'Toole left the hospital and moved out of Northmont. I never saw her again. The death of Mr. Fuchs at Pilgrim Memorial Hospital attracted no attention at all. Accounts of Rommel's death were published after the war, and all had him swallowing the cyanide capsule while in the car with his friend. If he made it all the way to Northmont with his capsule, no one ever admitted it.

A DR. SAM HAWTHORNE CHECKLIST

BOOKS:

Diagnosis: Impossible, The Problems of Dr. Sam Hawthorne. Norfolk: Crippen & Landru Publishers, 1996. Contains Dr. Sam's first 12 cases.
More Things Impossible, The Second Casebook of Dr. Sam Hawthorne. Norfolk: Crippen & Landru Publishers, 2006. Contains Dr. Sam's next 15 problems.
Nothing Is Impossible, Further Problems of Dr. Sam Hawthorne. Norfolk: Crippen & Landru Publishers, 2013. Contains 15 more problems.
All But Impossible, The Impossible Files of Dr. Sam Hawthorne. Norfolk: Crippen & Landru Publishers, 2017. Contains 15 more problems.
Challenge the Impossible, Dr. Sam Hawthorne's Final Problems. Cincinnati: Crippen & Landru Publishers, 2018. Contains 15 problems.

INDIVIDUAL STORIES:

All of Dr. Sam Hawthorne's reminiscences were first published in *Ellery Queen's Mystery Magazine* [EQMM]. Dates when the events took place are recorded below in brackets.

"The Problem of the Covered Bridge" [March 1922]. EQMM, December 1974.
"The Problem of the Old Gristmill" [July 1923]. EQMM, March 1975.
"The Problem of the Lobster Shack" [June 1924]. EQMM, September 1975.
"The Problem of the Haunted Bandstand" [July 1924]. EQMM, January 1976.
"The Problem of the Locked Caboose" [Spring 1925]. EQMM, May 1976.
"The Problem of the Little Red Schoolhouse" [Fall 1925]. EQMM, September 1976.
"The Problem of the Christmas Steeple" [December 25, 1925]. EQMM, January 1977.
"The Problem of Cell 16" [Spring 1926]. EQMM, March 1977.
"The Problem of the Country Inn" [Summer 1926]. EQMM, September 1977.

"The Problem of the Voting Booth" [November 1926]. EQMM, December 1977.
"The Problem of the County Fair" [Summer 1927]. EQMM, February 1978.
"The Problem of the Old Oak Tree" [September 1927]. EQMM, July 1978.
"The Problem of the Revival Tent" [Fall 1927]. EQMM, November 1978.
"The Problem of the Whispering House" [February 1928]. EQMM, April 1979.
"The Problem of the Boston Common" [Spring 1928]. EQMM, August 1979.
"The Problem of the General Store" [Summer 1928]. EQMM, November 1979.
"The Problem of the Courthouse Gargoyle" [September 1928]. EQMM, June 30, 1980.
"The Problem of the Pilgrims Windmill" [March 1929]. EQMM, September 10, 1980.
"The Problem of the Gingerbread Houseboat" [Summer 1929]. EQMM, January 28, 1981.
"The Problem of the Pink Post Office" [October 1929]. EQMM, June 17, 1981.
"The Problem of the Octagon Room" [December 1929]. EQMM, October 7, 1981.
"The Problem of the Gypsy Camp" [January 1930]. EQMM, January 1, 1982.
"The Problem of the Bootleggers Car" [May 1930]. EQMM, July 1982.
"The Problem of the Tin Goose" [July 1930]. EQMM, December 1982.
"The Problem of the Hunting Lodge" [Fall 1930]. EQMM, May 1983.
"The Problem of the Body in the Haystack" [July 1931]. EQMM, August 1983.
"The Problem of Santa's Lighthouse" [December 1931]. EQMM, December 1983.
"The Problem of the Graveyard Picnic" [Spring 1932]. EQMM, June 1984.
"The Problem of the Crying Room" [June 1932]. EQMM, November 1984.
"The Problem of the Fatal Fireworks" [July 4, 1932]. EQMM, May 1985.
"The Problem of the Unfinished Painting" [Fall 1932]. EQMM, February 1986.
"The Problem of the Sealed Bottle" [December 5, 1933]. EQMM, September 1986.
"The Problem of the Invisible Acrobat" [July 1933]. EQMM, Mid-December 1986.

"The Problem of the Curing Barn" [September 1934]. EQMM, August 1987.
"The Problem of the Snowbound Cabin" [January 1935]. EQMM, December 1987.
"The Problem of the Thunder Room" [March 1935]. EQMM, April 1988.
"The Problem of the Black Roadster" [April 1935]. EQMM, November 1988.
"The Problem of the Two Birthmarks" [May 1935]. EQMM, May 1989.
"The Problem of the Dying Patient" [June 1935]. EQMM, December 1989.
"The Problem of the Protected Farmhouse" [August or September 1935]. EQMM, May 1990.
"The Problem of the Haunted Tepee" [September 1935]. EQMM, December 1990. Also featuring Ben Snow.
"The Problem of the Blue Bicycle" [September 1936]. EQMM, April 1991.
"The Problem of the Country Church" [November 1936]. EQMM, August 1991.
"The Problem of the Grange Hall" [March 1937]. EQMM, Mid-December 1991.
"The Problem of the Vanishing Salesman" [May 1937]. EQMM, August 1992.
"The Problem of the Leather Man" [August 1937]. EQMM, December 1992.
"The Problem of the Phantom Parlor" [August 1937]. EQMM, June 1993.
"The Problem of the Poisoned Pool" [September 1937]. EQMM, December 1993.
"The Problem of the Missing Roadhouse" [August 1938]. EQMM, June 1994.
"The Problem of the Country Mailbox" [Fall 1938]. EQMM, Mid-December 1994.
"The Problem of the Crowded Cemetery" [Spring 1939]. EQMM, May 1995.
"The Problem of the Enormous Owl" [August-September 1939]. EQMM, January 1996.
"The Problem of the Miraculous Jar" [November 1939]. EQMM, August 1996.
"The Problem of the Enchanted Terrace" [October 1939]. EQMM, April 1997.
"The Problem of the Unfound Door" [Midsummer 1940]. EQMM, June 1998.
"The Second Problem of the Covered Bridge" [January 1940]. EQMM, December 1998.
"The Problem of the Scarecrow Congress" [late July 1940]. EQMM, June

1999.

"The Problem of Annabel's Ark" [September 1940]. EQMM, March 2000.

"The Problem of the Potting Shed" [October 1940]. EQMM, July 2000.

"The Problem of the Yellow Wallpaper" [November 1940]. EQMM, March 2001.

"The Problem of the Haunted Hospital" [March 1941]. EQMM, August 2001.

"The Problem of the Traveler's Tale" [August 1941]. EQMM, June 2002.

"The Problem of Bailey's Buzzard" [December 1941]. EQMM, December 2002.

"The Problem of the Interrupted Séance" [June 1942]. EQMM, September/October 2003.

"The Problem of the Candidate's Cabin" [October-November 1942]. EQMM, July 2004.

"The Problem of the Black Cloister" [April 1943]. EQMM, December 2004.

"The Problem of the Secret Passage" [May 1943]. EQMM, July 2005.

"The Problem of the Devil's Orchard" [September 1943]. EQMM, January 2006.

"The Problem of the Shepherd's Ring". EQMM, September/October 2006.

"The Problem of the Suicide Cottage." EQMM, July 2007.

"The Problem of the Summer Snowman." EQMM, November 2007.

"The Problem of the Secret Patient." EQMM, May 2008.

Challenge the Impossible

Challenge the Impossible, The Final Cases of Dr. Sam Hawthorne by Edward D. Hoch, is set in Goudy Old Style, with one small bit in Courier. It is printed on sixty-pound Natures acid-free, recycled paper. The cover design is by Joshua Luboski, and the introduction is by Josh Pachter. The first edition was published in two forms: trade softcover, notchbound; and one hundred fifty copies sewn in cloth, numbered and signed by the author of the introduction. Each of the clothbound copies includes a separate pamphlet, "*The Spy and the Suicide Club*" by Edward D. Hoch and Josh Pachter. *Challenge the Impossible* was typeset by G. E. Satheesh, Pondicherry, India, and printed and bound by Thomson-Shore, Inc., Dexter, Michigan. It was published in July 2018 by Crippen & Landru Publishers, Inc., Cincinnati, Ohio.

Milton Keynes UK
Ingram Content Group UK Ltd.
UKHW050728180724
445674UK00015B/528